Friends' Experience

Experiences: Book 6

Learning the Sublime Essence of Trust and Submission

Simone Freier

OTK Publications
www.OTKPublications.com

Friends' Experience

EXPERIENCES: BOOK 6

By Simone Freier

Published by OTK Publications
http://otkpublications.com

ISBN: 978-1-942054-15-3
v1.5

Manufactured in the United States of America

COVER DESIGN BY OTK PUBLICATIONS

This is a work of fiction. All names, characters, and incidents in this work are fictitious. Any resemblance to actual events or to real persons is purely coincidental. No humans or animals were harmed during the creation of this work.

Caution: This work contains mature content, including graphic sexual descriptions and scenes, and is provided for adults only. Neither the author nor the publisher intends to encourage or promote any of the activities depicted in this work. Many of the specific activities and scenarios described in this work can potentially be dangerous, and should not be attempted without special knowledge or training and, as appropriate, use of sterile single-use supplies. No information contained herein is intended to constitute advice or serve as instructional material, and this work should not be relied upon to ensure safe practices in real life.

Table of Contents

CHAPTER 1: MEET THE PARENTS

I sat on the steps outside the biology building, a cool breeze rustling through the mostly-barren trees, and dark clouds making it seem like winter, although it was still early November. It was hard to believe that I had been in Europe yesterday ... or had it been two days?

Sam and I had toured for nearly three weeks, but it now seemed like a dream ... although my bottom could still feel the sting of the cane wielded by the dominatrix that we had visited in London. I looked up from my notebook, as a flood of memories filled my mind.

The trip had begun in Amsterdam and, in my mind's eye, I could see the tree-lined canals, the gables of the old houses – each seemingly different, and the multitude of bicycles. I visualized the polders through the window of the first sauna we had visited, sheep grazing, as the sun set. And I saw the modern sauna complex in the small town near Henk and Zöe's house; Henk, who had surprised Sam as 'Helga' at the bar frequented by cross-dressers, and Zöe, his bi partner, who was into some kinky things, herself.

We had spent several days driving – over the dykes, through the 'little Switzerland' of Luxembourg, along the Mosel and Rhine rivers, and down the 'Romantic Road' into Munich. I couldn't help but chuckle, as I remembered Sam at the Oktoberfest – swinging his stein of beer along with thousands of other intoxicated merrymakers, and the terrified look on his face as we ascended high above the fairgrounds on the Sky Fall ride ... and then dropped a couple hundred feet in a few seconds.

I pulled up the zipper of my new jacket – the one I had worn when we had skied from Switzerland to Italy for lunch and then, that afternoon, had taken the gondola down from the 'little' Matterhorn to the cute town of Zermatt, falling asleep in our chalet with the Matterhorn towering above us.

And then there was Paris: Sam's 'electric' kiss, as twinkling lights surrounded us at the top of the Eiffel Tower. I knew that Linda would be jealous, when we shared some of the pictures that Sam had taken.

The wind blew my hair and I shivered, as I glanced at my watch: It was nearly time for the appointment with my advisor. I hoped that I had prepared sufficiently to explain my 'invention' to him. Although my dissertation topic had been finalized, my new concept could change everything ... if it actually worked. Sam had been skeptical, but after some research he had agreed that the use of genetic sequencing to understand the biochemical pathways of diseases, enabling the discovery of new drugs, could be an important contribution.

I closed the notebook, and walked up the steps and into the building, then up more stairs and to room 310A, where a small plaque read 'Dr. Rajit Desai, Biotechnology'.

I knocked softly on the frosted glass panel in the door, and let myself in. "Hello, Dr. Desai."

My advisor looked up from a desk piled with books and papers, and smiled. He stood and walked around the desk, clasping my hand warmly. Though short of stature, he always looked distinguished, and perfectly groomed: His black hair was combed back, his face was close-shaven, and his teeth were sparkling. He wore a grey V-necked sweater, the collars of his white dress shirt informally turned down outside the sweater, and setting off the dark skin of his kind but serious-looking face.

"Hello, Kelly. I see you made it back from Europe safely!" He smiled, and pointed to an adjoining room, where we sat at a table, similarly piled with more books and papers. He sat back and smiled broadly at me, "So how was your trip?"

Again, my mind was flooded with memories ... including quite a few that I wouldn't be able to share with him. "It was incredible. It seems like a whirlwind, now. We experienced a lot of local 'culture', in addition to seeing some of the famous sights. Sam knows people there, and we had some very unique experiences."

Boy, did we! An image of the sex club flitted through my mind, and I adjusted my position on the chair, my bottom reminding me again of one of our 'unique' experiences.

"Sam seems like a nice guy. After you introduced him, I looked at his LinkedIn profile, and read a couple of his papers. He has a great reputation in the pharmaceutical industry; actually, he's someone who I should bring in to give a few lectures to our students. The university would probably consider hiring him as a professor, if he were interested in teaching."

I chuckled, thinking about some of the things I had learned from Sam – not quite the curriculum that my advisor was envisioning! "I think he's happy with retirement, Dr. Desai, but I'm sure he would agree to give a few lectures, if you invited him."

"Kelly, it's about time you addressed me as 'Raj'. We're going to be working together closely on the research for your dissertation for the next year or two." Again, the thought flitted through my brain of how 'close together' Sam and I had been.

I quickly refocused myself, and informed Raj, "Actually, I did some research on the trip, and have a few ideas I'd like to run by you." Raj looked at me dubiously, then spread his arms, inviting me to continue. It took nearly twenty minutes to 'briefly' explain my concept, and Raj listened attentively, only asking a few questions along the way.

When I had finished, he squinted at me, then looked up at the ceiling for a moment, then closed his eyes for what seemed like several minutes. I knew that he was thinking the concept through, and I sat quietly, reviewing my own thoughts, hopefully ready to answer the questions I was sure he would have. It had taken Sam several days of research before he was willing to grant that my idea had merit.

Raj opened his eyes and smiled at me, his face now seeming even more kind, almost father-like, despite his relatively young age of just over forty. Slowly, the smile grew, and he began nodding his head. "Kelly, I think you're on to something; something wonderful ... something that could be big."

"Sam thought it might have great potential, although he wasn't sure it would really work." I had already presented to Raj my ideas for circumventing the problems that Sam had identified. Now, it appeared that my advisor had grasped the entire concept in just a few minutes.

"Kelly, can you come in on Monday? I think we should sit together and start putting this on paper, so I can help you write a patent application."

I must have given Raj a surprised look, as he quickly continued, "As much as I'd like to be a co-inventor, I think you've done most of the work in conceptualizing this, and we don't want to delay: The field is quickly moving, and we wouldn't want someone else to 'scoop' us."

Then, he thought a moment, and added, "There will be many more opportunities for inventions and patents as you do the research and, as your advisor, I would most likely be a co-inventor on those." Then, he squinted at me again, and said, "But if you think Sam contributed to the invention, he could be included as a co-inventor."

I sat there dumbfounded by Raj's evident enthusiasm, and nodded.

"Kelly, I've been looking for an opportunity like this for quite a while, and we should consider starting a company to pursue your idea. An advantage of my name not being on the initial patent is that the university won't have rights to the invention, so you could start a company and assign 100% of the rights to it. Then, if the research pans out – as I expect it will – I could join the company, either as a consultant ... or possibly even leave the university, and work full-time on it with you and Sam."

This was moving too quickly; I realized that my mouth was hanging open, and my mind was a blur of ideas.

Raj smiled, and held my hands in his, "You know, Kelly, even if it doesn't work out, you'll have a great dissertation. I'm on the program committee of the largest biotech society, and I'm sure that you would be invited to present your ideas, and will have several publications ... *after* we have done the research and filed the patents." All I could do was nod.

We stood, and walked to the outer office. Raj opened the door, and said brightly, "Well, I'll see you on Monday, then. Have a good weekend!"

I walked out of the building, and across the campus, in a daze.

Kelly had agreed to hold-off meeting with her parents until tomorrow, and I made reservations at the bistro where we'd first had lunch together, nearly five months ago. I sat back in my comfortable executive chair behind the desk in the playroom, and closed my eyes, reminiscing.

I saw Kelly bounding across the street, as I looked through the window of the restaurant, her long auburn hair bouncing behind her; then she was looking at me as we sat at the corner table, her hazel eyes bright, her teeth sparkling, and her youthful skin glowing.

She was still the most beautiful woman I had ever met, and she was mine; at least, in some ways, although I tried not to feel overly possessive. It was difficult: I knew that I would be devastated, if – or when – she ever left me ... for someone her own age. Or, for another woman (although she had assured me, and I truly believed, that wouldn't be likely to happen).

Then, I began considering seriously how she should let her parents know that she had decided to move in with me. I wasn't too concerned about losing Dave and Darlene as friends, but I didn't want to harm the relationship that Kelly had with her parents; although the relationship was already strained, to say the least.

Kelly couldn't relate to her 'jock' father, and she had said her mother had taken to drinking, presumably due to her inability to control her daughter's wild tendencies. But I hadn't known Kelly through those years, and she seemed quite a mature and serious young lady now.

Chuckling, I realized that I was perhaps a bad influence on her – having shared my kinks and fetishes, to which Kelly had responded with more enthusiasm than I could have ever dreamed ... and I had dreamed *a lot* about having a young woman to whom I could introduce my submission fetishes.

Of course, a little spanking role-play wasn't a big deal – *Fifty Shades* had become a big sensation, and was now mainstream to the extent that a movie version would be coming out soon.

And nudity had never been a big deal – even amongst strangers; Kelly and her friends had gone to nude beaches, and they had been comfortable having a skinny-dipping 25th birthday party here at my house, even when some of the games involved 'intimate nudity'.

But my medical fetish would be over-the-top for most people, although – again – her friends had surprised both Kelly and I with their acceptance (more-or-less) of even some needle 'play'. But, after debriefing her friends regarding the party, Kelly had warned me that I shouldn't push that aspect of my turn-on, which had developed from some of my own childhood fears and fantasies.

Thinking back, I also realized how much *I* had changed in the months I'd been with Kelly; I was now much more open to sexual encounters than I had been for more than two decades, since the early days after I had married Sarah.

My wife's passing had renewed the possibility of having sex with other women and, although my 'play' with Kelly had started as non-sexual (at least as I had defined it as 'transfer of body fluids'), it had quickly morphed into a sexual relationship ... which had been recently extended to a ménage with Julie, and even oral sex with my Dutch friends, Henk and Zöe.

Neither Kelly nor I had been 'possessive' of each other, but I wondered how long that would last. We didn't mind 'sharing' each other with our close friends, but neither of us wanted to lose the other. Things had become complicated ... as life usually does.

I took a deep breath, and put these things out of my mind, spending most of the afternoon unpacking, cleaning the house, and uploading the photos I had taken using my camera and my phone during our Europe trip. I was aware that Kelly was going to see her advisor at the university, but didn't think about it until I heard Kelly's car and greeted her at the door.

We kissed, and she bounded into the house with a surprising amount of energy, considering that we had taken a long flight yesterday, and were just beginning to adjust to the time difference. I didn't feel jet-lagged, but I was lagging, compared to Kelly.

Kelly took off her jacket, threw it over one of the living room chairs, and commanded, "Please sit down, Sam." Suddenly, I wondered whether Kelly had, in fact, visited her parents; something was up. I sat on the couch, and Kelly began pacing back and forth, making me even more uncertain of what she was going to tell me.

She suddenly stopped in mid-pace, and turned to me, smiling broadly. "I saw my advisor today." I nodded, now realizing that she must have good news about her 'invention'. She continued, "Raj thinks it's going to work! He wants me to start writing a patent application ... and he thinks we should start a company!"

"That's great, Kelly!" I hopped up and hugged her. I wasn't about to burst her bubble now, but it was concerning: How could anyone have evaluated her idea so quickly? And, what if her research didn't pan out? Getting started on a patent was fine, but it probably couldn't be filed until Kelly had some actual data that showed her idea really was technically feasible.

And, it seemed awfully premature to start a business, when the research hadn't even begun. Even if she did start a business, I didn't think she should get her hopes up of commercializing her technology rapidly, as these things take time to organize, plan, and obtain funding for; there were a million other aspects that weren't as easy or quick as she might think. And, what experience did her advisor have in running a company?

I was very happy for Kelly, and this would provide great motivation ... but there were just too many variables and uncertainties to start celebrating.

Kelly was overflowing with energy. She picked up her jacket and ran upstairs, with me lagging behind. When I got to the master bedroom, Kelly was sitting on the toilet, peeing. I lay on the bed, trying to assess her news; wondering whether – and how – I could inject some realism, in a way that wouldn't be a let-down for her.

As she emerged from the bathroom, her pants unzipped, I decided that it was premature for me to make any judgments. So I kept my mouth shut.

Kelly slipped her jeans off, and flopped down on the bed next to me. "What's wrong, Sam?" I guess she could see that I wasn't terribly excited. She put her hand over the mound in my pants, and rubbed softly. "Would a little sex cheer you up?" She smiled, coyly.

"Let's just talk for a while," I responded, unenthusiastically.

Kelly frowned, "Are you OK? Jetlagged? Or maybe feeling ill?" She took her hand off me, and lay on her side, her head propped up, as she looked at me closely.

"No, nothing like that. I'm OK." I took a deep breath, "I'm really happy for you, but would like to hear more details of the discussion with your advisor. Then, we should talk about how we will break the news of your move to your parents."

Kelly shook her head, "*We* aren't going to break any news." I looked at Kelly questioningly, and she continued,

"They're *my* parents, and I should sit down and talk with them. They don't even know that I went to Europe with you ... just with 'some friends'. It's about much more than just moving out."

I looked at Kelly, her face as beautiful as ever; actually she was radiant. I meekly offered, "I thought we could invite them over here for dinner, maybe take them into the sauna ... where your father might be less prone to slug me."

"Sam! We're not inviting them for dinner – at least, until they know I'm staying here. And we're *definitely* not going to get in the sauna with them ... even if they were willing, which I'm sure they wouldn't be. Please let me handle this by myself," she pleaded.

"You know, Kelly, we had already discussed making one of the bedrooms into an office where you could write your dissertation; maybe we could designate it as the 'corporate' office, if you start a company. I could be your consultant, which would make it practical for you to stay here," I said, hopefully.

Kelly laughed, "And you took me to Europe to 'do research'?" I nodded tentatively; it did sound ridiculous. "No, Sam! I want to let my parents know that we have a relationship; that I love you." I winced.

But Kelly was right – she should take the direct and honest approach with her parents. Kelly explained, unnecessarily, "That's the main message. Going to Europe with you and living with you is just a logical result of our relationship. They already know that we had lunch months ago, so that you could help me with my career choices ... and I think my parents know that you've met Raj. Our relationship grew out of that, naturally."

I was about to interject, but Kelly quickly added, "And, *no*, I'm not going to get into our kinky sex life." Well, that was good.

Kelly climbed on top of me, straddling my hips, and bent down to kiss me. Then, she explained her plan. "I'll stay here tonight. I'm probably going to get my period by tomorrow or Sunday, so let's have some casual sex, while we can."

"*Casual sex*? I never have *casual* sex with you – it's always totally serious." Kelly started tickling me, finally lowering herself to pin me to the bed, so I couldn't put up a fight – which was the last thing I wanted to do.

"You know what I mean, silly boy!" Smiling at me, she continued, "Then, I'll go back to my place tomorrow morning, and spend the day with my parents. Our little talk might take only a few minutes, but I'm hoping that they won't throw me out, and I'd like to spend some quality time with them. And, I'll have to start packing my things; it might take a few trips, since I only have a couple of suitcases."

"I can give you a few suitcases and cardboard boxes that you can use to carry your things." Kelly kissed me again, her long hair falling around our faces. I felt a stirring below, where she was grinding herself against me. Maybe some 'make up' sex wouldn't be a bad idea?

Kelly obviously felt my growing manhood, and sat up, smiling down at me, as she continued to grind even harder, her hips moving in an erotic circular motion.

She moved backwards, straddling my legs, and undid my pants, pulling them – and my underwear – down to mid-thigh. Then, she slipped off her own underwear, sucked me until I was hard enough, and impaled herself on my length, again moving her hips erotically.

I closed my eyes, and tried to relax, letting Kelly take control ... which I realized she had done since returning from school. She was also incredibly turned on, her wetness enveloping me, as she lowered herself, our mouths joining, and our discussion forgotten; at least for the moment.

We took a quick shower together afterward, and dressed for dinner. Then we went down to the playroom, where I decided to open a bottle of Champagne, despite my qualms about the challenges Kelly would face with her technology and her business.

She sat on my lap, as I flipped through some of the photos from our trip. It really *had* been an experience! Actually, a lot of experiences; new ones, for both of us.

Before leaving for the restaurant, I detoured into the basement bathroom and turned on the heat in the sauna. At least we would have one last fun night, before her father came after me with a shotgun. Kelly knew her parents better than I did; maybe it wouldn't go so badly?

Sam had finally decided to relax a little, and let me handle my parents. I was an adult, and they really had nothing to say about our relationship. And, with their *laissez faire* attitude towards me over the past half dozen years, I didn't think they would be too bothered, regardless of what I decided to do. If they didn't accept Sam as my partner, I probably wouldn't be seeing them for a very long time.

It was fun going back to the bistro where Sam and I had enjoyed our first lunch. We shared a big salad, and both ordered hamburgers, as we were somewhat starved for normal *American* food, after our trip.

I explained to Sam why Raj had wanted me to move quickly, both on the patent and on the company. I think Sam was surprised that Raj wasn't going to be listed as an inventor on the patent. "Kelly, I don't think *I* should be on it, either: You were clearly the sole inventor."

As I finished the last of my hamburger, I objected, "No, Sam. You were instrumental in helping me work through some important issues. And, I probably would never have come up with the idea, had we not been in a different environment, where I could think more creatively. The invention was at least partly the result of you taking me to Europe."

Sam tried to object again, but finally threw up his arms in a 'you win' gesture. Then, he ordered dessert.

The tight feeling around the waist of my pants reminded me that I would need to cut back on eating big meals and desserts ... but tonight was special. I was still on a high from the experience with Raj. He was a great teacher, and an even greater motivator. He had encouraged me to move forward, with no pressure as to his role – other than as my graduate advisor, and perhaps consultant to the company.

Sam educated me a bit on starting a company – the legal aspects, and issuance of founder's shares. I had already decided that both Raj and Sam would own part of the company, and I suggested that Sam consider being the president, but he flatly refused, saying that he was retired, and would remain retired.

He did offer, however, to consult for the company; so now, it appeared that the company would start out with a president (me), and two part-time consultants.

My research would be done at the university, and Sam offered to put up the initial capital – he suggested $10,000. It was a big bet that he was placing on my success ... but I guess we were both placing big bets on each other, regarding our relationship. Sam explained that this 'small' amount of capital would barely cover legal fees, the patent filing, a computer system, and a few minimal supplies which the company would need, such as business cards.

That brought up the question of what to name the company. After a short brainstorming session during our dessert, we came up with the name 'KS Biotech Corporation'; it sounded a little 'high falutin', and I thought 'KS Biotech, Inc.' might be more appropriate. We decided to sleep on it ... together.

That brought us back to reality, or surreality – including a nice time in Sam's sauna, and a nice romp on the playroom bed, before we retired upstairs.

Saturday morning, I dumped everything out of my suitcase. Sam designated drawers in the master bedroom dresser, and made space in the closet that I could use. He lent me a couple of large suitcases, and put those and a stack of flattened cardboard boxes in my trunk.

I kissed him goodbye, and drove to my parents' house, where I lugged the suitcases and boxes up the stairs to my over-garage apartment. Then, I walked to the house, feeling a bit nervous, for the first time, about having a discussion with my parents.

My mother greeted me at the door, hugging me as if I were a long lost relative, and ushered me into the house, where she insisted that she make my favorite breakfast – waffles and bacon.

My pants were already tight, but I relented, allowing her to pamper me; it felt like the first time in years that we had smiled and actually enjoyed each other's company. My father was playing golf, and wouldn't be back home until about 1PM.

Although I had planned to tell both my parents about Sam at the same time, my mother's questions about the Europe trip forced me to 'spill the beans' earlier than anticipated.

"Mom, before I tell you about my Europe trip, I wanted to let you know that I'm planning on moving out.

I've really appreciated being able to live here, rent-free, and being on my own ... but it's time that I 'left the nest'. I hope you guys are OK with that."

"Certainly, dear," my mother replied. She added, "Actually, we expected you to move out long ago ... not that we don't love having you here ... but you've got your own life. And we respect that."

She was making it much easier on me than I had anticipated. While she wasn't my birth mom, I loved her and had always considered her my 'mother'. Then, she asked, "So are you going to share an apartment with one of your girl friends? Maybe Linda, or Kathy?"

Now came the 'moment of truth' – well, at least one of them. "No, mom. Actually, it's more like a boyfriend."

My mother smiled, "That's great honey! I didn't even know you were dating seriously. Have I met him?" Oh, boy! Here we go ...

"Well, actually, it's more like a 'man friend' – maybe I should just call him a 'partner'." My mother was nodding, tentatively, so I continued, "And, actually, you *have* met him." There was a pang in my stomach, and I didn't think it was the waffles. I cleared my throat, and suddenly felt faint. "It's Sam."

My mother looked at me curiously, "I don't think you've introduced a 'Sam' to me ..."

I shook my head, "No. Actually, it's Sam Johnson." I had done it. The 'cat' was loose, and would never go back into the bag.

My mother squinted, "You don't mean our friend, Sam Johnson, who was married to Sarah ... *do you*?" Now my mother looked weak. I nodded slowly, and she put her hand on her forehead. Then, she looked at the oven clock, and announced, "Well, it's after noon ... on a Saturday ... I think I'll make myself a drink." It was probably a good idea, but I hoped that she wouldn't be knocked out before my father returned.

She opened the narrow pantry door, and pulled out a mostly-empty bottle of vodka, then put a couple of ice cubes in a small glass and filled it with the clear liquid. She sat down at the kitchen table again, and took a sizeable slug, tossing it back the way I'd seen Russians do, in some movie.

I reached out, and put my hand on hers. "Mom, Sam has been helping me figure out my career, and planning the research for my dissertation. We re-met when he came to your party a few months ago." My mother gave a small nod, and took another swig of vodka.

"And I have some really exciting news for you and dad about school and my career – something that I only found out yesterday. I'd like to wait until daddy gets home before I explain that part." My mother blinked a couple of times, and nodded again.

"But, now that you know about Sam, I can tell you about the Europe trip ... which was Sam's present to me for my 25th birthday." I didn't mention the beautiful pearl necklace or the satin nightgown, and certainly not the 'triple threat' rabbit vibrator!

My mother's eyes grew large, "That's quite a birthday present! And we just gave you the usual check, so you could buy something nice for yourself ..."

"Mom, that's fine. I love buying things for myself with my birthday checks."

I smiled, devilishly, "And, of course, Sam also enjoyed the Europe trip. He loves to introduce people to new experiences ... and this was a great opportunity for him, since everything was new to me." Not to mention all the *other* new 'experiences' to which Sam had introduced me!

Over the next hour, I told my mother the basics of the trip – which weren't that basic. From the first-class and business-class flights, to our hotel room overlooking Amsterdam, to running in *Vondelpark* and along the beach near the Dutch national park, to all the museums – the Van Gogh and *Stedelijk* modern art museum, and *Rijksmuseum* with its famous Rembrandt paintings, like the 'Night Watch', and Rembrandt's House ... and the Anne Frank house.

I told her about our sunset boat cruise through the canals, and our walking tour that included Amsterdam's red light district and the sex museum. My mother took another swig of vodka, nearly finishing her glass, when I explained the Dutch saunas – basically health clubs with different temperature saunas, steam rooms, whirlpools, and warm and cold pools, where everyone – of all genders – walks around nude.

I told her about staying in the small village with Sam's interesting friends (although I didn't mention *how* interesting they were!). And I spent some time recounting the special Dutch foods that we tried, including the Indonesian *rijstaffel*, the *Vlaamse frites*, the *pannekoeken* and *poffertjes*, the Dutch pea soup, and the smoked eels.

I probably had forgotten half the things we ate, but my mother was already overwhelmed. My parents had been to Europe once, a long time ago, but it had been a regular bus tour, and I don't think they had tried very many of the delicacies.

Then, I described our drive over the dykes (which really aren't 'dijks', but moveable sea walls), our wine tasting along the Mosel river, and our brief overnight stay in Koblenz, where Sam had bought me the jacket. I think my mother was getting tired by the time I described our Rhine River drive, the Neckar Valley *schlosshotel* (castle hotel), and the *Romantischestrasse* (Romantic Road) down to Munich.

She seemed to perk up, when I described our day at the Oktoberfest, with Sam in *lederhosen* shorts and me in a traditional *dirndl* dress, although I didn't go into detail about how soused Sam had gotten.

My mother yawned, and I skipped over the rest of the Munich sights, and just mentioned Zurich as part of our drive into Switzerland. I told her about our sail on the *Thunersee* near Interlaken, and driving onto the train, which went through miles of tunnels under the Alps, then taking the cog railway up to Zermatt, where we skied on the 'little Matterhorn'.

She perked up more when I described our tour of Paris, including the magnificent *Champs Élysée* boulevard, the Eiffel Tower, and the *Sacré Coeur* cathedral at the top of the *Montmartre* hill. I briefly mentioned Napoleon's Tomb, the Rodin Museum, the Versailles Palace, and the incredible cabaret show we had seen.

And then I described our tour of London – including Buckingham Palace, the Tower of London, the Egyptian mummies in the British Museum, and Madam Tussaud's Wax Museum.

My mother yawned again, so I skipped over the rest of London (just now realizing that my bottom wasn't sore anymore from our experience with the dominatrix), and described our first class flight home.

My mother's only comment was a sincere 'Wow', and I couldn't have agreed more. It had been a really incredible trip ... along with some even more incredible experiences that I couldn't share with her.

About that time, my father came home from his golf game. He also seemed happy to see me, and only a little surprised that my mother was already drinking so early in the afternoon. We sat in the family room, a football game on the television (fortunately with the sound muted), as usual. My father got up to get a beer from the fridge, and was surprised that I accepted his offer of one.

It wasn't until I had taken a few sips that I realized how bland it was, compared to the great beers we'd had in Europe. I repeated part of my story about attending the Oktoberfest which – apparently – my father had always wanted to experience.

And I told him about skiing– not only on the slopes near the Matterhorn, but also in the Jungfrau, high above Interlaken, in central Switzerland.

My mother put out some appetizers – including a slab of cheddar cheese and some little cocktail wieners in barbeque sauce. I knew that despite being a bit tipsy, she was softening my father up for the news about my moving in with Sam. Incredibly, he hadn't asked about my traveling companion, probably assuming that it was with one or more of my female friends. This was confirmed, when he asked how Julie was doing.

Again, my mind was flooded with memories – both of my realization that Julie had been a 'vixen', teasing my father when we had skinny-dipped in my parents' pool years ago; and my more recent experiences with Julie, including the incredible birthday party Sam had arranged with my friends; and, of course, the recent ménage with Sam and Julie.

I simply told him that Julie was fine, and segued into the news about school and my career.

It was impossible to explain the details of my invention to my parents, but I told them that the trip had invigorated my body and my brain, and that I had come up with an invention that my graduate advisor had informed me – only yesterday – was worthy of not only a patent, but on which a new business could be based.

That brought my mother and I full circle, and – before I realized what was happening – she blurted out, in slurred words, my intention to move out of the apartment over the garage ... and move in with Sam Johnson.

My father put his beer down, and looked back and forth from my mother to me, until she and I simultaneously nodded, and I explained that, yes, it *was* their old friend, Sam, who had been helping me with my career, *and* with whom I had toured Europe.

My father excused himself to use the bathroom, swinging by the kitchen as he came out, and grabbing himself another beer. Mine was still half full, the taste almost disgusting me – almost like dishwater, compared to the European beers.

"Do you realize how *old* Sam is, Kelly?" My father again looked back and forth from me to my mother, and back to me.

I nodded, "Yeah, about as old as you guys." That seemed to sting my dad, but not as much as I had hoped.

"So, you're moving in with someone your parents' age." It was a statement, not a question, and required no response from me. I just shrugged and nodded, again taking a sip of the beer only because my mouth seemed suddenly parched. My father was shaking his head, unbelieving – or not wanting to understand.

"Dad, at this point, I consider Sam to be a 'partner'. He's been very nice to me, and we really care for each other. I'm not planning to *marry* him, anytime soon."

I heard him grumble, "I should *hope* not!" He drained the last of his second beer; it was barely two o'clock in the afternoon. I wondered how many beers he'd already had 'with the boys' at the country club.

My mother rose, and announced, "Well, I've got to get dinner started." She smiled at me warmly, and added, "It's your favorite, Kelly – pot roast." I smiled and nodded.

It was at that point that I realized how far I'd come in the past few months, in recognizing and appreciating some of the finer things in life; in living a higher 'standard' of life, and appreciating Sam's high values and ideals. In a way, I felt sorry for my parents. But that wasn't really fair: They were both happy, in their own ways.

I heard – and smelled – onions frying in the pan, and told my father, "I'll see if mother needs any help. And, I want to get started packing my things – there's a lot of stuff I need to pack, and a lot of junk I'll probably leave here in boxes, if you don't mind." My father shrugged, and walked into the kitchen with me, where he grabbed another bottle of bland beer.

It was obvious that my father wanted to ask me, 'Why can't you meet some nice guy your own age?', but it was also obvious to me why I couldn't explain that to my parents. It would offend them to think that I was belittling their lifestyle, and what they had attained by working so hard for decades; and that I was now a snob for preferring a higher standard of living.

Not that Sam had much more money than my parents (although I didn't really know how much either of them had earned or saved) ... but he lived a distinctly different lifestyle, with what I considered – what I had *learned* – were higher values. And in my life, so far, I had never met anyone near my age who had the values, the sensitivity ... even the enthusiasm and *passion* that Sam had.

"Can I offer some help with the cooking, mom?" I had a lot of packing to do, but working with my mother in the kitchen was the least that I could offer ... and it would give us a little more 'bonding' time together.

Thinking back, I really couldn't remember the last time we'd had a real conversation ... until this morning. Even when I had come over for my parents' Labor Day bash, I hadn't spoken much to my parents, as the house had been full of guests, and it was deemed important for me to chat with each of *them*.

Actually, now that I thought about it, avoiding a discussion with my parents on Labor Day was one of the reasons I'd stayed only a few hours, targeted to when the guests would be here.

I loved my parents, but it had seemed like they never wanted to understand me, or spend time with me. Perhaps some of that was my own fault? Now that I would be leaving home, it seemed more important to at least try to relate to them; and they both were taking my news of living with Sam better than I had expected.

"No, honey. I've got everything under control, here." Her words were only slightly slurred, but I saw that she had refilled her drink. Perhaps she wasn't comfortable relating to *me*?

"OK. Then, I'll go over to my apartment, and start packing. I've got a lot of stuff to clear out of there!"

My mother stopped stirring the onions and put the spoon down. "That's fine, dear. But there's no rush – you can move a little bit at a time, if that would be easier." She took a sip of vodka, and continued, "We'll keep the room over the garage designated as yours, as long as you like. But, actually ..."

As she took another sip, I looked at her seriously, and said, "But, what?"

She made a giggling sound that turned into a burp. "Sorry. But your dad has been talking about someday converting the room into a place where he can invite his buddies. He's talked about putting a pool table in there, or maybe a giant screen television and card table, so they can play poker, smoke cigars, and do all those 'man' things that he knows I wouldn't want in the house."

Well, that was a surprise! But, not really. My parents were living separate lives at this point, and I knew my dad would love to have his poker games and football parties, watch porn, smoke, and generally raise hell with his cronies. I nodded, and said, "Yeah, I'm sure he would love that. I'll try to get everything cleared out as soon as I can."

My mother smiled, "As I said, there's no rush. I'd like to get him out of the house, but can only imagine the things he would do over there."

'Get him out of the house'? That stopped me, for a moment. I had thought more than once that my parents might get divorced, but I guess it was just easier for them to put up with each other, and live their own lives, than go through the hassle; and have to explain to all their friends. I really couldn't remember back to when they were actually 'loving' towards each other.

But I'd had my own issues, and hadn't paid much attention to my parents' problems. I nodded again, went out the side door, and walked the short distance to my 'apartment'.

Opening the door, and kicking the boxes aside, I looked around at all my junk; I really didn't feel like spending the next few hours packing. Nor spending the night here. I suddenly felt very tired. Picking up my phone, I flopped down on the bed and called Sam.

"Hi, Kelly!" Sam said cheerily. "How are things going at home? With your packing ... and with your parents?" He had said the last few words tentatively, undoubtedly expecting that there would have been fireworks when I announced that I would be moving in with him.

"Oh, things are fine. I'm just tired." I stifled a yawn.

"Yeah, I'm feeling it too: Jetlag." Oh! I hadn't thought about that, now that I was back in the 'real' world.

Sam asked, "Have you told your parents, yet?" There was a moment of apprehensive silence on the phone, before I could formulate my answer; an answer that only required one word ... but begged for much more explanation.

"Yes, Sam. They took it surprisingly well." I sighed, "Not that they were overjoyed that – or even understood why – I fell for an 'old man', like you." Sam made a loud 'harrumph!', before I could continue, "Like them. But I wasn't asking them to be happy, or to understand; I just hoped that they would accept the situation. Which I think they have."

I breathed heavily, then made an effort to relax when I heard my breathing in the telephone earpiece.

"That's great. I guess I can put away the baseball bat that I left next to the front door."

"Sam! My parents aren't violent people; although I wouldn't want to see you and my father duking it out." I heard Sam chuckle, and then he let out a long sigh, and I continued. "My mother said that my father is looking forward to converting my apartment into his 'man cave' ... and I think she'll be glad to give him a place to play with his pals."

At that moment, it occurred to me that perhaps he had his *own* female friend to 'play' with; but that was ridiculous – I had to be over-tired to even think of such a thing!

Sam replied, "Well, I don't think he'll ever invite me over ... not that he would have, anyway." That was true. Sam chortled, and I could tell that he was as tired as I was; we were both getting slaphappy.

"Anyway, my mom's cooking pot roast for dinner, and I thought I would start packing ... but I'm really too tired to face it right now." I thought about Sam sitting home alone. "What are *you* doing for dinner, tonight?"

"I'm making a simple pasta with pesto from a jar, with some garlic and an onion that was sitting in the pantry. I would normally add fresh vegetables, but haven't been to the market, yet, and the fridge is nearly empty."

Sam was a resourceful guy, and a very good cook; even his 'simple' pasta was better than taking a TV dinner out of the freezer. Although I doubted that he *ever* had anything like that in his freezer.

"Sam, if you don't mind, I'd like to come back over and spend the night with you. I can come back here tomorrow to do the packing."

"*Mind*!??! That would be wonderful! I miss you, already."

I had to interject, "But please don't expect too much 'fun' tonight – I really am very tired."

Sam harrumphed again, "Kelly, I love just *being* with you. We don't have to *do* anything. Just snuggling together and having a good night's sleep sounds great."

As I had realized several times previously, although Sam strove for a high standard of living, he was also willing to accept what he had, without complaint.

"OK. I'll be over in a couple of hours. I love you, Sam."

"I love you, too, Kelly. See you in a while."

As I put the pasta into a large pot of boiling water, I thought – again – how lucky I was to have found Kelly. Being alone for even a day seemed too much, now that I'd had a nearly full-time companion for the past few weeks. The jetlag was hitting me, also, and I wasn't sure that I could even stay awake until Kelly arrived. I'd already drunk nearly half a bottle of wine, and making dinner was sapping any remaining energy that I might have had.

It was great that Kelly's parents weren't making a stink over her moving out ... and moving in with me; but it would still be very uncomfortable seeing them again. I thought about my sons, and considered calling them tomorrow, to catch up on things. Then I wondered what *they* would think, when they learned that I was dating ... seeing ... living with a girl younger than them. I stirred the pasta, and turned off the heat on the sauce.

Kelly arrived around 8PM – early evening, although it was pitch black outside, and our bodies felt like it was the middle of the night. I greeted her with a long, passionate kiss, and we wordlessly climbed the stairs, and undressed for bed.

Although I knew that Kelly was due to get her period in the next day or two, we were both too tired – and I was too inebriated – to even consider making love. We did just as I had suggested earlier – snuggled, and fell asleep in each other's arms. The last thing I thought before sleep overcame me was how contented I was, just being with Kelly.

We slept nearly twelve hours, and woke feeling very refreshed. Kelly went into the bathroom, as I lay in bed making a mental list of the things I would have to get done in the next day or two: Going to the market to re-stock the fridge and pantry, finishing sorting and editing the Europe photos and making a little show, cleaning out more drawers and closet space for Kelly's things, working with Kelly on her patent and business startup, and calling my sons. The list kept growing, but I finally cleared my mind and thought of Kelly.

Now, my hand went under the covers, and soon something else was growing. I closed my eyes, and visualized a few 'scenes' from Europe: Kelly coming out to the narrow balcony of our hotel room in Amsterdam, modeling the fishnet dresses we had bought at the sex shop; Kelly satisfying herself, as she straddled my leg on the patio of our hotel room at the health spa in Valkenburg; and making love to Kelly in our chalet under the nighttime presence of the Matterhorn.

Kelly came out of the bathroom wearing a pair of cute pink bikini underwear. She climbed onto the bed, and lay down next to me, and I leaned over to kiss her. "Sorry, Sam." When I gave her a quizzical expression, she explained, "I just got my period." I gave her a peck on the lips, and let my head drop back onto the pillow.

Kelly ran her hand through my hair, and rolled against me, giving me a consoling kiss. Then, her hand went under the covers, and her eyes grew wide, as she curled her fingers around my hardened shaft. Giving me a cryptic smile, she said, "But, you *know* that there are many ways that I can satisfy you."

I smiled, thinking 'let me count the ways'. But it was true. I recalled our 'first experience' together, when we had played for 24 hours, each of us having numerous orgasms, without actually having sex. Until Kelly went down on me just before she left the next morning.

It seemed that Kelly was thinking the same thing, as her head went under the covers, and made its way to my groin, where she expertly took me into her mouth. I relaxed and closed my eyes, letting Kelly demonstrate her oral skills; which were considerable. It didn't take long before I came in her mouth, and she sucked me dry.

Laying alongside me again, she twirled my chest hairs with her fingers. "Well, now that I've had a nutritious breakfast, what shall we do, today?"

I laughed, "Don't worry – I'll make you a proper breakfast. I think I have a few eggs left in the fridge." We had cereal, but no milk; peanut butter and jam, but no bread; and whatever bacon that might be left was probably green, by now.

Kelly responded seriously, "Sam, I haven't weighed, but I know I've gained weight over the past month. I really have to start eating less, or you'll put me on a real diet, when I get too fat."

"Fat? You're perfect. And I love you for your mind, not your body." That was only half true; or maybe three-quarters.

Kelly laughed, and hopped out of bed, stumbling over a pile of clothing and other stuff she had dumped out of her suitcase. She frowned, then smiled broadly, bending down, and picking up something; she held the latex body suit up, and gave me an evil smile. "As far as 'doing' things today, I've got a lot of packing and unpacking to do. And I may need your help."

I smiled at her, and replied, "If you show me that sexy slippery suit any longer, you may just have to 'take care' of me again!"

She dropped the 'gummi-suit', and said sincerely, "I'd be happy to, Sam. But we really do have a lot of work to do, today."

"I know. Before you came out of the bathroom, I was making a mental list. But, somehow, you've made me forget most of it." She laughed, and I crawled out of bed. "It's my turn in the bathroom, and then maybe we can take a shower together downstairs. And I think we have some yogurt in the fridge; you've got to keep your energy up for all the packing you have to do."

She shook her head, "*We* have to do. You're going to come with me back to my apartment and help me start the move; I don't think I can face it alone."

It was nearly 10AM before we drove back to Dave and Darlene's house. I parked on the side of the garage, away from the driveway and nearest the stairs up to Kelly's apartment. We had only driven one car, but I had a large trunk and hoped that most of Kelly's stuff would fit.

Kelly looked at me and smiled, teeth gleaming. Her hazel eyes looked iridescent in the morning light, and contrasted with the auburn hair that framed her face. She turned and opened the door, and we stepped inside – the first time I had seen her place.

Other than the suitcases and flattened cardboard boxes taking up much of the floor space, and her shelves jammed with books and knickknacks, and her apartment was relatively tidy – the bed made, and the spread only slightly rumpled where I could tell she had lain.

I began assembling the boxes, as Kelly pulled open the sliding door of the closet, the rod filled with pants, tops, and dresses, and the floor a sea of shoes.

I handed Kelly a box, and she began dumping shoes into it. Amazingly, all her shoes fit, and I carried the box down to the car. When I got back into Kelly's apartment, she was putting knickknacks into a second box. I carried that down to the car, and we repeated the process, until most of the boxes had been used, and the trunk of my car was nearly filled.

Kelly looked around the room: The drawers were open, and it appeared that most everything in them, on the dresser and on the shelves had been packed. There were a few breakables, which she decided to leave until she could get a newspaper from the house, so that we could wrap them. She stared into the closet, and I grabbed an armful of pants and tops, still on hangers, and brought them down to the car, laying them across the back seat.

Re-entering her room, I saw her standing in front of the closet, holding up a beautiful dress. I said, "I don't think I've ever seen that one; it's really nice!"

Kelly nodded, "Some of these are older, and I'm not sure they'll even fit, anymore." Then she chuckled, and added, "Especially with the weight I've gained from all the great food in Europe." She unfastened her pants, and slipped them off her long legs, then unbuttoned her blouse, as I carried another load down to the car.

When I returned, she was modeling the dress in front of the mirrored closet door. "Well, at least I can get into it," she exclaimed. Taking it off, Kelly grabbed another dress – this one more suited to summer weather. Still in her bra and underwear, I stepped up to her and gave her a big hug.

"Kelly, you're beautiful, regardless of the clothes you're wearing ... or not wearing!" I gave her a peck on the lips, and she put an arm around my neck and pulled me close, still holding the lightweight dress loosely in her other hand.

Suddenly, there was a loud knocking at the door. "Oh shit! That's my dad!" She threw the dress over her head, and let it fall into place, as she walked toward the door. I followed her, picking up one of the still-flattened boxes, unfolding it, as the door opened.

Kelly's father smiled at her, then looked up at me. "I thought that might be you, Sam." I stepped forward and shook his hand, tentatively. Dave's grip was strong, and he continued to squeeze, until I thought he would break my fingers.

When he released his grasp, I took a step back, and held up the half-assembled box, and said, weakly, "I'm helping Kelly pack for the move." This was *déjà vu* in the most literal sense, as my mind's eye saw the vision I'd had a couple of months ago, when I had considered coming over to help Kelly select some outfits for the photo shoot. I smiled (the best I could muster) at Dave, and he nodded, grimly.

"Why don't you come over to the house for a drink, when you guys are done?" Dave offered. It was my turn to nod, grimly ... but I appreciated the offer. It was apparent that Dave was trying to accept the situation.

Kelly and I worked for another hour, completely filling both the trunk and backseat, and empting most of her room. Her parents would have to deal with the furniture, as there was nothing that Kelly had wanted to take, except for a Mickey Mouse lamp that evidently had some sentimental value.

We walked to the house, and Darlene greeted me warmly, although I suspect that she had already 'indulged' in some early libations. Taking me by the arm, she led us into the family room, where she had set out a bowl of chips. "Sam, I do appreciate all that you've done for Kelly ... especially taking her to Europe. She described the trip to us yesterday, and it sounded fantastic." If she only knew!

Dave offered us beers, which Kelly quickly declined; I realized why, when he brought out an ice bucket with several bottles of Bud Light. We toasted to Kelly's new adventures – both the move, and her new business.

Darlene excused herself for a few moments, returning with a stack of mail, which she dropped into Kelly's lap. Still standing, and appearing somewhat woozy, she held an envelope in her hand. "Kelly, I have something for you; it came, when you were on your trip." She glanced at Dave, and then back to Kelly. "It's from the court that approved our adoption of you."

Darlene's spoke slowly, and her voice was tremulous. "I'm pretty sure I know what it is ... and I'm a little nervous about your reaction. I'd like you to wait until you're alone, before opening it." She handed the plain-looking envelope to Kelly hesitantly, and I could plainly see that she was quaking. She excused herself again, and walked unsteadily toward the master bedroom.

Kelly looked shaken, glancing at me and then at her father. She rose, putting the stack of mail on the coffee table, and followed her mother, who was emitting soft, plangorous sounds.

I looked at Dave, but he looked away and took a large quaff of beer. It was uncomfortable, but this seemed to have a much deeper meaning than the discomfort of Kelly moving in with me.

I closed the bedroom door behind us, and my mother sat on the bed, visibly shaking, as she pulled a Kleenex from the box and sniffled into it. "What's wrong, mom? Why are you so upset?" I really couldn't imagine what was in the court letter, and didn't really care. What could be so distressing after 17 years?

My mother sniffled again, and looked up at me uncertainly, a tear running down her cheek. She took my hands in hers, and I sat down on the bed next to her.

"Kelly, this is something that I had put out of my mind a long time ago. I really didn't want to give you the letter ... but you have a right to have the information, if you want to pursue it."

I gave her a probing look, but remained silent. She continued, haltingly, "The court documents regarding your adoption were sealed ... but the judge ordered that you would have access to them upon your twenty-fifth birthday." She sniffled again, and blew her nose into the Kleenex.

"It is your decision whether to follow-up on this ... but I would like you to think about it for a while, and not act rashly. She looked into my eyes, her own now reddened and puffy. "My preference would be for you to not dig up the past, just focus on your future."

Now, I understood: My mother was concerned that I might search for my birth parents. "Mom," I said, putting my arm around her shoulder and pulling her close to me, "I love you. And nothing is going to change that." I leaned over and kissed her cheek, tasting the salty tears that were now flowing freely from her eyes.

She looked askance at me, and replied, "I know that, Kelly. I love you, too. But it's more complicated than you'll ever know." Then, in a very low voice, she mumbled, "I hope." She leaned on my shoulder, and it felt like I was now the consoling parent. My mother sat up, sniffled, and looked at me sincerely, "I just want you to be happy."

Now, I was nearly in tears, seeing my mother this way. "I know, mom. I *am* happy." I took a deep breath, and added, "And I can't imagine anything that would change that ... or our relationship." I kissed my mother again, and she lay on the bed, her eyes closed and her body trembling.

I stood, then bent over and kissed her again. "Sam and I are going to go, now ... but I'll come back soon, and we can talk again. In the meantime, I promise not to open the letter."

As I pulled open the door, my mother said, quietly, "Thank you, Kelly."

CHAPTER 2: SHARING WITH FRIENDS

It had been a very busy week! As I drove from the doctor's office back to Sam's house (I was still trying to assimilate it now being 'my' home ...), I thought about all that we had accomplished. I had moved my winter clothes into the master bedroom closet, and Sam had cleared out the closet of one of the guest bedrooms, which I had filled with the rest of my clothes, shoes, and other junk – most of it still in boxes that had not yet been unpacked from the move from my apartment.

Raj and I had outlined the basics of the patent, and Sam had spent two nights with me writing the 'specification' section, and brainstorming the 'claims'. It was still a work-in-progress, but my brain was now accepting how real – and important – the patent could be, as well as the business that we were starting.

Sam was visiting the attorney to begin the process of forming the corporation; I'd finally convinced him to forego watching my friends and I take our second round of HPV and hepatitis injections, promising him that he could be with us for our final round in five months.

Sam and I had marketed together this morning, re-stocking the fridge and pantry before I left for school. My friends and I had met at the clinic this afternoon, coming from different directions, and each having plans for the evening; so, despite all the questions they'd asked about my trip, I hadn't been able to share much with them.

Instead, I had invited them to dinner tomorrow night, and Sam had promised to finish editing the pictures and make a show that we would present on the big screen in the playroom.

The last few days had been a blur, and the trip now seemed in the distant past, although we had only returned a little over a week ago. I'd attended two seminar classes this week, and begun setting up the first of my experiments in the lab.

My mind whirled, as I pondered the future; it would be nice to spend a quiet weekend with Sam, although he would probably want to keep working on the patent. I think he was as excited as I was ... about the patent, the business startup, and 'playing around' a little – although we'd made love for the past couple of nights, despite my still spotting.

I pulled into the driveway, and carried my books and a briefcase loaded with my laptop and a bunch of lab notebooks, into the house. Sam had evidently not gotten back from the attorney, yet. I went up to one of the guest bedrooms that had a small desk, and plopped my books and briefcase down.

Opening the laptop, I checked my e-mails, and the latest biotech news. We had conducted several patent searches, and I was continuously scanning the published papers to make sure I hadn't gotten 'scooped'.

When I heard Sam open the door from the garage, I glanced at the desk clock, and was shocked to see that nearly two hours had passed since I'd returned home. I closed the computer and bounded down the stairs, excited to hear about Sam's progress with the corporate attorney.

"Hi, Kelly!" Sam put his arms around me, and I held Sam tight, as we kissed enthusiastically. We walked into the kitchen, and Sam put his own briefcase on the table.

Opening the fridge, Sam grabbed a Diet Coke, and asked if I wanted one.

"Sure, Sam. I'll take one also, or split one with you. Sam handed me a can, and I realized that I was probably dehydrated, not having drunk anything since my quick lunch at one of the small concessions at school. After taking a couple of swallows of Coke, I asked, "How did it go, with the attorney?"

Sam and I sat at the breakfast table, and he took a swig of Coke and smiled, "Well, the corporation has been formed: KS Biotech, Inc. I have some papers for you to sign, and the book of corporate bylaws to review. It's all pretty standard."

He took a few more gulps of Coke, and explained, "You are the majority founding shareholder, with 80% of the shares. Raj and I each have 10% ... but you have to realize that *all* our shares will be diluted, when we actually raise money.

"The attorney suggested that Raj get his share of the company for doing some initial consulting, and allowing you to file the patent in your own name; any additional IP he helps develop will probably have to be filed through the university, and we will have to negotiate an exclusive, world-wide license with them."

Continuing, Sam said, "We had a conference call with Raj; he has worked with the Technology Transfer office before, and told us he doesn't foresee a problem getting the license. The university will probably take 10% of the company, in exchange for paying for any patents they may need to file for things you and Raj invent at school. We also found out that 10% of the company is the most that Raj is allowed own, while he's still employed by the university."

Sam finished his Coke, and continued, "My 10% is for putting in $10K as initial capital. I'm OK with consulting for the company, if that becomes necessary, but I didn't think it fair to get any more stock for the time I spend while you're in school; I love working with you, and it's not about money."

Sam gave me an evil smile, and continued, "I love *playing* with you, too." Then, he looked at me sincerely, "I guess I just *love* you." We leaned over the table toward each other, and kissed again.

Sam chuckled, "So, Kelly, your company is currently 'worth' $100K – on paper. There's really nothing *in* the company, yet, except the patent application, which hasn't yet been filed." That sounded pretty good, as I hadn't really *done* anything, yet.

Then, Sam's face turned serious, "I hope that we won't have to raise money for a year or two. Your research will be done at the university, and I'll put up the additional cash needed to prosecute the patent; we'll set-up an office for you here, and keep the expenses low."

He smiled at me, "By the time we're ready to raise 'real' money – let's say in two years – you will have proven the technology, developed the prototype product, graduated – hopefully, and the patent should be issued."

Then, he grumbled "It could take four or five years for the patent to issue, if the patent office drags their feet. But the attorney said that these kinds of biotech patents should move faster, as the entire field is evolving so quickly. We'll have to see ..."

I followed Sam up to the master bedroom, and into the closet. He looked at me oddly, as he pulled off his tie, "I hope it's OK with you ... I made reservations tonight at the French restaurant. We haven't gone there for a while ... and I'm already dressed up. What do you think?"

My mouth was watering, already. "That sounds great, Sam. The last time we were there was on Linda's birthday, when you first met her and Julie ... and triggered that stupid vibrator that was inside me."

Sam chuckled, as I undressed, and pulled a dress off the hanger. It was black, and I would need to change my bra and underwear. As I turned, now naked, toward the built-in drawers and rummaged through my underthings, Sam fingered the small round Band-Aids on my butt.

"So how did the shots go, this time?" I knew that Sam would have liked to be there, but he'd had much more important things to do ... and he'd already seen us take our first HPV and hepatitis injections a month ago, just before we left on the Europe trip.

As I put on a lacy black bra, I laughed, "They went fine, Sam." Then, I decided to give him a bit more detail. "Actually, I had told my friends when I phoned them that the shots could be given in the arm, if they preferred."

Sam gave me a disgruntled look, and I continued before he could say anything, "But they all decided that getting them in the butt wasn't a big deal, and probably hurt less. I think the nurse had expected that we would take them in the arm this time, and she just shrugged when we told her we wanted them in the butt again."

Then, I remembered the conversations I'd had at the clinic with my friends, and – as I slipped on a pair of black bikini underwear – told Sam the rest. "Kathy and I arrived first, and we had an interesting talk in the waiting area."

Sam cocked his head and let me continue, "It seemed strange that she had been so open about needles at my birthday party, during the first round of our 'spank poker' game; I had expected my friends to take only the 'ante' of two needles, and not 'raise' ... but even Kathy had raised the bet, and ended-up with four needles in her bottom."

I saw Sam adjust himself through his pants; if he got any more turned on, I might have to 'take care of him' before dinner.

"But when you brought us to the clinic to get our first round of injections, Kathy really wasn't happy about getting the shots. So, I asked her about that." Sam's head was still cocked, and he was listening intently.

"She told me that she isn't bothered by needles that much – although she said her stomach turns when she sees one close-up ... like when we stuck you at the birthday party. But, she *really* hates getting shots – the feel of the medicine being injected. I can't blame her: Even if it doesn't hurt that bad, it's *not* a nice feeling." Sam was nodding.

Then, I told Sam about the other conversation with my friends. "While the nurse was getting our shots ready, I told my friends that you had wanted to be there; they know that you get turned on by this stuff. So, I made them promise that you could come with us when we take the final round, in a few months."

Sam smiled, and I could see that something was going through his head. He really wasn't going to push them for *more*, was he? I stared at him.

He said, casually, "I was just thinking that maybe I could take a few snapshots of you guys getting the shots next time. I have a few interesting ideas for some neat shots." As I continued to stare at him, he clarified, "I mean *camera* shots; photographs." I nodded, not wanting to hear any more right now.

I slipped the dress over my head, and asked, "Shall we go to dinner, now?" Then, I added, unnecessarily, "And, don't even *think* about putting that thingy in me, this time!" Sam smiled, and nodded. I hope I hadn't given him any more ideas!

It was a nice place; I really liked the tufted leather booths, Victorian feel, and subdued lighting – although we weren't planning on 'doing' anything tonight to take advantage of the relative privacy the restaurant afforded.

And, it was nice to have a waiter who already knew my preferences. George gave me a 'look', indicating that he was surprised to see Kelly with me again, after so many months. "George, I'd like to introduce you – or re-introduce you – to Kelly. I've been helping her with her career, and we just started a business together."

George nodded, and Kelly gave me a questioning look. I continued, "And Kelly has been helping me start 'living' again, so many years after I lost Sarah." George politely waited to see what else I would say ... and so did Kelly. I glanced at her, and then looked earnestly at George, "Kelly has become the love of my life."

George smiled, then said, "One moment, Sir." He disappeared, and I leaned over and gave Kelly a peck on the lips. A few minutes later, George re-appeared, delivering some wonderful, hot sourdough bread, and a crystal container with spouts for extra virgin olive oil and aged balsamic vinegar.

Then, from under his arm, he pulled a half-bottle of wine; from the gold foil around the top, I realized it was Champagne. George presented the bottle, holding it so that both Kelly and I could read the label: Perrier-Jouët Bell Epoque Rosé – a limited edition, with a beautiful bottle with artwork that showed flowers and a hummingbird.

As he opened it, George said, "This is on me, Sir. I think you'll enjoy it." It was incredible – even the half-bottle had to cost a couple hundred dollars (and would probably sell for much more in the restaurant).

"George! That's very nice of you ... and it will be greatly appreciated ... but that really isn't necessary." I didn't know whether this would be 'sponsored' by the restaurant, or if George would really be paying the cost ... but it was quite a treat.

"It's no problem, Sir. Anything for our 'special' guests. The restaurant is offering this as one of its top Champagnes, and we just received our quota of cases ... but they also provided a few promotional half-bottles. And I'm sure you will find it special."

The cork came out with a loud 'Pop!', and George poured a small amount into two crystal glasses, the fine liquid appearing peach-colored in the low light. "George, I insist that you bring another glass, and share some of this with us!"

George smiled, put the bottle on the table, and retreated. When he returned, I poured a half-glass for him, and we toasted – to Kelly, to the new business, and to friends. The thought of Kelly's friends coming over to hear about our Europe trip flitted through my brain.

George left us, and Kelly and I toasted again – to the same things. Kelly's dark hazel eyes sparkled with the flickering candlelight or, perhaps, due to her own internal glow. Once again I was mesmerized by this beautiful woman, her youthful face and delicious smile framed by her long, auburn hair, which fell to the seat around her.

I closed my eyes, and re-opened them ... and Kelly was still there, as beautiful as ever. It was not a dream; it was now an indelible – and hopefully, eternal – part of my life.

I ordered the escargots and a New York steak, medium-rare, something that couldn't quite be matched in

Europe. Kelly selected the spinach salad and turbot – which was served with a light Hollandaise sauce.

'Holland days' ... that brought back memories of our week in The Netherlands, less than a month ago. It had been quite a trip; and I was looking forward to sharing some of our experiences with Kelly's friends.

Our appetizers and main courses were great, as usual. Kelly stood firm on her refusal to order dessert. "Sam, my jeans are already uncomfortably tight, and I have no intention of gaining more weight. You fed me quite well in Europe, and now I'm going to have to cut back ... although this dinner didn't seem like much of a cutback."

She smiled at me, "Maybe, we should *both* go on a diet for a month or two?"

I shook my head, "First of all, you don't *look* any heavier to me. And, second, I will love you regardless of your body shape – I've told you that! I may have been infatuated with your looks when we re-met a few months ago ... but now I'm in love with your brain ... with *YOU!*"

It was true. I tried to give Kelly a disgusted look, but a smile kept creeping onto my face, so I finally gave up. Then, I followed with, "You don't think *I'm* fat now, do you?"

Kelly smiled, and moved her finger around the rim of her wine glass. Although the Champagne had been a good start, I'd ordered a bottle of fine Rioja to go with our dinner; it tasted like an aged Bordeaux, but was still light enough to pair well with Kelly's fish. We were floating, now, and needed neither dessert nor an after-dinner drink. Kelly looked up into my face, "You look fine, Sam." Then, she giggled, and added, "For your age."

I was about to get upset, then remembered our early friendship, when Kelly had been seething every time I mentioned her age. I took a deep breath, and let it out slowly. "Touché."

I thought a little more about Kelly's suggestion of dieting, and complained, "We can't start a diet now, Kelly; the holidays are coming up. We haven't even talked about Thanksgiving ... but I was hoping to make Christmas dinner, and invite my sons. And, it would be nice to have your family over, also." I thought about the four boys seeing each other again ... and Dave seeing them again ...

Kelly answered, "My brothers usually come home to visit over the holidays. Let's think about it." Kelly smiled, as she thought of the implications; although she certainly did not know *all* of the implications of such a get-together.

Kelly concluded, "Actually, that sounds nice – my brothers and your sons could see each other again, and catch up." More thoughts flitted through my head, which I realized was now well-muddled by the wine. I decided to focus on the here-and-now, and try to drive us home safely. To *our* home. How things can change, with time!

It had been a nice dinner. I guess I was getting used to having nice dinners, as I remembered quite a few we'd had in Europe. And, despite both of us feeling the wine, we enjoyed the evening, starting with a romp on the big bed in the playroom, and then retiring to the bedroom, where we made love slowly and passionately.

As I drifted off to sleep, I thought about some of the stories from Europe that we would share with Julie, Linda and Kathy – and the souvenirs that we'd bought for them. They seemed pretty minimal, now, but we really hadn't had much room to bring back anything else.

Then, I remembered a few of the things we *had* brought back ... wondering whether we would show them to my friends. I heard Sam already snoring next to me, and realized that he would certainly want to share a few of our more 'interesting' experiences with them. I closed my eyes, forced myself to relax, and put my thoughts aside; until tomorrow.

Sam decided to make pizza and a big salad for our gathering this evening, although he'd finally made the decision to buy pizza dough at the market, and not make his own – which, he explained, should have been done yesterday, so that it could have been refrigerated overnight.

We spent the early afternoon preparing everything: Me chopping vegetables, while Sam cooked his special red sauce for the pizza, and made a balsamic vinaigrette dressing for the salad.

While pizza wasn't the most slimming choice for my 'diet', Sam had explained that I could limit myself to a single slice, while others could take as much as they wanted. Sam, always the consummate host, never wanted his guests to go hungry ... so, as usual, we made way more food than was necessary for the five of us.

Sam had picked out a couple of bottles of inexpensive chianti – but had a difficult time finding the 'old style' bottles in the wicker baskets.

He had also insisted on stopping at an Italian bakery in town to pick up some cannolis, then whined all the way home that we hadn't really planned a dinner apropos to our trip – nothing Dutch, or German, or Swiss, or French.

By the time we got home, Sam had already planned to invite my friends over for another couple of dinners – one being an elaborate Indonesian *rijstaffel*, and the other being a Swiss fondue dinner ... with a dark chocolate fondue dessert. It sounded great, but I hoped that I would have time to lose some weight before either of those dinners!

After putting the vegetables in baggies, I went upstairs to wrap the gifts for my friends and set out several things I would be 'modeling' for them. It was silly, but Sam had insisted that this had been part of our Europe trip, and had to be part of our show for my friends. We had nothing 'sexy' planned for the evening, but the show would be sexy enough.

Of course, we had no pictures from the sex club, nor any of the saunas, as a camera would have been totally inappropriate.

But Sam had snapped a few pics of the outside of a few of the saunas – like the one we had walked to north of Amsterdam, the health spa in the far south near the Belgian border, and the one in Zurich, where he had actually used his phone to take a short 360-degree video from the end of the sauna deck that jutted out into the lake – showing the snow-covered mountains, our hotel on the hill, and the lights of the city that had just been coming on in the early evening.

I laid a few outfits on the bed, and then went back downstairs to see how Sam was doing with the dinner preparations. Sam asked me to set the table, and we used the fine china, crystal and silver – which seemed much too fancy for our simple 'pizza and salad' dinner with friends.

But that was Sam's style: Striving for the highest standards, even when they were not necessary or, in some cases, wouldn't really be appreciated.

And, he was always over-doing it; not settling for a 'normal' experience, when he could share something more special with friends. I guess it didn't really matter – we would be putting everything but the crystal in the dishwasher; but I couldn't remember back to when my mother had served us dinner on the fine china she'd had for decades.

That caught me suddenly, and I sat down at the breakfast table, thinking about the conversation with my mother, as Sam stood at the stove, now cooking crumbled sausage in one pan, while sautéing red, orange and yellow peppers with some sliced onions in another pan.

During the past few days, while I was in the lab at school, Sam had also thoroughly cleaned the house. I chuckled as I thought what a good 'wife' he would make someday. That brought back images of Helga – when she had first called to Sam in the bar, Sam looking around confusedly, not recognizing his long-time friend, Henk, transformed into a woman.

My thoughts returned to my mother, and I wondered what was in the envelope she had given me. I'd told her I would wait to open it, and was in no rush to do so today. As I stared toward the stove, my eyes did not see Sam, but the image of my birth parents, looking kindly at me. I couldn't help but wonder where they might be, today.

All my thoughts suddenly evaporated as the doorbell rang, and I realized my friends had arrived. I opened the front door, and Linda stood there, smiling at me. We hugged, and she informed me that Julie and Kathy would be driving over together, in a while.

I had suggested that my friends bring over a few things, in case they wanted to stay overnight, and I led Linda upstairs to drop her tote in one of the guest bedrooms. Then, we went downstairs, and into the kitchen, where Sam was stirring the contents of three pots, in turn, with a wooden spoon.

"Hi, Linda!" Sam hugged Linda, and then kissed her European-style: First on the left cheek, then on the right. Although I guess it depended on which country you were in ... and I didn't remember which was which, except for the

Netherlands, where three kisses were given, alternating sides.

Linda's eyes grew wide, as she looked at the pots on the stove, "Boy, it smells like an Italian restaurant, in here!"

Sam nodded, and complained, "Yeah, and we didn't even visit Italy on our trip! I promised Kelly that I would make an Indonesian dinner next time – like we had in The Netherlands." Then, Sam glanced at me, and continued, "or a German dinner, or Swiss dinner, or French dinner."

He smiled at Linda, "If you guys like my cooking, we'll have to invite you back for some different kinds of ethnic cuisine."

Linda was shaking her head slowly, "Well, Sam, if any of this is as good as your barbeque, we would be happy to come back for more." She leaned her head over the pan of vegetables, now partially caramelized, the aroma of basil and oregano clearly discernable. "And, I can already tell you that my mouth is watering for this Italian food – whatever you're making!"

Sam turned off all three burners, and explained, "It's just a simple pizza and salad tonight. Nothing fancy." I laughed inwardly, as I glanced into the dining room, at the formal place settings on the nice tablecloth. A vision of another 'simple' Italian dinner came to mind, when Sam had served me in the dining room, wearing his long chef's apron ... and nothing else!

As Sam uncorked one of the bottles of chianti, and poured a glass for Linda, we heard the doorbell ring, and I went to the door to let Julie and Kathy in. As we hugged, they were already sniffing, and Kathy exclaimed, "Wow! That smells great!"

I nodded, and explained, "Sam is making a 'simple' pizza dinner for us." Julie and Linda dropped their totes by the door, and we all walked into the kitchen.

Sam had a spice jar in one hand, and a spoon in the other, as he tasted the sausage. In a fake, overly-done Italian accent, he cried out, "Mama mia! That's a spicy meatball!"

We all laughed, and he put everything down, and exclaimed, "Hi girls!" Then he hugged Julie and Kathy, giving them both a kiss on each cheek, and immediately turning to pour glasses of wine for them.

Julie looked at me, and I shrugged. Sam was hyper 'hyper' today. He poured himself some wine – some *more* wine – and raised his glass. "It's great to see you guys again. I'm glad you all could come to our little party!"

We sipped the wine, and sat around the breakfast table. Linda licked her lips, saying, "This is a nice wine, Sam. And my mouth is watering, smelling that Italian aroma."

Sam nodded, "This is just a cheap chianti. Actually, there are some really great 'reserve' chiantis – as well as Amarones, Brunellos, and other famous Italian wines. Many people don't realize that Italy has some wines nearly as fine as the French ones. But tonight, I'm just making pizza and salad for you guys."

Before anyone could respond, Sam glanced at me, and back to my friends. "Kelly and I have been pretty busy since we got back from Europe." He looked at each one of my friends, in turn, and added, "Kelly just started a company!" Sam raised his wine glass, and my friends slowly followed suit, but their stares were blank, not realizing what this meant.

I explained, taking Sam's lead, "Due to jetlag, or whatever, I stayed up a few nights early in our Europe trip

... and imagined a way that the technology from my Ph.D. work could be used to help discover new drugs." I glanced at Sam, who's glass was still raised, and continued, "Sam helped me with some of the ideas, and when I met with my advisor a week ago, he agreed that the idea might work. And, if it does, it could be a big advance in designing new drugs to treat important diseases."

I took a sip of wine, "Both Raj – my advisor – and Sam suggested that we commercialize the concept as soon as possible ... so we're applying for a patent, and – as of yesterday – we formed a corporation."

My friends were stunned, still staring, as I took another sip of wine. "Sam is putting up some money, and Raj will be working with me to develop the technology, and ... I guess ... I'm now the CEO of a corporation; called "KS Biotech, Inc."

I looked around the small breakfast table. I think my friends were still dumbfounded – not able to get their heads around the idea that I was now president of a corporation. Actually, neither could I; it had all happened so suddenly.

Linda was the first to respond: She put her glass down, and clapped her hands, "Congratulations, Kelly! That's great! I hope you guys make it a big success!" Julie and Kathy nodded, and each took a swallow of wine.

As the table was silent, I introduced the evening, "Tonight, we're going to share a little of our Europe trip with you ... but it turned out to be a lot more than touring ... and sex."

I chuckled. The 'sex' was the least of it. I looked at Sam, and raised my glass to toast him, "I think Sam is as excited as I am, about the possibilities for our business. We'll give you the run-down on the trip, but we're both a little pre-occupied with everything else that's happened in the past week."

Julie's mouth was hanging open, and Kathy's eyes were glazed over. I added, "This whole thing has been a whirlwind ... but Sam has been really supportive." Then, I broke out into a full belly laugh. "Actually, the reason Sam and I first got together was so that he could guide me in my career." I smiled at Sam, coyly, "I guess he's done a pretty good job of it!"

Sam took a swallow of wine and put his glass down, shaking his head, "Actually, I didn't do anything; just listened to Kelly ... and her good ideas. I was afraid that Kelly was ill, or overly-jetlagged, as she was really tired the 4th or 5th day of our trip; but I soon found out why: She had been staying up all night doing research, while I was sleeping. So I can't really take any credit for all this."

Now, I had to shake my head, "No. Sam's questions and ideas were pivotal to my thought process." I laughed again, "And, maybe the Europe trip ... and saunas ... and sex ... relaxed me enough to spur my creativity, so that I could think of all this stuff. I give Sam a lot of credit for us getting this far with the idea."

Now, Julie was nodding, "Kelly, you've always been the smartest one of all of us." She glanced at Sam, and back to me, "And it seems like you've never been happier than in the past few months, being with Sam."

I nodded. That was true. It was hard to believe that all of this was real. But, as Sam had warned, we had a long way to go. Maybe we wouldn't be able to get the technology to work. Maybe someone else was working on this, and would beat us to the first patent and prototype machine. A million things could get in our way. But I was hopeful, and it really helped having supportive people around me, like Raj and Sam. And, my friends.

Sam suggested that we go into the living room, or down in the playroom, and talk for a while, as he made the pizzas. I thought about bringing everyone out to the patio, but it was already chilly. We were all wearing jeans and a sweater or, in Kathy's case, a sweatshirt; but it just felt more 'homey' here in the kitchen.

Sam shrugged, and began making the pizzas. He briefly explained, "I'm going to make two large pizzas – one with roasted vegetables, and the other classic Italian, with pepperoni, sausage, peppers, mushrooms, and onions." We all nodded, and continued our discussion around the breakfast table.

Kelly had exaggerated my role in her company; I had really just been a sounding board for her – she had done all the research, and creatively invented the concept. She was now in for a lot more work – both finishing her dissertation, and running the company.

I made two large pizzas, even trying to 'spin' one into the air – which worked OK (at least I caught it, before it hit the floor, and it actually turned out to exactly fit the pizza pan). I brushed the pizzas with olive oil, covered the dough with a generous amount of red sauce, and then added the toppings, mozzarella cheese, and pepper, dried oregano, and fresh basil on top, along with a sprinkle of freshly-grated Parmesan. I had already put the pizza stones in the ovens, and pre-heated them to 500 degrees.

As the girls chatted, I opened another bottle of chianti, and went into the dining room to pour it, leaving the bottle on the table, and lighting the candles. I turned down the dining room lights, then took out the already-washed lettuce and other salad-fixings, and made the salad. I tossed the salad with the dressing, and divided it onto plates, which I brought into the dining room; then I popped the pizzas into the ovens, setting the timer for 10 minutes.

I turned to the girls, and announced, "Dinnah is sahved, ladies!" The girls washed up and entered the dining room, 'Ooohing' and 'Aaahing' as they sat. They put the linen napkins in their laps, and looked around at the formal place settings, shaking their heads.

About the time we finished the salads, the timer on the oven dinged, and I removed the salad plates and checked the pizzas. Another 2-3 minutes, and they were done perfectly. I let them cool for a few minutes, while I sat at the head of the table, sipped the wine, and listened to the girls' conversation. Finally, I put a large plate in front of each of the guests, cut the pizzas into twelve wedges, and brought them to the table.

There was more "Ooohing' and 'Aaahing', as the Kelly's friends looked at the pizzas, took their slices, and passed the large round trays around the table. The girls must have enjoyed the food, as the conversation quieted, and I heard a lot of 'Mmmms', and smacking of lips.

At one point, Linda – holding a half-eaten slice in her hands – looked up at Kelly, and said, "If you get tired of him, I'll take him off your hands – or whatever – for a while!" Everyone laughed. I got up and walked around the table, refilling everyone's wine glasses. Kathy smiled, and seconded the motion, telling Kelly that it was the best pizza she'd ever eaten.

Then, Julie got up, came over to me, bent down, and kissed me on the lips. As she stood to my side, she put her hand on my shoulder, and announced, "Sorry, girls. If Kelly gets tired of Sam, I've got first dibs."

Everyone laughed but, as Linda helped herself to another slice, she shook her head, and said quietly, "I'm prepared to duel you for him."

Then, Kelly said, seriously, "Forget it! He's all mine, and he's not going anywhere." I just shrugged; what else could I do? As Kelly had said, I wasn't going anywhere ... and I was all *Kelly's*; mentor, lover, slave ... *whatever*.

When we'd all had our fill (or more), the girls carried the plates, silverware and glasses back to the kitchen, and insisted they would rinse them and put everything in the dishwasher. I retired to the playroom, where I set-up the show, adjusted the lighting, pulled the love seat around, in line with the couch, and piled the gifts that Kelly had wrapped on one of the chairs in front of the desk.

I pushed a button on the remote, closing the drapes in front of the bed at the far end of the room, and lowering the screen. I wasn't sure what would transpire after the show, but – just in case – decided to heat-up the sauna. Then, I chuckled, thinking that it was more likely that we'd all be *per*spiring, than anything *tran*spiring.

A few minutes after I'd finished the preparations, the girls came downstairs, and took their places on the couch and loveseat. Kelly stood by the desk, and I got up – taking the role of the official emcee, and introduced the show.

"Before we start the show, I have a few things to tell you. First, there *will* be dessert," the girls groaned, and Kathy held her stomach, "but I'll serve that a little later. I have some special wine to go with it." I looked at each of Kelly's friends; they were very attentive – I'm sure wondering what else we had in store for the evening's activities. It would be a 'mild' evening, but hopefully they wouldn't be disappointed.

I continued, "Second, we've been so busy that I could only make a 'simple' dinner for you tonight. But, I'll invite you guys over another time – or two – for some meals more representative of our trip. Like an Indonesian *rijstaffel*, which we ate in The Netherlands, or a Swiss fondue, or some German food, or classic French food."

Kathy piped up, "But, Sam – the dinner was great! You don't have to apologize for anything."

I nodded, "I know ... but it didn't exactly come out as a 'theme' dinner for our trip; we didn't even get to Italy." Then, I added, "This time." The girls were shaking their heads.

I then had to explain a few things about the show. "We only took snapshots on the trip; there are a few videos that I took with my phone, but we didn't make a professional production of it. As I'm sure you can understand, we really don't have any 'good' pictures of the saunas, or," I chuckled, "the sex club ..." At this, Linda gasped, and put her hands over her mouth; but I knew it was an act. "... and certainly not when we visited a dominatrix in London."

At this, all the girls gasped, and there was tittering back and forth across the couch and loveseat. I nodded, "So you'll only be able to see a small part of the trip. But, we'll try to explain some of the other stuff we did, even if we don't have pictures. You'll just have to use your imaginations!"

The girls were shaking their heads again, and I continued, "We'll show you a few of the things we bought, or brought back from the trip ... AND, we do have a few very small souvenirs for you." At this the girls' eyes lit up, and they turned to Kelly, and back to me. I explained, "Just like the pareos, you can switch, if you don't like what we got you ... but we brought a few extras, so I hope you'll all be satisfied."

I heard Julie, under her breath, say, "You can 'satisfy' me anytime, Sam." Everyone chuckled ... but I didn't think either Linda or Kathy were aware of our ménage, yet.

I looked at each of Kelly's friends, and hoped that they would take the next part 'in stride' – as they had done with everything else, especially at Kelly's birthday party. "Could I please ask a favor?" I saw Julie, Linda and Kathy nodding slowly, but Linda glanced questioningly to Julie, and Julie turned her head to look at Kelly – who kept a straight face. I knew she would make a great CEO. I asked, "If you wouldn't mind, could you guys undress to your bra and underwear?"

Now there was some groaning, and sniggering, but Julie immediately stood, and undid her pants, pushing them down. Linda shrugged, pulled off her sweater, and started unbuttoning her blouse. Soon, all three women were half dressed (and, half undressed), awaiting their fate. Except for Kathy who, as usual, was braless. Kelly stepped in front of Linda, and handed her a loosely-wrapped package. Kelly said, "Linda, we got this one especially for you."

Linda quickly tore the wrapping paper, and held up a long t-shirt, black, with a jeweled front that said, "Paris", with a thin jeweled line above and below it. I explained, "We thought you guys might have more fun, and be more comfortable, wearing these as a cover-up, during our show.

Linda 'Oooohed', and slipped the long shirt over her head, smoothing it down. It was nearly as long as a short skirt. "I *love* it!" She hugged Kelly, and then me. "Thank you, so much!" She sat down, still fingering the soft material, and running her fingers over the sparkling jewels. Now, both Kathy and Julie were smiling.

Kelly stepped in front of Kathy, handing her the next package. Kathy didn't waste time tearing it open, and holding it up: It was also black, with thin white lines outlining the gabled houses – and, below them, a canal – of Amsterdam. It was modern art, and had "Amsterdam" written across it in a modern script. She put it on, and hugged Kelly and I. "Thank you! It's really nice." It seemed to match Kathy's style – hip, abstractly modern, but classy. It didn't come down quite as far as Linda's but covered her well below her beige bikini panties.

Kelly handed Julie the third package, which she opened, and put on: It was a modern rendition of two female bodies intertwined – this time, thick pink lines on a black background – with "London Girls" stenciled across it. Again, Kelly and I were hugged, and Julie gave each of us more than a casual kiss (perhaps Kelly's being more intimate than the one she gave me). Once again, the tee came down far enough, and would look good tucked in or left out with jeans or grey slacks.

Kelly smiled and handed me a package. I was pretty sure I knew which shirt it was, but we had bought several extras – just in case. I opened it, and it was a black tee with a huge beer stein (a *Maas*, what Muncheners call a liter-mug of beer) on the back, frothing over, and small white letters on the front left, that said, "Oktoberfest, Munchen 2014".

I kissed Kelly, took off my shirt and pants, and put on the tee; it came down below my black European-style underwear.

Then, Kelly undressed down to her black bikini underwear, and opened the last package. It was another black tee – this time, with a drawing of the Matterhorn on the back, and a small line of skiers across the front. We all hugged and kissed each other. I suggested, "Why don't you guys carry your extra clothes upstairs? Kelly will show you to our guest bedrooms. When you come back, we'll start the show."

The girls followed Kelly out of the playroom, and up the stairs. It seemed like they all appreciated the small gifts we had brought back from Europe. It would have been nice to bring even more souvenirs – for Kelly's friends, and her parents – but we'd had barely enough room in our rolling cases and backpacks to stuff in the t-shirts; plus the 'other' stuff that Kelly would be modeling during the show.

When everyone came back down to the playroom, I took drink orders, and provided glasses with ice, and cans of soft drinks and (for Kathy) tropical juice. Kelly and I dragged the coffee table over, so that everyone could put their drinks down, and their feet up.

Then, I dimmed the lights, and projected the photos – and a few videos – that we had taken; it seemed like a random selection, and we had to fill in with explanations: About our flights (although we didn't mention the 'mile high club' experience); our hotel in Amsterdam, overlooking the canal; our boat tour, walking tour, the sex museum, and the trip to the sauna north of Amsterdam.

Before we continued, I turned up the lights. While I described our 'hash bar' experience, Kelly snuck into the exam room to change and, just as I was describing sitting out on the balcony of our Amsterdam hotel, smoking a bit of the good stuff, and mentioning that Kelly decided to try on the outfits we had bought at the sex shop – Kelly walked out, modeling one of the fishnet 'dresses' and G-string outfits. Her friends cracked up.

I refilled everyone's drinks, as Kelly got into the other dress. Her friends were hysterical when she re-appeared wearing the nearly see-through outfit – the one she had worn at the sex club.

I turned down the lights again, and continued the show, the girls cracking up again, when we explained Henk's (I mean Helga's) coming-out party at the cross-dressing and transgender bar. I had taken a short video clip with my phone of Helga singing her heart out ... and Kelly told them about being escorted to the ladies room by Helga.

Then, we showed pictures of Zöe, their home in Driebergen, and the sauna nestled in the forest in Soesterberg.

I had snapped a few pics of the *rijstaffel*, our 30-dish Indonesian dinner, and Zöe dressed as a dyke. We did not mention our submission and sex experience with Henk and Zöe, but did briefly describe the sex club. Again, Linda's hands were over her face, as Kelly narrated her experience spanking Max, and then masturbating as he watched her in the mirror.

We quickly flipped through the slides of our drive south, over the massive water project, and to the health spa in Valkenburg. I briefly turned the lights back up, and passed around brochures from *Thermae 2000*. Then, the lights dimmed again, and Kelly described our drive through Luxembourg's "little Switzerland", up the Mosel river, and our stay in Koblenz, at the confluence of the Mosel and Rhine rivers, as I flipped through the pictures.

Lights up again, Kelly modeled the ski jacket that I had bought her (wearing only panties underneath). Then, I suggested that we take a short intermission, while I got the dessert ... and dessert wine, ready. There was some groaning, but I think everyone was looking forward to the 'special' wine.

While Kelly brought the dresses and jacket upstairs, and Linda and Kathy used the downstairs bathroom, Julie came up to the kitchen with me. I put two small cannolis on each plate, then surrounded them with fresh blackberries, and a sprig of mint. Julie and I carried the plates, forks and napkins down to the playroom. Then, I opened the wine, and poured it into crystal glasses on the playroom bar. Everyone back in their seats, Linda's eyes went wide, and licked her lips. "That looks incredible, Sam!"

I apologized, "The cannolis should be great – they're from an Italian bakery in town … but they really don't represent our trip very well." Then, I carried the glasses to the coffee table. "But this wine is typical of the Mosel sparkling wines that we tasted. It's a Beerenauslese – a very sweet wine, not usually drunk in the U.S., but perfect with a very sweet dessert, like the cannolis."

Kelly took over, explaining the various levels (sweetnesses) of German wine, and described our incredible dinner at the *schlosshotel* in the Neckar Valley. Everyone tasted the wine, and began their desserts, as I dimmed the lights again, and showed pictures of the view from the castle hotel.

Kelly told them about the couple we met in the sauna there, and then we continued the tour of the Romantic Road – including such tidbits as our stop at the 'torture museum' – down to Munich.

There were more pictures than I had remembered taking – and they seemed random; scenes of Munich, a short video of the guys 'surfing' on the stream coming out of the *Englischer Garten* – the large park in Munich where people sunbathe nude; the *Rathaus* (city hall) with its clock performance – which I had captured in another short video; pictures of the *Hofbrauhaus* beer hall, and the pork shanks on spits in a window of the *Haxnbauer*.

Kelly described the sauna at the top of the skyscraper and the one in our hotel. And, then, we told Kelly's friends about our Oktoberfest experience.

I did have quite a few pictures – of the beer tents with thousands of people; a short video of the guy on the table quaffing an entire liter of beer in a few seconds; Kelly's ride on the spinning disk – in her *dirndl*; and even a picture of me in my *lederhosen*. Kelly wanted me to model them for her friends, but I suggested we try on our Oktoberfest outfits later ... or maybe not.

I had a good picture of the Sky Fall ride – from the bottom; but I had been too petrified to use my camera at the top. Kelly went on and on about my fear of heights, as I finished the first cannoli, and poured more wine for everyone. Then, she had to go on and on about my passing out in the field of 'dead bodies' – many thousands of other men who had drunk a few too many *Maas* of beer.

We took another short break, while Kelly changed in the exam room ... and came out in her bright-red, full latex outfit. Her friends screamed and squealed ... and so did I. It was an incredible outfit – form fitting (to say the least), with most of her breasts coming out of holes in the suit.

She wore a black mask (I would need to buy her a matching red one!), and she moved sensuously around the room, straddling Kathy's lap (Kathy was hysterical), and then Linda's.

Kelly concluded her performance in the latex suit by pulling Julie up, enveloping her, and kissing her zealously – full mouth, snake-like tongue moving around in Julie's mouth, then putting her hand under Julie's tee, and into the front of her black thong.

Julie returned some of the feelings (!), but Kelly's emotion was really over-the-top now, as I – and Linda and

Kathy – watched, our mouths open, Kelly literally *attacking* Julie with her passion.

After a few minutes, she pushed Julie back onto the love seat, and stalked out of the room, which was now silent, except for some heavy breathing coming from Julie … and the rest of us. Kelly emerged from the exam room wearing her tee, and sat down next to me. She leaned over and gave me a peck on the lips … and once again, I wondered whether I would lose Kelly to a woman.

I blinked, and Kelly laughed easily. Her friends – including Julie – could do nothing but stare at her for several long minutes. Finally, I dimmed the lights again, and re-started the show, again amazed at – or by – the incredible woman sitting next to me.

We showed pictures of our drive to Zurich, the video from the sauna deck that jutted into the lake, our drive to Zermatt, and even one from the small sailboat – of the waterfall and sheer cliffs descending to the *Thunersee*.

Then, we got to Zermatt, and showed some incredible views of the Matterhorn from our room at the small bed-and-breakfast at which we'd stayed. Kelly gushed about our Matterhorn skiing experience, including our ski down the Italian side, for lunch. She hadn't even mentioned our ski day on the *Jungfrau* above Interlaken.

When I showed a poor shot through the window of the plane over Paris, centered on the Eiffel Tower, Linda screamed, "*That's* what *I* want to see!"

We flipped through the pictures of Paris; I thought I had edited the images, but there were sure a lot more than I had realized. Kelly explained our 'electric kiss' at the top of the Eiffel Tower, as 20,000 lights turned on and twinkled around us. Unfortunately, I had no pictures of that … but soon we were showing the Montmartre hill, and the view of the lit Eiffel Tower from there, just after sunset.

I had a few short video clips made with my phone of the incredible cabaret show – including the nude girls with the snakes, and a bunch of other pictures during our boat ride, the Rodin Museum, the *Champs Élysées* from the top of the *Arc de Triomphe*, and many more.

Somehow, the pictures of London were a letdown – the Beefeaters standing guard in front of the Tower of London, some panoramas of London from the viewing deck of the *Shard* (now, said to be the tallest building in Europe), a few of the mummies in the British Museum (which didn't look very interesting in my pictures), the red double-decker busses at Trafalgar Square, and a few others.

I turned off the projector, and turned the lights up a bit, and Kelly spent a long time describing our Domme experience. Well, it sure seemed long, as she described needles through the skin on the underside of my penis; inserting a catheter through my urethra and into my bladder; injecting saline into my balls; and 'branding' me with an ice-cold branding iron (which I initially thought was hot, as I had been wearing a blindfold).

I closed my eyes, and shivered, just thinking about it again. It seemed like Kelly had had all the fun!

Kelly spent even more time explaining how she had been invited to take a dominatrix course – funded by some lecherous old guy; well, maybe not that old – probably younger than me. It was difficult for me to hear, but I was proud of Kelly: All the things she had done during the trip, and how impressed the real Domme had been with her.

I blurted out to her friends, "And here, I thought that *I* would be the Master (the 'Dom'), and *Kelly* the slave. Now, if she takes that course, *she* will turn out to be the fully trained dominatrix, and she'll want *me* to be *her* slave!" I realized my voice had risen, and beads of sweat were coming out on my forehead.

Linda laughed, "Well, Sam, you *did* ask for it! And, Kelly has put up with a lot of your submission challenges; so why shouldn't she get *her* chance?"

Kathy was nodding vigorously, "It's only fair, Sam." She glanced at her friends, "You put us *all* through a lot, at Kelly's birthday party. Maybe it's time to submit to her?"

Flustered, and blustering, I stuttered, "But I *have* submitted. To *her* and to *you guys*! I let you spank me at her birthday party, and then you guys insisted on sticking a butt plug in me, and making me come, while you watched!" I was getting riled up, and frustrated. Hadn't I submitted to Kelly, already?

Julie chimed in, "It didn't seem like you were suffering too much, Sam." She glanced at Kelly and smiled, then looked back at me, seriously, "And, after all, Kelly *is* the strong one."

This was too much. I stood, and paced back and forth. Finally, I said, "I'm going out to the patio to cool off!" I stomped out of the room, grabbed a beer from the fridge, and went out into the chilly darkness of the patio, not bothering to turn on the lights.

As I paced back and forth, I cooled down – both mentally and physically – and thought about the situation. The girls were right: Kelly should get her chance to 'top' me … seriously. I realized that I was reacting out of fear. The Domme experience had been much more intense than I had expected … or wanted to do again.

And, I guess, I was still a little upset that Kelly had been chosen to take a course … and that some guy was going to sponsor her. And that I might end-up being *her* slave!

I gulped the beer, and felt hot under the collar ... except that the tee I was wearing didn't *have* a collar. I shouldn't be so upset; Kelly deserved everything that her friends had suggested. She was a strong woman, and I loved her. And, I trusted her.

Sam really seemed upset; in fact, I had never seen him this way. I left my friends in the playroom, and went out to the patio, where Sam was chugging the last of his beer. It was really cold out here. As I approached him, Sam just stared at me. I took the bottle from him, and put it on the patio table. "Sam." He blinked a few times, trying to focus on me; I think he had been in a rage.

But, *why*? There was nothing new, in what I had told my friends. Or shown them. I put my arms around Sam, and – after a few moments – he relaxed, his shoulders sagging, and finally putting his arms around me. I kissed him deeply, although it didn't seem that he returned my enthusiasm. Finally, I suggested, "Let's go back inside." I took his hand, and led him inside, and back downstairs.

We sat back on the couch, but Sam said nothing. I shivered. "Sam, I'm sorry if I over-did the description of our experience with Mistress Elena. You know that I'm turned on by the idea of being trained as a dominatrix. But I haven't decided to go to London and take that course; and you *know* that the guy who would sponsor it means nothing – he just wants to watch, and maybe be dominated by the 'new girl on the block'."

Maybe that hadn't come out right. Sam was still upset. I glanced at Julie, and said, "And you *know* that I'll never leave you for another woman! I like Julie; I like *all* my friends. And, so do you." I shivered again.

Julie rose and walked slowly over to Sam, bending down, and kissing him on the mouth. Again, Sam didn't return the emotion. Julie straddled Sam's legs, and held his head in her hands. "Sam, I'm sorry if I showed too much emotion with Kelly. You know I love you both. And Kelly will always be yours. I would just like to be a friend ... to *both* of you." Julie went back to her seat.

Linda said, "Sam, I'm sorry, too. I *know* you have submitted – to Kelly, and to us, too. You've been great. Please don't feel hurt." Linda looked at me, and continued, "And you *know* that Kelly is a strong person. She loves you deeply; she's made that very clear to all of us."

Then, Kathy said, very softly, "Sam, we *all* love you. And respect you. It hurts us to see you so upset."

I shivered again – perhaps from the cold, and perhaps also from my emotions. I said, "Sam, I really got chilled outside. Can we please go in the sauna?" I looked around at my friends, "All of us?" Everyone nodded. Sam seemed to soften; but his eyes were wet.

"I'm sorry everyone. I don't exactly know what got into me, but I apologize; to Kelly, and to all of you." He sniffed, "This was supposed to be a fun evening, sharing our European adventure with you ..."

Linda stood, and stepped over my feet, standing in front of Sam, then bent down to give him a light kiss on the lips. Then, she stepped to the side of the coffee table, pulled her tee over her head, reached around and unhooked her bra, letting it slip off her arms, and quickly pushed down her pale blue underwear. "Well, I'm going in the sauna."

She looked around the couch and loveseat, "Does anybody want to join me?" With that, Julie and Kathy stood, pulled off their new t-shirts, and removed their underwear; Julie took off her bra, and headed toward the downstairs bathroom and sauna.

When my friends had gone, and I heard the shower running, I took Sam's head in my hands, and turned it toward me, kissing him until he responded – finally putting his arms around me and kissing me back. He said, "I'm sorry, Kelly. I guess I've been a little uptight about starting the business, dealing with your parents, maybe still a little jetlagged, and a little confused about my role in our relationship."

Sam finally smiled a little, "No, I'm not really worried about you running off with Julie ..." then he continued more seriously, "... but yes, I was a little shocked by our Domme experience, and your being invited to become a dominatrix, yourself." Sam looked down into his lap, and I tilted his head, so that I could look into his eyes.

"Sam, you have nothing to worry about. We will work on the business together. My parents responded very well to my moving out." I chuckled, "I think my dad has really wanted the room over the garage!" Sam sighed.

I continued, "And, your role in our relationship hasn't changed: You're my mentor and my lover, my hero and my partner, and I will always submit to you, if you ask me." I took a deep breath, "And I won't take the dominatrix training, unless you want me to."

I kissed him again, then stood. "Now, why don't we join my friends in the sauna?" Sam looked up at me with a crooked smile, and nodded.

Sam and I showered together and entered the sauna, taking the spaces between my friends; Kathy sat on the lower bench. After the huge saunas in Europe, Sam's sauna felt tiny.

It was very quiet, until I decided to start the conversation. "As I told you guys, we've been under a lot of pressure, this week. First, I had to meet with my advisor, and he wanted us to move quickly on the patent and starting the company. Then, I met with my parents ... and informed them that I would be moving in with Sam."

That brought some surprised looks, and Julie whistled. "So how did *that* go?" she asked.

I smiled, "Actually, surprisingly well. I haven't seen them much, anyway, and it came out that my dad had been wanting to convert the room over the garage into his 'man cave'." Julie laughed, and Linda and Kathy nodded.

I continued, "My mother was upset, but not about me moving out: I got a notice from the adoption court. Maybe she thinks that I will try to find my birth parents, and is insecure about what will happen."

Kathy said, "Why? She's been your mother since you were a little girl. I'm sure she can't be worried about 'losing' you. That doesn't make sense." I shrugged. But Kathy was right: I really wasn't sure what had upset her so much. Maybe I *should* open that envelope and find out what it was about?

I continued recounting the events of our tough week. "We've both been jetlagged a little, and have spent several nights working on the patent. Then, Sam spent most of yesterday with the attorney, forming the corporation. I've still got a lot of papers to read through and sign."

I looked at Sam as I told my friends the next part. "And the experience with the dominatrix in London really was more serious than either of us – especially Sam – had expected. Sam had told her that he wanted some new experiences, and she really laid it on ... with some things that surprised both of us. Sam was strapped down a lot of the time ... and you guys know how that feels."

Kathy nodded, "Yeah. We know: That 'spank poker' game. It was scary, not knowing what was going to happen, and not having any control."

I looked at Kathy, "Exactly! We had no idea what Mistress was going to do to us. Sam told her that he was interested in medical fetish stuff ... but I don't think he expected anything like what happened."

I chuckled, then stifled it. "Even *I* was scared, and I wasn't the one strapped down having needles stuck through my sensitive parts. And that catheter ..." Sam was looking down into his lap, and shaking his head slowly.

I concluded, "I haven't decided whether I would actually get trained ... and if Sam doesn't want me to, I certainly won't do it. It sounds interesting, but isn't worth either of us getting upset about. I love Sam, and won't do anything to jeopardize our relationship." I looked at Sam, and he glanced at me, and nodded sheepishly.

Sam said, softly, "I'm sorry, guys. And Kelly. As Kelly said, we've been under some stress lately ... and to finish our trip with that experience and then immediately get into this business stuff ..."

Shaking his head again, Sam said, "I don't know. I've been retired now for several years, and – I guess – I haven't had to face much stress." Looking into my eyes, Sam assured me, "And I love Kelly, too. I want her to be happy." Then, he coughed, and added, "I guess I might have been a bit nervous about her moving in, also."

That was news. Then I remembered, "Sam even offered me one of the guest rooms, in case I was uncomfortable not having my own space." I turned to Sam, "But I *am* comfortable ... with you. I *love* being with you, Sam. Unless *you're* uncomfortable ..." This was getting to be a delicate discussion to have sitting with my friends.

But Sam replied immediately, "Kelly, I love being with you, too. And I'm *not* uncomfortable sharing my home with you. It's *our* home." Then, he smiled, "You and I have been together just about every minute of the day for the past month. And I've loved it. I'm very comfortable with you."

Looking down into his lap again, he shook a few drops of sweat from his nose and chin. "I guess I'm just tired."

Linda stood, and stepped down to the tile floor. "Now, I'm getting overheated." She opened the door, and we all filed out and got under the shower together. Silently, comfortably, we bathed each other. It felt really good to have such close friends; close enough that we could shower together. Close enough that Sam and I could have that discussion in front of them.

We dried off, and gave three of the robes to my friends, and I took the last one; Sam wrapped his towel around his waist. We would have to get a couple more robes, if we expected to entertain so many guests. We all put back on our underwear and tees. Sam took bottles of water from the bar fridge, and handed one to each of us.

I went upstairs with my friends, Linda and Julie taking one guest room, and Kathy the other. Sam followed us, after turning off the electronics and most of the lights. When he peeked into the guest bedrooms, my friends were already in bed.

Sam walked over to Linda, bent down, and kissed her on the forehead. "Thank you, Linda. I hope you enjoyed our show ... up to the point that I ruined it."

Linda said, "Sam, I understand. You guys seem to have had a pretty smooth relationship, so far." She chuckled, and added, "Far longer than any I've had with a guy!"

Then Sam stepped over to Julie, in the kitty-corner bed, bent down, and kissed her on the forehead. Julie pulled his head toward her, and gave him a kiss on the lips. "Thank you, Sam. Your cooking was great, as usual ... and we did enjoy the show. It looked like a fantastic trip. Kelly is very lucky to have someone who love's her like you do."

Sam walked to the door, and turned off the light. "Good night." I stood in the hallway, as Sam walked into Kathy's already-dark room, bent down, and kissed her on the forehead.

She said, "Good night, Sam. Thanks for everything. I really enjoyed the food, and the wine, and the pictures."

"Good night, Kathy." Sam and I walked into the master bedroom, and soon were in bed, also. We held each other until we were asleep, which didn't take long.

I felt much better when I woke, but was embarrassed that I had caused such a scene last night. When I went downstairs, Kelly had already put out cereal and milk for her friends, and was standing at the counter cutting some fruit. I kissed her, and sat at the breakfast table.

The girls chatted about the coming week, and I listened to them vaguely, trying not to think about the work we had to do in the next few days. It would take a while to get back in the groove, after five years of retirement.

Julie and Kathy thanked us, and left early. Linda stayed, and helped Kelly strip the beds and put the sheets and pillow cases into the washing machine. When they were through, we all sat at the breakfast table.

Linda smiled at me, "Sam, that was an incredible trip that you gave Kelly for her birthday. I can't even imagine all the things you guys did, in only three weeks." Then, she looked down, and back up – glancing at Sam, then me, and back to Sam. "I have to admit, I'm a little jealous of Kelly. You're both lucky to have each other."

I nodded, "I agree. We've been very good for each other. Our relationship started by me trying to give Kelly some new experiences, and show her a more open lifestyle ... but it has evolved to her showing me that I was never very open about certain things."

I smiled at Kelly, "But I think she's making progress with me, too; opening me up a little." Kelly was nodding.

Linda glanced at Kelly, and then asked me, "Sam? ... Kelly? This might not be the right time ... but I wanted to ask you something." She looked at Kelly, and added, "To do something for me."

I looked at Kelly and she shrugged; neither of us had any idea what Linda was going to ask. Linda coughed, and then looked me in the eye. "Sam, if it's OK with Kelly ... would you want to do a 'role play' with me, sometime?"

Now, I was shocked; *happily* shocked. Linda was clearly a sexual woman, but this was coming out of left field. "What kind of role play, Linda?" I was intrigued, but didn't want to make any assumptions.

Linda looked at Kelly, and back to me. Then, she looked down at the table, and mumbled, "A schoolgirl spanking scene." Linda kept looking down, and there was a moment of silence. I could hear the oven clock ticking.

Then, Kelly erupted in laughter; she was laughing so hard, she was almost crying. "OF COURSE, it's OK with me, Linda! And I *know* that Sam would love it." Kelly glanced at my growing smile (not to mention something else that was also growing, down below).

Before I could say anything, Kelly added, "And, I wouldn't want to get in the way ... but maybe you could let me play a small part?" Then, she quickly changed course,

"But, of course, if you just want to play with Sam, that would be fine with me. I'll be in the lab most of the time, so you guys will have the house to yourselves."

Again, before I could say anything, Linda shook her head, "No. It would be great if you wanted to be part of the scene. Maybe we could *both* be in Sam's class ... and misbehave. Now Linda was smiling, and added, "Like we used to do. Although Julie was the real rabble-rouser." Kelly was nodding, but couldn't stop laughing.

I looked at Linda curiously. "Linda, that would be really fun." I explained unnecessarily, "And it would be a great turn-on for me." Kelly was nodding, and still laughing, although trying hard to stifle it.

Linda looked down, and said quietly, "I know. For me, too."

What a surprise! I wondered what role Kelly wanted to play ... but it didn't matter. My mind overflowed with ideas, fantasies. Kelly had finally stopped laughing; almost. I looked at Linda, and asked, "When would you like to do it?"

Linda replied immediately, "Anytime, Sam." She glanced at Kelly and was unsuccessful at trying to not smile. "My calendar is pretty open." Kelly was unsuccessful at trying to not laugh again.

I looked at Kelly, "Well, Thanksgiving is in a couple of weeks. How about the week after Thanksgiving?"

Linda smiled at me, "That would be great, Sam." Then, she frowned, "I have a few 'real' schoolgirl outfits ... but I don't think any of them will fit me, anymore. It might take that long for me to get something together."

This was an amazing turn of events – one that neither Kelly nor I would have expected; although we had both seen how turned-on Linda had been months ago, when I gave her a 'birthday spanking'. We helped Linda collect her things, and walked her to her car.

The mood had flipped 180 degrees, since the scene I had made last night: We were all intrigued by the possibility of 'playing' together, and I was excited for Linda to have volunteered something like this. *Especially* her desire to role-play a schoolgirl scene.

I pictured Kelly and Linda, in their schoolgirl outfits, one misbehaving more than the other, and both getting spanked. Or strapped. Or paddled. The possibilities were amazing.

CHAPTER 3: SCHOOLGIRL LINDA

My sons updated me on their situations, and I asked if they would consider coming home over the holidays – and, specifically, to a Christmas dinner party that I wanted to organize. Robert and his wife said they would be delighted to come home for a visit, and would fly back the day after New Year's.

Although I had originally wanted to tell my sons about Kelly when they were here, I realized that would not be fair to anyone, so broke the news the best way I could – by being direct. Robert laughed, and congratulated me for having a 'girlfriend', and didn't seem at all concerned that Kelly was younger than him by a few years.

I mentioned having Kelly's parents and her brothers come to the party, but Robert had no particular thoughts about that; he remembered Dave's sons, but hadn't seen them for more than half his life.

Mark was a bit unsure about coming home, but when I insisted that he bring his partner, he accepted the invitation, and thanked me, then said that they had plans for New Year's eve, and would have to fly back a few days after Christmas.

He also laughed, hearing that I had a young female friend, commenting that he always knew that I was 'oversexed', whatever that meant. He did make a comment about playing with someone my own age, but was happy that I had companionship, now that his mother was gone.

He became nervous again, however, when I mentioned Dave and his sons. "Dad, you know how Dave was always talking to us about 'being a man'. I can't even imagine how he will react to my situation." I assured him that I couldn't care less how he would react.

I loved my sons, and he loved his daughter, and the families would be thrust together due to the fact that I loved Kelly. However, I was also nervous, and could only imagine what Dave would think. Hopefully, he would keep his thoughts to himself.

Kelly invited her parents to the party, and asked that they make sure her brothers knew that they were also invited. It would be important to have everyone together.

I also suggested that we make an impromptu Thanksgiving dinner for Kelly's parents, but she didn't think that would be wise; tempting fate once during the holiday season was all that she was willing to gamble.

I didn't see it as a big deal, but Kelly admitted that she was also nervous about her mother getting upset again about the adoption ... although she still had no idea exactly why her mother was so upset.

I thought about making a 'practice' dinner for Kelly and I – a trial run of turkey and stuffing, homemade cranberry sauce, and sweet potatoes, but Kelly suggested that we go out for dinner. That seemed strange to me, as even when I was alone for the past few years, I'd made Thanksgiving dinner, if just for myself. The leftovers had fed me for the next week.

We decided to go back to the French restaurant for Thanksgiving dinner. Although they did offer a gourmet version of the standard Thanksgiving meal, both Kelly and I ordered from the regular menu. George had been off that night, but the food was as good as ever.

I'd made a slight concession to the holiday and ordered duck à l'orange, one of my favorite old-time classics. Kelly ordered fish again – a seared ahi tuna, and marveled at how well-prepared a simple dish could be.

By then, Kelly was in a routine of going to her seminars and working in the lab. KS Biotech, Inc. had been fully-formed, and the stock issued to Kelly, Raj and I.

I decided to utilize the pool room as the corporate headquarters, and went to a surplus store, where I bought an old wooden desk, and several legal-size file cabinets. The room wouldn't have the same 'playful' feeling anymore, although I left the massage table in there ... and the turntable against the wall, behind the file cabinets – probably never to be used again.

In looking for used furniture at the surplus place, I amazingly found a large, well-used school blackboard, some old United States and World maps, and several old-style school desks with built-in seats, probably from the 1940's or 1950's. They were in terrible shape, the desks marked with ink, and carved with initials. But I decided to buy four of them, and spent a full day sanding them down, and re-varnishing them. I put two in the pool room, and left two in the back of the garage.

The school desks had been an amazing find, and fortunately, the varnish was dry by Wednesday – 3 days before Linda's role play experience. I put the two school desks in front of the large 'teacher's' desk, and hung the blackboard behind the large desk – taking up most of the pool room's side wall at the kitchen-end of the room, opposite the end with the half bath.

Then, I put screw-hooks into the ceiling, and hung the U.S. and World maps. The U.S. map was more-or-less accurate (although neither Alaska nor Hawaii were shown as states), but the World map was quite out-of-date. But I could still use it, if I avoided Africa and parts of Asia.

I printed some sheets with 50 math problems on each sheet; they were simple addition-subtraction and multiplication-division problems, the difficulty being determined by how long I allowed the student to complete the tests. I also found a nice map of the U.S., only showing state outlines, and printed several copies.

I went through my collection of punishment implements, and selected a 'lesson' paddle, two different 'school' paddles (one with holes and one without), a heavy-leather replica Scottish tawse, and several canes (mostly thin, whippy ones, that would sting like hell, but not cause bruising). I already had a straight-backed chair that I brought up from the playroom and put alongside the desk in the pool room.

Other than the file cabinets against one wall, and the sliding glass doors and massage table making up the other wall, the room now looked like a miniature 'school room' – ready for Linda's role play.

On Friday evening, Kelly and I went to a local Japanese restaurant, where we ordered a variety of sushi rolls, and discussed some ideas for Linda's experience the next day. I suggested that Kelly be a second student, and she agreed to put on the outfit, but thought that Linda should be alone with me through most of the experience.

Kelly did, however, have some very creative ideas, which we decided to incorporate, pending Linda's cooperation. I decided that the scenario would be a 'detention' class, with Linda the only student ... and I would discuss her prior school corporal punishment experiences with her at the beginning of the session.

Kelly made her own plans, and got everything ready Friday evening, before we went to bed.

Linda's 'detention' class was scheduled to start at 1PM on Saturday, giving us plenty of time to review the scene, and 'get our act together', before she arrived. Kelly e-mailed Linda the basic scenario, and a few instructions.

Saturday morning, we both made our preparations; then, we waited for Linda to arrive. As we had a couple of hours available, I did some research on the Internet regarding corporal punishment in U.S. schools, circa 2010-2014.

I knew that slipperings, tawsings, and canings had been used in English and Scottish schools up to at least the mid-1980s, but was amazed to find that there were still more than 30 states in the U.S. that allowed corporal punishment. In 2006, more than 200,000 students in the U.S. were punished on their bottom – usually with a paddle, including both boys and girls; that was roughly when Julie and Linda had been punished (when they had been in middle school) down in Texas.

I would have to find out the details from Linda after she arrived ... and wondered whether I could avoid getting really turned-on – and having to masturbate – as I listened to her stories. Well, she had seen me come, so it wouldn't be a big deal ... but it might ruin the scene. I certainly did not want any 'sex' involved, just school punishment, as Linda had actually experienced it.

Well, perhaps we would do a bit 'more' than she'd actually experienced.

Just before 1PM, we heard the doorbell ring. Kelly quickly got into her assigned position, and I went to the door to let Linda in. "Hi, Linda." I chuckled, "*Schoolgirl* Linda." We hugged, and I asked, "Are you prepared for your 'schoolgirl' experience?" Linda looked down guiltily, and nodded once. I smiled; she was already 'in the role'.

Linda wore a schoolgirl outfit similar to Kelly's: A short plaid skirt (although this one was red and gray), a white blouse, bobby socks, and low-top tennis shoes. She did not wear a jacket, but one wouldn't be required for today's informal session. I had been concerned that Linda would wear jeans, but Kelly had spoken to her, and suggested a more typical skirt-based private-school or religious-school outfit.

Kelly and I had discussed asking Linda to select a 'safeword', but finally agreed that it wouldn't be necessary: None of the punishments would be that severe, and as Linda had requested this experience herself, we would be sensitive to her feedback throughout her 'ordeal'.

I led Linda to the pool room – now our old-fashioned 'school room' – where she would be spending most of her time today.

As Linda stepped through the door from the kitchen to the pool room, she gasped, and brought her right hand up to cover her mouth. Kelly was in her schoolgirl 'uniform', and was seated at one of the small desks, her hands folded on top of it, and her expression grim. There was a notebook and pen on the desk in front of her.

"Kelly!" Linda glanced back at me, then entered the room, stifling a laugh. Kelly looked at Linda, then straight ahead, her expression still serious - although I could see that she was making a big effort not to laugh and greet Linda as she normally would.

I walked through the door, behind Linda, and said, "Have a seat, young lady. I'm almost finished with this student, who was in the prior detention class. We'll start your session when I'm done with her."

Linda quietly slid into the too-small desk-chair, and I realized that I hadn't thought about her 'fitting' into the old grammar-school desk ... but it appeared that she would be

"OK; a little discomfort wouldn't matter, once she had been given a few spankings.

Kelly handed me a notebook as I walked up to her, and I brought it to the teacher's desk and sat down, opening the notebook, and scanning the contents (there was actually nothing there, but we were acting these roles, anyway).

A few moments later, I announced, "Your essay is acceptable. But I'm finding a number of grammatical and punctuation errors; and you *know* the penalty for mistakes in each lesson." I pretended to count, and looked up at Kelly, who now had slightly reddened cheeks. She was either being a very good actress, or really was nervous about the punishment I was about to met out.

Waiting a few more moments to build the suspense, I told Kelly, "There are nine mistakes here. So you will receive nine swats with the 'lesson paddle'. When those are finished, I will compute your final detention class score, and administer your 'final grade'. Then, you may leave. And, I don't expect to see you in here again, young lady!"

I closed the notebook, and grabbed the 'lesson paddle' (a standard, smooth-sided Ping-Pong paddle), and commanded, "Now get yourself into position for the lesson paddle!"

Kelly immediately stood, walked around to the front of her small desk, and bent over the desk, her hands holding the wooden seat. I walked around the large desk, and approached her, glancing at Linda, who was sitting at her desk, hands clasped, and smiling at me.

Then, I lifted Kelly's short, plaid school skirt onto her back, and smoothed the full-size, cotton, 'regulation' school underwear. Placing the paddle against Kelly's bottom, and holding it there firmly, I asked, "Are you ready for your essay 'correction', now, young lady?"

Answering immediately and loudly, Kelly responded, "Yes, Sir!"

With that, I brought the paddle back, and gave Kelly a hard swat on her left buttock. I heard her release a large breath, but otherwise she was silent. Continuing at the rate of about one swat every two seconds, and alternating sides, I gave her the other eight strokes with the thin paddle. When I was finished, I went back to my desk, and pretended to fill-in a 'punishment log'. Kelly remained in position.

I looked up at Linda, and said, "*That* is how a punishment should be taken. I hope this has been a good example for you, young lady, as you will undoubtedly be getting your own paddling – or paddlings – in the next couple of hours." Linda just nodded, but she was no longer smiling. I thought I could discern a slightly reddened complexion on *her* cheeks, too.

"OK, Kelly, you may rise." Kelly stood, and flipped her skirt down. She started to get back into her seat, and I continued, "No, young lady! It's time for your 'final grade', now. Please approach my desk." Kelly immediately walked to the front of my desk, and assumed the 'standing position', her legs shoulder-width apart, and her hands on her head.

I shuffled through some papers, and looked up at her, "Well, you haven't done that badly: You will only receive four hard strokes of the school paddle, today. Are you prepared to take your final punishment, now?"

Kelly nodded, "Yes, Sir. I'm ready." Her cheeks definitely looked cherry red, now.

"OK, young lady. Bend over the desk, spread your legs farther apart, and take hold of the far edge. If you get out of position, the stroke will be repeated." Kelly did as she had been told, bending over the desk, and holding onto the edge closest to me. She held her head up, and gazed forward. Then she gave me a smile and a wink – Linda, of course, not being able to see this.

I retrieved the school paddle from its place hanging next to the blackboard. It was about 18" long and about 4" wide; it was the one without the holes, but was at least ½" thick. This could be a bruising implement, if wielded at full strength. Kelly and I had decided that her swats would be relatively hard, to give Linda something to ponder (or look forward to?) throughout her detention.

I walked around behind Kelly, and again lifted her skirt, folding it onto her back; and, again, I smoothed her full-size underwear against her nicely-rounded bottom.

Standing to Kelly's left, I placed the large wooden paddle across her butt, and told her, "You will count the strokes, young lady; and give me a 'Thank you, Sir' after each stroke." I held the paddle against her bottom, and slid it back and forth a few times. "Are you ready for your 'final grade', now?"

Kelly immediately and loudly answered, "Yes, Sir! I'm ready for my punishment, now."

I slowly pulled the paddle back, and then swung it in an upward arc. Accelerating as it impacted Kelly's bottom, there was a loud gunshot-like sound that reverberated throughout the room. Kelly murmured a quiet, 'Ow!', but held her position. She called out 'One. Thank you, Sir'.

I again placed the paddle against her butt, and slid it back and forth. And, again, I brought the paddle back – this time holding it for a few seconds so that Kelly could not anticipate the timing of the swat.

The paddle swung again, with another loud sound when it impacted her buttocks. I could see the flesh below her underwear ripple outward, and Kelly issued a slightly more urgent 'Aaaghh'. Again, she called out the stroke and thanked me, holding her position admirably.

Turning briefly, I looked at Linda, who had her hands over her face, but I could tell that she was smiling, and undoubtedly enjoying the sight of Kelly getting paddled over the old wooden teacher's desk. I returned my focus to Kelly's bottom, and gave her the third stroke. This time, Kelly's middle lifted off the desk, but her fingers still grasped the far edge, and her feet were still perfectly in place.

Kelly called out, "Sorry, Sir." She immediately lowered herself back down onto the desk. "Three. Thank you, Sir." Perhaps it was the experience I had given her over the past few months, of taking hard spankings ... or perhaps it was her innate strength ... but she was a fantastic model of how to take a hard spanking well.

"OK, young lady, you're onto the last stroke, now. As you know, this will be the hardest one." I heard a very quiet, 'Yes, Sir' from Kelly, and she moved her bottom side-to-side slightly, before stilling herself.

This time, I gave her a really hard swat – nearly as 'full strength' as my energy would allow. Kelly cried out, "Aiyeeee!" She started to lift up again, but quickly forced herself down against the desk. "FOUR!!" She breathed heavily, then added, "Thank you, Sir!"

I let Kelly remain in position for nearly a minute, then rubbed her bottom through her underwear. Then, I flipped her skirt back down, and told her that she could rise. I hung the school paddle back on its hook next to the blackboard, and sat down at my desk.

I had to stick my hand down my pants and adjust myself slightly, and Kelly smiled at me, although she was sniffling. I handed her a tissue from the box on the desk, and she got back into the standing position.

"Thank you for cooperating, young lady! That made it easier for me ... and MUCH easier for you!" I gave Kelly the most fatherly smile that I could muster, and added, "That completes your detention session. You may collect your things, and go now."

Kelly returned to her desk, and piled the pad, notebook, and pens together, as I walked out of the room. I went into the kitchen to grab a Diet Coke, opening it and taking a few swallows, letting Kelly and Linda have a few moments alone together.

I sniffled again, and rubbed my nose with the tissue; this was *not* an act, as Sam had really paddled me hard. I had expected it, and it served to demonstrate to Linda both the severity of the punishments she could expect, and act as an example of how she should behave, in this pseudo-detention scene.

Linda turned to me and smiled, "That was pretty impressive, Kelly." She laughed, "It probably made a pretty good 'impression' on your *butt*, also!"

I nodded, now laughing myself. I got out of the tiny seat, and turned my backside to Linda, lifting the short blue-and-green plaid skirt and pulling down one side of my underwear. Linda whistled softly. I looked over my shoulder, and could see that my bum was quite red. Linda would be receiving much more, on her large bottom, over the next two hours.

I put the underwear back up, and skirt down, as I turned to Linda and said, getting back into the role, "He was pretty gentle on me, today. I've been in here before ... and it's not fun." Although I knew that Linda would have 'fun' with the experience.

Then, looking into Linda's eyes seriously, I informed her, "At least I got to keep my undies on. The male teachers aren't supposed to paddle girls' bare bottoms ... although they *are* allowed to examine them, if they think their punishment may have caused damage."

Linda just shook her head. I had no doubt that she had expected me to be her 'friend' today; but we were all in the scene, and I was certainly not going to break my role. Well, at least my *first* role. Linda had no idea of what was to come over the next couple of hours.

I sniffled again, picked up my notebooks and pens, and walked to the door. Before I exited, I turned to Linda, and said, "Good luck!" Then, I left the room. I would have a while to relax, before I had to don the next costume and get into my next role for today's scene.

I put my stuff down on the breakfast table, and Sam put his can of Coke down, then hugged me tightly. He let his hands drop to cup my bottom, which really *was* pretty sore. I kissed Sam, and gave him a knowing smile.

"Thank you, Kelly. That was a great performance!"

I nodded, "Yes. I think Linda now has some idea of what's going to happen." Then, I giggled, "But she doesn't know the half of it!" We had planned a *lot* more for today's scene, and I was sure that Linda had no idea what her 'challenges' would be.

Sam said, "We'll come down in about half an hour. Go ahead and put the sign on the door. You can work upstairs or, if you like, at my desk in the playroom." I nodded, kissed Sam again, grabbed my stuff, and turned to go upstairs. I may as well get my outfit on for the next act, even though I had plenty of time.

Sam took another swig of Coke, put the can on the kitchen counter, and walked toward the pool room door. He looked back at me and smiled ... and I smiled sweetly back at him. Then, he entered the pool room, and closed the door.

I sat at my desk, and looked at the script that we had written. Then, I looked up at Linda, who was sitting nervously, her body barely fitting between the desk and the seatback. The hard wooden seat would probably accentuate the feeling of her spankings, which wasn't a bad thing.

"OK, young lady." I glanced at the large commercial clock I had mounted over the blackboard, and back to Linda. It's 1:15PM, and your detention will begin now." Linda nodded slightly, her hands still folded on the desk in front of her.

I looked at her, and asked, sternly, "Do you know why you're here – in detention – for *two* hours?" I wanted to make sure we both understood the basis for the scene we were role-playing.

Linda said, meekly, "Yes, Sir. I cut class." She looked down, and then back up at me, a smile creeping onto her face, and added, "Two days in a row."

I nodded, "Yes, young lady. But that wasn't all: You claimed to have a bad cold, AND the note you brought from your parents was forged! You have not only missed your classes, and not turned in your homework, but you were dishonest. That was unfair to the school, your fellow students, *and* your parents."

Then, in a much louder voice, I exclaimed, "Appalling! Really inexcusable."

Linda nodded, and looked down, her cheeks now clearly flushed. I had really learned how to build suspense, and anticipation! I explained, in my best 'schoolteacher' voice, "For each day of class missed, you are receiving an hour of detention. So, today, you will be with me for *two* hours." Linda nodded again.

"Each detention will consist of simple lessons – math, geography, English, and so on. Things that you should already know." I took a deep breath, "After each short lesson, you will take a test. And you will be paddled – as you saw me do with that other girl – for each incorrect answer on each test."

Now, Linda looked up at me; she was just beginning to understand what would be involved today. Of course, we could have simulated her real-life experiences, by just having her bend over the desk and giving her a couple of swats with the school paddle. But that wouldn't have made a very full, or fun, day for her. Or, for me.

We would continue to surprise her throughout the scene. It was something that turned me on – exposing young girls to new experiences, and surprising them by giving them more than they had expected; much more. I would explain only a portion of Linda's day to her now.

"At the beginning of each detention session, I give a 'warm-up' spanking: Over-the-knee (or, 'OTK'), with 100 hard spanks using my hand. This is to prepare your bottom for receiving corrective swats with the 'lesson paddle'." I held up the Ping-Pong paddle, and saw that Linda's eyes were focused on it. She swallowed hard, and nodded again.

"As you are getting two detention sessions today, we will begin with 200 warm-up spanks. I think you already know that you MUST cooperate and stay in position for all of your punishments, today. If you get out of position, I may repeat the stroke, give you extra strokes, or even re-start the punishment from the beginning." Linda swallowed again.

"As you saw, the conclusion of the detention will be a paddling with the 'school paddle' – the number of strokes depending on your cooperation and performance on your lessons and tests. If you do not do well on the simple tests, your bottom is going to really be sore by the time we finish your two detention sessions." Linda nodded again, now looking a bit pale, her red cheeks contrasting nicely.

She should be almost ready for her warm-up ... but I continued. "Finally, as you were dishonest with the school, and forged your sick-leave note, you will visit the headmistress for a mandatory caning." Linda started to speak up – I could see the 'What?' forming on her lips; but she then subdued herself, and looked down at the desk.

I explained, "It will be up to the headmistress – and my recommendation, depending on how well you've cooperated during this detention, but I believe you will receive a minimum of six strokes of the school cane." I smiled at her, and added, "On the bare."

Linda looked up at me, a bit shocked, but then nodded curtly. I could see that she was now certainly 'prepared' sufficiently to begin her detention session. I rose, and pulled the old, wooden, straight-backed chair in front of the desk and sat down, facing the short row of pupil desks (consisting of only two of the desks I had bought and refinished).

"OK, young lady. Get over here, and over my knee, for your warm-up spanking!"

Linda rose uncertainly, and slowly walked up to me. I separated my legs, and patted my left thigh. Guiding her between my legs, she bent awkwardly over my left leg, dropping her head, and putting her hands on the Berber-carpeted floor.

I moved my right leg over her legs, not taking any chance that she would get out of position for her warm-up spanking – that I intended to administer hard and fast, to give her a bit more 'feeling' for what she (or, more correctly, her bottom) would face, today.

I smiled as I looked down at her wide hips and full bottom, the short skirt not even covering all of her underwear, now. I lifted the skirt, and smoothed it onto her back. I hadn't been sure what to expect, but now realized that Linda would be getting an additional punishment.

"Young lady! I see that you're not wearing your regulation knickers! I guess you'll need to get *more* punishment, after your warm-up spanking."

Linda gurgled, truly surprised, and stammered, "But, Sir ..." Then, she realized her error, and let her head drop again. I tried not to laugh and said, unsympathetically, "Do *not* 'But, Sir' me!" I gave Linda a moment to absorb that, and commanded, "You will now request your warm-up spanking. And, when I'm done, you will thank me."

I saw Linda trying to nod her head, as much as her position would allow. "Yes, Sir," she said quietly. Then, a bit louder, "May I please have my warm-up spanking, now? Sir?" I couldn't help but smile again; this was really fun!

Answering her, I said, "Yes, you may. Prepare yourself, girl." I put my hand on her full-cut white bikini underwear, not bothering to smooth them. Then, I began a hard hand spanking, alternating sides at the beginning (the first 25 or so), then spanking her at random positions all over her wide bottom and thick upper thighs.

Linda did well, mostly staying in position; actually, she couldn't move very far out of position, as I had my leg locked over hers, and her upper body was hanging down, barely able to move. She gave a couple of small yelps after the first few spanks, then settled down, the only indication of her distress being a bit of heavy breathing.

I increased the intensity and speed of the spanks approaching 100, and then stopped, and rubbed her bottom over her underwear. As I smoothed them, I told her, "That is the halfway point – the warm-up for your first hour of detention. Now, we'll finish the rest."

With that, I began spanking her again, even harder, the speed slowly increasing, her fleshy globes bouncing and rippling. It was a mesmerizing sight.

Boy! We had come a long way, since her short birthday spanking several months ago! By the time I had given her 150 spanks, she was grunting and groaning, and by the time we'd reached 180, she was emitting short squeals, and taking large gulps of air. I spanked her even harder and faster, as her 200-spank warm-up concluded.

As I rubbed her bottom lightly, Linda was gasping for breath and whimpering. I flipped her skirt back over her bottom, and continued rubbing – a bit harder now; almost giving her a butt massage. I continued to rub, until Linda's breathing slowed, and the whimpers diminished.

"You may get up, now, young lady." I patted her bottom a couple of times, and helped her stand. As she lifted her head to face me, I could see that her eyes were slightly wet – she was not crying yet, but would be, soon.

Although I had forgotten, Linda hadn't, and quickly said, "Thank you, Sir, for the warm-up spanking." Then, she chuckled, and added, "I think my bottom is pretty warmed-up, now."

She was obviously not suffering much from the hand spanking, even though it had been respectably hard. I realized that *I* had not gotten 'hard', yet. But there was much more time for that. I stood and turned the chair around, facing the large desk, and asked Linda to sit, as I went around and sat in my own chair behind the desk.

"Linda, you took your warm-up well. This may be getting slightly 'out of role', but I wanted to ask you about your real-life school spanking experiences. For example, what were you wearing? Did you have to raise your skirt, or pull your pants down? Did you take the spankings alone, or with Julie or others who had misbehaved? How many strokes did you get? And, with what implement?"

I took a breath, "I guess I have a lot of questions. I was never spanked in school ..." I chuckled, "... Even way back, in my day." Then, I remembered the one swat I'd gotten in high school gymnastics.

Linda smiled, and I continued, "So, maybe you can tell me how it was. Was it a teacher, or the school principal who spanked you? Was it during class, or after school? Did you always tell your parents about it? Did they also spank you , when you got home? Did you actually get turned on while you were at school – either before or after your spankings ... or only after you got back home?"

Linda's mouth was open, and I decided to let her speak, even though I had a thousand other questions.

She took a deep breath, and began, "Well, Sir ..." She looked at me, and smiled, "Julie and I were usually the ones being punished – usually together, but sometimes separately; and there was at least once when a bunch of us were punished; I think it was for a food fight in the cafeteria."

Linda was quick to point out, "But it was someone else who started it – Julie and I just joined in, after food was flying everywhere." She chuckled.

"We usually wore jeans to school. Actually, I don't remember ever being paddled when I was wearing a skirt or dress." She looked up at the ceiling and back to me. "Our paddlings were always given by the Girl's Vice Principal. And, almost always given over our jeans."

Then she smiled, obviously remembering the details of her experiences. "But I think we had a choice of dropping our jeans twice – and both times, Julie and I decided to get fewer swats on our underwear. I remember that at least one of those times – maybe both – the secretary from the outer office was asked to come in and be a witness."

She grimaced, "We were always paddled with one like that." She pointed to the school paddle that I had used on Kelly, now hanging tranquilly next to the blackboard. "And, usually we only got one or two swats."

I raised my eyebrows, "That's *all*?"

Linda was nodding. "They were real zingers, Sir. We felt even one stroke for at least an hour. But we got three swats a few times." Then, Linda smiled, "And I heard that one girl got five swats ... but I never did, and I'm pretty sure Julie never did, either."

Then, she continued, "Usually, we were sent to the Vice Principal from one of our classes. And, I think most girls – and boys – were paddled alone. But since Julie and I were known to cause trouble together ..."

Linda chuckled again. "I think I was paddled about half a dozen times ... and Julie was in there with me most of the times."

I asked, "Were you paddled together – I mean bent over the desk at the same time, or one after the other?" I put my hands into my pants, and re-adjusted myself. It was more of a turn-on listening to Linda's story, than actually spanking her. So far.

Linda said, "I think in our freshman year, we were spanked one after the other. Julie was usually the ring leader, so she got hers first. And sometimes, she got one more swat than I did. But I do remember in our sophomore year – at least once – bending over the desk together. That was a time when we lowered our jeans.

Then we each took three swats – with the Vice Principal going back and forth."

She smiled, "That was probably our worst punishment in school.

"And, no, my parents never spanked me when I came home from getting a licking; but they always knew when it happened. I think the school called them before I even got home. My mother would hug me, and warn me about getting in trouble again; she always thought that it was because of Julie." Linda smiled at me again, "But there were a few times that it was my fault for starting something."

She was silent for a moment, and I asked, "And you got turned on when you got home?"

Linda nodded. "Even though we knew what to expect, we were always scared – or at least had 'butterfly stomachs' – when we were told to go to the Girl's Vice Principal's office. And I certainly wasn't turned on during the lickin', or at school afterwards. It was usually when I went home, shut myself in my room, and lay on the bed."

She smiled again, remembering back, "And I don't think I got turned on until at least my junior year; but I certainly did in my senior year. I was looking at it more sexually, by then. I would go home – hoping my mom wasn't there – then go up to my room and close the door. I would lower my jeans and underwear to my knees, and lie on my stomach."

She glanced up at me with a smirk, "And then, I would masturbate." She chuckled, and added, "I had a few good orgasms, then. By that time, I'd had sex with a couple of guys ... but had never orgasmed with them." She thought for a moment, and concluded, "Maybe that's why I started fantasizing about it, after I graduated?"

I told Linda to go back to her seat, and I moved the chair alongside my desk. I left the room for a moment – sure that Linda would think I needed to masturbate ... but I was only bringing her a bottle of water, and my can of Diet Coke, into the 'classroom'.

"OK, Linda. Let's get started on your lessons ... and your tests." Linda nodded, and I asked, "Shall we start with math, or geography? These are all simple things, arithmetic; there's no algebra, trigonometry, or calculus."

Linda's eyes went large, "I should hope not! I never even took calculus, and don't remember much algebra ... or any 'trig'. I guess we can start with the arithmetic."

I smiled, and shuffled through the pages I had made-up. "I don't think we have to spend time with a real 'lesson'; let's just see how you do on the tests." Linda nodded, adjusting her position, as the small seat was obviously uncomfortable for her.

Walking over to her, I put two pages face-down on her desk, and handed her a pencil. "We'll start with some addition and subtraction. It will be a timed test, and you will get a swat with the 'lesson paddle' for each problem that you get wrong – or don't finish. I'll give you ten minutes to complete both pages."

Linda looked at me inquiringly, and I'm sure she expected single or – at most – double-digit problems. But these were 3-, 4-, and 5-digit addition and subtraction problems. When I pulled out my phone, set the countdown timer for 10 minutes, and said, "Go!" she turned over the first page and groaned.

I knew she could get them all right, and I had taken these tests myself, finishing the problems on both pages in a little over 7 minutes. I had made up an answer key, using my calculator to be certain of the correct answers.

I watched, and sipped my Coke, as Linda hurriedly worked on the problems. It seemed like a much longer time than necessary, but she was cooperating, and I didn't want to make her take *too* many swats, as she had a lot more coming. I saw her move to the second page, and she groaned – most of the 4-digit subtractions not being 'doable' in her head.

The timer buzzed, and I called out, "Stop! Put down your pencil." Linda's head was shaking; she knew that she would be getting at least a few swats. I walked over, and picked up the pages, then walked back to my desk, checking her answers against the key. She had actually done quite well, getting all but one of the addition problems correct, but missing three of the subtractions ... and there were five problems that she'd not had time to finish.

"Well, Linda, you did pretty well: You only missed one addition and three subtraction problems." I looked up at her, "But you didn't finish the last five. So that will be nine swats, in total." Her shoulders sagged, and then she shrugged, and stood up. I instructed her to bend over the front of her desk, like Kelly had, and I slowly walked over to her, holding the Ping-Pong paddle.

Linda had gotten into position well – there was nothing I could correct. I lifted her skirt, and then realized that I hadn't punished her for the non-regulation underwear she was wearing. I had to chuckle; this was almost as good as the first time I'd spanked Liz. That had been more than four years ago.

"Linda, I just realized that you haven't yet been punished for wearing these sexy bikini panties." They weren't that 'sexy', but I think she appreciated the comment; her response was a loud groan. I told her, "We'll take care of that after your nine swats, so stay in position."

I heard a soft, "Yes, Sir," and placed the paddle against her left buttock.

"Are you ready, now?" I asked, giving her a chance to prepare herself mentally.

"Yes, Sir," she answered promptly. I pulled the paddle back, and swung it with a medium force. It landed on her full bottom with a 'SMACK!', and I saw her flesh ripple outward. She hadn't moved or made a sound. I waited a few seconds, then pulled the paddle back, and gave her the second swat. Again, she behaved perfectly.

These weren't really very hard, but again I knew that she would be getting many more, over the next couple of hours. 'SMACK!' 'WHAP!' 'CRACK!' The paddling continued, and was over in less than a minute. Linda had done quite well, hardly reacting to the swats with this light paddle.

I was surprised when Linda – still facing ahead – offered, "Thank you, Sir." She may not be getting turned-on, yet, but I knew that this would be an interesting experience for her, by the time it was over.

I walked back to the large desk, pulled open a drawer, and took out the tawse. This was a 'mean' implement, originally used in Scottish boarding schools on miscreant boys' bottoms ... although it had later been used on girls, as well (probably mostly on their hands).

Linda was still in position over her desk – as she should be. Walking around her desk, I held up the tawse, and said, "Now, *this* is what you will get for wearing the wrong underwear ... *and*, if you misbehave or don't cooperate during your detention sessions with me."

I heard Linda draw in a breath, but she didn't otherwise react. I continued, deciding to be a bit 'easy' on her. "Linda, this can be a very severe implement. In this case, you may not have known what to wear for your detention, and I'm not going to be too hard on you."

Before I could say anything else, Linda closed her eyes, and said, "Thank you, Sir. I appreciate that."

I stood before her, and made a quick decision. "So, I'm only going to give you a *taste* of this implement: Three strokes on your underwear." It didn't sound like much, but even 'medium' strokes of the heavy leather tawse would produce thick red lines across her bottom – even through her panties.

Positioning myself behind her, I laid the tawse across her buttocks. Then, I drew it back, and let it fly. 'THWACK!!' It was a harder stroke than I'd intended. There was a second of silence, and then Linda yelled, "Oowww!"

I gave her time – about 15-20 seconds as she calmed, holding herself in position. I pulled the tawse back again, and swung it – aiming for a slice of butt just below the prior stroke. 'WHACK!' Linda squealed, "Ooowwee!!" She lifted up, but got herself back into position, and didn't try to reach back with her hands.

I let nearly a half a minute pass, before I placed the tawse across her bottom, and she flinched when she felt it. Ten seconds later, I gave her the final stroke. 'WWHAAPP!!' Linda shrieked, and lifted up, her hands willing themselves to go to her sore bottom, but she smartly put them back down on the seat, only wiggling her bottom and breathing hard.

I heard a sniffle, and she said, "I'm sorry for dressing improperly, Sir." I felt a bit sorry for hurting her so badly for an offense that she hadn't even considered. So, I flipped her skirt back down, asked her to stand, and hugged her – not exactly the proper response of a teacher, but very appropriate for a role-play that Linda herself had requested. She sniffled again, and I told her to sit back down at her desk.

Back behind my own desk, I pulled out the next two pages – one multiplication, and one division. "Shall we finish the math tests, young lady?" Linda nodded, and I walked to her desk, and put the pages face-down in front of her. Then, I walked back to my desk, reset the phone timer, and told Linda, "I'll give you 15 minutes for these tests." Linda shook her head.

It seemed like a long time to make her solve math problems, but with the number of problems, and their difficulty, I felt that she would be doing very well to finish them all. It had taken me ten full minutes of working as fast as I could to do them myself.

I started the timer, and said, "Go!" Linda turned over the first sheet – a bunch of 3- and 4-digit multiplication problems – and groaned. Then, she got going, and I sat back and sipped my Coke.

After a few minutes, I got bored, and decided to leave the room; I hoped that Linda hadn't brought a calculator – or had any thought of cheating. *That* would have really brought some hard discipline – REAL discipline – to her already-sore bottom!

I went down to the playroom, where Kelly sat behind my desk, wearing her second costume of the day, and doing some research on the computer. She looked up and smiled at me, "How's it going with Linda?" Chuckling, I told her what we'd done so-far, including tawsing her for not wearing the proper underwear.

"Sam!" Kelly chided. "That wasn't really fair; I hadn't told her to wear anything specific under her school skirt and blouse."

I nodded, and said, "Well, I thought she might want to try more than just that thin Ping-Pong paddle." Kelly shook her head, and went back to her research. I added, "I'm going to give Linda a 10-minute break after her math test ... and then I'll start the geography lesson. So why don't you plan to interrupt us in about twenty minutes?"

Kelly nodded, without looking up, and said, "OK. I'll set a timer."

I went back upstairs, and into the 'classroom', where Linda was still hard at work on her math problems. I pulled out the phone, and saw that she only had a few minutes left.

When the timer buzzed, I looked at Linda, and asked "How are you doing?"

Linda looked up at me, and said, "I only have three more problems to finish." She looked exasperated.

I said, "OK, Linda, I'll give you one more minute, then ask you to stop." She thanked me, then looked down, and continued working. I couldn't expect that everyone would speed through math problems like I did – I had been in science for my entire career, and could probably have done most of these problems in my head, without slowing down much.

I watched the seconds tick by, and gave her nearly a minute and a half. "OK. Please stop, now." Linda put down her pencil and looked up.

Collecting her test forms, and comparing them with the key, I found that Linda had again done quite well, only getting two of the problems wrong ... and not quite finishing the last problem. I looked at her and smiled, "You did very well, young lady: You'll only need three swats."

Linda shrugged, stood, and walked around her desk, then bent over and flipped her skirt onto her back. As I walked toward her with the Ping-Pong paddle, she announced, "I'm ready for my punishment, Sir."

I smiled, "OK, Linda. This shouldn't be too bad." I placed the paddle against her wiggly bottom, and gave her the three swats quickly, one after the other: One on the left side, then one on the right, and the last in the middle – taking only about ten seconds for the whole thing. I flipped Linda's skirt down, and told her that she could get up. Hugging her again, I kissed her on the cheek, and asked, "Would you like to take a ten-minute break, now? Then, we'll get started on your geography lesson?"

Linda hugged me back, and said, "That would be nice, Sir." As I put the paddle down on the desk, Linda said, "I think I'll go out to the car for a minute." I nodded, and went downstairs to let Kelly know that we were taking a break.

Kelly shrugged, not looking up, still doing her research. So I decided to go back upstairs and grab a beer; it was Saturday afternoon, after all. And here, I was teaching math and geography. Well, not really. I was having a spanking role-play with Linda, who had shown herself to be more open and sexual than Kelly had realized. And, interested in corporal punishment as a turn-on.

I quaffed the beer, as I thought about Kelly's friends: They were all very open and enthusiastic about 'playing' with us. It was amazing that Linda had actually requested this experience.

I looked at my watch, and wondered where Linda was; if she was only getting something from her car, she should have come back in several minutes ago. I opened the front door, but didn't see her in her car ... or around it. I stepped out onto the walkway, and took a few steps to the front of the garage; Kelly's car was parked outside the garage in the driveway.

Then, I saw smoke curling around in the still air, and over Kelly's car. Taking a few more steps, I found Linda, leaning on the hood of Kelly's car, smoking! Then, I realized that she was smoking weed!! While I knew that she smoked grass sometimes – and so did I, occasionally – she was playing the role of a middle school or high school student. "LINDA! What are you doing, young lady?!!?!"

Linda jumped, and exhaled a large puff of smoke. She tried to hold the joint behind her, but – of course – couldn't hide it from me.

"Hand it over! Right now!" She did so, guiltily. It was mostly smoked down. I yelled, "Get back in the classroom! NOW!!" This was very upsetting: Not that she was smoking grass, but that she would do it in the middle of her role play.

I calmed myself, and then realized one reason that I was so upset: She hadn't invited *me* to join her! Well, that wouldn't have been part of the role play ... but at least, I might have allowed both of us to take a break from the scene.

I looked at the stubby joint – still smoking – and took a few puffs. I knew that I shouldn't have done that, but it would calm me down. And, at least I could benefit a little from Linda's brash behavior. I took another couple of puffs, then stomped the stub into the driveway, and went back into the house.

When I entered the pool room, Linda was in the standing position in front of the large desk, facing forward. I had been very upset, but the grass was hitting me, and I felt a little calmer. I sat behind the large desk, and stared at Linda. I wasn't sure what to say.

I took a deep breath, and began, "Linda, I'm very upset with you." I paused, and Linda nodded. I tried to give her a 'fatherly' look, but utterly failed. I scratched my head. Even *I* wasn't sure why I was upset. I picked up the mostly-empty can of Coke, and drained it.

Looking at Linda, I said, "I may be going in and out of 'role' ... but I'll try to be honest with you."

Linda nodded curtly, and said, "I appreciate that, Sir."

I continued to stare at Linda, the grass now having more effect on my thought process. "First of all ... in the roles we were playing, I can't believe that I gave you a 10-minute break ... and you smoked marijuana! What would have happened down in Texas, had you been caught smoking grass?"

Linda stared at me, finally shrugging, "I probably would have been expelled." She chuckled, and then answered solemnly, "They don't go for that, down there." She tried to smile, and added, "At least, officially."

I shook my head. "Here, I'm asking you to memorize things, and take tests ... and you'll be punished if you do poorly." I looked into her eyes, "If you really wanted more punishment, you could have said so ... and I would have been happy to tan your bottom as much as you wanted." Linda nodded, and then swallowed hard.

Continuing, I said, "And, personally ... I'm not sure what to think. If we were both going to get out of role, then I would have appreciated turning on *with* you ... being invited to be social with you ... instead of you hiding in the driveway."

I thought about it more, and added, "And, what about the neighbors? Our backyard is private, but the driveway isn't; I'm sure the smoke could be smelled by people in at least half a dozen houses around us. I'm not friendly with those neighbors ... and they're pretty conservative: They could have called the cops!" I was exasperated, but still not exactly sure why I was so upset.

Linda nodded, "I know, Sir." She swallowed again, and her face looked pale. "And I deserve to be punished."

I just stared at her. "You didn't do this just to get caught and be punished, did you?" I really had no idea *why* Linda had done this. It wasn't that I was against recreational drugs, per sé ... but this was tantamount to a break of trust between us.

Linda shook her head, "No, Sir. I'm not sure why I did it. Maybe, I *was* still in the role – and acting out, like I did in high school – rebelling, and doing 'my own thing', regardless of the consequences."

This was incredible. I wasn't sure whether to be upset, glad that Linda was being open with me, or turned-on because I had another reason to punish her. At this moment, I was fairly certain it wasn't the latter. Maybe, it was my *own* hang-ups? But I'd already turned-on with Linda at Kelly's birthday party, and we'd told Kelly's friends about the hash bar in Amsterdam.

I was very confused; I really didn't know what I was feeling, or why. Finally, I said, "Linda – as you just said, you *know* you'll be punished for this. Whether 'in the role' or out of it (now *I* was feeling pretty 'out of it'), hiding and smoking grass just doesn't seem like the best thing you could have done."

Linda was almost in tears. I really had wanted to have a 'happy' experience with her – even if her bottom hurt, she would be getting turned-on. Now, the whole experience seemed negative. My stomach was hollow: I somehow wanted to salvage the situation, but really couldn't decide the best course of action. Perhaps I should ask Kelly for a recommendation?

"Linda – you *do* deserve to be punished, as far as I'm concerned. Will you agree to the punishment that I deem appropriate?"

Linda looked down, and then back up at me. Finally, she said, weakly, "Yes, Sir. You may do whatever you think is appropriate."

Well, that was something. But I still didn't know what I should do, or how I should act – 'in the role' or outside of it. At the moment, I was very confused. And I didn't think it was the few puffs of grass that I'd smoked.

I looked at Linda and blinked. "OK, Linda. I'm going to 'top and tail' you." She looked confused, and I explained, "You will receive two strokes of the tawse on each of your outstretched palms ... and then two dozen strokes on your bottom."

I realized that I really was upset; and I wasn't sure why. I'd been feeling stressed, lately – including acting immature during our European show for Kelly's friends. It felt like I was going through menopause – with hot and cold flashes. That was ridiculous: I was just upset that Linda had seemed to have broken the trust in our relationship – whether we were role-playing or in real-life.

Linda gulped, "That seems like a pretty harsh punishment, Sir. But I will take it, if you ask me to." Linda's shoulders sagged, and she stared at the floor.

I felt a little sorry for Linda ... but not much. I had obviously seen her nude (for a whole day, during Kelly's birthday party), and decided to offer her a choice. "I will give you the choice of getting two dozen hard strokes of the tawse on your underwear ... or a dozen strokes on the bare. Please decide."

Linda didn't have to think about it long, and replied, "I'll take a dozen strokes of the tawse on my bare bottom, Sir."

I nodded, opened the desk drawer, and pulled out the tawse; I hadn't planned on using it again today. As I walked around the desk, Linda turned to face me. I told her, "Hold your hand up, palm stretched, and your other hand underneath to support it." Linda did as I had instructed.

I lifted the tawse, and held the 'tail' with my other hand. Quickly, I let go, and the tawse swung down, impacting Linda's outstretched hand with a loud 'Crack!'. She mimed an 'Ow!' and pulled her hand toward her, rubbing her palm with the other hand. Then, without being told, she raised it again, and I let the tawse do its job again – reddening her hand. She yelped, and put her hand between her legs, giving me a painful look.

Then, without being told, she repeated these steps with her other hand, and I repeated the strokes, not being gentle with her. Now, both of her hands were red – nearly raw. The heavy leather implement was really too much to be used at this strength on the hands, but Linda had taken it as well as could be expected.

"Bend over the desk, now, and I'll administer the rest of your punishment on your bottom." Linda bent over the desk, spreading her feet, flicking her skirt up and onto her back and pushing her underwear down to her knees, before lowering her chest to the desk, and holding the far edge with her fingers.

I positioned myself, and laid the tawse across Linda's quivering buttocks. I was breathing heavily, and did not want to punish her out of my own emotions. Perhaps I should ask Kelly to be a witness? But I wanted to get this over with ... and it seemed that Linda wanted to be done with it, also. "You will count the strokes, young lady. Let me know, when you're ready."

I heard Linda take a deep breath and release it slowly, "I'm ready, Sir." Her voice was cracking, and I thought she might cry before I'd delivered the first stroke. But Linda held her position resolutely, and I began the most severe tawsing that I'd ever delivered. Linda counted the strokes, but was in tears after the fourth or fifth time the tawse landed on her quickly-reddening bottom.

I extended the time between strokes, to nearly a minute for the last few strokes. Linda was bawling, now, and I had no doubt that the tawsing had made an impression on her. However, I still wasn't exactly sure what the 'lesson' had been. Only that she should have been more open with me, and not snuck around behind my back, doing something that would have been grounds for expulsion in any 'real' school.

After the sound of the last stroke had died out, I rubbed Linda's now beet-red bottom. She continued to cry, and reached over to grab a tissue. After a minute or two, Linda looked over her shoulder, and asked, "Would you please 'do' me now, Sir?"

What? This had been a 'real' punishment, as far as I was concerned. And now, she was going to get *pleasure* from it? Suddenly, I was more confused than ever. I replied quickly – too quickly – saying, "No, I will *not*, young lady. This was supposed to be a punishment."

Then, I thought a bit more and, as I calmed, offered, "Well, maybe I could get you started … and I'll allow you to 'do' yourself." This was getting more confusing by the minute!

Linda said, softly, "Thank you , Sir."

Now, I put my hand under Linda, and moved it , grazing her labia, and letting my fingers straddle her clit. I was not turned on, but realized that Linda would be, soon. I slid my fingers up and back, occasionally squeezing her clit between them.

Then, I took my hand out from under her, and walked around the desk, sitting in my chair, and looked into Linda's eyes. I shook my head slowly. "I guess I'll allow you to 'do' yourself, if you want. But you must keep your eyes on mine. I want to *feel* your pain ... and your pleasure."

Linda nodded, and mumbled, "OK, Sir." She put her hand under herself, and began masturbating, as she stared into my eyes. Tears were still falling onto the old desk.

When Linda's breathing quickened, I whispered, "We're obviously 'out of role', now. May I kiss you, Linda?"

She moaned, and answered, "Oh, *please*, Sir." I took her head in my hands, and kissed her fully, intimately. As she breathed through her stuffy nose, she continued to move her hand, until she was bucking, moving back and forth over the desk, as I held her and kissed her deeply. It wasn't 'love' ... just raw emotions.

Finally, Linda came, pulling her head back, and shrieking at a pitch that I thought might break the sliding glass doors. I ran my hands through her shoulder-length hair, as she continued to come. Time was suspended, and I don't think either one of us could have related at that moment to 'time' in the real world.

Finally, Linda let out a deep breath, and lowered her chest to the desk, put her head sideways, and closed her eyes. I continued to stroke her hair, as she calmed. The door was closed, but I fully expected Kelly to come bursting through, any moment, wondering what the animalistic sounds had been. But Linda and I were alone in the room, now quieting, almost silent.

Linda lifted her head from the desk, turning toward me, and said, very quietly, "Thank you, Sir. I deserved that." I really wasn't sure to what she was referring – deserving the tawsing, or the orgasm, or both. It didn't matter. The episode was over. I would try to 'forgive and forget'. We had a lot more role-play to do.

I'd heard a loud shriek, and wasn't sure whether it was from pain or pleasure ... or possibly both. But the timer had only a minute to go, so I quit the browser on Sam's computer, and walked upstairs with the note I had printed, knocking on the pool room door.

Sam opened the door cautiously, and I handed him the note, being careful to not be seen by Linda. I did not see her at her desk, and wondered what had just transpired. But it was time for the next act in Linda's schoolgirl role-play scene. I left the door open and, as I turned to walk through the kitchen and down to the exam room, I heard Sam read the note to Linda.

When I got downstairs, I made sure the sign on the exam room door – 'Nurse's Station' – was straight, and I went inside to wait for Sam and Linda. I knew that Sam was reading the note to Linda: "Please come immediately to the Nurse's Station. Your teacher will accompany you." I laughed inwardly, awaiting Linda's reaction, when I opened the door.

It didn't take long – I soon heard a loud knocking on the exam room door. When I opened it, Linda was staring, apparently quite baffled, as Sam stood behind her. I watched, as Linda looked at me briefly, then moved her eyes downward, examining my nurse costume.

Then she squinted beyond me, at the waiting exam room – the exam table, instruments on the wall, the counter on her right, with various medical supplies ... and the faint smell of formaldehyde. Julie had been the only one of my friends who'd already seen Sam's 'exam room'.

Suddenly, Linda's eyes went from squinting to wide, and back to 'beady', as she looked at me again, and a belly laugh emanated from her core. She was laughing so hard, she bent over, coughing, and Sam pushed her gently into the 'exam room'. I took control. "OK, young lady, please get up on the exam table."

As Linda stepped slowly into the exam room, and looked around, I smelled something strange, not the formaldehyde or alcohol swabs; something familiar, but unexpected. I was momentarily baffled, and then realized what it was. I glared at Sam, and he smiled weakly and shrugged.

Linda hopped up on the exam table, her school skirt now seeming much shorter – that, and her puzzled expression made her seem younger. As she continued to gaze around the small space, her mouth fell open, and finally she looked at me in wonderment - or just confusion.

I spoke tersely, loudly, firmly. "I was notified that you were out of school for the past two days." It wasn't a question, but Linda nodded slowly, surely wondering where this was going ... and I'm sure not being able to fathom what Sam and I had planned. I continued, "And you said you had a bad cold – perhaps even pneumonia?"

Linda glanced at Sam, who was trying to play it 'straight', but I could see the smile creeping onto his face, even while his eyes communicated a blank expression. Linda hesitantly nodded again. I tried to play the part of a 'battle-axe' nurse, speaking loudly, forcefully, in full control of the situation.

"Well, young lady, it is *my* responsibility to ensure the health and safety of all the girls in this school. And I won't take the chance that you will infect the entire school; many other girls would lose class time, and possibly fall behind in their studies."

Linda was now shaking her head, "But, Miss, I didn't *really* have pneumonia. I'm sure you heard that I forged the note – just to skip classes." She was looking more and more nervous, as she tried to explain the situation.

"I'm sorry, young lady, I just won't take that chance. Your voice sounds hoarse now," (it really did) "and if there is even a small chance that you're infectious, it is my duty to protect the other girls – and instructors – in this school. I won't take that chance. Maybe, if you lied before, you're lying now? We don't know what to believe, but I am required by law – and ethics – to do the 'right' thing. I'm going to make sure you're 'cured' by Monday morning, so you can come back to school, and everyone will be safe."

Linda was nodding slowly, still unsure of what this meant. So I clarified, "I will, therefore, give you a large dose of penicillin, to make sure you and the rest of the students and faculty are protected."

Now, Linda understood, her mouth dropping open, and her eyes darting between Sam and I. "But ... but ..."

I held up my hand, "There are no buts ... but there *will* be *your* butt, getting a big shot in a few minutes." I couldn't help but laugh, and I turned around, facing the counter, and tried coughing to cover up the laughter. I glanced at Sam, and he turned into the hall, probably also nearly hysterical at the situation we had created ... and Linda's reaction.

I picked up the syringe that I had already filled with 6cc of sterile saline, and a big (20-gauge, 1.5" long) needle attached, and turned back to Linda. Her eyes went wide, and it appeared that she was suddenly faint.

She stammered, "But I wasn't *really* sick!"

And I replied, "But I can't take that chance. You're going to get this big shot in your butt. Now, lie down on your stomach, and we'll get started."

Linda's reaction was predictable; it was insanely funny, and I turned around – presumably to get the alcohol swab, but actually coughing again and trying not to laugh riotously. Sam was in the doorway again, observing the scene with fascination and – I'm sure – sexual excitement.

I turned to Linda again, who had not moved a muscle, and raised my voice, "NOW, young lady!" Slowly, Linda turned onto her stomach, and I lifted her skirt, and began to pull down her bikini underwear. Then, I stopped, and said, "If you don't want your teacher to watch, I can close the door."

Linda stammered, "It's OK ... he's already seen my butt." I pulled down her panties, and examined the red stripes, and general dark red color of her bum. I now knew what I was smelling; this was getting more and more interesting!

I looked at Sam, and asked, "And why did you see her bare bottom, may I ask?"

Sam shrugged, and said, "I caught her smoking, and she had to be tawsed. I offered her the choice of two dozen strokes on her knickers, or one dozen on the bare."

I tried not to smile. "Mr. Johnson! You know the rules: Male teachers are *not* allowed to punish our girls on the bare bottom. Only the headmistress may do that!" I glanced at Linda, who was intrigued by the tone of the conversation, and then I looked back to Sam. "This is a reportable offense! You could get fired for this."

Sam's mouth fell open, and he said, "But ... but ..." just as Linda had done, a few minutes ago.

Now, I had him! I stepped up to Sam, and said, "I would like to smell your breath." Sam had been holding his breath, but now breathed out, the distinct smell of marijuana very apparent. "Mr. Johnson!! You were 'smoking', too? Did you give drugs to one of our students?"

Sam was shaking his head vigorously. We really hadn't anticipated this – it wasn't part of our original script.

I shook my head slowly. "You will be duly reported, and I'll leave it to the headmistress to decide the best course of action." Then, I looked back at Linda, "But now, I'm going to give your student a shot of penicillin ... just in case."

I took my time swabbing Linda's butt – on the right side, and then pulled the needle protector off, and squirted some of the saline from the syringe. It made a long, thin arc, landing on Linda's forehead (my aim hadn't been perfect, but close). She flinched, and dropped her head to the small pillow on the exam table.

Using the thumb and forefinger of my left hand I stretched her skin, and plunged the needle into her. I heard a soft 'Ow!' from Linda. Then, I pulled back the plunger of the syringe to check for blood. I left the syringe sticking out of Linda's butt, and announced that I had forgotten something.

Linda opened her eyes, and saw that I was now holding a lubed rectal thermometer.

I looked sweetly at her, and said, "We also need to take your temperature, dear. Let's get this started, while I give you the shot." Separating Linda's full buttocks, I roughly inserted the thermometer, moving it around a little, before letting go of her globes, and then began her injection.

Linda groaned quietly, and I informed her, "This is a big shot – it's going to take a while. Just relax."

Sam was staring at Linda's butt, both the thermometer and the needle now in her; he smiled, and gave me the 'OK' sign. I gave him a dirty look, and re-focused on slowly injecting the 'medicine' into Linda's bottom. When about 4cc had been injected, Linda began to groan.

I told her, "Just suck it up, young lady. It was *your* idea to get pneumonia!" Linda closed her eyes again, and lay quietly, as I finished the injection ... and then left the needle in for another 30 seconds, while I moved the thermometer around.

This hadn't been part of her fantasy ... but might be part of her *future* fantasies. Finally, I pulled the needle out, and disposed of the syringe, putting a small round bandage on the injection site – just like the nurse at the real clinic had done, after our HPV and hepatitis shots.

A few minutes later, I pulled out the thermometer. Reading it, I announced, "Well, your temperature is normal now ... but maybe I should check it when you get to school Monday morning?"

Linda groaned again – perhaps not remembering that we were still in role-play mode, and that there would be no 'Monday morning'. I cleaned the thermometer, and told Linda that she could get up. She pulled up her panties, and slipped off the exam table.

Sam, right on cue, commanded, "Come along, young lady. We've lost enough time. Let's get back to your detention class!" Sam and Linda went upstairs, and I cleaned up the exam room. It had been an interesting – and not entirely expected experience.

Now, I had to change into my third costume – that of headmistress – and figure out what punishment I should give Sam. I really didn't know if he had suggested turning on with Linda, or if he had caught her doing it ... but it didn't matter. He was going to be punished severely for his indiscretion.

We walked back into the classroom, and I closed the door and sat at the desk, as Linda squeezed herself into the small student desk-chair combination. She looked up at me, and I shrugged. "Now, *I'm* in trouble. And I'm not looking forward to what the headmistress will do to me, for tawsing you on the bare, and smoking the last of your weed."

Linda just nodded, her hand going down to her butt, and rubbing it where the shot had been given. We had planned some surprises for Linda, but Kelly and I were now being surprised ourselves ... and we would have to adapt to the new situation. My hand subconsciously went to my own bottom, which I fully expected would be as red as Linda's an hour from now.

The rest of Linda's detention session went as planned. I let her study the U.S. map for five minutes, and then handed her one of the maps I had printed, with outlines of the states, but no labels. I gave her five minutes to fill-in the state names. She did pretty well, only getting two pairs of states out of order (Nebraska/Oklahoma, and Vermont/New Hampshire), and missing three others (Delaware, Maryland, and West Virginia). That was seven more swats with the Ping-Pong paddle, which Linda took without comment.

Then, I gave her ten minutes to study the state capitals – both from a list, and from an annotated map. On the subsequent test, she got 15 of the capitals wrong – probably better than I would have done!

She groaned as she bent over her desk again – was this the fourth, or fifth time? I paddled her quickly, alternating sides, and she had trouble maintaining her position ... but she tried, and I didn't make her take any 'corrective' punishment.

By this time, we were both tired, and anticipating a visit to the headmistress' office. Linda probably guessed that the headmistress would – again – be Kelly, but she didn't ask or comment. I decided that this had been enough role-play, and told Linda to take the standing position in front of the large desk, in preparation for her 'final score'.

I went downstairs, where Kelly was just finishing getting dressed in her 'headmistress' outfit – basically a grey suit, with a white blouse, and small black tie. It seemed that she really was upset with me.

"Sam, what happened? Did you decide to have drugs with your 'student'? And, what *else* did you have with her?" I knew Kelly wasn't worried about my relationship with Linda, but she seemed peeved that I had strayed from the script.

I tried to explain. "Kelly, I gave Linda a break, and she wanted to go out to her car. When she didn't come back in, I went looking for her, and she had finished nearly a whole joint on the driveway, hiding between your car and the garage door."

I took a deep breath, still not sure what to say, or what my motives had been. "I decided to punish her – both in the role-play (as a student smoking), and in real-life. The neighbors could have seen her and called the police. That's all we needed!"

I was exasperated, finally explaining, "I decided that an appropriate punishment would be 24 strokes of the tawse ... but she had already taken a lot, and I made the executive decision to offer half that number of strokes on her bare bottom. I didn't think that would be a big deal."

Kelly hugged me. "It wasn't that big of a deal, but why did *you* smoke?"

I chuckled, "Well, I had taken the joint from her, and sent her back to the classroom ... and saw that there was a little left. Again, I didn't think it would be a big deal."

Kelly nodded. "OK, I understand. But we're still in the scene, and you *will* be punished, when you visit the headmistress." All I could do is shrug and nod. Fair was fair, after all. I told Kelly that we would be down to the playroom in ten minutes.

As I entered the pool room, Linda was standing in front of the large desk, as I had requested. I sat down, and put my head in my hands. The only thing left of our script here in the classroom was to take the school paddle to Linda's butt. She'd already taken quite a lot, and I didn't know how many strokes would be appropriate – or 'appreciated' by Linda. I decided to ask her.

Linda thought for a few moments, and said, "Well, Kelly took four when I first got here ... and I didn't do that well on the tests ... and I did get you in trouble." She looked at the ceiling, and back to me, "So, I guess that six hard strokes would be fair." I had been tempted to give her eight strokes, but had to agree with her suggestion. It was *her* fantasy role-play, after all.

"OK Linda, please bend over the desk, and let's get this over with. I have a feeling I'll be getting the same, when we visit the headmistress." I coughed, and now *I* was the one swallowing hard. "And, I'm just hoping that she doesn't take the cane to *my* bottom!"

Linda chuckled, bent over the desk, and flipped her skirt up. There was no way I would paddle her on the bare, after all that had transpired; if I did, Kelly probably *would* take the cane to my rear.

I took the school paddle down from the hook next to the blackboard, and positioned myself behind Linda and to her left. The portion of her bottom that I could see looked dark red, and I could still see faint stripes from the tawse extending out from under her panties. But I didn't want to disappoint Linda; she had selected the number of strokes, and was now holding her position awaiting her fate.

I placed the school paddle across her bottom – the length of it almost perfectly sized for her big butt. I said –

more quietly than anticipated – "Please count the strokes, and give me a 'Thank you, Sir' after each one. Then, you can say 'Ready' when you want the next stroke. I'm not going to go easy on you, Linda. But you've taken a lot, already ... and still have six strokes of the cane coming."

Linda wiggled her butt back and forth, then settled and forced her chest down to the desk. "I know, Sir."

I brought the huge paddle back, in anticipation, and Linda took a couple of big breaths, letting each one out slowly. Then she said, "Ready!" The paddle flew in an upward arc, impacting the fleshy mounds of her bottom fiercely, with a loud 'WHAP!!'

Linda whimpered, but held her position, and she yelled, "One. Thank you, Sir." A few seconds later, I heard 'Ready!' again, and I let the paddle do its work. Linda's reaction predictably increased in intensity, as each swat landed on her bulbous buttocks. Amazingly, she continued to hold her position. It was clear that she'd had experience with this, prior to our role-play, today.

The paddling continued, the full six strokes being delivered, and covering most of her bottom, from the upper middle of her buttocks, down to her upper thighs. Linda was sobbing at the end, but proudly called out 'Six, thank you, Sir' on the last stroke. I rubbed Linda's bottom, and asked if I could lower her underwear to survey the damage. "Please do, Sir."

Despite the over-the-knee spanking, the light paddlings, the tawsing and, now, the six hard swats with the mean school paddle, Linda's bottom looked OK. It was dark red, but there was no broken skin, or bruised areas. However, she still had the cane coming. I could only hope that Kelly would go easy on her; and on me.

I pulled up Linda's panties, running my fingers around the inside of the waist band and leg bands, to make sure they were on properly. Of course, they would be coming down in a few minutes. But I had done my job for the day. I asked Linda to stand, and we hugged again.

"Linda, I am very proud of your performance today. And, if you want, I'll tell Kelly that you've had enough." I chuckled, "And maybe she'll skip my punishment, also."

I breathed deeply and continued, while holding her waist, "This experience was your suggestion, and we don't want to overdo it. You are welcome to call it quits, if you feel you've had enough." I looked at Linda in the eyes, trying to convey my sincerity.

I wasn't that surprised when Linda replied, "I'm OK, Sam. I knew it would hurt. And you've done a great job. I'm the one who decided on the bare-bottom tawsing, so you shouldn't be punished for that. And, I'm sorry that I didn't skip the grass ..." she smiled at me, "... or invite you to smoke with me. I guess, subconsciously, I was acting as I really did in school – perhaps actually *wanting* to be punished."

I kissed Linda on the forehead, and she kissed me back lightly on the lips. Then, she asked, "Shall we go see the headmistress, now?" I laughed, took her hand, and led her downstairs to the playroom.

I watched Sam and Linda come down the stairs, hand-in-hand. Having had time to think about it, I wasn't really upset with Sam. But it seemed only fair that Linda see him take a punishment, as well; I had a feeling that she would leave even more turned on. Or, at least, have the fantasy fodder for getting herself off at home ... tonight, and probably for many nights to come.

And Sam would undoubtedly get off on the memory of this role-play plenty of times in the future. I had moved the chairs from in front of Sam's executive desk to the side walls, and cleared the desk.

Linda and Sam walked up to the desk, Linda immediately taking the standing position. "Reporting for my caning, Miss, as you requested." Linda blinked a couple of times; she was really taking this seriously. And I intended to give her a serious caning.

I smiled at Linda, but turned to Sam, and said, "First, the *teacher* will be punished for his unseemly conduct with one of our female students." Sam flinched, and was about to say something, but smartly kept silent.

I continued, "The charges are 1) punishing a female student on the bare – which is not allowed at this institution, and 2) smoking marijuana during school hours." I smiled at Sam, "I am willing to dismiss the possibility that you provided the drugs, or encouraged the student to use them." Sam was nodding, but said nothing.

Standing behind the desk, I pronounced, "Your punishment will be six of the hardest strokes I can muster with the school paddle." Sam's face dropped, and he put his hands over his face, as Linda had done many times.

I picked up the 'other' school paddle – the one with ten holes drilled through it. Sam looked up, and I added, "On the bare."

"But ... but ..." Sam was pleading, whining. He knew better than that.

I raised my voice, and spoke in the sternest tone I could, "Mr. Johnson! You have set a bad example for our student. Don't set another one: I expect you to take your punishment cooperatively, and with dignity."

Sam was about to comment on the 'dignity' of being spanked on his bare bottom in front of his student. I reminded him, "You punished your student on the bare, and now it's only fair that she see you punished the same way."

I glanced at Linda, who was smiling, but unable to put her hands over her face, as they were still on her head. Smiling sweetly at her, I suggested, "You may stand more casually, young lady, until it's time for your own punishment. Why don't you stand farther back, so you'll have a good view?"

Linda put her hands down, and giggled, "Yes, Miss." She took a few steps back.

I glared at Sam, as I imagined a real headmistress would, and commanded, "Drop your pants and underpants, now! And bend over the desk!" Under my breath I mumbled, "I think you know what to do." Sam unbuckled his belt, unzipped his pants, and let them drop to the floor. Then, he pushed down his underwear, and stood in front of the desk. He was only slightly turned on.

I realized that he would not be able to spread his feet wide enough, and instructed him to remove his pants and underwear entirely. Sam gave me a sour look, but complied, putting them on the chair next to the wall. Then, he spread his feet, and bent over the desk.

Taking the school paddle, I walked behind him, positioning myself to his left side, and placing the paddle across his bottom. I chortled, "I have half a mind to let the student do the paddling," Sam immediately raised his head and was about to protest, as I continued, "but I think, with my experience, I'll be able to give you a harder 'lesson'."

I looked back and smiled at Linda; she was smiling broadly, and nodded once. Turning back to focus on Sam, I said loudly, "Prepare yourself!" As an afterthought, I ordered Sam to call out the strokes, and a 'Thank you, Miss' after each one. Sam coughed and nodded, "Yes, Miss."

Sam had taken several very hard strokes of the belt by my hand, acting surprised at my strength. And, he had witnessed my abilities when we had visited the Domme. I decided that this would be another submission 'challenge' for him ... and one that I hoped would impress Linda.

I took two steps back, and then quickly stepped toward Sam, swinging the paddle – with a wrist-snap at the end (as my dad had taught me to do, playing baseball, golf, and a number of other sports). There was a cannon-shot sound that echoed in the room; and a second later, Sam screamed. "Owwww!! Kelly!"

He lifted his head, and I quickly commanded, "Get back down! Right now! Or, you'll be getting extra strokes." Sam was whining already – after only a single stroke! He really was a baby. It was Linda who would be caned in a few minutes; Sam was lucky that he was only getting six strokes of the paddle.

Sam finally called out 'One; Thank you, Miss', and I continued, stepping back again, and doing a two-step run-up while swinging the paddle. It took three strokes before I had the method perfected, and Sam screamed after every stroke. But he counted them out and held his position – more or less.

After the fourth stroke, I looked back at Linda, and she appeared weak – almost about to faint. I asked, "Are you OK, dear? Would you like something to drink?" She shook her head, but still appeared wobbly.

I gave Sam another two very hard swats with the thick paddle. He probably would be black-and-blue by tomorrow; this would be an experience he would remember. I laughed inwardly; *another* one.

Sam wept, wetting the desk with his tears, and I handed him a tissue. Then, I went to the coffee table, and retrieved the already-lubed butt plug that I had prepared.

Showing it to Linda, I pointed to her; she cocked her head, and I nodded. Perhaps it wasn't in the schoolgirl script – but neither was the marijuana, or tawsing Linda.

Without saying a word, Linda took the huge plug from my hands, and stepped up to Sam. I spread his buttocks, as Linda took her time inserting the butt plug. Sam flinched, but soon realized that he would be getting a 'corner time'; at least, *our* style of corner time. I had no doubt that this – and watching Linda being caned – would turn him on.

The butt plug was mostly in, but Linda was having trouble advancing it further. I said, "Sam, you're going to have to relax your anal muscles more. Try to push out, as the plug goes in." He tried, and Linda tried. After several attempts, Linda shoved the plug into Sam's rear, Sam yelping once, and then relaxing himself onto the desk.

I gave Linda the 'OK' sign, and indicated that she should move back a few steps. Then, I instructed Sam to stand, turn around, and stand by Linda.

When Sam turned, Linda and I could see that he was getting hard, his dick at 'half mast', already. Sam looked at Linda, and shook his head resignedly, then took his position next to her.

Without being told, Linda took off her skirt and underwear, placing them on the chair on top of Sam's clothes, then stepped up to the desk and took the standing position. "I'm ready for my caning now, Miss." I was impressed, and I knew that Sam was, also.

I walked around the desk to the credenza, and picked up the small-diameter, whippy cane that I had selected. This would not bruise Linda, but give her six really good stings across her bottom. "You may bend over the desk, now, young lady." As Linda was doing so, I added, "And don't even *think* about getting out of position!" I wasn't going to make Linda count the strokes.

Stepping behind her, I slid the cane back and forth across her butt. "This caning is for being dishonest with the school – forging the sick note. I hope you learn a lesson, today."

Linda mumbled, "I'm sure I will, Miss."

It was time. I decided to make it quick. The cane flew, striking Linda's bum with a loud 'SNAP!' I administered the strokes evenly, like a metronome, with one stroke every five seconds.

Linda squealed after the first stroke had landed, screeched after the next, wailed after the third stroke, shrieked after the fourth stroke, howled after the fifth, and screamed at the top of her lungs after the last stroke. But she had held her position, and never tried to bring her hands behind her. Now, I *knew* that both Sam and I were impressed!

Linda was crying – almost as loudly as Sam had – and I handed her a bunch of tissues. Then, I opened a bottle of soothing lotion, and smeared it on Linda's big butt. When I looked back at Sam, he had a full-on erection. I saw that he was stroking himself, but I decided not to punish him further.

I asked Sam to bend over the desk again, and I think he was nervous that he would get more punishment. But he complied silently, and I smeared lotion over his butt, also, rubbing it in.

With both Linda and Sam bending over the desk, I walked around and sat in Sam's executive chair; they both looked up at me, wondering whether their ordeal was over ... or what I had in mind next. I was now a CEO, and decided to take 'executive action'.

"You've both taken your punishment well, and I think you're ready for a reward." They were both smiling, now. "As it was Linda's idea to do a schoolgirl role-play adventure, I'm going to let *her* make the final decision." Now Sam and Linda were looking at me cautiously, then glanced at each other. Sam shrugged, and I smiled.

"I will offer Linda a choice: You may get dressed, and leave, now; you may masturbate in front of us; or you may ask *Sam* to masturbate you. And you may also choose to let Sam 'get over' his erection, get him off with your hands, get him off orally, or you may ask *me* to get him off orally". Both Sam and Linda were now opening and closing their mouths, like two fish out of water.

Finally, I smiled at them broadly, and said, "Or, you could accept *my* choice." I waited, and realized that the room was completely silent – the two fish in front of me not even breathing. "My choice is for Linda to remain in position, and Sam to take her from the rear." There was gasping from both Linda and Sam.

Then, I added, "But, Sam, you will *not* wear a condom. Linda has already gone down on you, and she's been taking shots at your suggestion. You'll just have to accept the small risk that having unprotected sex with her will mean."

Then, I looked at Linda, "You *don't* have to accept my suggestion; it's entirely up to you. I just thought – as you're both obviously turned on already – that it might be a nice way for you two to complete the experience."

Linda's blank expression slowly turned into a smile. Sam looked at her, and shrugged, then gave her a crooked smile. I was surprised that Sam wasn't objecting ... and happy to see that he was finally loosening up, a little.

Sam and Linda were still bent over the desk next to each other, Sam with a large plug up his butt. Sam leaned over, and kissed Linda on the cheek. He told Linda, "This was *not* part of the script; I'm as surprised as you are." He looked at me, and I nodded. Then, he turned to Linda, and said, quietly, "Only if you want, Linda."

Linda leaned over and kissed Sam on the cheek. I really wasn't sure which way it would go. Then, Linda batted her eyelashes at Sam, and said, quietly, "I want." I was a little shocked, but happy for both of them.

Sam moved behind Linda, and rubbed his dick on her butt crack for a minute, then, lowered it, stepping closer to her. Linda reached under, and put Sam inside her. I sat back in the executive chair – now, a 'real' executive – and watched the action.

The two fish were already very turned on, as was evident by the fervent movements of their bodies. Sam – the considerate man that he was – reached around, and fingered Linda's clit, as they continued their coupling motions.

Linda's breathing was heavy, and her motions more urgent. Suddenly, Linda stopped for a moment, grunting, and then thrust herself back against Sam. Sam closed his eyes, making his final thrusts into Linda, as he came.

Our ménage with Julie had been the first time I'd seen two people – live – making love. This was even hotter, both Linda and Sam fully ready, after the schoolgirl experience that had turned both of them on. Sam's paddling and Linda's caning had brought them both to the edge. And, now, they were in the climax of their experience with each other. It was beautiful.

When they were finished, we all walked the short distance to the downstairs bathroom, where Linda sat on the toilet, and I took the butt plug out of Sam. Then, we got under a warm shower, and bathed each other. Silently. And, kissed each other. With passion.

CHAPTER 4: HOMECOMING GAEITY

While I stood in the lab, watching the lights on the gene sequencer flash and the computer screen scroll through the software steps I had written, I thought about Sam, his late wife, Sarah, and his two sons. Sam and I now knew each other well; *very* well. Sam's energy, enthusiasm, and sexual prowess continued to excite me, as did his intelligence.

I had understood for many years that I was sapiosexual – intelligence being almost as much of a turn-on as the physical characteristics of a man. And Sam always strove for higher standards – in everything: His openness, honesty, and considerateness, not to mention food, travel and the intensity of his various interests ... just the way he lived. It had opened my eyes to new possibilities.

I barely remembered Sarah – a couple of times at the soccer field, a few times at the country club, and once or twice at my parents house. My impression of her was that she had been very self-confident and poised, but down-to-earth; I would be happy to be like I remembered her.

Sam had been devastated by her death in a car accident in England, and he had closeted himself – developing his fantasies, but no real relationships – for several years before we had re-met at my parents' party.

My memories of Sam's sons were vague – I tried to picture them playing soccer with my brothers, but couldn't see their faces. I did have a couple of images of them diving into the country club pool, when we had all been kids; but they were several years older than me, and we had never gone to the same school. I guess I had always associated them with sports – and I had always rebelled against the importance my father had placed on team competitions, and his macho attitude.

I still viewed my dad as rather 'coarse', and he certainly was, compared to Sam. It wasn't that Sam was feminine, but he appreciated finer things, less physical things ... although I couldn't deny that sex with him had been very physical. But even Sam's perspective on his fetishes – submission, spanking, BDSM – were at least as much focused on the mental as the physical.

Recently, in relation to the upcoming Christmas party, Sam had described his sons to me – and they both sounded very intelligent. I had known that one of them, Robert, was married; he was into finance and real estate development. His wife, Jessica, had graduated with an accounting degree, but had a job with a company that developed software for small businesses.

Sam said they were both liberal, and went to jazz concerts and art films, as well as supporting human and animal rights. It seemed unusual for people who were into usually-conservative professions. But then, it seemed unusual that Sam would be turned on by medical fetishes, having come from the medical industry.

Sam hadn't mentioned anything about their sexual proclivities, but I assumed that they must be fairly 'open' people.

I had been quite surprised to hear that Sam's younger son was gay. There had been research indicating a possible X-linked genetic disposition towards homosexuality, but as the X chromosome could come from the mother or the father, it didn't imply anything about Sam; he certainly wasn't homosexual and, in fact, had told me that he was somewhat homophobic. Not against gay – or, more generally, LGBT – individuals, but having a discomfort with close male interaction.

Of course I realized that the world – and especially biology – wasn't so simple: Any given trait could depend on multiple genes and biochemical pathways, plus the epigenetic makeup of the individual, as well as their environment and upbringing.

As I watched the genetic machinery in front of me, I chuckled; it had seemed to me that people involved in some of the most 'macho' activities – such as football or wrestling – appeared homoerotic ... although I very much doubted that any of those people would recognize or admit to those tendencies. My mind was wandering.

Sam had told me that Mark was an artist, but hadn't mentioned what his partner did for a living. I was looking forward to getting re-acquainted with both of Sam's sons ... and it would be interesting to see how my father would reconcile his memory of Mark playing soccer on the team he had coached, with the gay Mark with whom he would be having Christmas dinner.

Chuckling again, I shook my head, hoping that my father wouldn't cause a scene at Sam's house. One would have thought that in the 21st century, everyone would have become more accepting of diversity ... but I knew most people hadn't. Especially older ones, like my father, who seemed to always be living in the past, with fixed ideas about how the world was ... or should be.

The computer dinged, and I clicked the 'Analyze' button to complete the calculations based on the genetic profile of the bacteria that I was testing. This was only a simple 'model', but it would help validate the hardware I had integrated, and the software that I had written to run the whole system.

I had done pretty well to build this complex of a system and begin testing before the holidays. Most of the basic components had already been available in the lab, and I'd had to write only the interface software to get everything to work together ... and the analysis software – still evolving – that was the crux of my invention.

I shut down the computer, turned off the various systems, and cleaned up the area; it was time to break for the holidays. This would be my first holiday season spent with Sam, and I was looking forward to a little 'holiday cheer'.

As I walked down the aisle of the market, stocking up for the Christmas dinner, I reminisced about the development of my relationship with Kelly over the past six months ... and with her friends. Kelly and I had really 'hit it off' – in a manner of speaking. Now, our loving relationship was maturing, both of us finding our 'sweet spot', in terms of domination, submission, and the level of openness in our relationship.

Kelly had really opened me up to new experiences – at least as much as I had with her. Especially surprising to me were the relationships we were developing with Kelly's friends; I'd now had actual intercourse (and much more) with two of her friends – totally unexpected, and something which I would never have accepted just a half year ago.

Julie, Linda and Kathy were all incredible – individuals with very different personalities and interests, but clearly sexual beings who had enjoyed playing with us, and who had been a turn-on for both Kelly and I.

Linda's schoolgirl role-play had been amazing, and Kelly had surprised me with her desire to see Linda and I move our relationship into a sexual realm. Despite her heavyset figure and outwardly conservative personality, Linda had been amazingly sensual and sexually open. She was a very nice girl, and very intelligent; I wondered what type of guy she sought for a longer-term relationship.

We all had our stories, and we were all sexual creatures ... but the socially shallow ways that most people meet didn't typically allow us to share our desires, our true needs. Perhaps that wasn't fair: The evolution of our relationships – through dating, sexual contact, and discussion – should allow us to gauge each other and select mates (or at least companions) who have similar interests and desires.

But how many of us really shared our innermost fantasies, our basic sexual needs – sometimes formed in our early childhood, and often (it seemed) hidden, even from our partners?

I threw the last items into the basket, and headed to the checkout lines.

Sam and I had finished as much prep work as feasible for the dinner party, and he was on his way to the airport to pick up Mark and his partner. Robert and Jessica would be arriving tomorrow, and renting a car – both to get here from the airport, and to tour the area, Robert wanting to share with his wife some of his childhood haunts.

The dinner would be on Christmas eve – two days from now, and I was busy setting the dining room table, using Sam's crystal, silver, and china, on a beautiful cream-colored Irish lace tablecloth. A pair of silver candle holders were set near each end, and a exquisite flower arrangement that we'd picked up yesterday was the centerpiece.

Mark and his partner would be staying only a few days, as they had New Year's eve plans in New York city, while Robert and his wife would be joining us for a small New Year's eve celebration, including a special dinner at the French restaurant, and fireworks at the largest park in town.

I had thought that everyone would stay with us at Sam's house, but both Robert and Mark had opted for a room at a local hotel, where Sam had reserved two suites. I guess neither couple was interested in sleeping in single beds. There was the king size bed in the playroom, but that was deemed 'uncomfortable' for putting up guests.

Neither Robert nor Mark had seen the finished basement, having not come 'home' since Sam's wife had died, nearly five years ago.

I wondered whether they would notice any difference in Sam's personality or behavior, since he'd lived alone for so many years ... and then been with me for the past six months. I wasn't really nervous about what Sam's sons thought about the relationship between he and I, as Sam had already told them about me, and they had not been surprised – simply finding it amusing.

Well, I found it 'amusing', too, although in a totally different way.

Sam had stored the old-time school desks in the garage with the others, and I was now using the large desk for writing my dissertation – which so-far only consisted of the 'background' sections, as my main research would be ongoing for many months – perhaps more than a year. Large file cabinets lined the back wall, and the massage table still sat on the opposite side of the room, along the sliding glass doors.

Sam had given me two massages since he'd massaged Alex on Labor Day; I really enjoyed them, even though they had been 'normal' massages – not the sensual, electrified experience we'd had during my first long weekend with him.

Our patent had been filed, based on the limited data I had collected in the lab, and now we had the long wait until receiving feedback from the U.S. Patent Office.

I really enjoyed living with Sam; he was loving and considerate, and we seemed to be very compatible. It had only been a month since I'd moved in, but I was already getting used to – and preferred – living with someone.

The holidays would be interesting – meeting Sam's sons and their wife/partner, and seeing my own brothers again after more than a year. Especially interesting would be the Christmas dinner that we were hosting; I hoped that my parents would 'behave themselves', and not cause a scene. I were pretty sure they would be OK.

I thought, again, about the envelope that my mother had given me, now stored in the big desk in the pool room. Maybe I should open it, and see what it was about, before my parents came over for the party? I could ask Sam's advice, but it was my decision, and I didn't think he would offer much helpful input.

I ushered Mark and Greg, his partner, into the house. They had checked in at the hotel, and dropped their luggage in their suite. Greg seemed to be a nice guy – he was in the advertising field, more on the commercial side, while Mark was trying to be a 'real' artist – not willing to cater to corporate desires ... but also not making a lot of money.

Sarah and I had set up a trust for both sons – in addition to paying their college expenses – and they'd had access to the funds when they turned 25. Robert had not touched his trust, but Mark had utilized a portion of it, already. Being with a partner, his living expenses were somewhat lower, but living in New York, they were still sky high, compared to most other places in the country.

In any case, he appeared to be happy, which was the most that a parent could hope for ... or, at least the most important thing, according to the value system that Sarah and I had taught our kids.

Kelly skipped into the living room from the pool room, and I introduced her to Mark and Greg. Her eyes lit up, I'm sure finding both of them quite handsome and, as she shook Mark's hand, she gushed, "It's great to see you, Mark, after all these years. Sam has told me so much about you. It sounds like you're living an interesting life in the big city as an artist."

Mark nodded, "Yes, it's pretty 'happening', and I may have started to make an impact. I've done some 'public art' projects – like painting three-dimensional images of plants growing down steps, which have made some of the public spaces more accessible to many people. The city is really vibrant." He glanced at Greg, who was nodding.

Kelly shook Greg's hand, and he commented, "Yeah, Mark is making his impact as an artist, while I pay most of the bills, working for a large ad agency." Then Greg put his arm around Mark's shoulders and pulled him close, "But our arrangement is working out pretty well." Mark smiled and nodded.

I led everyone into the kitchen, where I opened a bottle of Chardonnay, and poured glasses for everyone. "Could I give you the nickel tour?"

I had been really talking to Greg, but Mark spoke up, "Yeah, Dad. You've told me a little about your basement 'project', but you never posted any pictures on Facebook, so I've been trying to visualize what you've done with it."

He turned to Greg, "When Rob and I were young, we played in the basement – and dad had set-up a workbench, where we built model planes, and did some fun stuff. But most of it was a storage area."

Before I showed them my 'play room', we all took our wines, and stepped outside to the patio. It was quite cool, but I'd put on the pool lights, and lit the grounds. The trees were bare, and the grass was mostly brown, but Greg was still impressed. There wasn't much new, since Mark had been here five years ago.

We walked through the sliding door into the pool room, which now was the 'headquarters' of KS Biotech. I think this room was also being used as a storeroom, when Mark had last been here.

"Kelly got her Masters degree in biotech last June, and is now working on her Ph.D. I took her to Europe recently for her 25th birthday present, and – while I was sleeping off the wine tastings, Kelly was inventing a revolutionary approach to new drug development. Her advisor suggested we file a patent and start a company ..."

I waved my hands around at the desk, file cabinets, notes and technical figures on the blackboard, and papers and notebooks stacked everywhere, and continued, "So this is now the official world headquarters of 'KS Biotech, Inc.'. I winked at Kelly, "Kelly is the CEO, and she hired me as a part-time consultant for the company."

Kelly was shaking her head, but before she could comment, I led everyone back through the kitchen, and down the stairs to the former 'basement'. The Berber carpeting from the playroom continued up the stairs, and

Mark whistled as he saw the finished 'basement' ahead of us. We passed the exam room on the left – the door still locked, and the only indication of the room being something more than a closet being the numeric keypad. We also passed the bath on the right; I would show Mark and Greg the sauna as we headed back upstairs.

Mark whistled again, as we entered the playroom. The curtain at the far end of the room to our left was drawn, hiding the king size bed, and I had lowered the screen, the documentary, "Winged Migration" now being projected, but with the sound muted. The lights were in their 'normal' configuration, with highlights on the desk area, couch area, and bar, with the rest of the room lights slightly dimmed.

I pointed directly across the room from the stairs, "That's my office area – I mostly play around on the Internet, now that I'm retired." The large walnut and steel executive desk still looked classy, with my black leather executive chair behind it, and two small grey-cloth armchairs in front.

Ahead of us, to the right, was the bar, which wrapped around a corner. The back bar was black glass with a thin gold abstract pattern giving it a three-dimensional feel. The bar top was grey granite, with black veins, and flecked with various colors, from gold to silver. Behind the bar was a small refrigerator, and glasses were in wood cabinets on either side of the back wall.

To the right was a walk-in wine cellar, that took up the corner behind the bar, and to the right of the wine cellar door, in the corner, was the Christmas tree that Kelly and I had selected together. The room smelled like pine, which was one of my favorite parts of Christmas.

To our left, across the room, was a couch, loveseat, and chair, and the large coffee table – grey with a wide diagonal brushed-aluminum band crossing it. On the wall to our left, next to us, there was a small side-table, and straight-backed chair – my 'spanking' chair, although I didn't point it out as such.

Mark said, "I guess you really do have a 'man cave' for your retirement activities!" I nodded, although Mark would never know the extent of the 'activities' that had gone on in this room. Kelly remained quiet, but caught my eye – as Mark and Greg watched the video on the huge screen – and gave me a knowing smirk. She had been my main partner for 'playing' in this room, along with her three friends.

Mark and Greg turned to us, and we led them into the small bath, and through to the shower room outside the sauna. "And here is the sauna!" Turning to Mark, I said, "I guess you've seen it, already; it was the only part of the basement I had finished when your mother was alive."

I opened the door, and let Greg stick his head in. The sauna was at a 'warm-up' temperature; it would only take half an hour to heat it. Mark and Greg gave each other a 'look', and I flashed on an image of 'gay saunas' in New York, although I had never actually seen one.

"You guys are welcome to use the sauna facilities, if you like, while you're visiting." I hoped that I hadn't said anything wrong. Of course, Kelly and I could give them the sauna and playroom to 'play', if they wanted.

Greg laughed, "Only if you and Kelly come in with us." I chuckled, not sure if Greg was serious or joking. Somehow, the whole prospect made me uncomfortable: Going into the sauna with my gay son ... and his partner ... and Kelly. It felt weird.

Kelly smiled, her eyes bright, "That would be fun!"

We continued back up the stairs, to Mark's old room – now being occasionally used as a guest room. Kelly's

Mickey Mouse lamp was on the table backing the kitty-corner beds. I turned to Mark, "You certainly could have stayed here, if you wanted ... or still could, if you don't like the hotel."

Mark shook his head, "We're fine in the hotel. You're going to have a lot more visitors here." Then, he tilted his head, "When are Robert and Jessica coming in?"

"They'll be here tomorrow evening. The party is Wednesday, on Christmas eve, and they'll be staying a week, and leaving on Saturday." I added, "They also preferred to stay in the hotel."

Looking at Kelly, I remarked, "I guess my kids don't want to be with me that much." Mark and Greg would be departing on Friday, only Robert and Jessica staying through New Year's eve.

As I showed Greg the other guest room and the master bedroom, Mark explained, "It just seems that staying in the hotel will be more comfortable, and should make it much easier for you and Kelly – not to have to host us (or Robert and Jessica), *and* get the house ready for the party." We walked back downstairs, to the kitchen, where I refilled the wine glasses.

"Well, there is one thing you could help us with, if you don't mind: We need to decorate the Christmas tree tomorrow; maybe we can all bedeck it with ornaments and lights together?" I still had to bring the boxes of Christmas stuff in from the garage; there hadn't been a tree in this house – or a Christmas celebration – since before Sarah had died.

Mark and Greg smiled, nodding, and Greg offered, "That sounds like fun!"

We had taken Mark and Greg to dinner, and dropped them off at their hotel last night. This morning, we'd met them, and taken them to the local zoo. It was small, but nice to walk a couple of the trails through the forest, where some of the animals were in large fenced or walled areas.

I got to know Mark a little, as he explained some of his public art projects and philosophies, and told us about his life in New York – the restaurants, gallery openings, and parties he attended. And Greg mentioned a few of his agency's clients – which were some well-known company names across the U.S.

It was an interesting mix of a very successful business person and a very successful artist, who both happened to be male and gay. It was also interesting how Sam's two sons had diverged, both socially and in their values – especially their focus on business vs. art.

After visiting the zoo, we went to 'our' bistro, where we had an early dinner with Mark and Greg. Sam had bought some holiday desserts for later in the evening (and for the Christmas dinner) at the bakery where he had gotten my incredible birthday cake.

When we got back to the house, Sam and Mark climbed into the attic space over the garage to retrieve the Christmas lights and ornament boxes, while Greg and I went down to the playroom to continue our conversation. Greg said that he would like to try the sauna, so I turned up the temperature, and then got us a couple of sodas.

Greg seemed interested in my Ph.D. project and business, but his eyes glazed over as I tried to explain the technology involved. One of his company's clients was a large pharmaceutical company, and he offered to provide suggestions on our initial marketing pieces and eventual ad campaign. But my project was far from a commercial stage; we probably wouldn't need Greg's services for quite a while.

Sam and Mark carried in the boxes, and we had a nice time decorating the tree. There were a couple of ornaments that Sarah had bought, and I saw tears in Sam's eyes. Mark and I hugged him; the tree-trimming had turned out to be an emotional experience.

Finally, the tree was done, and Sam plugged in the cord: Let there be light! Everyone cheered. The tree was beautiful, rising to the tall ceiling of the playroom, festooned with ornaments, lights strung through the branches, and tinsel draped over the pine needles. It smelled wonderful.

There were no presents under the tree, yet, but Sam and I had bought gifts for my parents and brothers, and for Sam's sons and their wife and partner.

Sam went behind the bar, and brought out a bottle of Schramsberg sparkling wine, holding it up, as he expounded on the history of the winery.

"This is a Napa, California wine, from one of the oldest wineries in northern California, founded in 1862, just five years after the first commercial winery – Buena Vista – was founded in Sonoma, California. Jacob Schram was from the wine region along the Rhine River, where Kelly and I visited recently."

Sam continued, "After the Transcontinental Railroad was completed in 1868, Jacob hired hundreds of Chinese laborers to dig caves in the mountain behind his vineyard and house, to age and store the wine.

"Jacob was originally a barber, and he cut the hair of Robert Louis Stevenson, who later brought his bride back to Napa, and visited the Schramsberg winery, among others, which he wrote about in his book, '*Silverado Squatters*'."

As Sam twisted the wire of the cage counter-clockwise, he added, "All wines made using the champagne method – *methode Champagnoise* – have a wire cage over the cork, called a *muselet* ... and it takes precisely six half-turns to open it." He continued twisting, and took off the cage, then pulled out the cork with a resonant 'Pop!'.

After pouring crystal fluted glasses for each of us, he lifted his in a toast. Turning to Mark, he said, "Here's to our family reunion," then turning to Greg, Sam added, "and good friends."

Smiling at Greg, and turning to me, he concluded, "And lovers. And to the holidays and great success in the coming year." We all lifted our glasses, and I hoped that I would have success with my project, and in my relationship with Sam.

We sipped the sparkling wine standing around the tree in the playroom, and then Sam brought the bottle to the coffee table, and we sat on the couch and loveseat.

I couldn't help but visualize some of the things that had transpired around this coffee table, including my punishment of Sam, when I'd come over for a first spanking experience; Linda taking her birthday spanking over Sam's lap, and Julie masturbating in front of us all; and, more recently, my own birthday spanking experience with Julie, Linda and Kathy; and Sam, of course.

Sam picked up his customized remote control, and tapped one of the light profiles; immediately, the lights in most of the room dimmed, including over his desk, while the light over the coffee table dimmed only slightly. Mark exclaimed, "Boy, you've really put your technical skills to good use, Dad. Quite a 'man cave' down here."

Little did Mark know ...

Sam smiled, and said, "Yes, I call this the 'playroom'. It's not only my office, a bar, and a nice social setting, but also a place where I can bring young women to play."

"What!?!?" I screamed. I knew that Sam was joking, as he and I had been together nearly constantly for the past six months. Then, I thought about our ménage with Julie, the birthday 'play' with my friends, and the recent schoolgirl role-play with Linda.

And then there was Fiona. Alex had to be considered an 'older' woman; and Sam had told me about his neighbor Liz, who'd been here just after the room had been finished. I guess Sam *had* brought several young women – and a couple of older women – down here to play.

Giving me a smirk, he turned to Mark and Greg – who were sitting together on the love seat – and explained, "Actually, Kelly was the first 'young woman' I played with in this room." He looked at me lovingly, "And she has become the love of my life. But she's brought a few of her own friends over – for example, when we celebrated Kelly's birthday. It's been a great room for a number of things."

At that, he pressed a button, and the giant projection screen rose. Before it had disappeared into the ceiling, Sam pushed another button, and the drapes parted to the sides of the room, exposing the king size bed, dressers, and artwork.

"Dad!" Mark gave his father a 'look', and shook his head.

Greg had a big smile on his face, as Mark continued, "If we'd known you had that huge bed down here, we *might* have taken up your offer to stay here!"

Mark looked down, and his face seemed flushed, "And I don't think we want to know about how you 'play' down here." I should hope not. I glanced at Sam, and was quickly reassured that he wouldn't be talking about spanking and fetishes with his son.

Then, Greg spoke up, "And that great bathroom down here ... with the *sauna!* You could really party!" Greg – and Mark – had no idea. And that was probably for the best.

However, for some reason, I suddenly felt playful, and wondered how Sam would react. "Would you guys like to try out the sauna with Sam and I?" I saw Sam flinch, and his mouth drop open, and I quickly looked at Mark and explained, "Your dad is turned on by openness."

Although I was referring to a mental turn-on, rather than a sexual one, I could see Sam's jaw stiffen, his mouth open, as he stared at me.

I continued, unfazed, "For example, we toured many saunas in Europe, where everyone is comfortable with nudity, and he has taught me the pleasures of openness – mental, physical, and sexual." Sam hadn't said a word; he seemed to be tongue-tied, perhaps the first time I'd seen him like this.

I smiled at Greg and Mark, "So what do you think? Sam built a really nice sauna, and it would be fun to share it with you guys."

Mark and Greg looked at each other, Greg nodding his head, as he'd already indicated to me that he wanted to try the sauna. Mark looked at me, and said, "That would be nice, Kelly."

Sam coughed, and sputtered, "I think I'll let you young'uns use the sauna; maybe I'll sit this one out."

Giving Sam a stern look, I said, "No way, Sam; you're coming in with us!" I hopped up, and took Sam's hand, pulling him up from the couch. Sam was shaking his head, and he looked uncomfortable.

I led Mark and Greg into the bathroom, as Sam stood at the door. Opening the narrow closet just inside the shower room, I handed them robes, and took a couple for ourselves.

"You can leave your clothes on the chaises and get showered, and we'll be back down in ten minutes, and join you in the sauna." Then, I took Sam's hand, and we walked out of the bathroom, and up the stairs to the master bedroom.

As I unbuttoned my blouse, I asked, "What's the problem, Sam? Why are you so uncomfortable?" I unbuckled my belt, and slipped off my jeans.

Sam stood at the doorway to the closet in his slacks and dress shirt. "I don't know, exactly, Kelly. You know that I'm more comfortable being with women than with men."

I nodded, "I thought that was because you don't want to compete with men in a macho way. But I don't think you have anything to worry about with Mark and Greg. They seem like sweet guys."

Sam flinched again. "I guess I'm even more uncomfortable with gay men." Sam was shaking his head, "I'm not uncomfortable being with Mark, but going nude in the sauna with both Mark and Greg ..."

I took off my bra and underwear, and stepped out of the closet into the master bath, pushing Sam into the closet, then sitting on the toilet to pee. "Get undressed, and let's go downstairs."

Sam reluctantly took off his clothes and put on the robe. Then, we went downstairs for what would be – given Sam's attitude – an 'interesting' experience. Once again, I realized that Sam was not quite as 'open' as he professed.

When we entered the shower room, Mark and Greg were relaxing on the chaises in their robes, obviously having already showered. Sam and I hung our robes, and took a quick shower together. Sam checked the sauna temperature setting, surprised that I had already turned it up, then we all entered the red-lit, Cedar-scented space, and sat on the top bench.

Mark and Greg knew to sit on their towels, letting the ends drop to the lower bench for their feet, and we all settled in for a relaxing course of the dry heat.

Opening the conversation, I remarked, "I guess Sam is a bit uncomfortable sitting in a sauna with a couple of gay guys." That woke everyone up, and Sam's mouth again dropped open, but there was nothing he could say.

Greg spoke up first. "It's all about cultural stereotypes. Men are expected to like women, and feel that they might be criticized, or perhaps judged to be gay, if they admire a male body. Most men don't compliment other men, or talk about their physical attributes – unless it's about being tall or short, fat or thin."

Mark nodded, and added, "And there's a double-standard involved: Men – and most women – enjoy watching two women touch each other, play together, or have sex ... but don't want to see two men together."

Greg laughed, "Although some men are OK with watching or being part of a ménage à trois ... they focus on the woman, or their own bodies."

Mark thought a moment, and said, "And many men are uncomfortable being around gays because they're afraid that they will be hit on." He looked at Sam, who was nodding, almost imperceptibly. "Or, they're afraid they will see two men show emotion toward each other, or perhaps kiss, or touch each other in a sexual way."

I had to jump in, here. "But Sam thinks he's very open, and nonjudgmental regarding people's turn-ons."

Sam's voice was hoarse, and he said defensively, "I don't think I judge other people. I'm OK with Mark being gay, and being with Greg. It's just the way I've been brought up ..." He glanced at Greg, "Maybe you're right: I may be afraid that I will be judged to be gay, or criticized, if I look at another male body, or appear to be feminine."

"Sam," I said, "you *are* more feminine than most other men." I had to chuckle, "Especially, men like my father, who act so macho." I looked at Mark, "I still don't know how my dad will react, when he finds out that you're gay."

Mark nodded, "I know. But the crux of a lot of the social 'stigma' is based on the misunderstanding that homosexual men have made a choice; that we have chosen this as a lifestyle. I'm sure you know that it isn't something we've selected ... it's how we are, our basic nature."

Greg, getting a little more animated, explained, "Sexual orientation – whether you are heterosexual, gay/lesbian, or bisexual, is about someone's emotional attraction to men, women, or both sexes; that usually leads to their romantic and sexual attraction, as well."

He sighed, "And, it's not the same thing as gender identity – whether someone feels the psychological sense of being a male or female. While biological sex (such as anatomy), gender identity, or age are characteristics of an individual, sexual orientation is defined in terms of their relationships with others."

I explained, "Sam is most comfortable being around women – not just sexually, but just having conversations. As you know, Mark, he's not really a 'macho' guy, not into team sports or other things most guys are into ... except women." I laughed, but realized that I was beginning to confuse myself.

Sam said, "I guess I've always been a little homophobic." At that, Greg stiffened. Sam explained, "I'm uncomfortable being around men ... especially men's bodies – like in a gym, or touching activities, such as wrestling. In fact, when I watch wrestlers, it seems to me that they must be a little gay, to have such close contact with other men." Now we were all shaking our heads.

Greg said, "No, Sam, you're wrong on two counts. First, wrestlers – as far as I can tell – are generally *not* gay; they're macho men, the same as men who play soccer, baseball, or other sports. It's just a sport. And, second, the word 'homophobic' doesn't mean what you think: It's usually used to signify someone who is *against* homosexuality ... people who hate gay men. In fact, some homophobes are actively militant or violent against gays."

Sam nodded, "OK – you're right. I'm not *against* gays ... just the idea of me being homosexual, myself, or being touched in a sexual way by another man."

Sam breathed in deeply, "As you said, it's the social mores, the way I was brought up, that – I guess – makes me afraid that I'll be labeled homosexual, even by myself." The sauna was quiet for a minute or two. We were now all sweating, and Sam adjusted his position, and lifted the corner of his towel to wipe his face.

Greg said, "Sam, I've studied this for quite a few years. In college, I took a lot of psychology classes, and learned that there is no single cause for someone being gay – although there may be some genetic, some hormonal, and – yes – even some social and cultural components. Most of us knew that we were attracted to people of the same sex as a child; certainly, by middle-childhood, or early adolescence at the latest."

Then he chuckled, "Although some men try to hide it, and don't want to admit to it, until they are an adult. And, due to religious or other reasons, some men have been convinced by those around them that their preference is just behavioral; but they eventually recognize that it's 'who they are', not a behavior that they can voluntarily change; or, even change through training, hypnosis, or other active approaches."

Looking at Sam, Greg continued, "In fact, those who have gone through programs – usually sponsored by religious groups – to change have often come out psychologically disturbed, because being gay is part of them – a characteristic, not merely a behavior."

Mark joined the discussion, "Until the mid-1970's, psychologists labeled homosexuality as a mental disorder. So there was a stigma placed on gays, lesbians and bisexuals even amongst professionals. If it is a disorder, then it should be treatable, but we now know that it's an inherent part of us, and not something that can be changed."

He quickly added, "And, if you think that men in prison are likely to become homosexual, you're wrong: Some men accept male relationships, even sexual ones, as a convenient way to satisfy their sexual needs, a temporary behavior, but it doesn't change who they are."

Now, I was curious, and needed to ask some questions; I flashed on Helga, and had a déja vu moment, thinking about all the questions I'd had for her, regarding transvestite and transgender individuals. "It seems that gay men have good relationships with straight women ... and lesbians. Is that true?"

Greg laughed, "Well, I can speak for myself: I enjoy friendships with women, for a couple of reasons. First, I can relate to women, as I share many of their sensitivities and values. And, second, it is a way to have a close – sometimes even intimate – relationship, without the tension or pressure having to do with sex."

Greg wiped his face with his hands, and drops of sweat fell onto his chest and dripped down his body. He was in good shape, muscles well-toned, and would appear as a 'hunk' to any straight woman. His mannerisms weren't feminine, and I doubt that most people would recognize that he was homosexual, if they didn't engage in an intimate conversation with him.

He continued, "It could be comfortable for me to have a close relationship with a straight male, also ..." He glanced at Sam, "As long as they were not intimidated by talking frankly with a gay male. And, most women can relax and feel comfortable with a gay guy, as they know we're not after sex. The only problem comes if they begin to have a romantic attachment, in which case it can become uncomfortable for both of us."

Greg chuckled again, "Sometimes a woman who doesn't know that I'm gay will gravitate to me, as she see's me as a perfect gentleman, more interested in her mind than her body; but if she's straight, she may eventually want to have a sexual relationship, and that – obviously – goes beyond my interests in being with her."

I turned to Sam, "That sounds very much like how you approached me: Interested in my mind, and doing things – that although intimate – didn't have to do with 'sex'. There may have even been a moment or two, during our first lunches or even when I came over the first time," I had to control myself to not mention 'for a spanking session', "when I might have thought you might be gay ... as you kept avoiding the subject of sex with me."

Sam nodded, but seemed flustered as he replied, "But you knew that I'd been married, and had two sons. And, I'm sure you knew that I also loved your body, and – certainly when you came over for the first time – got turned on by you."

I shook my head, "But there are many married men, even with kids, who turn out to be gay. And, maybe you were just getting turned on by the things we did, not by the fact that I was female?"

This was becoming an interesting conversation, but difficult for us to continue without letting Mark and Greg know that we were both turned on by dominance and submission. Which, I think, neither of us wanted to divulge.

We were all hot now – from the sauna. I suggested, "Shall we get out of here, and cooled off under the shower?" Sam nodded, as did Mark and Greg. We all filed out of the sauna, and I got the shower going – including the huge rain shower head, and the leg jets.

We all crowded under the rain shower, letting the cool water stream down our bodies. Both Mark and Greg were good-looking guys: They were handsome, and fit. Greg had much more chest hair than Mark, but they were both very pleasant to look at – for a heterosexual (perhaps bisexual) woman.

We rinsed off, then grabbed our robes, and sat on the chaises – Greg with Mark, and Sam with me – and continued our discussion.

Mark opened up to his father, "I feel a simpatico with women. I understand how they must deal with the emotions of desire and love, rejection and pain. And I can easily see the double-standard that society has created; the inequality, male show of superiority, and male aggression towards women."

Mark said, seriously, "I enjoy talking with gay men, and most women – straight and lesbian – about *feelings*. That's something that most men don't do; they're focused on objective, measurable things, like sports scores, and their possessions – things that seem competitive, not things that create emotional bonds."

Mark took a deep breath, and continued, "Most women are interested in peace, togetherness, and developing relationships, while most men seem more focused on competition, aggression, and violence. I think gays, lesbians and bisexuals are somewhere in-between ... perhaps some gays being more on the female end of the spectrum and some lesbians being more on the male side. But it's a continuum."

Sam was listening, and hopefully learning, but not saying much. Greg jumped in, looking at Sam, "Something else that may be related to your fear – or at least discomfort – with homosexuals may be the idea that gay men are always looking for sex with other males; that would be intimidating for most straight males, if they thought they might be the target of the gay's desires. For example, heterosexual men may think of a gay bar as merely a place for hook-ups."

Greg laughed easily, "Well, it's partly true – as much as straight men go to bars to pick up women."

Mark was shaking his head, but Greg continued, "But mostly, we're there to meet like-minded people, to have conversations that are non-threatening to us, and not necessarily for sex. In fact, I think gays may be much more relationship and emotion focused – like many women – and *not* thinking about sex, as much as men."

Mark was now nodding, "I think that's right. Believe it or not, *sex* is not the most important thing – at least to me ... and I think many gays. It's the relationship, the emotional bonding, the closeness we feel with another man."

Sam changed the subject. "Unfortunately, the pool and spa aren't heated." He looked at me, "Please remind me – we should at least heat up the jacuzzi, since we have so many people visiting this week." Then, he turned back to Greg and Mark, "Shall we go back into the sauna?" We were all a bit chilled from the shower, and everyone nodded.

Once we were again in our places in the sauna, I asked, "Is there usually a 'top' and a 'bottom' with most gay couples?" Sam looked at me sharply. I clarified, "I mean, a more masculine and a more feminine partner?"

I took a breath, and continued, unsurely, "And, I guess I'm wondering whether one partner takes the 'male' role, and the other the 'female' role ..." This was getting more than a little personal, and Mark looked away, perhaps being embarrassed to talk about this with his father sitting here.

Greg chuckled, "If you're thinking about anal sex, some gay couples probably have their 'way' of doing it ... but you have to realize that there are many ways to get to an orgasm: We sometimes use our hands, sometimes our mouths, sometimes prostate stimulation ... it just depends how we feel at the moment; what we're 'up' for."

That brought chuckles from all of us. I should have known this, as it was the same with Sam and I; we didn't always get off with vaginal sex, even as a heterosexual couple. I nodded, communicating my understanding

Continuing, Greg said, "And, as prostate stimulation can be a large part of our turn-on, both the top and bottom – as you called them – can have a sexual response; it's not one-sided ... just as it hopefully isn't in a heterosexual relationship." Now, I felt a little ridiculous – having learned these things over the past six months with Sam, but somehow thinking that it would be different between two males.

Perhaps this was also silly, but I asked, "I guess I've seen some ménages on porn movies with two guys and a woman ... but would you guys ever consider being part of a ménage with a woman? Or, would that turn you off?"

Sam coughed loudly, and I thought he might have a fit, picturing his son and partner making it with me. Or, perhaps, he was visualizing himself as part of the scene. He was still obviously hung-up and fearful about homosexuality.

Mark and Greg looked at each other, and shrugged; but a slight smile on Mark's face made me think that this wasn't a theoretical question for them. Greg shrugged, "That might be possible. But it would probably have to be with a straight – or, at least bisexual – woman ... and I doubt that would happen." Then, he said, under his breath, "Unless we were all drunk." I saw a thin line of a smile on Mark's face, again.

I knew that we were all nearly ready to get out of the sauna again. But, I decided to venture one more comment, "Well, I've recently discovered that I might be bisexual." Sam coughed again, then stood, and walked down the steps and out of the sauna. Perhaps I'd gone too far?

With just Mark and Greg in the sauna with me, I clarified, "Although I am sure that I would want a male as my main partner, I've recently found that I can get turned on – and even have an orgasm – with another woman. Sam is well aware of this, and sometimes jokes worriedly that I might leave him for a woman. But, he is the love of *my* life, so he has nothing to fear."

I had been sitting cross-legged, and now I pulled a corner of my towel up, and wiped my face.

Continuing, I said, "But, like most guys – heterosexual guys – Sam's had fantasies about being part of a ménage." Of course, I didn't mention that we'd already had a ménage with my friend, Julie. I laughed, "He doesn't mind the idea of me getting it on with another female, if he's part of it; double the pleasure, double the fun – and lots of female bits to look at and touch."

Mark and Greg nodded, and we all laughed. Then, we stepped on the lower bench and down to the floor, exiting the sauna into the shower room. Sam was still in the shower, and I kissed him, and began soaping him.

As I had expected, Mark and Greg helped bathe each other. It was only natural. But Sam faced the tile wall, letting me soap his backside, without having to watch his son with another male.

We all put on our robes, and went upstairs, where Sam served the dessert on the kitchen table, as I'd already set the dining room table for our big dinner party tomorrow evening.

Robert and Jessica were arriving tonight, and driving themselves to the hotel. I wondered if Sam's other son would be as interesting as Mark had been. I would find out soon.

CHAPTER 5: HOLIDAY CHEER

Robert and Jessica drove Mark and Greg to the house shortly after noon. My family had been invited for a 4PM gathering, and we had planned dinner for 6PM. Sam had spent all morning stuffing the turkey and had just put it in the oven. Now, he was finishing some last-minute appetizers for the party, including deviled eggs, guacamole, and cheese puffs made from *Challah* bread he had picked up at the bakery.

I made the simple appetizers: Cashews (which we would roast in the oven when my family arrived), and cream cheese with jalapeño jelly, circled by crackers. Next, I would get the salad ready; Sam had made a Green Goddess dressing yesterday. He had also prepared the sweet potatoes with marshmallow topping, and traditional green beans with fried onion topping, both of which were being stored in the refrigerator out in the garage.

Sam answered the door, and I washed my hands and entered the living room, just as Mark and Greg were stepping through the front door. I hugged them, and they continued to the hall closet to hang their coats. Sam greeted Robert and Jessica warmly, and introduced them to me. Robert was a handsome guy, and I could see a strong resemblance to Sam. He was taller than Sam, and obviously very fit.

Jessica was about my height, and good looking, but not quite as fit; she was probably 10-15 pounds overweight, with a round face, and I could tell – looking at her sweater – that her breasts were large. She had beautiful red hair, just a little frizzy; I wondered if she also had an Irish background. She also had a great smile, and a vivacious personality. She hugged me warmly.

Robert stepped up to me, and I put out my hand, but rather than shake, he hugged me affectionately. "So you're the woman my dad couldn't stop talking about! I do have some vague memories of you when we were kids, but you certainly didn't look like this, back then."

I smiled at him, and glanced quickly at Sam, who shrugged. Robert continued, "My dad has really needed someone, since my mom died. I hope you're taking good care of him." Robert smiled.

I was taking good care of Sam when he was good, and good care of him when he was bad. "We're taking good care of each other," I said. I took Robert's and Jessica's coats, and hung them in the hall closet, as they continued into the kitchen. As I caught up with everyone, I could hear a lot of 'Mmmm's', they all smelled the great aromas coming from the oven.

Sam offered everyone drinks, he and Robert taking beers, and Mark, Greg and I deciding on a rosé that Sam pulled from the fridge. Jessica drank the water we had put in a pitcher, now infused with flavor from the lemon and lime slices that Sam had dropped in. Sam asked if anyone wanted to start on the appetizers, but they declined, as they'd all had a big breakfast together at the hotel.

Sam led us downstairs to the playroom – which elicited a reaction from Robert similar to the one Mark had shown us. "Wow, dad; you've really done a lot of work down here!" Jessica was nodding, and they both scanned the room, the giant screen being down again, and the curtain closing off the end of the room with the bed. This time, Sam was playing a video that showed mountain scenes: Snow in the winter, wildflowers in the spring, and rushing streams in the summer. The sound was turned down, but we could hear the wind, and gurgling of water in the background.

We sat around the coffee table, Sam in the chair, and me on the couch with Mark and Gregg, while Robert and Jessica took the loveseat. Sam had stacked some card chairs in the back of the playroom, which we would have to put out when my family arrived.

Sam started the conversation with a few questions to Robert and Jessica about their work, and it progressed with the two sons updating each other. It was great for Sam to have his family here, although a few comments elicited sadness as he remembered Sarah. The Christmas tree was lit, and we had put all the presents under it.

When Sam went upstairs to finish the cooking, Robert looked at me, holding up his beer, and toasted, "Here's to Kelly, the newest member of our family."

Everyone sipped their drink, and Robert continued, "I think dad has really been lost since mom died, looking for things to do ... and trying to make new friends; but you're the first person he's really been excited about. And I can see why: You're beautiful, and dad's told us about how smart you are – coming up with a new invention and starting your own company."

I felt my face flush. "Actually, Robert, Sam's been a big part of that. I met him at a party my parents gave for a few friends, and asked him to help me with some career guidance. We immediately hit it off, and our relationship has grown to the point where he invited me to move in with him recently.

"Sam's been very nice to me. He took me to Europe for a birthday present, and I was able to relax enough to think up a few new ways to use the technology I'm developing for my Ph.D. project. And, he was instrumental in helping me see some of the limitations, and help me get over the hurdles to make it practical. Now, I'm building and testing it at the college ... and it looks like it really might work."

Then, Robert turned to Jessica and chuckled, "I barely remember Kelly from when we were kids ... and never would have recognized her, now that she's grown up to be a beautiful woman." Turning back to me, he asked, "Where did you guys go in Europe? Dad mentioned the trip, but didn't give us any details." I sure hoped that was true! There were a lot of 'details' that his sons would never know.

I described the trip – mainly the itinerary, and some of the tidbits such as our Oktoberfest experience, skiing in Switzerland, and touring Paris. I did not mention the saunas, sex club, or dominatrix. Everyone listened with rapt attention, and shared some of their own European experiences. Both Mark and Robert had been to Europe several times.

When Sam returned, and he heard the discussion about Europe, he put the show of our trip on the big screen. He mentioned his friends Henk and Zöe, whom his sons had never met, including the part about Henk's 'coming out' as a cross-dresser. And – when pictures of *Thermae 2000* popped onto the screen, he casually mentioned our touring of saunas in The Netherlands and Germany. Robert nodded, and turned to Jessica, "My parents were always open about nudity; I remember the family going to nude beaches a few times when we were little." Mark was nodding.

We heard the doorbell ring, and Sam sprang up, and ran up the stairs; it seemed too early for my family to arrive, but I looked at the digital clock on Sam's credenza, and saw that it was nearly 4PM. By the time I stood, my brothers were already coming down the stairs.

"Kelly! It's great to see you!" I hugged Pete and Tom, and turned to introduce - or re-introduce – Sam's sons and their partners. I hadn't seen my brothers for a year, and they hadn't changed, much. Both were husky guys – not overweight, but solid-looking. They were both into sports, and both had gone to out-of-state colleges, and had settled near them, one in the Midwest, and one in the southeast.

"Tom, Pete, I'm sure you remember Robert and Mark, Sam's sons?" Everyone stood, and walked over to where we were standing – near the Christmas tree. "And this is Jessica," I pointed, as she stepped up and shook their hands, "and Greg." Everyone shook hands, and I saw a flicker of curiosity in Tom's eyes, when he shook Greg's hand.

"Can you guys help put those extra chairs around the coffee table?" Everyone pitched in, and we soon had seating for 10 around the coffee table; the table was pretty large, but the seating was a bit tight. I ran upstairs to help Sam carry the appetizers downstairs.

"Hi mom, dad. Merry Christmas!" My parents hugged me, and both seemed to be in good spirits, figuratively, and probably literally. Sam was in the kitchen, putting the cheese puffs in the oven, and I hung my parents' coats in the closet.

My father carried wrapped boxes of presents, so I gave my mother a platter, and I took another platter of appetizers down to the playroom, where we put them on the bar. Everyone was still standing, and I introduced my parents to Sam's sons and partners – again avoiding specifying exactly who Greg was.

My father put the presents under the tree, and asked, "Where do we get a drink around here?"

Sam walked into the room, carrying the opened bottle of rosé, and an unopened bottle of chardonnay, and announced, "The bar's now open! What can I get everyone?" My father asked for a bourbon and ginger ale, my mother for a vodka and tonic – light on the tonic.

My brothers each took a bottle of beer – but winced when they tasted the hoppy beer that Sam stocked. Mark and Greg selected the chardonnay, and the rest of us opted for a pinot noir that Sam had opened.

We heard the oven timer buzz, and Sam asked me to take the cheese puffs out. As I took out the baking sheet, and used tongs to move each cheese puff to the serving platter, I began to relax; perhaps it was the wine ... but it felt like the evening was going well, so-far.

Back down in the playroom, everyone was still standing around, talking. Sam winked at me, and I smiled thinly at him. The Europe show was still on the screen, flipping mutely from one image to the next.

My mother glanced at the screen, and turned to me, "Is that Paris?" I recognized the images of our walk up the *Montmartre* hill, and nodded. She asked, "Did you go to the top of the Eiffel Tower? At that moment, images of the Eiffel Tower flashed on the screen, and I realized that the show wasn't exactly in chronological order.

I pointed, "Yes. It was really nice." More images flashed, looking down from the middle level, and then an incredible panorama from the top, showing the pink sunset clouds and the city below. I closed my eyes, remembering our 'electric' kiss, with 20,000 lights flashing around us.

My mother sipped her vodka and complained, "Your father only took me to Europe once, and we took a bus tour. We saw the Eiffel Tower from the bus, but never got to go to the top." I remembered that they had taken one of those typical tours – 14 countries in 9 days (or something like that). They had never really experienced any European culture, only seen a few of the major sights.

I expected my mother to ask about the images now on the screen of London, or to continue complaining about her own life; but she surprised me, and said, "Kelly, dear, I've thought a lot about it ... and I guess I'm OK with you opening that letter from the court. You have a right to know. I just want you to be happy, and not be hurt."

This was something! I thought that *she* would be hurt if I showed any interest in finding my birth parents.

"I haven't had time to look at it, mom. And, I'm really not that interested in my past life, anymore. You're my mother ... and I love you." We hugged gently, trying not to spill our drinks. I could see that my mother's eyes were moist, but she just nodded, and drank a gulp of vodka. I offered, "Let's talk in a week or two; maybe I can bring it over, and we'll open it together?" She nodded again, and looked away.

I gravitated over to my brothers, who were talking with Robert, Mark, Greg and Jessica. They were providing a little of their recent history – my older brother now working in an auto dealership near Chicago, and my younger brother, Pete, having taken a job as a high school athletics coach, after graduating with a degree in kinesiology.

The culture differences between Sam's sons and my brothers couldn't have been more apparent.

I heard my father say something loudly; he was pointing to the large screen, and asked Sam if he could turn on one of the college football games. Sam caught my eye, and I shrugged; if he turned it on, it would occupy my father for the rest of the evening ... which might not be such a bad idea ... or distraction.

Sam and I carried the appetizers to the coffee table, and we all sat down, continuing several different conversations. My mother was now sitting next to Jessica, and was asking her how she liked being a housewife ... with Jessica looking funny, and then explaining that she was a professional in a software company.

Then, Jessica cleared her throat, catching Robert's attention. Robert picked up the knife from the cream cheese and jalapeño platter, and dinged the edge of his wine glass. The noise level in the room fell immediately, and all eyes were on him.

He cleared his throat and smiled at Jessica. "I guess this is as good a time as any ... Jessica and I have an announcement." I glanced at Sam, and his face turned in an instant from questioning to smiling. Robert held up his glass, across the table from Jessica, and she nodded demurely.

In a quiet voice, Jessica said, "We're going to have a baby! I'm about 12 weeks pregnant, now ... but I was only sure a few weeks ago, and we decided to wait until Christmas to tell everyone. So the baby should be born in June."

The table erupted in applause and cheers, and Sam smiled broadly as he held up his own glass, "Congratulations! That's great!" Then, a brief flash of seriousness crossed his face, and he mumbled, "I guess I'm going to be a grandparent!"

I got up and walked around to Jessica and hugged her, and then went behind the couch and put my arms around Sam's neck, "Congratulations, granddad!" Now, our age difference had suddenly emerged again, this time in a totally different – and unexpected – context. I leaned over the couch, and kissed him on the cheek.

The conversations around the table picked up, again, my father now asking Robert and Mark what they did. He nodded, when Robert explained that he was developing commercial properties, but seemed flustered when Mark said that he was an artist. He took a gulp of his bourbon, and looked at Greg, "And what do you do, Greg?"

Greg casually answered, "I work for a big ad agency ... doing creative projects for our clients." He smiled, and added, "For example, we just did a new concept for merchandising in the Victoria's Secret stores." That was impressive. It probably helped everyone understand his work, by dropping a name that we could relate to.

But my father, squinted, and said, "So you tell people how they can sell women's underwear?" Greg shrugged, and nodded cautiously. My father drained his bourbon, and set the glass on the table. "And Mark works with you?"

Greg answered carefully, "No. Mark is a friend."

Mark and Greg were much more than 'friends'. I had to jump in, "No, dad. Mark is Greg's partner. Just as Sam is my partner." It was direct, but I still didn't quite go as far as to say that Mark and Greg were lovers. My dad rolled his eyes.

Sam took my dad's glass, stood, and made his way around the coffee table and to the bar. "I'll refill your drink, Dave." Now, Tom and Peter were tittering and snickering, which I thought quite unbecoming for men of their age; but, in many ways, they were still boys.

I smiled at my mother, and she held out her empty glass; I took it, smiling back at her, and brought it to the bar, where Sam refilled it. He then brought the bottles of wine to the table, and refilled everyone's glasses. Just as he finished making the rounds, the buzzer went off in the kitchen, and Sam announced, "I'll go take out the turkey. Dinner will be served in 20 minutes."

"Fuck!" My dad shouted, and all eyes around the table were on him. He cried, "That was a simple field goal. That guy can't kick worth shit!" My brothers turned to the large screen, and shook their heads.

The rest of us rose, took our glasses, and made our way upstairs. I suggested that Mark and Greg sit on one side of the head of the table, and Robert and Jessica on the other side. I put my wine glass at the 'tail' of the table, and went into the kitchen to help Sam. He was taking the stuffing out of the turkey, and asked me to light the candles on the dining room table, and then take the sweet potatoes and beans out of the oven.

Ten minutes later, Sam had carved enough turkey to fill a large platter, and we set out all the dishes on trivets on the kitchen table, which we would use as a buffet. I filled the water glasses on the dining room table, and then poured the Bordeaux wine that Sam had opened for everyone, except Jessica. Sam tossed the salad, and divided it onto salad plates, which I brought into the dining room. The football game finally ended, and my family came up and took their places at the table.

Sam sat at the head of the table, and raised his wine glass. "Here's to good friends and good food, to loving, and living … and to appreciating what we have." He looked around the table, "I would like to wish you all a Merry Christmas, and great success in the New Year. It's wonderful to have you all here with Kelly and I."

Then, he focused on Jessica, and said, "And here's to having another member of the family join us next year!" We all sipped the wine and ate our salads in silence.

After I had collected the salad plates, I ushered my family and then Sam's family into the kitchen, where they loaded their plates with turkey and stuffing, gravy that Sam had made with a thick brown roux as base, the marshmallow-topped sweet potatoes, onion-topped green beans, and cranberry sauce. It was an incredible spread, and Sam had made it look easy.

Everyone returned to the table carrying plates filled with food, and we dug in to our Christmas dinner. My mother would probably have made a ham, with whipped potatoes, green beans, and a cranberry mold. But we all were enjoying Sam's dinner.

My mother asked Jessica her plans for a nursery, and how many kids she hoped to eventually have, and the conversation re-ignited. Robert talked about looking for a new home, and my father – finally joining the discussion – talked about his plans for my former room over the garage.

I asked my brothers whether they had serious female friends, and Peter surprised me by going on and on about an English teacher at his school. It sounded more serious than he was willing to admit. Tom always had a girlfriend, but there were evidently none that he considered worthy of a long-term relationship.

The conversation came full circle with more discussion about babies, and I turned to Mark and Greg and asked, "Is there a baby in your future?" My father had a coughing fit, and had to excuse himself. Greg smiled at Mark, and then replied, "Well, we've thought about adopting ... or using a surrogate." Sam was nodding, but my mother pushed her chair back, and said, "I'll help you clear the table, dear."

My parents were of the age – or mentality – that females had their 'role' in the family: Cleaning the house, making the meals, having the babies, and taking care of the family.

As I carried the dirty plates and silverware into the kitchen, I thought about the traditional roles and relationships, and those that I would want. I didn't reject outright the tasks that my mother valued, but they wouldn't be my entire life, either. I saw myself sharing the responsibilities with Sam; perhaps Sam even taking most of the traditional 'female' role, as he was such a good cook, and so neat.

But I saw my life as something greater – giving something back to humanity, with my technology, my company, and setting higher standards as a role model to those around me ... as Sam had done for me.

It was strange: I had nearly thought, 'I wouldn't be subservient to a husband, to a man' ... but in some sense, that was part of what I craved; perhaps not subservience, but submission. And not in a one-sided relationship, but at some times, or in some situations, taking the dominant role. In fact, I now saw myself primarily being the dominant – in business and in the family, with periods of submission to break up the monotony of a single role.

As far as having kids, I couldn't imagine it at the moment; perhaps that would change sometime in the future? But Sam had had a vasectomy. Would I also be looking for a surrogate, or adopting? My mind was a little muddled from the wine, and there were many questions I could not answer; but there was no question that I would not be following my mother's footsteps as the traditional 'housefrau'.

I went downstairs, and cleared off the coffee table and bar, bringing the leftover appetizers and dishes up to the kitchen, then put on a pot of coffee. Darlene and Kelly had put the china and silver in the dishwasher, and had washed the crystal by hand. I ground fresh Kona coffee beans, and started the coffee maker. Then I kissed Kelly, and turned to Darlene, "I hope you enjoyed the dinner."

Darlene nodded, and replied, "Yes, Sam. It was very nice. I can understand what Kelly sees in you." She hugged Kelly, then looked at me and added, "Please take care of my baby." Her words were a bit slurred from the alcohol, but it was clear that she was being sincere ... and becoming more accepting of our relationship.

I hugged Darlene, and told her, "I certainly will. I only want the best for her. She's very special."

Darlene hugged me back, and said, "Yes, she is."

I asked Darlene and Kelly to help me carry the desserts, plates and silverware into the dining room. As usual, I had slightly over-done it, providing a selection from the bakery that included a flourless chocolate cake with caramel filling, a *tarte tatin*, and a New York style cheesecake decorated with fresh berries on the top.

As everyone helped themselves, I poured the coffee, and announced that we would have after-dinner drinks downstairs, while we opened the gifts. There were 'Mmmm's' around the table when the desserts were tasted, and as I glanced at Kelly – who had taken tiny slivers of each of the desserts – she patted her stomach. We would start our diets after New Year's eve.

All of our stomachs were bulging, as we made our way downstairs. I poured brandy, liqueurs, and soft drinks, and Kelly reached under the tree, pulling out each present, and handing it to the person listed on the tiny cards. Dave had given me a bottle of Johnny Walker scotch, and Robert had selected B&B Brandy. Mark gave me a small framed piece of abstract art on ceramic, signed by one of his artist friends.

Kelly and I gave her mother two framed pictures of her from our Europe trip, and her father a bottle of his favorite bourbon. I had selected several DVDs for my sons – some of my favorite recent movies that I thought each of them would like, and a gift certificate for Jessica at a major department store. Kelly gave her brothers some DVDs that she thought they would like – including '*42*', '*Million Dollar Arm*', and '*Draft Day*' for Peter; and '*Rush*', '*Red Army*', and '*Foxcatcher*' for Tom. Kelly's mother gave her a very nice Cashmere sweater from the entire family.

Presents opened and after-dinner drinks consumed, everyone departed in a festive mood. Kelly and I cleaned up, and dragged ourselves upstairs to get ready for bed. "That didn't go too badly," I said, as we got undressed in the closet.

Kelly nodded, "My dad behaved himself, mostly; and my mother seemed to be accepting us as a 'couple'. I thought there would be more conversation between my brothers and your sons ... but I guess they didn't have much in common. It's interesting how they've all grown apart, since middle school."

That was true ... but I wasn't so sure they'd had much in common back then, either; except being on the same soccer team, and swimming at the country club. I remembered that they'd all taken golf lessons around the same time, but wasn't sure whether they had ever actually played even 9 holes together.

We climbed into bed and turned off the lights. I asked, "Can we make love in the morning?" As I spooned Kelly, it was obvious that I wouldn't be 'getting it up' tonight.

I could hear the smile in her voice, as she whispered, "Sure, Sam. I'm tired, too." Then, she turned around and we kissed. She said, "That was a nice dinner, and a nice way for everyone to re-meet, after so many years." Then, she giggled, and added, "And congratulations on being a future grand-dad!"

She turned around, before I could answer, and I spooned her again. That *was* a surprise, but I guess I should have expected it.

"Good night, Kelly." I knew she could hear the smile in my voice, also. I put my arm around her, and we were both asleep within a few minutes.

Sam's sons came over on Christmas day in the afternoon, and Sam weathered the cold to make hamburgers on the barbeque, along with his famous potato salad, and a garlicky coleslaw. We drank beers, and it almost seemed like a summer dinner, except that we sat at the dining room table.

Sam's sons showed us pictures on their iPads, which Sam had networked into the large screen projector downstairs. Mark showed us a lot of pictures of his 'city art' projects, and Robert and Jessica showed us pictures of their home, that they had recently remodeled ... just in time to put it on the market and buy a bigger house for the addition to their family.

The next day, Robert and Jessica visited old friends of his, while Sam and I drove Mark and Greg to the airport. It had been a short trip for them, but I had really enjoyed meeting both of them; and learning more about the gay lifestyle and perspectives. Sam seemed very comfortable with them, although I think he was still uptight and now somewhat conflicted about his own views on homosexuality.

On Sunday, we spent the day with Robert and Jessica. Sam had heated the spa, and I assumed they would wear bathing suits. They had brought them, but Jessica said that she wanted to try the sauna, asking Sam if he thought it was safe for the fetus. He had said that her body would regulate the temperature inside the womb, as long as her core temperature didn't exceed 101 degrees.

He and Jessica sat at the computer doing Internet searches, finding a lot of misinformation, and only a few scholarly articles. The decision was that, to be extra safe, the hot tub shouldn't be set higher than 99 degrees, and the sauna to a much lower temperature than normal. Also, she shouldn't stay in either for more than 10 minutes at a time. I wondered whether Sam would suggest measuring her core temperature with a rectal thermometer ... but he was respectful to Jessica, and didn't offer that.

We supplied robes to Robert and Jessica, and began in the sauna; it was nice, but none of us were sweating when we got out. Sam and I sat on the chaises, while Robert and Jessica showered, and then we took our turn. Sam made sure that we all were hydrated, serving water in plastic cups on a tray. I flashed on my first experience with Sam, when we'd mixed up the cups, and he had announced that – per his definition of fluid transfer – we'd had 'sex' with each other.

Our robes on, and wearing flip-flops, we went outside, immediately getting chilled. We got into the jacuzzi, which felt very nice at 99 degrees, which was nearly 60 degrees warmer than the air temperature.

Sam wore his watch, his count-down timer set for ten minutes. When the timer buzzed, we all went back down to the sauna. It was a delightfully different experience, not getting ultra-hot. I learned that Robert and Jessica were very open people, and very committed to environmental causes. Much of our discussion related to global warming, and they were much more knowledgeable on the subject than either Sam or I.

Sam asked, "Isn't the decrease of snow on Kilimanjaro due to global warming? I'm sure I've read that several times."

Robert shook his head, "Yes, it's been publicized, and still promulgated by a few scientists ... but most believe that it is deforestation that's been the cause. So, it's still due to man, but not associated with global warming."

As Sam nodded slowly, Robert explained, "The top of Kilimanjaro has always been near zero degrees – way below freezing, but energy from the sun causes sublimation – the change from ice to vapor, without melting; only mist and clouds protected it, and deforestation changes the evapotranspiration, the amount of water vapor at different levels on the mountain."

This was more information than either Sam or I needed, but it was interesting that the effect was still manmade, although the global warming hypothesis in that case had been debunked.

Robert told us that global warming particularly affected the polar regions, with the permafrost in the arctic melting, and releasing even more greenhouse gases. We learned that the Northwest Passage had become ice-free by 2007, the first time in recorded history. Even the glaciers in the Alps appeared to be disappearing. It was a much more complex subject than politicians described, but still dangerous for the future of the earth.

Robert and Jessica got out of the sauna after 8 minutes, and took a cooling shower. When they had gone upstairs to get dressed, Sam and I took a shower together. Sam prepared a dinner of leftovers – which included all of the dishes he had made for the Christmas dinner. There was still some of each dessert left, and I knew that I'd have to start dieting soon.

On New Year's eve, we enjoyed a leisurely dinner at the French restaurant, starting at 9PM. There were hats and noisemakers for everyone, as well as streamers that people were throwing into the air. It wasn't the usual atmosphere at the restaurant, but George was working, and Sam insisted that he join us in our booth for a few minutes, to sample the Burgundy that Sam had selected.

We toasted to the New Year, and left the restaurant stuffed ... again. Then, we drove to the largest park in town, and sat on a blanket, bundled up, watching the fireworks show.

As a nod to our new year's resolution to diet, Sam and I had yogurt and cereal for breakfast, and he made a big salad for Robert and Jessica and us in the early afternoon. The rest of the day, as we all visited, he made a great turkey vegetable soup.

He had bought a seeded baguette yesterday morning, and heated it to go with the soup. Unbelievably, he didn't take out the butter, and I don't think any of us missed it. Sam even skipped the alcohol ... until the evening, when he couldn't resist opening a beer.

We said our goodbyes to Robert and Jessica, and they left for the hotel to pack for their flight in the morning. It had been a nice holiday, and I'd enjoyed meeting everyone. I felt a bit guilty about not spending more time with my own family, although my brothers had left before New Year's eve. But we'd all visited during the Christmas dinner, and even my father had behaved himself.

My parents had not been overly inebriated at the dinner; well, no more than the rest of us. Sam and I would need to cut down on the alcohol, as that was a major source of our 'extra' calories. My pants still fit, but I knew that I had gained nearly ten pounds since we had departed for Europe – about a pound per week.

I was ready to get back to school and into the lab, excited to really test my system and finish writing the analysis software. Raj had provided guidance, but I was on my own in the lab. I hadn't even updated him about the successful initial trial of the automated hardware, run by my prototype software, the day before the holiday break.

We had no more vacations scheduled or trips planned, and I would put my nose to the grindstone and work as hard as possible to prove my technology, submit my dissertation, and start development of a product that KS Biotech could sell.

CHAPTER 6: PARTING SHOTS

It was hard to believe that it was already the middle of March. I was spending every day at school, in my symposia classes and in the lab; so-far the project was going well, although not as fast as I had hoped. Raj and I had written a couple of new invention disclosures, and Sam was negotiating with the college to license all of the inventions resulting from our work.

On the home front, nothing much had changed. Sam and I were enjoying living with each other, and I hadn't seen my parents since the holidays. I'd spoken with my mother on the phone, and heard that my dad was already converting the room over the garage.

Sam and I were invited to dinner over the weekend, and my mother suggested that I bring the unopened envelope from the court that she'd given me more than four months ago. I still had no idea why it had upset her, and wasn't really that curious about it, although I would have to consider whether I would seek my birth parents, if the documents gave me a lead.

Over the past few weeks, I'd had several dreams in which I'd seen them briefly, and I tried to remember exactly what had happened when I was eight. But although I could picture a few scenes – such as sitting in the car alone in the parking lot, being taken from my parents, and looking up at the judge – I really couldn't remember many other details.

Today was Friday, and my friends and I were scheduled to meet at the clinic for our last round of HPV and hepatitis vaccinations. Sam would be meeting us there, and my friends had agreed to humor him. He'd said that he wanted to take some pictures of us, and my friends weren't too happy about that, although they'd agreed to wear a black top, jeans and white bikini underwear, as he had suggested.

Getting a couple of small shots wasn't a big deal for any of us – even Kathy, who'd finally realized last time that they were quick and didn't hurt much. But Sam was still turned on by the idea of seeing us bend over the table, and take our shots, a remnant from his childhood fear of needles. I would have thought he'd be over it by now, with all the needles we had played with over the past year.

It was amazing: It had been nearly a year, since we'd had our first lunch together. There had been a few arguments early in our relationship, but we'd gotten along incredibly well over the past four months, since I'd moved in with him. I still found sex with Sam hot, although we hadn't engaged in many of his fetish activities lately, other than the role-play with Linda.

We hadn't discussed it, but I was still considering taking Mistress Elena's domme course during the summer. I was turned on by the idea of having Sam submit to me, especially when it came to some of his hang-ups.

But I had to admit that Sam had loosened up considerably since we'd first met – when he had been reluctant to have any sexual contact, at least other than with me. My friends had broken the ice by giving him oral sex the morning after my birthday party, and now we'd had a ménage with Julie, and Sam had made it with Linda after her schoolgirl role-play. And, he'd had sexual contact with Zöe which, by extension, meant with Henk (or Helga), also.

Now, I thought about his fear of closeness with men –
he'd called it 'homophobia', which Mark had said was not
the proper terminology. I don't think I'd ever seen Sam
touch, or be touched, by another man, except for shaking
hands.

We were all meeting at the clinic just before 3PM, and
Sam arrived a few minutes after me, carrying his camera
bag and a tripod. I shook my head, as I approached him,
"Sam, I hope you aren't going to make a big production of
this. I don't think my friends really want to star in your
home video."

As Sam began to nod, Julie, Linda and Kathy came
through the door of the clinic and walked up to us. We all
hugged and took a seat, waiting for the nurse to call us. It
didn't take long, and soon we were marching in single file
down the corridor of the clinic, and into the exam room.

The nurse followed us in with our files, and Sam put
his camera equipment on one of the chairs. Sam looked at
the nurse, and asked, "Would it be OK if the girls all got
ready, and you gave them all one shot and then the other
one, this time?" Both the nurse and my friends looked
askew at Sam, the nurse rolling her eyes, Linda and Kathy
shaking their heads in disbelief, and Julie just smiling. The
nurse looked at us, and we all shrugged. Putting the files
on the counter, the nurse said sourly, "I'm glad this is the
last time we'll have to do this."

As she stomped out of the room, Kathy – under her
breath – said, "I'm glad, too." Linda laughed.

We all turned to Sam, who explained what he wanted
us to do. "I'd like you guys to stand at the exam table, next
to each other, then first lower your pants to your knees,
then your underwear to mid thigh, and bend over the table.
I'm just going to take a few shots – I mean pictures –
before the nurse comes back in."

Again, we all shrugged, Julie finding it amusing, but Linda and Kathy less so. We lined up next to each other with the exam table in front of us, and lowered our pants. Sam was taking a video and, when our pants were down, he took a couple of snapshots with his camera, as we looked over our shoulders and smiled at him.

Then, we lowered our underwear, Sam again taking a video of the process, and a few more still pictures. Finally, we all bent over the table; Kathy, on the far left, would be the first to get a shot, next Linda, then Julie, and finally me.

As we waited for the nurse, Sam took a few more snapshots, and then came around the table and set up the tripod with the small camcorder, aiming it at us. "When the nurse comes in, I'd like you to smile at the camera, and then – when you feel the needle go in, give the camera a 'thumbs up' sign. When the needle comes out, you can put your hand back on the table. OK?"

Kathy grumbled, but we all nodded our assent. Sam started recording the video, and walked back around behind us. He said, "The video is just going to catch the table, your arms and hands, and your faces. I'm going to take a few close-ups of the needles going into your butt; so none of you will be identified in the pictures from behind."

That was my Sam; the perverted and anal man I loved. Once again, he was really asking a lot of my friends ... and once again, they were cooperating with him, if not enthusiastically, this time. The nurse came back into the room with two paper cups full of syringes. Sam reminded us, "Please smile at the camera, until everything is finished."

As the nurse got things ready, Linda commented, "It's too bad Sam isn't getting any shots, this time .. or he could be lined up with us." Kathy muttered, "Yeah. That would have only been fair."

I looked to my left, as Kathy looked into the camera and forced a smile, putting her thumb up, as she took her first shot. We heard the nurse step back, and get the next syringe and, a few seconds later, Linda put her thumb up. The nurse went down the line, each of us getting our injection no more than 15-20 seconds after the person on our left.

I felt the alcohol swab on my left hip, and put my thumb up as needle went in. The shot was over in a few seconds, and the nurse quickly pressed a bandaid onto me.

Then, the entire process was repeated, each of us taking the second shot on our right side. None of us made a sound, but we could hear the clicking of Sam's camera as he got *his* 'shots'. I had to admit, it was quite efficient, all of us being done less than three minutes after the nurse had come back into the room.

The nurse walked out, closing the door behind her. Sam snapped a few last shots, and asked us all to wave to the camcorder. As we pulled up our pants, Sam stopped the recording, put everything back into his camera bag, and grabbed the tripod. As she buckled her belt, Linda turned to me, and said, "He really *is* perverted, you know."

We all laughed. Before we left the exam room, I offered, "Well, I think Linda and Kathy are right: Why don't you all come over, and we'll make Sam take a couple of shots in the rear, as he smiles into the video camera?" We were roaring again, as we left the clinic. I had been serious, but my friends had to go in the opposite direction.

Linda said, "We'll take a rain check, Kelly." Then she turned to Sam, hugged him, and said, "And don't think we're going to forget!" Sam chuckled and nodded; now he was the amused one in the group.

I should have expected Kelly's friends to suggest something like that ... it was only fair. I knew they wouldn't forget, and knew that I wouldn't mind taking a couple of shots for them. But I had no idea when we would all be getting together again.

As I drove home, Kelly following me in her car, I thought about the four girls lined up, bent over the table, needles going into their butts. Kelly and I had discussed the possibility of giving her friends a submission experience – or 'training' – as she'd had the first time she came to my house.

But, with the birthday party, the ménage with Julie, and Linda's schoolgirl scene, I'd done a lot with them, already. I'd given Linda a birthday spanking; I'd spanked and paddled Julie; at Kelly's birthday party, I'd spanked them, done rectal insertions, and even stuck them with needles; then we'd had the ménage with Julie, and she'd taken enemas and a couple of shots; and, finally, I'd spanked, paddled, and tawsed Linda, and she'd gotten a shot during her schoolgirl scene.

It was amazing how far we'd gone with Kelly's friends, and they had all been cooperative – even enthusiastic – about playing with us. They had submitted to a wide range of experiences, and they didn't really need to be 'trained'. It didn't seem as if there were many more things we could do that would surprise or shock them.

But as I daydreamed, I came up with a few interesting ideas, more along the lines of a competition. In a way, that's what I'd intended the Spank Poker game to be ... but being strapped down on the turntable – the 'Lazy Sam' – hadn't been exciting to them. It would be even more exciting for me, if they would engage in a spanking competition voluntarily. And some videos I'd recently seen on the Internet gave me the idea for a few more possibilities ...

When we got home, Kelly went upstairs to take a bath, and I started preparing dinner. When I had everything in the oven, I poured some wine, and brought it up to Kelly, sitting on the side of the tub while she enjoyed the fragrant-smelling bubble bath.

"What's for dinner?" she asked. I smiled, thinking how our responsibilities were reversed from the 'normal' gender-based family roles.

"Prime rib and rice pilaf; and fresh asparagus – but I'm not making Hollandaise sauce, this time."

"Mmmm. Sounds great." Kelly sipped her wine and smiled at me. "Sam, you pushed my friends again, and I thought they were very cooperative, letting you line them up for their shots, and take pictures of them."

I sipped my own wine, and nodded, "I agree. Should I send them thank-you cards?" Kelly splashed soapy water at me, fortunately none of it falling into my wine. "And, I was thinking ...."

Kelly shook her head, and mumbled, "Oh, no." I cocked my head, and she explained, "Sam, when *I* think, I come up with new inventions; but when *you* think, you come up with submission challenges for my friends!" She knew me well, by now, and knew what was coming.

I nodded, "What we've done so-far hasn't been that 'challenging' for them. I think they've all enjoyed it." Kelly gave me a doubtful look, but I continued on, "Maybe we could do a combined training and competition for your friends? I have some ideas for some new things that might be interesting; and, yes, 'challenge' them again." Kelly sighed, shook her head, and took another sip of her wine.

Then, Kelly looked up at me, a smile growing on her face. "OK, let's think about that. But, your birthday is coming up in a little over a month, and you'll need to get your birthday spankings. I think there should be a party."

I chuckled, "I'll let your friends spank me, if they want to. But you don't have the time to organize a party ... and I've already had enough birthday parties to last me a lifetime."

Kelly picked up her wine, "No, I don't have the time ... but *you* do. It doesn't have to be a big production like the party you gave me." I was going to say how special her 'quarter century' age was, but decided better of it; I'd had my *half-century* birthday last year, but nobody to celebrate it with, having re-met Kelly just a couple of weeks later.

We had been together nearly a year! I would have to plan something special for the 1-year anniversary of our first lunch together.

Kelly persisted, "You can get the balloons and the cake, and I'll organize the activities." She sipped her wine, and smiled sweetly at me, but then she grinned devilishly, and added, "Oh boy! I can think of quite a few activities ... to 'challenge' *you*."

I shook my head, "Haven't I been challenged enough? I've had sex with your friends, they've stuck me with needles and spanked me; they've done to me just about everything I've done with them."

Kelly retorted, "Yes. But you still want to challenge them, more ... so why shouldn't they get their chance with you, first?" I really had no idea what *else* they could challenge me with.

Nodding, I stood, and said, "Take your time in the bath; dinner won't be ready for another couple of hours." I sighed, and stalked out of the room and down to the kitchen to make a salad.

I was laughing inside: It served Sam right for coming up with another challenge experience for my friends. Now, my mind whirled, as I thought of the possibilities. It was true – he *had* submitted to my friends: They had spanked him, inserted butt plugs, masturbated him, and gone down on him. And he'd had intercourse with two of them.

Sam had grown over the past ten months that I'd known him. But there was always more growing to do. I would have to ask my friends what they wanted to do; perhaps I should give Sam to each of them for an hour to be their slave?

I thought back to our domme experience in London, with Sam strapped to the table. Elena had put fear into him within minutes after we'd begun our session with her. I finished the glass of wine, and lay back in the tub. Yes, there were a *lot* of possibilities!

On Sunday, we went to my parents' house in the early afternoon. My father was in the family room, finishing a college basketball game, beer in hand. My mother greeted us, walked us into the kitchen, and offered us something to drink.

Sam had wanted to bring beers, but knew that my father wouldn't like the hoppy beer that we had in the house; so we had stopped at the market, and bought two six-packs – one that my father would drink, and one for Sam and I. Sam pulled them out of the paper bag, and placed them on the table. My mother handed Sam a bottle opener, and he opened beers for himself and me. My mother picked up her glass of vodka, and sat at the table with us.

I pushed the envelope toward her, and she looked at it warily. "You can open it, dear. I don't know exactly what's in it ... but if all the information is not there, then I would like to tell you a little more about what happened."

I still had no idea what she was talking about. My parents had been very good to me, and I loved both of them. But when they had left me in a car alone in a shopping center parking lot, someone had reported it to the police, and I'd been taken away from them. Then, the judge had decided that I would live with Darlene and Dave.

I tore off the end of the envelope, and slipped the official-looking documents out, placing them on the table in front of me. There was a lot of small print, but my eyes immediately gravitated to the names written in bold, at the top: Jake and Dorothy Flynn. I closed my eyes; something was very confusing. My middle name was Lynn; I was Kelly Lynn Walsh.

I tried to remember back to my first years in grammar school, but could only see a few images that had been burned into my memory. I perused the documents, and there was an address given, but it had obviously been from 17 years ago. I began to pull my iPhone out, but my mother put her hand on my arm. I could see tears in her eyes.

"Kelly, what do you remember from back then?" My mother was looking down at the documents, avoiding eye contact with me.

"I don't know. I can visualize a few scenes – sitting in the car coloring, the police coming, an old lady who took me away, the judge, and then living with you."

My mother nodded, "And, do you remember your name, before you came to live with us?"

I closed my eyes again. I had remembered being eight, but perhaps I'd only been seven years old when the traumatic event had occurred. "I thought it was Lynn ... my middle name."

My mother nodded again. "And, do you know my maiden name?"

This was surreal ... I don't remember my mother ever mentioning her maiden name. She was Darlene Walsh. I strained to remember. "I don't think so," I said tentatively. What was happening? It was like I was in a dream. Certainly, I should know my mother's maiden name.

"It was Lynn," she said. I was 'Darlene Lynn', before I married your dad." I nodded. That made sense: My middle name was my mother's maiden name. Perhaps I *had* known that? Suddenly, the earth was moving, and my entire frame of reference shifted.

My mother continued, her hand still on my arm, "Dear ... my name was Darlene Lynn." Her hand pressed down harder, willing me to be calm, stay still. "And, my sister ... your mother ... was Dot. That's what we called her. Dorothy Lynn." I wasn't exactly sure what I was hearing. My adoptive mother was my birth mother's *sister*? My mother was nodding, slowly. I glanced at Sam, who was sitting as still as a statue, his mouth having fallen open.

My mother continued, "I am one year older than your mother. We were very close." A tear dropped from her eye, and splashed on the kitchen table, seemingly in slow motion. "Your birth mother met a scoundrel named Jake. She was enthralled with him ... but on their second or third date, he raped her. Dot and Jake got married, and had a baby girl ... Kelly Flynn."

My mother looked up at me with teary eyes. "That's you." I couldn't believe what I was hearing. How could I not have known? How could she have kept this a secret, all these years? And, why? I didn't want to believe it.

"My sister had gone into a store, and Jake was supposed to be watching you. But he decided to go into a bar for a drink; we don't really know the whole story ... but he locked you in the car. When somebody reported a small girl sitting alone in a car, the police were called. When your mother returned, your father wasn't there, and he didn't come back for more than an hour.

"The police took you from the car, and your parents were arrested. There were several judges, a lot of hearings. I had stayed away after my sister married Jake; we were all afraid of him.

"But when a preliminary hearing concluded that you should be sent to a foster home, we approached the court, and offered to care for you. You're a blood relative, Kelly. Your mother readily agreed, happy that her daughter would be loved and taken care of."

I still couldn't understand this; it didn't make sense. My father had loved me; he was a good man. And my mother certainly loved me; I could picture her kind face, and I remembered touching the smooth skin of her cheek.

Now, Darlene was sobbing, and Sam put his arm around me. I felt cold; lost. My mother continued, "Jake was a violent person, a bad person." I felt myself shaking my head in disbelief; this didn't match my memories.

My mother said, "He abused your mother ... and less than two years after we adopted you, she committed suicide. At least that was what the official report said." My mother looked at me, tears now flowing down her cheeks.

"My little sister. Dead. We never believed that it was suicide; we all thought that Jake had killed her. But there was never any evidence. She died of an overdose of drugs and alcohol, and nobody could prove that Jake had done it. It was a sad time for the family.

"My parents – your mother's parents – died in an auto accident, and Dot was the only real family I had ... except for the family I made with Dave. I had married Dave more than a decade before all this happened, and we already had two sons; a happy family. Then, we adopted you, and shortly thereafter my sister was murdered. There was nothing we could do. I went into a long period of depression, but still tried my best to be the mother of my sons ... and your mother."

I was in shock. This could explain a lot of things, but I wasn't thinking straight, and couldn't put everything together.

"Jake disappeared for a long time, but we always worried that he would try to return and take you away from us. Dave became your protector; we couldn't imagine what would happen, if Jake took you. It was seven or eight years ago, after we had mostly recovered – you were in high school – that we found out that Jake had been arrested for armed robbery, and sentenced to ten years in prison. The last time we checked, he was still there.

"We moved shortly after we adopted you, and – as far as we know – Jake doesn't know where we live. But I've always been afraid that he would find out, and come after you ... or us. We testified against him in court; we knew how rotten he was. And we've lived in fear ever since."

My mother looked at me, and then Sam, "Excuse me." She pushed her chair back, and got up, unsteadily from the table, making her way into the back bathroom.

Sam held me tight. I still couldn't believe this incredible story. "But my father was a nice man, he loved me." I still saw an image of my parents, looking at me lovingly. Now, I was in tears. Sam pulled me to him, as the dam broke, and a flood of tears poured down my cheeks. This couldn't be happening; it had to be wrong. My whole world had turned upside-down.

What we had just heard from Darlene was incredible; I couldn't imagine what Kelly was going through, right now. All I could do was hold her, console her. After a few minutes, Kelly looked up and said, "Sorry, Sam. I have to lie down for a while." I escorted her to her parents' room, where she flopped onto her stomach on the bed, weeping, the lights off, and the room darkening as the sun set. I closed the door and returned to the kitchen.

Darlene had come out of the bathroom, and was now cooking, making a racket, as she stirred the meat and vegetables in the large Dutch oven on the stove.

I opened another beer, and sat at the kitchen table, staring into space, deep in thought. How could this have been hidden from Kelly all these years? How could Dave and Darlene have lived with this, not sharing these incredible events with their friends? Why hadn't Darlene enlisted the help of a psychologist to break the news to Kelly? And, why had they waited so long?

While Kelly was now attached to her adoptive parents, she had always told me that her birth parents had loved her, had been good to her. I was confused, and not even sure that it had been the best strategy to inform Kelly of her past, now, although if Jake was really dangerous, she should know about him.

Dave walked into the kitchen, and threw his beer bottle in the trash, then took another from the fridge. I walked with him back to the family room, where he sat on a recliner, taking large swigs of beer, and shaking his head.

Finally, he said, "It's been difficult, Sam. We've tried to take care of Kelly, we've loved her, and made her part of the family; but her situation put the family at risk, and there was no way that we could explain things to Kelly when she was younger."

He took another gulp of beer, and continued, "Darlene had hoped we – and Kelly – would never have to face this; but it would also be unfair to Kelly for her not to know. Darlene has been terribly disturbed by everything, from the rape of her sister, to taking on the responsibility for Kelly, to her sister's death.

"I thought she was adapting, and moving beyond it all, until we saw the news about Jake, and that opened up the past again. That's when she started drinking, and Kelly became too wild for her – us – to handle. It's really been a tough situation for all of us."

Now, I understood much better, with more perspective, Kelly's background. I could understand – at least partially – Dave and Darlene's dilemma, and why Kelly had reacted the way she had. The strength of Kelly's character had allowed her to overcome the tribulations of her upbringing, and she had become a self-confident, independent woman.

It still wasn't clear whether Kelly had a lack of trust of men, based on those in her life who had let her down or, perhaps, an insecurity stemming originally from the adoption, and later based on her perception that her adoptive parents hadn't cared about her. This was psychology far above my ability to comprehend.

Fortunately, Kelly seemed to have developed her own self-confidence, and she'd shown great trust in me, since our first experience ten months ago.

I didn't know whether to leave Kelly alone or show her some compassion, but finally decided to see how she was doing. I went into the bedroom, closing the door behind me, and lay on the bed next to Kelly. Putting my arm around her waist, I whispered, "How are you doing, Kelly?"

Kelly turned her head to me, her eyes wet and swollen. "I'm upset, and confused."

"You can't take responsibility for the actions of your birth parents. And the situation provides some insight into how your adoptive parents have loved you, but also had deep concerns about your safety, and your future. Darlene lost her sister, and felt threatened by Jake. It was a tough situation for everyone, Kelly ... and you not only survived, but came out strong and self-confident, earning an advanced degree, and now developing technology that could benefit mankind.

"I'm sure it hasn't been an easy journey – for you, *or* your parents. But I'm incredibly proud of you, and I know your parents are, too."

"Thank you, Sam. It's just going to take me a while to get my head around all this. Go visit with my parents, and I'll wash my face, and come out shortly." I kissed her on the cheek, and left her in the room.

I helped Darlene set the kitchen table, and opened another beer for myself. When Kelly came into the kitchen, her mother hugged her, and stroked her hair. "I love you, Kelly. All your dad and I want is the best for you."

"I know that, mom. I'll be OK." Kelly sat next to me, and Darlene served the salads – which were pineapple rings from the can, on a bed of lettuce, with grated American cheese on top, and a dollop of mayonnaise. Dave sat down with us, and we ate in silence.

Darlene served the main course, which was a hearty American stew, served over wide egg noodles. It was actually quite good. I couldn't help but visualize chicken instead of beef, some bacon, and a little red wine, which would have turned the dish into a nice *coq au vin*.

We all drank beer, and were stuffed by the time we had finished the main course. Darlene had baked chocolate chip cookies, which she served with vanilla ice cream. Kelly and I had done well with our diets, weighing a bit less now than when we had departed for Europe. We were doing fine with our diet, but needed more exercise.

Kelly updated her parents on her research, and said she expected to graduate by a year from June. That might have been optimistic, but it seemed Kelly's lab experiments had been running without too many problems, so far.

Dave updated us on his man cave project, offering to walk us down to the garage, but we took a rain check, opting to come back in a couple of months when it was due to be completed.

Kelly helped her mother rinse the dishes and wash the pots, and I did the drying. Then, we said our goodbyes, and I drove us home.

We climbed into bed, and I held Kelly for a long time. She sniffled, and wept for a few minutes, but finally drifted off to sleep. It would take some time for Kelly to grasp her new history, but I was confident that she would come through it fine.

CHAPTER 7: FIONA VISITS

The weekend after we had visited my parents, I got a call from Fiona. She informed me that her boyfriend had proposed to her, and that the wedding would be in late June. Sam and I were invited, and the timing seemed good, as my symposia would be done, and I could take a break – although I planned to work through most of the summer in the lab.

As she and her fiancé, Justin, lived in Toronto, I considered the possibility of leaving from there for London, and taking the domme training from Elena. But I hadn't mentioned this to Sam, yet, and was nervous about doing so. Sam had been upset on the plane back from Europe, and during our Europe show for my friends, because I had been selected for the training ... and, because it would be sponsored by a wealthy benefactor in London.

Fiona also told me that she would be bringing Justin to visit Alex, Sam's neighbor in a couple of weeks, and hoped that we could attend the engagement party, and perhaps spend some time together here at the house.

She had laughed, and said that she was amazed that Alex had let Sam massage her, and that she had gone in the sauna and jacuzzi with us ... nude. I told her that Alex had been very open with us, and that Sam had been very proud of her willingness to relax and enjoy her Labor Day experience.

We put the engagement party on our calendar for a week from Friday, and I invited Fiona and Justin to spend Saturday with us, if they were available.

We'd had stormy weather over the past few weeks, and the rains continued on and off for another week; then, the temperature soared, and it felt like summer had arrived. There were still huge cumulus clouds breaking up the deep blue sky, and Sam spent time in the backyard, planting the flower beds, despite having a gardener that came weekly.

The lawn was bright green, and all the trees were full of leaves. The grounds looked better than I'd ever seen them. We got into a habit of using the jacuzzi every evening, either just after I came home from school, or just before bed – with the lights off and stars blazing between dark islands of clouds.

We sometimes played a game as we sat in the still water of the spa, each of us trying to see satellites passing overhead, looking like a quick-moving star; whoever found the most would take the dominant role for the rest of the evening. That sometimes meant the loser submitting to a spanking, but most often gave the winner the choice of how we would make love – the position, whether vaginal, oral or anal, or using certain 'toys'.

We enjoyed sex almost every day – sometimes both in the morning and at night. During my periods I usually treated Sam to oral sex, sometimes getting him ready with my hands ... or feet. Or, he would 'make love *on* me', as he had described on the first night we slept together – rubbing himself against my 'landing strip' of pubic hair.

Early in the new year, I had let Sam give me a 'touch up' waxing, and he did pretty well. I considered just shaving myself, but finally made an appointment with Barbara, the esthetician, who did a professional job, as expected, leaving a long, thin rectangular landing strip about the length and width of my pointer finger. Barbara convinced me to get waxed at least every three months, and I saw her at the beginning of the week that Fiona was to arrive. Fortunately, the redness had disappeared by the end of the week.

Fiona and Justin flew in late Thursday, and stayed with Fiona's aunt, Alex, who lived only a few blocks from Sam's house. Their engagement party was scheduled for Friday. They would be spending the afternoon and evening with us on Saturday, then visit with Alex on Sunday, before their red-eye flight back to Toronto on Sunday evening.

Although an engagement gift was probably not required, Sam had bought a Perrier-Jouet gift set that included a full bottle of bubbly decorated with the winery's flower pattern, and two fluted glasses, with a matching flower pattern, all in a fitted box. There was a satin ribbon tying the box, with "Happy Engagement – Fiona and Justin" engraved in gold.

We just hoped that they could fit it in their luggage for the return trip to Toronto. In the worst case, we would carry it to them when we went to their wedding in June; their wedding present would probably be something selected from things they had put on the registry of a department store near them.

On Friday, I came home from school in the early afternoon. Sam and I used the sauna and took a shower together, and then I soaked in the tub with bubble bath. I decided to wear the black dress that I'd worn in Europe, with a pair of ultra-sheer pantyhose and no underwear underneath. I also wore the pearl necklace that Sam had given me for my birthday along with the trip to Europe. I chuckled, thinking of the slave collar he had also given me, which was still in a drawer, not yet worn.

Sam looked very elegant in a dark navy camelhair blazer over grey slacks, a shirt with a tiny checkerboard blue and white pattern, and a navy tie with tiny silver squares. He wore a thin gold watch, with a brown leather band.

We drove the few blocks, arriving just after 7PM. Alex greeted us warmly, hugging both of us, and kissing us alternately on the cheeks, in the European style. We hadn't dressed too formally: Alex wore a stunning gold metallic lace sheath dress, with a scalloped 'V' top in front and back, and four solid bands crisscrossing her waist. There was a nude-color liner underneath, and hundreds of sequins making up a flower pattern on the sheath.

She wore a thin chain necklace with a gold nugget pendant, and an elegant gold bracelet with a tiny watch face built into it. Overall, the effect was striking. We knew that Alex was a classy woman, but we had never seen her dressed for a party, like this.

We walked into Alex's family room, and Fiona smiled and walked up to us, Justin in tow. Fiona wore a pleated, turquoise halter-top dress, her shoulders bare. The hem was much shorter than mine, and she sported double, thin black belts. Fiona's ginger-colored hair was short, and her eyes sparkled. Sam congratulated the couple.

Fiona hugged him warmly, then she took my head in her hands, and gave me a full-on kiss, her tongue exploring my mouth; I wondered whether both of us would have to re-apply our lip gloss.

Then, Fiona stepped back and introduced Justin. Sam shook his hand, and I hugged him. He was also dressed quite casually, with a light, long-sleeve turtle neck sweater in black, over dark blue/purple woven pants.

Justin was not what I had expected; somehow, given Fiona's description of his body jewelry, I'd half expected to see a Mohawk, or some other wild hairstyle. Instead, he had long reddish-brown hair, combed straight, along with a thin short-trimmed reddish-brown beard and narrow mustache. His face was oval, with a pointed chin, and he had piercing brown eyes. He was quite handsome. Now, Sam seemed older, by comparison, and over-dressed for the occasion.

We handed Justin the wrapped gift, which he put on a card table in the corner. A bar ran nearly across the width of the room, and appeared to be staffed by a bartender. There were hors d'oeuvres already on the bar top, and Sam munched on a couple of canapés, as he procured glasses of wine for us.

Alex brought two more couples into the room, and introduced everyone. She leaned over to Sam, and said, "I use Bill and Martha, a husband-wife team who cater small parties. They do a great job – perhaps you might want to use them sometime." Sam had done all the work for our get-togethers, but we'd never had a formal party, other than the Christmas dinner, and that had only been for ten people.

Alex's backyard was lit with colored lights, and we went out on the patio to survey the property; it was cool, and stars filled the sky. Sam kissed me lightly on the lips, and smiled at me. "You're beautiful tonight," he said. Then, he shook his head, and said, "You're *always* beautiful, Kelly ... but you look especially gorgeous tonight."

I knew that wedding parties often softened-up single men to the concept of marriage, and wondered whether engagement parties had a similar effect. But I didn't think Sam was thinking about a long-term commitment, and I was in no rush; we were enjoying the relationship we had at the moment.

We went back inside, soft jazz playing in the background, and at least two dozen people now filling the family room, kitchen, and living room. It was a nice group of people, all of them apparently between Fiona's age and Sam's age; most of them Alex's friends from the art world, and a few neighbors. We wouldn't meet Fiona's friends, until we visited Toronto.

Martha, the caterer, circled the rooms with one platter of appetizers after another. Around 8:30PM, the dining room was opened, the table filled with food; the chairs had been taken away, the buffet being approachable all around. By 10PM, the guests were starting to leave.

We hung around for a while longer, and Alex approached us, "I hope you enjoyed our little party. Fiona is my only niece. My sister and her husband died a few years ago, when the small plane he was piloting crashed. It was determined to be pilot error – he flew into a storm that hadn't been predicted, and didn't have an instrument rating. Fiona was already out of high school, but I've been her 'surrogate' mother, since then."

A tear came unbidden to my eye, thinking about my own birth mother and Darlene.

Sam hugged Alex, "The party was great, Alex. Congratulations." Then, Sam glanced at me, and turned back to Alex, "Can you come over for a while with Fiona and Justin, tomorrow? We'd love to have you." I nodded. We had no specific plans for the day, just visiting, and Alex would certainly be welcome.

She smiled, "I'll ask Fiona if it's OK with her, but I'd love to. I do have a dinner commitment, but maybe I could spend a couple of hours with you guys."

Sam said, "That would be great, Alex. We look forward to seeing you tomorrow. Thanks again for inviting us to the party." He kissed Alex on the cheek, and I hugged her. We told Fiona and Justin goodbye, and suggested they come over around 2PM. Sam suggested, "Why don't you have Alex bring you, and then we can drive you back after dinner?" The plan was set, and we drove the short distance back to Sam's house.

As we entered the master bedroom, Sam's hand slipped under my dress, softly running from my thighs to my hips, and he held my bottom. I smiled, pulling away from him, and he seemed disappointed; but he wouldn't be for long. I walked to the foot of the bed, and took the standing position. "I think I could use a little 'warming up', Sir." I smiled sweetly at him, "If you don't mind ..."

Sam grinned broadly, and walked over, putting his hand down the front of his pants and adjusting himself before sitting on the end of the bed. There were no more words spoken.

I walked around to his right side, and put myself across his lap, diagonally, with my head on the bed. Sam stroked me, the feeling electric through my pantyhose, as his hand ran up and down my legs, traveling higher and higher, under my dress. He flipped the dress onto my back, and lightly circled my bum, gently squeezing each of my buttocks, then massaging them.

I felt his hand leave me, and knew what to expect. It came down hard, on one side, then the other, spanking me first slowly and softly, and then more and more rapidly, harder and harder, until I was bouncing on his lap.

Although I enjoyed taking the dominant role, I could easily get excited by realizing how much Sam was getting turned on. He continued to spank me, and I closed my eyes, feeling the warmth, the closeness, my bottom stinging; but it was a good kind of pain. Sam reached across to my outside hip, and pulled me to him, and I felt his hardness against me. As I bounced with each stroke, I knew that I was getting him off.

I didn't count the spanks, but Sam continued until he knew that we were both ready. I got off Sam's lap, and lay back on the bed, my feet up, as Sam removed my pantyhose; I hoped that he wouldn't run them, but it didn't matter. He only lowered them (or raised them?) to my knees, then quickly removed his own clothes and stood at the edge of the bed, pulling me to him.

He entered me roughly, and pounded into me, his hands grasping my hips and pulling me to him on each thrust. I let my hands wander down, fingering my clit as Sam continued to plunge into my depths with raw energy.

We both came suddenly, and simultaneously, an eruption of hot lava filling me, our breathing heavy, panting in synchrony. Sam continued to pump, savagely, until we both began to calm.

As he came out of me, he smiled, then continued removing my pantyhose. He took my hands, and pulled me up, took the hem of my dress, and pulled it over my head, then reached around my back and unclipped my bra. We stood, pressing against each other, and he kissed me desperately, our bodies melting into one.

When we got into bed, Sam smiled at me. "Are you thinking what I'm thinking ... about tomorrow?"

I shook my head, "Sam, don't push. Let's see how things go." Then I laughed, "But it *would* be fun to see if Alex will relax with her future nephew-in-law ... and Fiona's reaction, when she sees how open her aunt can be." We were both excited about the possibilities. I reached down and curled my fingers around Sam's re-hardening shaft; *he* was certainly excited.

I looked at him questioningly, and he smiled and shrugged. It didn't take long before he was ready again, and I climbed on top of him, putting him into me, and taking long, leisurely strokes as we made love a second time. Our lovemaking seemed to have an additional spark tonight, both of us having enjoyed the party, and looking forward to tomorrow. I glanced at the clock, and realized that it was *already* tomorrow.

When Sam came, I lowered myself onto him, pulling the covers over us, and we fell asleep joined together. I hoped that we would always be joined together; I loved this man.

Fiona, Justin and Alex came over in the early afternoon. I had heated the pool and the sauna, and Kelly had cleaned up the KS Biotech office (AKA the pool room), but we had no idea what we would actually be doing with our guests, today. The weather was beautiful, puffy clouds dotting a deep blue sky, and the temperature was in the upper 70s; not quite summer, but very nice considering the cold, wet weather we'd had for the past few months.

Everyone was dressed casually, although 'casual' for Alex still seemed dressier and more elegant than was necessary for an afternoon get-together.

Kelly and I greeted our guests at the front door, and ushered them into the house. I hugged Alex, "That was a nice party last night – we really enjoyed it."

I pointed to the backyard, and then to the stairs down to the playroom and shrugged; Kelly pointed to the backyard, and I led everyone out to the patio table. I had set-up an umbrella over the table, and brought an extra chair from the garage for seating the five of us.

Justin surveyed the backyard – the black-bottom pool lined with huge boulders, the jacuzzi running, spilling water over a rock waterfall to the pool, the huge trees, now full of leaves, the bright green lawn, and the flower beds. It was now in the best shape it had been in a long time. "Sweet! Nice yard! Fiona had told me you had a pool, but this is incredible."

We all sat down, and Fiona turned to me, "Thank you, Sam ... and Kelly, for the nice gift. That was very thoughtful of you, and not really necessary; but we appreciate it."

I smiled and nodded, "Well, it isn't often that we have friends getting engaged. And, thank *you* for inviting us to the wedding. We'll have to confirm our plans, but we hope we can attend."

Kelly looked at me a bit strangely; we hadn't really discussed the trip to Toronto, yet, but I knew that she would want to go, assuming she could take a break from her research. The end-of-June timing was good.

I thought about the possibility of a driving trip: Perhaps we could fly into Rochester, New York and make the short drive to Niagra Falls, stay the night, and drive to Toronto for the wedding; then, we could drive up to Montreal and on to Quebec; and, finally, drive down through the White Mountains of New Hampshire to Boston, and fly home from there. It would make a great week-long trip.

Justin wore tan cargo shorts, a lightweight, pale blue, checkered dress shirt, and sandals. "What do you do, in Toronto?," I asked, genially.

"For work? I manage a night club in a suburb south of Toronto." He glanced at Fiona, and she stared at Alex, who obviously knew this, already.

Then, Fiona said, "But it's not your 'usual' nightclub." Alex cocked her head. Fiona laughed, "Alex, if you're as open as Sam and Kelly say you are, perhaps Justin can give you more details. It's a pretty interesting place."

Alex looked perturbed, "You've been hiding what Justin does for a living? I thought you were open with me; I shouldn't have to prove anything to you in order to hear the details about your fiancé." Alex looked down, visibly shaken, and then looked into Fiona's eyes. "And you don't believe what Sam and Kelly told you?" She shook her head, and reminded Fiona, "I went in the pond nude when you and I first met Sam and Kelly."

Fiona rose and stepped over to her aunt, bending down and hugging her. "Alex, I'm sorry; I was just teasing you. You were very open with us at the pond, and of course I believe Sam and Kelly. You don't have to prove anything." Fiona kissed Alex on the cheek, and added, "I love you, Alex. You've been great to me, and to Justin." Fiona shook her head, and sat down again, giving a prompting look to Justin.

Justin shrugged, and said, "I'm one of the managers of a membership-only sex club. Actually, most of our members are couples – whether married or not – and are only looking for some excitement, to meet new people, and to have a great time in an open environment."

Justin explained, "There's no pressure for anyone to have sex, but our members are very open-minded. Sometimes they just want to have a good time together; sometimes, the woman wants to hook-up with another female; and sometimes, there's a full-on orgy going on."

He continued, "We have great music by some of the best DJs, great drinks, and a sexy atmosphere. There's really nothing to tell; there are many clubs like that in most big cities. But ours strives to set the standard for high-class entertainment."

Kelly asked, "Is everyone there a 'couple'?"

Justin shook his head, "No. Most are, but single females are also allowed to participate, and a very small number of pre-screened single males may also come, on certain nights. In addition to the normal weekend nights, we have special themed events – such as lingerie nights, fetish nights, body painting nights and, of course, special occasions like Halloween, Valentine's Day, and New Year's Eve."

He continued, "On some nights, couples may ask permission to bring a single guy or girl. The most important thing – and the one 'absolute' rule of the club – is that the members respect each other. Our members trust that they will not be harassed, or hit-on by another member."

Alex asked, "What does your job as a manager entail?"

Justin replied, "Mainly organizing the events, booking the entertainment, making sure that all our employees have the things they need to do their job, and scheduling the employees. There are two other managers, so I'm not at all the events, but it's a pretty big production to get the club ready for a party."

Kelly followed-up, "And what is the age of most of your members?"

Justin laughed, "Well, probably between about your age and about Sam's age. But attitude is much more important than age; our members are very 'young at heart', regardless of their age ... and they are very open to new ideas and experiences."

Kelly looked at me, and smiled. It sounded like the things I stressed, and I knew that she would want to visit the club when we were in Toronto.

Alex stood, and said, "Thank you, Justin, for sharing the details of your job. I don't see how managing a sex club is any different than working at a regular nightclub. I'm really not as uptight as Fiona may have told you." Then, she turned to me, and asked, "Sam, is it OK if I go in the pool for a while?"

I nodded, but Alex had already started unbuttoning her blouse. In a few moments, she was standing in a white thong, and lace bra, and in another moment, she had divested herself of those, and walked casually to the ladder at the deep end of the pool. Lowering herself into the cool water, she pushed off, and floated on her back, looking up at the sky.

I turned to Fiona, "That wasn't very fair to Alex; she's taken herself out of her comfort zone to be open with us. And she has found that she enjoys it. I don't think Alex has had much opportunity to relax outside of her professional life ... or to have close relationships, since her divorce. We're trying to provide a safe and encouraging environment for her to explore some new things, without pressure or judgment."

Fiona nodded, "I know, Sam. I'll go talk to her, and make sure she understands how proud I am of her. She may have always been a sensual woman, but I never saw it." Fiona smiled at Justin, "Maybe she really is much 'younger at heart' than I ever knew?" Fiona undressed, putting her clothes on her chair, and slipped into the pool.

I stood, and announced, "I guess I'm ready for the jacuzzi." With that, I took off my Hawaiian shirt, pushed down my shorts and underwear, and headed for the spa.

Justin turned to me, and chuckled, "Sam is an interesting man." Well, that was an understatement.

I nodded, "Sam and his wife were always open, but after Sarah died, he's had a focus on hedonistic pleasures, including developing fetish interests based on fantasies stemming from his childhood experiences. He likes to challenge people with openness, and is turned on by submission, but he's not a sadist."

Now, I was the one to chuckle, "He's really not strong enough to be an effective Dom, and I've found that he has his own hang-ups. I've been asking *him* to submit to some experiences that he's always been uncomfortable with. One of his sons is gay, and brought his partner to visit over the holidays; Sam was uncomfortable being with them in the sauna. Sam and I are always challenging each other, and we're both becoming more open in the process."

Justin was listening intently. "I've seen a lot of people – and couples – blossom, in terms of new sensual and sexual experiences, when they're given the chance. That's one of the useful functions of our club: It gives people the opportunity to try new things, in an environment where they won't be judged – and where they can see that others are also trying new things."

"We'd like to visit the club, if there's time, when we come to Toronto for your wedding." Justin smiled. I pointed to the pool, "Shall we join them?" Justin nodded, and we undressed in silence. Justin had a gold bar through each of his nipples, and several small tattoos – on his biceps, and upper chest. They seemed to be abstract, but I could see lightning bolts, and a yin-yang symbol.

He removed his shorts and boxers, and I glanced down at him, but could not see the frenum rings that Fiona had said were on the underside of his penis.

Justin headed for the pool, and I joined Sam in the jacuzzi. We watched, as Fiona and Justin spoke with Alex in the deep end of the pool. After several minutes, Alex climbed the steps, Fiona and Justin following, and they all joined us in the jacuzzi.

Sam cocked his head, and Alex shrugged, "I'm OK, Sam. Fiona just pushes too hard, sometimes." Sam waded over to Alex, and hugged her; despite their nakedness, Alex hugged him back. Then, Sam sat next to me, and shook his head.

Fiona was flustered, "I'm sorry everyone. I didn't mean to make Alex upset. And I know it wasn't right to link information about Justin to Alex's openness. I know that she's been very open ... with all of us."

Alex stood, her back to the wall of the jacuzzi that separated it from the pool, the water just below her C-cup breasts that still looked beautiful, despite her age.

Fiona continued, "We don't keep anything secret from you, Alex. I'm sorry we hadn't given you more details about Justin's job. But, as you said yourself, it really isn't any different from managing any other nightclub."

Alex closed her eyes and nodded. "And I'm sorry for getting upset with you, Fiona. I've been under pressure, lately. One of our benefactors pulled out, and I've been scrambling to find funds to replace his contributions."

Alex looked at Sam and I, "That's why I can only stay a while ... I'm having dinner with an HNWI in the region – a 'high net-worth individual', who I'm hoping will help us out. We may have to considerably scale back our activities, something we never anticipated. Most of our funds are in long-term investments, but some of our commitments depend on ongoing funding. Our accountants are working overtime to understand how this could have happened."

We could tell that Alex was shaken.

We got out of the hot tub, and Sam ran downstairs and brought up towels and robes for all of us. Alex dried off and got dressed. As she buttoned her blouse, and picked up her slacks, she apologized, "I'm sorry, but I need to get home and prepare for my meeting tonight. I probably shouldn't have come over at all, but I wanted to be with you guys for a while." She pulled up her pants, and buckled her belt, as the rest of us donned the robes.

Sam said, "We understand, Alex. I'll walk you to the door." We all said our goodbyes, and Fiona told Alex that they would have time to talk tomorrow, before they had to catch their late-evening flight to Toronto.

After Sam and Alex went into the house, Fiona explained, "Alex hid her stress well. It seemed like all her efforts were focused on preparing for our engagement party." She shook her head, and I hugged Fiona; then, Justin hugged her.

Sam came back out to the backyard, and said, "She'll be OK. She's a very strong woman. The foundation will be fine, but it may be embarrassing for them, if they have to reduce their support for some of the programs they're funding."

Fiona looked at Justin, "I guess we didn't know much about Alex's work, either."

We gathered our clothes, and followed Sam downstairs to the playroom. "Shall we show Justin the sauna?" Sam asked. We nodded, and followed him into the downstairs bathroom. Hanging our robes, we went directly into the sauna. We all sat on the top bench, letting our towels hang down onto the lower bench, so that we could put our feet on them.

It was again interesting how small Sam's sauna felt, with four people inside, compared to the huge saunas we had visited in Europe. Fiona and I sat in the middle, with Sam and Justin near the corners.

We warmed quickly, dots of sweat already breaking out on our bodies. I glanced at Fiona's face, and smiled, remembering how her freckles and droplets of sweat had covered her face the last time she'd been here. Then, I thought about the sensual – and sexual – experience we'd had afterward.

Fiona smiled back, and put her hands on my thigh. We turned toward each other, and she leaned forward, giving me a soft kiss on the lips. "I told Justin about our fun experience, last time I was here."

I wasn't sure exactly *which* 'fun experience' she was referring to, as we had taken a shower together during which she'd gone down on me. And, Sam and I had given her a needle experience, after she'd shown us her nipple and vertical clit hood piercings.

And then, we'd had an incredibly sensuous experience in the playroom, with me going over her lap for a spanking, then undressing each other, and finally sexually satisfying each other – my first girl-on-girl experience.

Fiona added, "You know, Justin's bi, also." I didn't know; Sam adjusted his position, and I knew that the idea of Justin being bisexual made him uncomfortable.

Justin reached around Fiona, holding her small breasts in his hands. A moment later, Sam followed suit (birthday suit?), and put his arms around me, holding my much-larger mammary assets. Fiona and I kissed each other again.

The sweat was streaming down our bodies, now. All I could think about was holding each other and moving our bodies against each other, letting the sweat lubricate our motions. But we were all getting hot.

Finally, Sam tapped my shoulder, my fantasy disappearing as quickly as it had formed. "Shall we take a shower together?"

Fiona smiled, and removed Justin's hands from her breasts. Then, we all stood, and shuffled out of the sauna. Sam and I got the shower going, water shooting from all the heads, as we huddled together under the warm rain shower, and feeling the cool spray from the leg jets.

We all squeezed soap into our palms, and began bathing each other. As Sam concentrated on Fiona, I washed his back, and then Justin took over the task. Then, I washed Justin's back, and ran my hands around to his front, and turned him around. Fiona turned Sam around, and soaped his front, as I did the same with Justin, working my way down his fit body.

My fingers glided through his pubic hair, and lightly circled around his cock. I felt the frenum rings, and lifted him to examine them; Fiona had exaggerated slightly, as he had 'only' seven rings, not the 'eight or ten' that Fiona had told us. Still, they were impressive, spanning the length of his dick, and spaced just enough for me to grip him, with his rings between each of my fingers.

I washed his genital area, and then Fiona tapped my shoulder, and we switched positions again. Looking into Justin's eyes, I pointed to Sam; I hoped that Sam would not back away from this experience. Fiona washed Sam's back – although it had been washed at least twice in the past few minutes.

Justin moved around to Sam's front, and soaped his chest, while I stood behind Justin, and soaped his butt, slipping my fingers down between his buttocks, and over his anus. I continued on, moving my hand under him, and feeling the bar of his guiche piercing. I pressed it, giving him some prostatic pleasure, before moving back to his anus, soaping him again, and inserting my finger deeply, pressing against his prostate.

At the same time, Justin was bathing Sam's front, moving downward, and bending, allowing him to reach Sam's privates, and also allowing me to press even harder against Justin's prostate. I looked at Sam, and his face showed discomfort, but I gave him a 'look', and he nodded slightly, and closed his eyes.

Although Sam had no soap in his hands, he reached out, and ran his hands over Justin's chest. With my free hand, I squeezed some soap down Justin's chest, Sam finding it, and lathering it with both hands, his eyes still closed tightly.

I looked behind Sam, and realized that Fiona had her finger inside Sam; both men were now getting a prostatic massage while they bathed each other. As Sam concentrated on Justin's shoulders and chest, Justin put his hand under Sam, pressing on his perineum.

Even without a guiche bar, I had no doubt that the combined efforts of Justin from the outside, and Fiona from the inside, was working, as Sam was now smiling, and breathing more heavily.

I held my breath, as Justin's hands now held Sam's cock, circling it, stroking, and eventually seeing the result of his efforts, as Sam grew in length, and in breadth.

Sam did not return the favor, but I realized that he was already being pushed to his limits, and beyond. I put my hand around Justin, and began stroking him. Fiona took her finger out of Sam, and I took mine out of Justin, as we switched places. Justin stepped aside, as Fiona kneeled on the hard tile floor of the shower, and took Sam in her mouth.

Sam's eyes suddenly opened, and he looked down, relieved to see that it was Fiona fellating him. I moved behind Sam, and put my hands over his eyes. At the same time, Justin kneeled down, and took Sam in his mouth. I heard Sam moan, but I wasn't sure whether it was from his happiness due to what he was feeling, or from being disturbed, if he realized that it was Justin's mouth that was now doing the stimulating.

Fiona tapped the insides of Sam's legs, and he spread them widely. Then, she put her hands over Sam's eyes, allowing me to bring my hands down Sam's back, and over his bum. I knelt, and put my head between Sam's legs, taking Justin's growing length into my mouth – rings, and all. It was another surreal experience.

The position was uncomfortable for me, my head nearly on the ground, but it was an amazing experience, knowing that Sam was receiving oral sex from Justin, as Justin was being satisfied by me. I realized that I could reach up with my left hand, and insert it into Sam's butt; able reach his prostate, as my fingers were curling downward. I opened my eyes, Justin's middle in front of me, then guided my right hand under him, inserting my middle finger into *his* bum, and curling it back toward me, definitely pressing against *his* prostate.

Only Fiona was being somewhat left out, having one hand over Sam's eyes, and the other over Justin's eyes, as she pressed her front against Justin's back.

I closed my eyes, and saw the scene we were making: Sam standing, his legs apart; Justin kneeling, his mouth taking Sam's length in, and his hands now holding Sam's butt, and pulling Sam to him; And me, taking Justin's jewelry-laden cock in my mouth, one finger in Sam's rear, and another in Justin's rear.

I didn't know how far we would go, but nobody was complaining, so we continued, Justin coming first, and then – amazingly – Sam achieving his orgasm by Justin's mouth. I was sure that Sam must realize that he was engaging in homosexual activity, and I really had to give him credit for the growth – or at least, acceptance – that had occurred, since his sauna experience with Mark and Greg just four months ago.

Justin and I stood, and we did one last wash. We were all laughing, as Fiona took her hands from over Sam's eyes, and he looked around, seemingly bewildered. But it had to be an act: He must have known that he'd had sex with Justin, but didn't want to admit it.

It was funny; but it was also amazingly open of him. Perhaps he saw it as submission to my desires, my need to push him to be more open, and get over his hang-ups?

We dried off, and Fiona took Justin by the hand, and led him into the playroom, walking the length of it to the king-size bed. I put my arms around Sam and kissed him passionately, 'thanking' him for being open to the new experience in the shower. Then, Sam and I followed Fiona and Justin to the bed.

Fiona crooked her finger, making the 'come here' signal to me. It was our turn, now. We lay across the bed, our knees up, feet on opposite sides of the bed, and our heads together, turned so that we could kiss each other. The men knew their roles, positioning themselves between our legs, and going down on us with their mouths open, tongues swirling, partners swapped.

It was again nice, knowing that Justin would be doing me, and Sam doing Fiona. I had every confidence in Sam's ability to get Fiona off, and we both relaxed, letting our men do their job. Fiona and I focused on each other, our heads turned, our mouths engaged in slobbery, wet, upside-down kisses, tongues swirling, lips swollen, pulling each other's head to our own.

I had to admit that Justin's oral skills were as good as Sam's, as jolts of electric energy passed through my body, my back arching, and my muscles clenching. Fiona was rapidly reaching her peak of excitement also; our heavy breathing made our kissing intermittent, but we showered each other with tiny kisses over our necks and faces, as we came nearly simultaneously.

Now, Sam lay over Fiona, kissing her sweetly, as Justin lay over me, doing the same. Justin raised his head, and turned it to Sam; I watched, as Sam sighed, closed his eyes, and let Justin kiss him on the lips. Then, Justin leaned into Sam, opening his mouth; Sam made a short, whining sound, but finally relented, letting his own mouth open, allowing Justin's snake-like tongue to enter.

Justin didn't dwell on the kiss, obviously aware of Sam's discomfort. He gave me a peck on the lips, and then pulled me into a sitting position. We all repositioned ourselves, Justin and Sam sitting on the bed, next to each other, facing opposite directions, while Fiona sat in Sam's lap, and I sat in Justin's lap, our legs wrapping around our partners, and rocking with them.

Fiona looked into my eyes, and commented, "This was an amazing experience. You guys are *both* really hot!" Those were the first words that had been spoken – as far as I could remember – since we'd been in the sauna.

Justin agreed, "I have to say, this was as creative and interesting as anything I've seen at the club." He chuckled, "You guys are welcome to visit the club any time you want – comp." We all laughed.

I had to comment, "I don't know, Justin. We seem to have a pretty good 'club', right here in Sam's house." Justin and Fiona could say nothing, just nod. But I still wanted to visit Justin's club in Toronto. And, I still had to discuss with Sam the possibility of spending a month in London with Elena.

We cleaned up, got dressed, and Sam took us out for sushi. We made up for the lack of conversation earlier, and learned a lot about each other. Fiona and Justin were another interesting couple – both were bi, but neither were particularly into fetishes ... although Justin and Fiona had tried a needle play experience, after Fiona had sampled it in Sam's exam room. But, this time, Justin had been on the receiving end, with Fiona the artist.

As we munched on sushi rolls, Fiona showed us pictures of her 'artwork' on Justin's backside – it was actually much more elaborate than the needle art that Sam had fashioned in my skin.

But our experience today had involved no spanking, no shots or needles, no butt plugs or other toys ... just our bodies and appendages. There had been no talking, and very little human sound, other than some heavy breathing.

We found out that Justin was 41 years old, five years older than Fiona, who was about ten years older than me. And Sam was ten years older than Justin. So, our sensual-sexual experience today included participants in their 20s, 30s, 40s, and 50s.

I remembered back to the first – and second – lunch that Sam and I had eaten together, when Sam had made several comments about my young age. And, I had to admit that in those early days, I'd had a few thoughts about Sam's old age.

But today had been enlightening: It really was about being 'young at heart', being open and creative, being willing to experience new sensations and relationships; it had very little to do with chronological age.

We dropped Fiona and Justin off at Alex's house, saying our goodbyes intimately, congratulating them again on their engagement, and telling them how we looked forward to their wedding. Justin promised to bring us to the sex club, and that prompted another loving kiss from Fiona.

Sam and I drove home in silence, made our way up the stairs, and undressed. As we got into bed, I told Sam how proud I was of him – being receptive to new experiences with a male, something that he'd strenuously avoided all his life – more than half a century.

That reminded me that his birthday was coming up in a month. But now, as I reached under the sheets, I noticed that something else was 'coming up'.

Our sex life hadn't waned. Nearly a year into our relationship, we were still very much in love; in fact, our love had only increased with time. I hoped that would continue. By the end of our first long weekend together, I wouldn't have imagined that there was much more to experience together, sensually, sexually.

But over the past ten months, we'd continued to experience new things, to move beyond our prior limits, to open ourselves to each other – and to other people; and to grow. This seemed to me to be the essence of life – continual excitement, new experiences, and growth. It was what I had been seeking for many years, without being able to define it so succinctly.

I helped Sam get ready, and then took the top position, and put him in me. As we moved in unison – against each other, but together – I also realized how we had evolved and changed in our roles. Although I was willing to submit to Sam and, in fact, get turned on by it, Sam was willing to let me be the 'top', the dominant one, in many respects. I thought again about London, and Mistress Elena.

And, as we neared our mutual release, I remembered many of the experiences we'd had in Elena's 'dungeon': Taking Sam over my knee for the spanking of his life; Sam being strapped down on the table, while Elena gave him some very new needle and injection experiences; the mock branding; and Sam offering to take a caning for me.

I was more interested than ever in pursuing my training as a domme, continuing to put Sam to the test, and getting off together on new submissive challenges.

My orgasm exploded, and I was calming before I realized that Sam had not yet finished. But he did, in his own time.

We turned off the lights, and I spooned him, as I thought about the day's experiences ... and the year's experiences. And wondered what new experiences we would have in the future. Our future together.

CHAPTER 8: LUNCH WITH FRIENDS

I hadn't seen my friends for a month, since we'd gotten our final HPV and hepatitis shots, and we hadn't had a chance to talk then. So I called them, and set-up lunch with them on Friday. I had suggested the bistro where Sam and I had first eaten nearly a year ago, but was out-voted, so we ended-up going back to the Mexican restaurant in the mall.

We hadn't updated each other since November, when Sam and I had shared our pictures and purchases from the Europe trip ... and, of course, we had role-played a schoolgirl scene with Linda the first week of December.

Kathy and I walked into the restaurant at the same time, coming from opposite directions in the mall. A few minutes later, Julie and Linda showed up, and we sat in a booth in the corner. Hopefully, this time, we wouldn't be getting as tipsy as we had last time, but the booth was better for a private conversation. The lunch hour guests were mostly leaving, and we would have the restaurant to ourselves soon.

Linda ordered a pitcher of margaritas, without even asking us, and she already had a grin on her face.

Kathy seemed unhappy, and Julie asked how she was doing. "I'm ready to forget about men, altogether." She got stares from around the table, but before we could ask, she smiled and added, "But I don't really think I would be satisfied by sex with a woman."

Well, I hadn't either. And, I still planned on staying with Sam or, if worse came to worst, find another man; as difficult as that would be, now that I'd experienced life with Sam. But I had to admit to myself that I'd had no trouble getting off with both Julie and Fiona; our experiences had been hot, and they certainly beat taking care of myself.

Julie asked Kathy, "Do you want to tell us about it? I thought you went to Mexico over the holidays to be with the guy you met down there?"

Kathy harrumphed, "Yeah, that's what *I* thought. I did go down to meet him ... but caught him making out with another woman the night I arrived! We had talked a few times about my itinerary, but when I confronted him, he shrugged his shoulders, and said he thought I wouldn't be arriving until the next day."

Kathy licked some salt off the rim of her margarita glass, and took a swallow of the pale green liquid, before continuing. "He didn't seem to think there was a problem with hooking up with other women until I arrived, and couldn't understand why I was upset. So, I spent a few days sitting on the beach by myself, and flying home early."

Linda was shaking her head, "That sucks. Maybe it's the mentality of those Latin guys ..."

Kathy sputtered, as she tried to talk with drink in her mouth, "But he's American! We hadn't talked about having an exclusive relationship, but I certainly didn't expect to find him like that ... and he didn't even seem bothered, or regretful about it."

Julie chuckled, "Well, maybe you should have found someone else, while you were there? A rich, single, American guy at one of the big resorts?"

Kathy was shaking her head, as if none of us were 'getting' it. "Most guys go down there in groups on their vacations, or are already hooked-up with someone; it isn't that easy. And, I didn't want anyone else. I was just steaming that this guy treated me like shit." She took another gulp of margarita. There was nothing we could say to make it any better.

Our food came, and we ate in silence for a few minutes. Then, Linda said, quietly, "I've gone out with the schlub a few times, since the beginning of the year. He's fun for a movie or dinner ..." Linda smiled, "I even let him stay over one night" Now, she had gotten the attention of all of us; Julie's mouth hung open. None of us had met him, but Linda had told us enough about him that we were surprised that she would invite him over for the night.

She took a sip of her drink and continued, "We had gone to a movie, and he was dropping me off at my apartment. It was raining so hard, I invited him to come in ... and I thought I would give him a chance; he *has* been very nice to me, even though he's not much of a hunk to look at."

Linda took a bite of enchilada, drawing out the suspense, as we waited attentively to hear what happened. "As soon as he came in, he was asking me if there was anything good on TV." Linda chuckled, "I told him that I was tired, and we should just go to bed. Now, for most guys, that invitation would have been irresistible."

She looked at me, and smiled, "Maybe it's all the 'open' experiences I've had with Sam ... and you guys ... but I was ready to seduce him. He sat on the bed, and watched, as I got undressed in front of the closet, and hung my clothes.

I had to use the bathroom, and suggested that he undress, also. But I forgot to bring my nightie in with me; I had taken off my bra, and walked out in my underwear, heading for the dresser. He was lying on the bed, in his boxers and socks." We all laughed, visualizing the scene; but the story wasn't over.

Linda wiped some salt off the rim of her glass with her forefinger, and put it into her mouth, sucking on it. I wasn't sure whether that was part of the story or not. She continued, "I brought my nightgown to the nightstand by the bed, and slipped off my panties, before getting under the sheets. I suggested that he finish getting undressed ... and he asked me to turn off the light!"

Now, we were in an uproar; it was lucky that the restaurant was nearly empty. She nodded, continuing the story, "So I did. I don't think he is a virgin, but he sure acted nervous. He couldn't keep his hands off me – especially my breasts; he was enthralled by fondling them, but he was too rough for it to feel good.

"I reached under the sheets and found his dick, and tried to get him turned-on, but he couldn't get it up. We'd each had a glass of wine at dinner, but that was hours before, as we'd just come from the theater. I told him to relax, and said it wasn't a big deal if we didn't have sex, and that we could try again in the morning, if he wanted. I took his hand, and put it on my privates ... and he stroked my pubic hair for a while, and then tried to put his finger in me; I guided him, but he lost interest pretty quickly."

Linda chuckled, "Maybe he *is* a virgin? I guess I should have asked him, and offered to be the 'teacher' ... but I didn't want to make him feel any worse. I turned him on his side, and spooned him, putting my arm around him and pulling him close to me. He seemed to enjoy that, but I heard him snoring after about five minutes."

We were all smiling, but not laughing; we'd all had our own experiences with guys who couldn't get it up, for one reason or another, and who'd fallen asleep before getting us off.

Linda concluded her story, "When I woke up in the morning, he was already dressed. He told me he'd had a nice time, but had to go, and we didn't discuss the previous night." Linda looked around the table, "So, I guess he's someone I can safely share a bed with, anytime."

We hooted, and I realized that the pitcher of margaritas was nearly empty. I flagged the waiter, and ordered another pitcher, telling my friends that the lunch – and drinks – would be on me, today.

Julie looked at Linda, shaking her head, "You should invite him back, and say that you want him to act like a little boy, and let you play with him. Then, you could teach him a few things. Maybe give him some prostate stimulation. Or, maybe he has fetishes that he's hiding; you could tell him about a few things that we did at Kelly's birthday party, and that might open him up ... and turn him on?"

Linda shrugged, "I don't know. He's very private with his body, and might freak out if I stuck a finger up his ass. And, I would have thought he would get at least a little hard, just seeing me nude." Then, Linda laughed, "I guess I could tell him that I always wanted to make it with a virgin, and ask if he qualified?"

Kathy offered, "Maybe, he's gay? That might explain a few things."

Linda just shrugged again, "I don't know. I don't think so." Then, she brightened, and looked at me – perhaps for approval; but I wasn't sure what she wanted. Looking directly at Julie, she said, "Well, I had a really hot experience with Sam and Kelly last December, a week or two after we saw their Europe show."

Now, I knew what she was going to tell them. She glanced at me, and I nodded. She looked at Julie again, smiling, "I did a schoolgirl scene at Sam's house." I could hear in her voice how excited she was to tell the story.

"I have to admit that Sam really goes all out: He had real old-fashioned school desks, a blackboard, and even printed tests." Linda smiled at me, and added, "And Kelly played three roles – a student, the school nurse, and the headmistress." I smiled and nodded.

Julie asked, "How did it compare to the 'real thing' – when they used corporal punishment on us in school?"

Linda laughed, "Sam and I spent several hours role-playing; there was a lot more than bending over the desk and taking two or three swats over my jeans." She hadn't mentioned going into the exam room, or the 'climax' of her experience – having sex with Sam.

This was my cue; there wouldn't be a better time. I began slowly, "You may be wondering why I invited you all to lunch today." I doubt if any of them had thought about anything other than catching up with old friends. "I'd like to talk to you guys about two things. First, Sam is having a birthday in a couple of weeks ... and I thought it would be fun to 'repay' him for the birthday party he gave me."

Linda was already smiling, "Yeah. I *told* him that we wouldn't forget about giving him shots while he waves to the camera."

I nodded, "There are a lot of things we can do. Of course, he should get his birthday spanking ... and we could pull out the 'Lazy Sam' turntable, and put *him* on it. I'm open to your suggestions." There was now twittering around the table.

"But it *will* be his birthday, and I'd like to reward him, also, if he submits to whatever you guys do with him." My friends made some suggestions, and I decided to make a list of them on the computer when I got home, and develop an agenda for the event.

Now, came the more difficult thing I wanted to suggest. "And, Sam and I would like to ask you guys if you would be interested in a submission experience ... Sam views it as 'training' in how to behave when taking a spanking, and testing you guys on your ability to control yourselves – your mind and body – when receiving some pain and embarrassment." I looked at my friends, and they were listening, awaiting the details of our proposal.

"Basically, he would like to see how you will do, when participating in an experience similar to the one to which he subjected me, when I first visited him. And, he wants to turn it into a competition between us ... but not like his 'Spank Poker' game; this time; we would be doing everything voluntarily, trying to see who can take the most."

My friends looked at me probingly, and I explained, "Mainly the positions, implements, corner times, and corrective punishments; challenging you with being able to stay in position, and accept some pain on your butt. Sam's idea of submission involves both physical and mental aspects – the physical usually some kind of pain, and the mental usually embarrassment. "

Kathy said, "But haven't we already gone through most of that? He's seen us nude, seen our private parts, spanked us, put things up our ass, stuck us with needles. Even watched us put in and take out a tampon." Linda and Julie were nodding, and Kathy summarized, "What else is there to do? We've been more open with Sam than with almost any other males – or, females, for that matter." I nodded.

Kathy added, "Does that mean he wants to give us *more* shots? I'm getting better with them, but still don't like the experience."

I explained, "I told Sam that he would have to lay off the injections ... except maybe in *his* butt." My friends chuckled. But I knew that they were still worrying about what else Sam would come up with. "As you said, I don't think there should be much that will embarrass you guys ... and he's not into really hurting people – just challenging them. So I can't imagine that you'll have a problem with whatever spankings you might get."

Our second pitcher of margaritas came, and I refilled everyone's glasses. "Sam knows that at least two of you might get turned on by being spanked, and I think he wants to demonstrate that he can get you guys off ... like he did with me ten months ago."

Kathy shrugged, "It doesn't sound like a big deal. I think we've done most of what he'll throw at us."

Julie nodded, "Sam is a pretty sexy guy – he may be twice our age, but he's also twice as sensual and creative than any of our boyfriends."

Kathy whined, "Don't even mention 'boyfriends'." She drained her glass, and I refilled it again. Maybe we *would* be getting tipsy, again?

Kathy announced, "I'm not as turned on by spanking as you guys ... but it's been interesting 'playing' with you and Sam. I guess I might be OK with having another 'experience', if Linda and Julie want to do it." Linda and Julie nodded, and smiled.

We talked about the schedule. Sam's birthday was two weeks from today, so we decided on two weeks from tomorrow for the party. Fiona's wedding was in June, and I would need to finish-up my classes and turn in the work I had done on my dissertation in mid-June, so we decided on having the spanking training, submission challenge and competition four weeks from now. We would confirm the exact timing at Sam's birthday party.

The restaurant was now almost empty, our plates had been removed from the table, and we were finishing the second pitcher of margaritas. I was glad that Sam and I had gotten our weight under control over the past three months. My friends and I spent another thirty minutes brainstorming some of the things that we could do at Sam's birthday party.

I also spoke seriously – well, as seriously as I could be after two pitchers of margaritas – with each of my friends, to make sure they were OK with coming over for a weekend of submission. I was honest with them: It would undoubtedly be uncomfortable, their butts would hurt from the spankings, and they could expect to be embarrassed. I made sure they knew that they didn't have to agree to this – it would be entirely voluntary.

The general consensus was that they'd all been very open with Sam already, and they couldn't imagine that he would make them feel embarrassed. Only Kathy was concerned about the spankings, as that had been contrary to the culture in her hippie family, and she'd never taken a hard physical punishment. Julie and Linda were not concerned, and it was clear now that Linda actually was turned on by being spanked.

Regarding discomfort, I couldn't tell them exactly what the experience would entail. They said that they did not want to go on Sam's turntable again. And Kathy said that she wasn't too bothered by small needles, but didn't want injections to be part of the submission challenge.

I assured my friends that I would work with Sam to design an experience that would be interesting for them; perhaps it would be challenging, but we would try to avoid the things that turned them off.

They seemed to be much more interested in Sam's birthday party – both giving *him* some challenges, and also making sure that he had a 'rewarding' birthday celebration. It wouldn't be as elaborate as the party that Sam had given me, but it should be interesting to see Sam take some of his own medicine, in a manner of speaking.

Over the next week, as my experiment ran in the lab, I designed some of the games we might play at Sam's birthday party. It was cooler again, and raining on and off, so I couldn't count on having the party in the backyard.

I printed out a page with my indoor game ideas: They included "wave to the camera", "pins and tails on the doggie", "musical dares", "turn around", "bobbing for Sam", "Sam says", "dirty dancing", "hula hooping", "birthday roast", "whipped cream challenge", and "spank poker – girls edition". I hadn't worked out all the details, but would e-mail the list to my friends and let them contribute to the rules for each game.

One minor detail was that Julie and Linda were expecting to have their periods – perhaps being at the end of them, while Kathy could be getting her period around that time, if it came early.

We decided that it might be fun, and more embarrassing for Sam, if the girls were dressed in fancy outfits, while we made Sam spend the day nude or, at the most, dressed in his Europe tee and skimpy underwear. We would be 'calling his bluff' (or 'buff'?) regarding being comfortable and not embarrassed ... but I also wanted to give him an experience that would be fun, and a turn-on, overall.

I suggested that we all wear dresses with pantyhose or nylons, and also bring skirts and tops; I had some ideas that might be a surprise and a turn-on for Sam. I also invited my friends to stay over Saturday night, and they said that they had assumed they would be spending the night at the house. We discussed the possibility of putting out the Aerobeds again, for a special slumber party, but finally decided to leave that decision until Saturday night.

It was interesting that Julie and Linda had already had intercourse with Sam, and I thought about the possibility of a group sex scene ... but they might not be over their periods, and Kathy might get hers. I wasn't sure that Kathy would even be up for something like that; she had been receptive to playing with Sam and I, but it had never progressed to anything sexual.

And then there was Sam's present: I had worried about this for the past couple of months. What could I possibly buy for a man who had everything he wanted? I was still a student, and didn't have a huge budget ... but I had to get him something different, something that he would appreciate. So, I had taken the plunge and ordered something that I was sure he would like. Perhaps I would also buy a few smaller things – practical things?

While the experiment continued to run in the lab, I fired up my browser, and did a little last-minute shopping. I thought briefly of the outfits Sam had bought for the pirate scene at my birthday party, and considered buying similar Victorian dresses for each of my friends, but they would be too uncomfortable to wear the entire day.

I bought Sam a few very small clothing gifts – just the type that most men hate, before clicking onto some sex shop websites, where I found some things that Sam (and my friends) would find much more interesting.

I also stopped at a super-size, discount department store – part of a huge national chain – to buy a few things that would be useful for a couple of Sam's submission challenges during his birthday party. The store was located near the college and had only been open for the past couple of years. It had been responsible for putting several of the smaller shops on Main Street out of business, as they couldn't compete with the prices and selection.

I also bridled at the thought of any store espousing or supporting any religious views, as this one was known to do. But it was the most convenient place to shop for the miscellaneous items that I needed. I visited the pet section and the baby section, and also picked up a couple of DVDs, for good measure.

Over the next week, I discussed a few details of the party with Sam. Although he had wanted to cook dinner, I convinced him to only make lunch – if he insisted on cooking at all – and that I would bring in Chinese food for dinner. As the party would be the day after Sam's actual birthday, he was OK with that.

To compensate, he said he wanted to go to the French restaurant for his birthday on Friday night; we hadn't been there since New Year's eve, and we'd both lost enough weight that we could even feel good about ordering dessert. I had to admit that it was one of the best restaurants in town, and had become one of my favorites.

The week of Sam's birthday, the weather continued to be unpredictable: One day it was sunny and in the mid-70s, and the next it was blustery and in the mid-60s. We just couldn't count on having an outside birthday party – especially, not a skinny-dipping one, as my party had been.

But, hopefully, my friends and I had planned enough 'events' that could be enjoyed indoors. It would be interesting to see whether Sam would actually submit to them, without whining. But we had also planned to reward him for his cooperation.

Julie had asked how many orgasms Sam could have in one day, and I'd had to admit that I didn't know. He was able to get turned on easily enough, and I was sure that he had the stamina for a half dozen orgasms in a day ... but there was undoubtedly a limit that we hadn't found, yet.

I thought about bringing some test tubes home from the lab, and letting my friends compete to see who could fill one with Sam's semen first, but that didn't seem practical for a number of reasons ... and we agreed that his orgasms should be for his own enjoyment, and not for ours.

It was amazing, now that my friends had played with Sam and I, how creative – or, as Linda would say, 'perverted' – our ideas could be. None of us could possibly have imagined thinking of any of these things a year ago, when the most exciting time we could imagine with our dates would have been actually coming, while we had sex with them.

CHAPTER 9: GETTING THE POINT ACROSS

I took off from school on Friday, Sam's birthday, and began the day by making love to Sam, letting him try various positions on and off the bed. But I had to laugh when he finally was ready, and decided to make love in the standard missionary position. I 'gave' myself to Sam for the day, but he didn't really take advantage of my offer; until we were getting ready to go out to dinner.

We went into the closet to dress, and Sam smiled at me, pointing to the heavy leather belt hanging on a hook. It was his birthday, and I was happy to humor him; I couldn't remember the last time we'd had a spanking experience. I shrugged, and nodded. He took the belt from the hook, and followed me back into the bedroom, where I lowered my bikini underwear and bent over the foot of the bed.

I didn't know what to expect, but trusted Sam, and trusted my ability to control my mind and my body, and take whatever pain Sam wanted me to experience. There were no words spoken. I felt the belt being laid across my bare bottom, and tried to relax myself, my hands clasped together on the bed in front of me. Then, the belt left me for a moment, and came down with a 'CRACK!', a line of white-hot pain across my bum. "One. Thank you, Sir!"

Sam hadn't asked me to count the strokes, but it was my intention to show the utmost cooperation, which I knew would turn him on. A few seconds later, the belt was raised, and again came down with a 'CRACK!', searing a second line just below the first one. "Two. Thank you, Sir!"

I realized that I was gritting my teeth, and willed myself to relax, closing my eyes. Sam applied four more strokes, my bottom now blazing. But, while my eyes were damp, so were my feminine tissues down below. Sam put the belt on the bed, and rubbed my sore bum.

Then he commanded, "Please stand, and pull up your underwear." I did so, and he said, "Now, sit on the edge of the bed." He removed his own underwear and turned to me, "I'm ready for my birthday spanking, now." He laughed, "At least my first one." As he maneuvered himself across my lap, he whispered, "You may spank me as hard as if Mistress Elena were watching."

Sam adjusted himself, as I rubbed my hand lightly over his bottom. I gave his butt a couple of pats, and then began his birthday spanking. At one hard spank every second or so, it took nearly a minute to complete the 51 spanks.

Then, I reached over and picked up the belt, folding it over, and placing it against Sam's bum. I don't think he expected that, as he flinched, and then forcibly relaxed himself. I raised the belt, and let it come down hard against Sam's rear. "One for good health!" Another hard stroke followed. "One for good wealth!" Sam was remaining in position, and I really laid it on – in a manner of speaking – for the last stroke. 'CRACK!!!' I chuckled, "And one for long life!"

Helping Sam up, I saw that he was at half-mast, and reached for him. I was turned-on, also, and assumed we would be having a little before-dinner nooky.

Sam gave me an enigmatic smile, and asked, "Would you be interested in getting yourself off on top of me ... like you did before we went to the French restaurant the first time?" Well, this was interesting! I smiled, stood up, and pointed to the bed.

We didn't bother with the blindfold, this time. Sam lay along the width of the bed, his nude body trim and fit, his bottom well-reddened by the spanking. I took off my bra, and climbed onto the bed, and on top of him, pressing my breasts against his back, my legs straddling his.

It was a déja vu scene, but this time I was turned on both by the strapping Sam had given me, and the hard over-the-knee spanking I'd given him. And, this time, I would take care of him *before* dinner. I relaxed my full weight onto Sam, and slipped my hands along our sides, to our hips, and then ground my front, in a circular motion, into Sam's rear.

Pushing my knees into the bed, I lifted my middle enough to bring my hands between us, and into position to satisfy myself. I closed my eyes, and focused on my own needs, now urgent, lustful. My legs squeezed against Sam's, grasping and releasing, as I thrust my pelvis. My fingers slid along each side of my clit, over the hood, pressing, pulsing, as my mind went blank, and I found my release.

Taking my hands back out from between us, I reached up and held Sam's shoulders, as I let my body move in waves against him. I showered his upper back with small kisses, before slipping a hand under him, and curling my fingers around his manhood. The motion was limited, but I squeezed my fingers, one after another, along his length.

Finally, I rolled off Sam onto the bed, and helped him turn over. Then, I took him in my mouth, swirling my tongue around him, sucking, and moving my head to take him in fully, as my lips closed on him. Sam began thrusting slowly, and I tasted his pre-cum on the back of my tongue. Soon, he was erupting into me, his hot, thick liquid further lubricating his motion within me.

It had been another incredible experience: Feeling Kelly masturbating on top of me, and then taking me into her mouth and satisfying my needs. She crawled up my body, and kissed me, the taste of my own cum no longer seeming objectionable. Now facing each other, she lay on me again, and I held her tight. Kelly licked my lips, and bit them gently.

As we kissed again, I let my hands move down her body, taking the twin globes of her bottom, squeezing, and molding them. My own butt felt the residual sting from the spanking she had given me. My birthday spanking.

Then, I chuckled, remembering that it was only the first of my birthday spankings. I had no idea what Kelly and her friends had planned for tomorrow, but I knew that it would be interesting ... and probably challenging. They knew that I planned to challenge them – again – in a month. It was only fair that they have their turn.

Our dinner was very nice; George took good care of us. Kelly and I shared a dessert, a gooey, messy dessert, as we'd had the first time I'd taken her here after our 'first experience' together.

It was just short of a year since we'd had our first lunch together, and about eleven months since she'd come over for a spanking and much more. Although she'd had several orgasms by my hand, we'd kept it non-sexual, per my original definition of 'sex' as transfer of body fluids.

But we'd come a long way since then; not only the two of us, but our relationship with her friends, as well. And, we'd had intimate relations with Henk and Zöe ... and

Fiona and Justin. My life had dramatically changed in the past year.

But despite all of the things we'd done, my fantasies hadn't abated. If anything, they were as strong as ever, the difference being that now I could implement them, share them with Kelly and others. I had enjoyed the renewed social contact, and I was loving my life with Kelly.

I could only hope against hope that our life together would continue. Perhaps it was selfish? I still had occasional pangs of guilt that I was preventing Kelly from developing a relationship with someone younger, someone able to live a long life with her, someone who could give her children.

I was very much in love with Kelly; it had grown far beyond my initial infatuation. I wanted the best for her: A comfortable life, a loving relationship, mental and physical growth, and fulfillment. Hopefully, I could give her all of that. She was a strong woman, and I knew that she would find success in everything she did; and have anything she wanted, with enough focus and effort.

It is said that a person is not old, until regrets take the place of dreams. I had now lived for 51 years, but still had a lot of dreams; for Kelly and I – working, playing, loving together. Kelly and I made love again, holding each other until we were asleep. I felt very contented – not thinking about tomorrow or the future, but enjoying the moment; the warmth, the love, of being with Kelly.

In the morning, we went to the market to pick up a few things for the party. She suggested that we prepare a simple lunch buffet, getting everything from the market, rather than having me do any cooking.

I had only planned to make a few appetizers, but I accepted Kelly's suggestion, and we bought sandwich fixings – including meats and cheeses from the deli department, some coleslaw, and potato and macaroni salads, along with pickles, olives, and already cleaned and cut fresh vegetables.

We laid out the spread on the kitchen table, along with paper plates and plastic utensils. I had offered to make sangria, but Kelly wanted her friends – and me – to remain sober, at least until dinner.

I put on a pair of shorts and a Hawaiian shirt, and went out to the backyard; there were still five chairs around the glass patio table, but the sky was mostly clouded, the weather looking threatening. There was a breeze, and the temperature was comfortable, but the humidity was high; I hoped that we could have lunch out here ... and then maybe go in the pool for a while.

As I walked back into the kitchen, I heard Kelly welcoming her friends at the front door. Entering the living room, I was surprised to see that everyone, including Kelly, looked like they were ready to go out to a nightclub: They wore dresses – even Kathy – and had on nylons and high-heel shoes.

Smiling when they saw me, they crowded around and wished me a happy birthday. Julie took my head in her hands, smiled at me, and gave me a deep and lingering kiss. When we had come up for air, Linda took her place, hugged me, and then she too gave me an open-mouth and intimate kiss.

Kathy smiled, and stepped up to me, "Happy birthday, Sam." I bent and gave her a quick peck her on the lips, but as I pulled back, she smiled and leaned forward, giving me a brief, but very nice French kiss.

I looked at Kelly's friends and chuckled, "Well, I guess Kelly has gotten me over my discomfort with sharing saliva. And, we don't consider kissing – or eating after each other – part of our definition of 'sex', anymore." The girls laughed easily.

Julie reached down, cupping her hand over the mound in my pants, "Well, we've all had sex with you, Sam." When I started to look shocked, thinking about the ménage with Julie – that, I assumed, her friends were not aware of – Julie continued, "By your definition, we all had sex – at least oral sex – during Kelly's birthday party."

She glanced at Linda and Kathy, and then stared at Kelly, as she announced, "And the ménage we had cleared up any doubts about us having had sex ... by *anybody's* definition." Now, I really was shocked; I had expected that the experience between Julie, Kelly and I would have remained private.

Kathy exclaimed, "Ménage?!??" She looked at Kelly for confirmation, and received an almost-imperceptible nod. "I guess you guys really *do* share each other."

Linda, looking down at her feet, quietly commented, "Yeah, they do. After our schoolgirl scene, Kelly insisted that Sam take me from behind ... with her watching!" Now, it was pandemonium, Julie making exaggerated gasps and expressions, and Kathy grinning broadly and shaking her head.

Linda turned to me, and added, "And, it was really nice, Sam. Thank you." She pulled my head to her, and gave me another slobbery, wet kiss.

Kelly said brightly, "Shall we have lunch, now?" We all laughed, and proceeded into the kitchen to make our sandwiches.

There was some tittering as we filled our plates, and Kathy, turning to Linda, said, "You didn't share *that* part with us, when we had lunch!"

Linda just shrugged, but looked at Julie, and remarked, "And *you* didn't tell us about having a ménage with Kelly and Sam!"

Julie shrugged, and said, "I don't usually 'kiss and tell' ... but since we've all agreed to be so open today, I thought it would be a good 'ice-breaker'."

I harrumphed, and held the door open for the girls to go out to the backyard. Julie shook her head, as she passed me, "Sam, it *is* your birthday, and Kelly has told us how much you stress *openness* ..." We sat around the glass table; we hadn't bothered with a tablecloth, as it would undoubtedly be raining soon.

There was nothing I could say in answer to Julie's comment: I did believe in openness and honesty ... but knew there had to be a limit. It seemed OK to share within this group of friends, as we'd all shared some intimate physical experiences with each other. But I would not have been as comfortable, had Alex overheard this exchange.

At the time – each time we had gotten together with Kelly's friends – our activities had seemed natural, but perhaps we *had* been overly promiscuous? Once again, I was confused, my thoughts confounded by a combination of ideals and practicalities, fantasies and realities. I shook my head, and took a bite of my sandwich.

About the time most of our food had been consumed, we saw a huge bolt of cloud-to-cloud lightning, and almost immediately heard the crack and the rumble of thunder. A few seconds later, drops of rain began to fall and, by the time we filed back into the kitchen, there was a downpour. We cleaned up the buffet, and Kelly suggested that we go downstairs to the playroom where, it was now clear, most of my birthday party would take place.

Linda announced, "Well, we've waited long enough, and I don't want to let Sam off the hook: He should get his shots now, while he waves to the camera." It was something I had expected – I had certainly not forgotten; but it was still a surprise that I would have to take my shots so soon. Kelly nodded, her friends looking at me expectantly.

I shrugged, and fetched the small video camera and tripod from the credenza behind the desk. "It's a bit cramped in the exam room, so how about if I set it up out here? I can bend over the back of the couch." There were silent nods all around, and I asked Julie to position herself behind the couch, near the corner table, and bend over, as I mounted the camcorder on the tripod, and aimed it at Julie's smiling face.

Then, I stood, faced Kelly and her friends, and made them an offer. "I would like to give you guys a choice: Kelly can give me two big shots, while you watch. Or ..." Kelly was shaking her head, already, but I continued undaunted, "I'll let each of you give me a small shot on each side." The girls glanced at each other, and nodded.

Before anyone could answer, I added, "But there will be a condition for anyone but Kelly giving me shots." I heard a quiet, 'Oh no' from Kelly, as Linda rolled her eyes, Kathy looked up at the ceiling, and Julie smiled at me, awaiting my 'condition'.

I nodded, "In order to be safe, I would like to give you all a very brief 'shot training' experience; teach you the details of how to give an intramuscular injection." Kelly was still shaking her head, while Linda's mouth dropped open.

It was Kathy, who looked at me, and asked, "And what does that involve?"

I nodded, "We'll go into the exam room, and I'll give you all the information, while I demonstrate on Kelly." Kelly was smiling, but had her hands on her hips, in a mock-defiance posture. "Then, you'll bend over the exam table, and I'll do exactly what I demonstrated on Kelly."

There were questioning looks, so I elaborated. "You'll each get three needle sticks, and one small shot. The first two needles will be very thin, and will show you what it feels like to get a quick insertion and a slow insertion ... and to have a couple of needles in your but for a minute or so. Then, those will come out, and you'll get a quick insertion with a much larger needle – just to feel the difference; I won't leave that one in more than a few seconds." The girls were nodding their heads, slowly.

"Finally, you'll each get a 2cc injection – just a little larger than the ones you got at the clinic, and the same size that you'll be giving me."

I smiled, and only Kelly immediately realized that I hadn't finished. "The shot will be your 'graduation exercise' – to show that you understand two things: 1) that needles, and even small injections of saline don't hurt much, if given properly, and 2) that you're confident that you can insert the needle and inject the medicine properly."

I was receiving blank stares all around. It was time for the 'climax' of my proposal. "So, to do that, you'll be giving *yourselves* the shot."

Linda moaned, and Julie chuckled. Kelly looked upset with me. Kathy exclaimed, "Sam, I don't think I can do that. I'm getting used to the needles, and even with the small injections we got at the clinic – when I don't have to look ... but I don't think I'm strong enough to actually give *myself* a shot." She looked around at her friends, who had neutral expressions.

I replied, "You *are* strong, Kathy. But if you get as far as inserting the needle, and don't want to inject the saline, then you can ask me to do it for you."

Kelly looked like she was going to explode. "Sam! It's not such a bad idea to train my friends ... but I promised them that you wouldn't start with things they didn't want to do – like getting shots. And now, you want to start the party off that way?" She shook her head, glaring at me.

I shrugged, "It wasn't *my* idea to start the party with shots ... it was Linda who suggested it. And, I'm not making anybody take any shots – just offering to let them give me shots, while I wave to the camera ... but only if they're trained."

I smiled at Kelly, trying to defuse the situation, "And you know it would be much easier for me to take two big shots from you, than six smaller ones from your friends."

Kelly harrumphed, "Well, if they agree to it, you're going to get the smaller shots from them, AND the two big ones from me."

I winced, and my bottom hurt, already. I guess Kelly was punishing me for making the offer to her friends. I realized that my mouth had dropped open, but there was nothing I could do. Kelly had already explained to me that my birthday party would be a combination of things that turned me on, and challenges from her friends; at least partially in anticipation of the 'challenge' to which they would be submitting a month from now.

Kelly looked at her friends, "You guys *don't* have to do this!"

Julie said, softly, "Kelly, it *is* Sam's birthday. And, I would like to be 'trained'. I've already given you shots, and don't mind what Sam is proposing."

Linda shrugged, "You know, Sam, you're even more perverted, than I realized." Everyone chuckled, as Linda continued, "I'm OK with it ... if the rest of you are. I'm looking forward to giving Sam *his* shots."

Kathy's shoulders fell, "Oh, all right. If you guys are going to do it, I guess we can do it. But I still don't know if I can insert a needle in my own butt, let alone inject anything. I might wimp out on that part."

Kelly was smiling now, and so was I. Reaching into my shorts, I adjusted my growing erection.

Kelly stared at me, "Just so you know, Sam, my friends and I *will* be taking care of you today ... relieving any tension we cause to be built up ... but NOT until all this shot and needle stuff is over!" I nodded, mutely.

I led everyone into the exam room; only Kathy hadn't seen it yet, and her eyes darted around nervously. I asked Kelly to lie down on the table, and she hiked up her dress, and lowered her pantyhose; she was not wearing underwear.

Julie, Linda and Kathy stood next to me at the exam table, as Kelly got settled, and put her head on the pillow, turned toward us.

I explained the purpose of an intramuscular injection, and pointed out the various possible injection sites – in the deltoid muscle of the arm, the vastus lateralis muscle of the thigh, the ventrogluteal muscle (hip), or the dorsogluteal muscle (butt).

Then, I demonstrated assembling a syringe and needle – using a 5cc syringe and 25 gauge needle, and filling it with 2cc of sterile saline. I demonstrated how to safely uncap the needle, and assembled a second shot, this one left empty.

Setting Kelly's shot on the counter, I provided materials to her three friends, and they turned to the counter and assembled and filled their own shots, as I observed, and reminded them of all the steps.

With the four shots lined up on the counter, we turned back to Kelly, and I took out two 25-gauge needles and an alcohol swab. I carefully explained how to find an injection site in the upper-outer quadrant of each buttock.

Kelly demonstrated how to find the site on herself, by putting her right thumb in the small of her back, and the tip of her little finger on the outermost bony protrusion of her hip, her three middle fingers now lying on the area for safe injections on her right buttock.

I ran my finger from her spine diagonally down across her butt, and down the back of her leg, showing everyone where the sciatic nerve was – to be avoided when inserting a long needle.

Finally, I tore the end off the alcohol swab package, and demonstrated how to clean the injection site. I told them that it would hurt less if the alcohol was dry, either by wiping with a sterile pad, or just letting it air-dry. Then, I took the empty shot, uncapped the needle, and held the skin of Kelly's right buttock taut.

I said, "Then, you quickly dart the needle all the way in, up to the hub, going vertical to the skin." With that, I inserted the needle into Kelly; she was silent, but I heard a quiet gasp from Kathy. I let go, the syringe now sticking out from Kelly's butt, and wobbling a little.

Turning to her friends, I said, "So that's how you quickly insert a needle. It doesn't take much force, but you want to keep it going, until it's all the way in."

The syringe was standing straight up from Kelly's bottom, as I asked, "Do you have any questions?" Julie, Linda and Kathy shook their heads, their eyes fixed on the syringe.

I asked Kelly, "So how does it feel? How would you rate the pain, on a scale of one to one hundred?"

Kelly, her head still on the pillow, glanced up at us, and said, "It feels OK. Like a mosquito bite. It doesn't hurt much, maybe a two or three." I smiled at her friends. Kathy was shaking her head dubiously.

I then swabbed Kelly on the opposite side, and uncapped another needle. "This time, I'm going to use the same size needle, but insert it slowly, which hurts a bit more. You'll see the skin pushing down, and then the needle popping through.

I slowly pushed down on the needle, and it took only a second before it was all the way in. Again, Kelly hadn't made a sound.

I turned to her friends, and said, "You should always try to do a quick insertion, which is easier for the patient." I glanced at my watch, "And now, we'll leave the needles in for about a minute or so. Kelly has, of course, already felt this; quite a few times."

I chuckled. "As she's said before, it gets a little annoying, but still doesn't hurt much." The girls had their eyes on Kelly's bottom, the syringe still sticking out on the right side, and a small blue hub against her skin on the left side.

Glancing at my watch again, I pulled each of the needles out about a quarter of an inch, so that her friends could see the stainless needle going through her skin. I said, "If you don't have any questions, I'll pull the needles out, now."

Kelly's friends shook their heads, and I pulled the needle on the left out, quickly. Then, I pulled the one with the syringe out very slowly, dumping it into the sharps container mounted on the wall on the other side of the exam table.

I looked at Kelly's friends, and they nodded. Kathy had a blank expression, but it didn't look like she was getting faint. I then swabbed Kelly's left side again, and unpackaged a 20-gauge needle; uncapping it, I held it up for her friends to see.

"This is a much larger needle, but shouldn't hurt much more, if it is inserted quickly." Without further explanation, I inserted it quickly into Kelly's left buttock, an inch below where the first needle had been.

Kelly exhaled, and I asked, "How does this one feel?" Kelly shrugged, "It does feel bigger, but I guess it doesn't hurt much more than the thinner one." Smiling, I pulled it out, and dumped it into the sharps container.

"Now, for something that even Kelly hasn't done, yet." Picking up the filled syringe, I asked, "Are you ready to give yourself a shot now?"

Kelly shrugged again, and said, "I guess so." I handed her an alcohol swab, which she opened, then located the injection site, and swabbed herself. I took the swab and dumped it in the trash, and handed her the syringe and needle.

Kelly uncapped the needle, and held it up, tapping on the syringe, and then pushing the plunger, a tiny stream of saline squirting across the exam room. Then, she lifted her head, and reached back, positioning the needle over her hip.

"Kelly won't be able to stretch her own skin in this position, but if she inserts the needle quickly, it still shouldn't hurt, much." Kelly exhaled again, and plunged the needle into her butt. She glanced up at me, and smiled proudly.

Then, she held the syringe with a couple of fingers, while pulling the plunger out a little; there was no blood coming into the syringe. She pushed on the plunger, holding the tab of the syringe with two fingers, and we watched, as the saline went into her. Then, she pulled the syringe out, and handed it to me to discard.

I smiled at Kelly, as I put a small, round bandaid on her butt. "Congratulations! You graduated!" Kelly shook her head, and climbed awkwardly off the exam table, her friends stepping back to make room for her. She pulled up her pantyhose, and smoothed down her dress.

Looking at her friends, she said, "That really wasn't so difficult. I'm sure you guys can do it." Linda grumbled, and Kathy 'harrumphed', as Kelly stepped into the exam room doorway.

I smiled, "OK, guys, get yourselves ready, and bend over the exam table." The three girls didn't argue, just stood next to each other and lifted their dresses. Julie lowered her pantyhose and bikini underwear, not quite to the bottom of her buttocks. Linda did the same. Kathy was wearing nylons, and lowered her black bikinis down to mid-thigh. They all bent over the exam table, just as they had at the clinic.

I opened six 25-gauge needles, still capped, and took three packages of alcohol swabs from the counter. I opened the first package, and swabbed Julie's bottom, on the left and on the right; then I repeated the swabbing with Linda, and with Kathy.

As the alcohol dried, I announced, "Since you're cooperating so well, I'm going to use only two thin needles on you guys; we'll skip the larger needle. You'll just have to take Kelly's word for it that it doesn't hurt much more than the small ones."

I heard exhaling of breath, and Kathy looked up at me, "Thank you, Sam." I nodded.

"I'm going to insert the left one first for each of you, then come back and insert the right one – just like at the clinic ... except I'll leave the needles in, so you can feel what it's like to have two needles in you, for a minute or so." I uncapped one needle at a time, sticking Julie, then Linda, then Kathy, and repeating, until each of the girls had two blue hubs showing on their butt.

I glanced at the wall clock, and asked each of the girls how they were doing. "It's no big deal," Julie said quickly.

"Not much different than at the clinic," Linda said, softly. She added, "Like Kelly said, it feels like a couple of mosquito bites."

Kathy nodded, then looked back and smiled at me, "I guess I really am getting used to it. They're not so bad." Then, she whined, "But I'm still not sure that I can give myself a shot."

It had been a full minute, and I pulled out all the needles, depositing them in the sharps container. I took one of the shots from the counter, and handed it to Julie. "Why don't you watch each other do this?" Kathy and Linda stood, and stepped back, while Julie looked over her right shoulder. I said, "You can find the site, and I'll swab it for you; then you can insert the needle, check for blood, and inject the saline."

Julie did as she'd been taught; she pointed, and I swabbed the area for her. Then, she held the needle over her own skin. "Here goes nothing ... I hope." She darted the needle in, and it disappeared into her flesh. She glanced at me, and I smiled at her and nodded.

After she checked for blood, she injected herself, and then pulled the needle out. We all clapped. It looked like she'd done this all her life.

Julie reached over and dropped the syringe and needle into the sharps container, and I handed the next shot to Linda. She didn't have a problem, either, although the needle only went in about an inch, and she had to push it the rest of the way.

Linda injected herself and, leaving the needle in another moment, said, "I still don't like the pinching feeling." Then, she pulled the needle out, and disposed of the shot.

Linda and Julie pulled up their pantyhose, and pushed their dresses down, standing back for a good view of Kathy. They smiled at her, Kathy giving them her trademark 'sourpuss' expression.

Then, wordlessly, Kathy found her injection site, I swabbed it, and handed the shot to her. She uncapped the needle, and positioned it over her butt, still shiny from the alcohol. We all held our collective breath, as Kathy breathed in and out a few times, the needle moving around slightly, before she finally plunged it all the way in.

"Good job!" I cried. Kathy glanced up at me, and gave me a dour look, before focusing again on the shot, and finally injecting the saline. We all clapped, very proud of how far Kathy had come in the past several months.

As she pulled up her panties, and lowered her dress, Kathy said, "And now, it's *your* turn!" I guess it was. I asked Kelly to prepare the shots, and her friends and I went into the playroom, where I got everyone something to drink.

Soon enough, Kelly came out of the exam room with a tray full of syringes, alcohol swabs and a sharps container. My stomach felt hollow; I didn't mind getting shots that much, but there would be a lot of them, this time. Kelly put the tray on the corner table, and I took one last swallow of Diet Coke.

Her friends were smiling, as Kelly looked at me, and said, "You can take off all your clothes for this, Sam." I did as I had been told, dropping my shorts, underwear and shirt onto one of the chairs facing the desk. I walked around the coffee table, and pushed the 'Record' button on the camcorder, then went behind the couch, and bent over, resting my forearms on the couch back. Julie and Kathy sat on the loveseat, looking very nice in their fancy dresses, as Linda moved behind me, Kelly handing her an alcohol swab.

I looked into the camera, trying to smile, and gave a 'thumbs up', as Linda gave me a 2cc shot on each side. Then, it was Kathy's turn. She gave me the first shot on the left side, and it didn't feel too bad. I relaxed for the second needle, but Kathy did a slow insertion, and I let out an 'Ow!'

The girls laughed, as Kathy injected the saline; they obviously had gotten the 'last laugh', after I'd made them take their series of HPV and hepatitis injections, filming them during the final course. Finally, Julie came around, and swabbed both sides of my butt. It was already hurting, and we hadn't even begun the birthday spankings, yet. This was going to be a long afternoon.

Julie injected me on the left side, and it didn't feel any different than it would have at the clinic. But then, I felt the second needle go in, and the injection starting – while the first needle was still in me! I didn't know if it had been Julie's or Kelly's idea, but I soon had two needles in me, with 2cc of saline having been injected on each side. I involuntarily groaned.

Julie laughed, and then whispered, "That's a good boy!" Then, she pulled out the needles. I was already sore, and not looking forward to two *big* shots from Kelly.

Fortunately, Kelly laughed, and asked, "Would you like to wait a while, before I give you the big ones?" I nodded vigorously, glad that Kelly had sensed my discomfort, and offered me a break.

I stood, and stepped back from the couch, a slight erection causing me to bob. As I turned to get my clothes, Kelly said, "Stay there, mister. We're not through with you, yet!" Uh oh, what now?

I turned back toward the couch, and got into the standing position. Julie rose. "I guess I'll take the first shift," Julie said, as she approached the couch, got on her knees, and took my penis in her hands. She looked up at me, smiling, as her hands stroked me.

It was clear that this wasn't going to be a punishment, so I let my hands drop from my head to hers, letting my fingers run through her bangs, and down each side of her parted, dark brown hair. It didn't take long for me to 'rise to the occasion', and Julie took me into her mouth, her head bobbing, the feeling exquisite. I closed my eyes, and let my fingers twirl Julie's hair, as she gave me head.

All of Kelly's friends had seen me orgasm, and I came in Julie's mouth, as she continued to suck and lick me. Then, taking a swig of her soft drink, she washed it down.

Julie came around the couch, and led me by the hand into the bathroom, where she took a washcloth, ran warm water through it, and cleaned me with care. When we came back into the playroom, Linda and Kathy clapped, and Kelly exclaimed, "Well, it looks like you've gotten the point (in a manner of speaking): Your birthday will be a combination of pain and pleasure."

Kelly said, "Maybe you can understand now that my friends are willing to accept challenges from you ... but they have already taken enough needles and shots. I'll let them vote later – maybe they'll decide not to give you the two big shots, if you'll promise they won't be getting any during their challenge in a few weeks."

As I headed to the chair to retrieve my clothes, Kelly – in a bit kinder tone, now – said, "No, Sam. It's your birthday: You can stay in your birthday suit." We all laughed. Now that the shots were done, it was starting to feel like a fun birthday party, again.

CHAPTER 10: BIRTHDAY SPANKING REDUX

I asked Sam to sit on the chair kitty-corner to the couch, and he retrieved a towel from the bathroom, covered the chair, and sat down, looking a little uncomfortable that he was in his birthday suit, while the rest of us wore fancy dresses; this despite his openness, and the fact we'd spent my entire birthday nude with each other.

Smiling, I turned to my friends, "I thought we could give Sam a short break, before his next 'challenge'." They nodded. Sam looked at me questioningly, but he would just have to wait to find out what we had planned.

"I will ask you guys a few questions. Any of you can volunteer to answer them, and your answers can be serious or joking. But, it may be interesting for all of us to hear the answers, especially Sam." My friends did not know what I would be asking, and I hoped to receive candid answers from them.

I looked down at the sheet I'd printed. "First, please finish this sentence: 'The first time I met Sam ...'"

Linda immediately raised her hand, and I pointed to her. She smiled, ".. he shocked me by suggesting that he give me a 'birthday spanking' that same night!" Julie and I laughed; Kathy had been in Mexico at the time, but we'd all related the story to her.

Then, Julie piped up, "... I wondered who this old guy was with you, and why you were squealing, every time you started to talk." Yes, Sam had asked me to insert that crazy remote-controlled vibrator, while we sat in the booth of the fancy French restaurant, and he'd triggered it when I tried to reply to Julie's and Linda's questions.

Kathy volunteered, "... I nearly cracked-up, seeing him in his tiny European-style underwear." Even Sam had to laugh at that one. My friends were all smiling, and nodding, awaiting the next question.

I continued, "OK. Fill in the next line: 'I wish I had a picture of the time ...'"

Julie immediately answered, "... you came outside in the Victorian dress Sam had bought as a costume for your birthday party, and you first saw him dressed as a pirate!" Again, we all laughed, everyone nodding.

Sam said, "Well, actually, I do have video of most of the party ... but I've never looked at it. I don't know if the cameras caught Kelly's expression." My friends were a little shocked to hear that they'd been recorded ... and I'm sure their minds were considering the possibility that Sam had a video of the spank poker game.

Sam added, "Maybe, I should edit some of the footage together – that would make an interesting show for you guys." Linda groaned, and shook her head. I think we all agreed that it would be interesting, but didn't feel like we had to see it, anytime soon.

Continuing down the list, I read, "I knew that Sam was a true friend when ...'"

This time, Kathy answered, "... he let me masturbate on top of him, without touching me inappropriately, or asking for me to satisfy him, afterward." We all flashed on the night of my birthday party, when Julie and I had been in the playroom bed, and Sam had 'made the rounds' to satisfy Linda and Kathy, in the pitch black room.

This was fun, but I wanted to get on to the next 'event'. I looked at my friends, and asked one more question,

"Finally, what are the top reasons why you are surprised that Sam made it to 51?"

Julie laughed, "Because there are only a certain number of orgasms a man can have in his lifetime, and Sam must surely have used them all up, by now." Everyone applauded, except Sam.

Sam whined, "That's just not true." He gave us the 'evil smile', "I have a *lot* more orgasms in me!" We were hysterical.

Linda gave her answer, "Because I would have thought, with all his pushing, that somebody would have killed him, by now." That was funny, sort of; Sam did push too hard. But, then, all of us had come a long way – in our openness, and in our mutual relationships – due to Sam's pushing.

Although there were several questions left, I walked over to the desk and put down the paper. Then, I picked up a small box that I'd stored in the credenza. As I walked back to the couch, I said, "Well, Sam, you wanted to have a version of this game during my birthday party ... so now we'll have a different version at yours."

Sam looked at me inquisitively, and I could see his brain processing all the things he'd planned for my party. I didn't make him wait long.

Smiling at him sweetly, I said, "I first thought we could play 'pins and tails on the doggie' ..." Now Sam sat back, and closed his eyes, probably expecting more needles. I explained, "But, as I think we can all agree there have been enough needles today ..." Sam nodded and smiled, as I continued, "We'll just have a little pet play." Sam sat motionless, waiting to hear exactly what this would require of him.

I looked at my friends, "Sam has introduced me to a lot of different fetishes, but there are also a lot we haven't tried." I smiled at Sam, "Some of them wouldn't be much of a turn-on for Sam, considering how much we've all done together, already.

For example, some men have a pantyhose fetish; we could hike up our dresses, and let Sam caress our nylon-covered legs. But we've already hiked them up in the exam room, and I don't think seeing our pantyhose is much of a turn-on for Sam."

He shrugged and nodded, so I continued, "And many men love 'up-skirt' – looking up women's dresses, and maybe taking pictures surreptitiously. But, for the same reasons, I don't think that would excite Sam very much." Sam nodded again, still waiting for me to divulge his next challenge.

"But 'pet play' is one of the kinks that we haven't really tried, yet ... although Sam introduced you to the concept of 'pony play' at my birthday party." Looking at Sam, I continued, "So, I thought it might be fun for us to have a little 'puppy' that we could play with for a while."

Sam smiled, and nodded, instantly 'getting it'; at least part of it. I instructed, "Sam, you can get in the 'chair position', now, while we have you try a few 'tails'.

Without discussion or delay, Sam turned around, getting on his knees, widening them against the sides of the chair, and putting his head on his arms, resting on the low back of the chair. He knew what to do, and arched his back, thrusting his butt into the air.

His 'package' swung beneath him, and there was no part of him left to the imagination ... although my friends had already seen him this way, so they didn't need to imagine anything.

I opened the box, and pulled out a few different 'tails' that I'd ordered from one of the Internet sex shops. There were long ones and short ones, bushy ones and thin ones, and they all had a butt plug at the end, for inserting into Sam, to hold them in place.

Handing a couple of tails to each of my friends, I put on an exam glove, and opened a small tube of KY. As I lubricated Sam's anus, my friends passed around the KY and lubed the butt plug portion of their tails. I pushed the tip of my finger down, inside him, pressing on his prostate. Sam moaned.

When my friends were ready, I removed my finger, and pulled off the glove, turning it inside-out, and putting it on a folded paper towel on the coffee table.

Each taking their turn, Kathy, Julie and Linda inserted their tails, and we discussed how they looked, as though Sam was not there hearing us. We asked Sam to shake his butt a few times, some of the longer tails swishing back and forth. We decided that Kathy's long 'tail' looked best on Sam, so she re-inserted it, and we left it in place.

I leaned over Sam, and whispered, "You're a little doggie, now. If you get out of role, you can expect to be punished." Sam began panting, nodded his head, and gave us a couple of confirming 'woof's.

"OK, boy, get off the chair. You know you're not allowed on the furniture!" Sam obediently put his legs on the floor, and backed himself off the chair. Then, he went around the coffee table on his hands and knees, smiling up at us and panting eagerly.

I handed Julie the bag of 'treats' – which really *were* treats – several varieties of Hershey's 'kisses'. Julie knew what to do. "Let's see how well this little puppy is trained: Sit, boy!" Sam sat, his tongue hanging out, and continued panting. Julie continued, "Now show us how you beg, Samo!" We hadn't actually picked a name, but that was as good as any. Sam got up on his knees, putting his arms up, and letting his 'paws' drop down; he smiled and panted.

When he saw Julie unwrap a treat, Samo barked loudly. Julie popped the treat into his mouth. Samo ate the candy and licked his lips. "Now, roll over, boy!" Samo did as he'd been told, rolling over on the playroom's Berber carpeting, then sitting up, ready for another treat. Julie unwrapped another 'kiss', and Samo leaped up to eat it from her hand. "Good boy!"

Linda got up and knelt on the playroom floor next to our puppy. She looked up at us, and said, "I love dogs. Maybe I should get a puppy?" She stroked Samo's back, and then put her hand underneath, rubbing his stomach. Samo panted, and Linda let her hand move over and stroked Samo where it counted most.

Samo rolled over, put his feet and arms in the air, and let Linda continue 'petting' him, stroking, until Samo was getting hard. Linda had seen what was in the box, and said, "I think our puppy is thirsty. Do we have anything for him to drink?"

I smiled, and pulled out a dog's chow bowl, then went behind the bar, and pulled out one of Sam's favorite beers. I spread the towel from the chair on the carpet, then put the bowl down, and poured the beer into it. Samo wagged his tail, and lowered his head to drink from the bowl. He tried lapping, but finally put his lips into the liquid and slurped it into his mouth.

Linda petted him on the back, "You like that, don't you, boy?" Samo wagged his tail again, and 'woofed' a couple of times. We thought he would finish the beer, but when there was still a little left, Samo barked loudly; repeatedly.

Linda asked, "What is it, boy? Are you hungry? Do you hear someone at the door?" Samo barked again, and then lifted one of his rear legs. Now, we knew what he wanted. Linda looked at me, and asked, "Shall I walk him?" Julie and Kathy were in stitches, as I pulled out the collar and leash I had bought at the discount store.

I walked over and fitted the collar around Samo's neck, and attached the leash. Handing it to Linda, I suggested, "Why don't you see if he heels properly?" Linda stood up, and walked across the room to the bed, Samo heeling nicely, and sitting on his haunches every time Linda stopped.

"It looks like he's pretty well trained, for a puppy!" Linda exclaimed. As she walked back, Samo in tow, she picked up the towel. I'm sure that Sam had expected – we *all* had expected – that Linda would walk Sam into the downstairs bathroom. But, instead, she took Samo up the stairs.

I shrugged, and signaled Julie and Kathy to follow me. Linda took Samo out the kitchen door to the patio, which was still wet, but it had stopped raining. I took Julie and Kathy into the pool room, where we watched through the sliding glass door.

We heard Linda loudly say, "Come on, boy!" But Samo shook his head, and pulled back on the leash. I had thought of buying a choke chain, but that could have been dangerous; we didn't want to hurt Sam – it was his birthday, after all.

Linda bent down to whisper something in Samo's ear, and Samo shook his head again, but finally walked with Linda, as she took him across a short strip of grass next to the garage, just beyond the barbeque.

Samo barked a couple of times, but finally lifted his leg and peed into the grass. Julie had her hand over her mouth, and Kathy was laughing loudly. I was amazed that Sam had actually done that for Linda; it was something beyond what I had envisioned.

When Samo was finished, Linda walked him back to the kitchen door, and then took the towel, and wiped his paws (actually, Sam's hands, knees and feet). Then, she opened the door, and Samo pranced inside, panting, as we followed them back to the playroom.

Samo sat, while Linda removed the leash, leaving on the collar. I would have to have a "Samo" nametag made that we could hang from the collar! Sam had given me the 'slave' collar for my birthday, and now he would have his own collar.

As Julie, Linda and I sat on the couch, Kathy smiled and pulled the armchair back from the coffee table. She said, "I've always wanted to try this."

We had no idea what she was talking about, until she reached under her dress, and removed her black bikini panties. Then, she hiked up her dress, and sat in the chair, her legs straddling the arms; she moved her butt to the edge of the chair, then reached down to separate her labia.

Now, we knew what she was going to do ... but it was almost unbelievable to see Kathy in this position, doing something so wild. It looked like the whole day was going to be 'wild'.

"Come on, boy!" Kathy called Samo, who pranced over to her, nodding his head, and panting. Kathy gave the final command, "It's OK. Go for it, boy!" With that, Samo licked and lapped, eventually putting his paws on the edge of the chair, so that he head was buried in Kathy's privates.

We couldn't see much – only Samo's head moving up and down and around, as Kathy lay back, her head on the back of the chair, facing the ceiling, her eyes closed.

Samo was very good at this task, even without using his paws. It probably took five minutes, but Kathy was now panting, thrusting her middle toward Samo, and licking her own lips, eyes still closed. Finally, she emitted a keening tone, obviously unabashed, as we watched silently.

I noticed that Julie had her hand under her dress, and Linda's mouth was hanging open. It really was a hot scene, watching Kathy get off to the licking and slobbering of our new puppy.

Looking totally spent, Kathy put her legs down, her dress still hiked up to her waist, as Samo licked her face. Then, Samo woofed a few times, and pulled himself against Kathy's leg, humping it in true doggie style.

"Just a minute, boy," she said, as she smiled at Linda, and asked, "Would you please bring the towel over here?" The towel was a little wet and dirty, but Linda tried to drape the cleanest part of it over Kathy's leg.

Samo jumped up again, and Kathy reached under and stroked his hardened shaft. Then, Kathy put her arms around Samo's shoulders, and pulled him close, as he humped her leg. The panting became louder, and Samo emitted some human-like groans; but he made a token effort to 'woof', as he came on the towel. Kathy stroked his head, and rubbed his ears.

Kathy wadded-up the towel, as Samo pranced over to the couch and sat proudly, his tongue hanging out, and his panting gradually becoming less urgent.

I looked at my friends: Julie's hand was still moving under her dress, and Linda's mouth was opening and closing, her eyes showing a smile, as she adjusted her position on the couch.

She looked up at me, "That was really hot! I never thought I could be turned on by watching a dog hump a leg." We all laughed. I took the towel from Kathy, and dumped it into the washing machine, and then returned to the playroom.

I pet Samo on the head, and leaned down to kiss him, doggie-style. We licked each other's tongues, and I had to agree with Linda that it had been fun to have a little puppy to play with; at least, this one. I took off the collar, and told Sam he could stand up. Then, I held him tightly to me, kissing him fiercely, lustfully.

Turning to my friends, I asked, "Shall we go up to the pool room, now?" They got up, and followed Sam and I upstairs.

As we entered the pool room, Sam commented, "You cleaned off the desk!" Yes, that was going to be used for one of our next 'events'. Sam had stored the student desks in the garage, and the room now had a large open area, with only the large desk at one end, file cabinets along the side opposite the sliding glass doors, and the massage table centered on those doors.

I asked Sam, "Can you please take out the turntable, now? The 'Lazy Sam'?" Sam's shoulders dropped, and he stared at me, at once understanding that we were going to 'turn the table' on him, this time.

The turntable was behind the file cabinets and, fortunately, no longer strapped to the wall. Sam was able to get his arm behind the cabinets and roll the turntable out; then I helped him lower it onto the Berber carpeting, in the center of the room. Pointing to it, I said, "OK, Sam, it's *your* turn to get on the table."

He didn't look too happy, and finally said, "I don't think it will balance with all my weight on one side." That was a weak excuse.

I replied, "OK, then go get one of the cinder blocks I saw in the corner of the garage." Sam shrugged, and left, coming back into the room straining to carry the heavy block. He put it on one side of the turntable, then got into position on the opposite side. "Good boy," I said, as I put the Velcro straps around his ankles, then reached over to strap down his wrists.

Now, Sam would understand how uncomfortable it was being strapped down, while the four women had their way with him. Sam grumbled, and started to ask, 'What ...'

But I was prepared: I opened the lowest desk drawer, where I had stashed stuff bought from the Internet sex shop, and pulled out a ball gag – similar to the one that Mistress Elena had used. I walked over and inserted it into Sam's mouth, surprising him, and fixed the strap around his head, as he whimpered.

My friends and I pulled up our dresses and sat cross-legged around the turntable. This time, it would be four-on-one, rather than one-on-four; the women now in control. Julie and I spun the turntable, and it soundlessly rotated, moving Sam around the circle in front of us. I smiled, "Shall we play 'Spank Poker – Girl's Edition'?"

Julie chuckled, "That sounds like fun. What are the rules?"

I shrugged, "Why don't we play ten hands of five-card stud? We will ante up giving Sam a quick 'hand' spanking – one spank the first hand, and doubling for each additional hand." Sam was very familiar with the concept of a geometric series, and started whimpering again. Quickly doing the calculation, I realized that it might actually be too much – about 1,000 spanks in total.

I said, "Maybe, I should go downstairs and get those big shots; if Sam complains, that can be his 'corrective' punishment?" My friends laughed. But I hoped that Sam wouldn't need to get any more shots, and would agree to not give my friends shots during their upcoming challenge.

I decided to give Sam a bit of a break; "OK. Maybe we should just play eight hands. How about we each give him ten hard and quick spanks for each ante?" Then, I continued with the rules, "Whoever wins the hand will use the next heavier implement on Sam."

I turned him, so that he was facing the sliding glass doors, and walked over to the desk, pulling out the spanking implements I had stored in it. Then, I laid them out, in order of severity – first the ruler, then the wooden spoon, then the belt, then the Ping Pong paddle, then the flogger, then the hairbrush, then the tawse, and finally the thin, whippy cane.

"The number of strokes will start at 100, and go down by 20 for each next hand. When we get down to 40, the next hands will be 30, 20, 10, and 6 strokes." Sam began to whimper again, but quickly caught himself, lest I go downstairs and get the big shots, which I knew he didn't want.

My friends agreed, and we began the game, each of us giving Sam ten hard and quick hand spanks, then rotating the turntable to the next player. I watched, as Sam stiffened, and then forced himself to relax and take the spanking. I dealt the cards, and we played the first hand. Sam was watching the action, and I decided that he should be subjected to just a little more fear.

Putting my cards down, I rose, walked to the desk, and pulled out a blindfold, which I put around Sam's head, and pulled down over his eyes. I brought my phone from the desk, and took a couple of snapshots of the game – my friends sitting around the turntable, Sam's rear – sticking up and ready for his spanks, and Sam's face – his eyes covered by the blindfold, and the ball gag in his mouth.

Julie won the first hand, and took the ruler to Sam's bottom. We watched intently, as Julie gave Sam no quarter, the ruler making parallel red lines on his butt. One hundred strokes was a lot, and Sam whimpered again.

As we gave him hand spanks for the next ante, Sam made a guttural sound, and I leaned over to him, and whispered, "Do you *really* want those shots, young man?" Sam silenced himself, and we played the next hand.

This time, Linda won, and she took the wooden spoon to Sam, giving him 80 good pops all around his bottom. We got into a routine, playing each hand quickly, and following-up on Sam's bum.

Linda won again, and gave Sam 60 strokes of the belt; they were not as hard as I had expected, but Sam had plenty more coming.

I won the fourth hand, and gave Sam 40 good swats with the Ping Pong paddle. By this time, Sam's bottom was red all over, and I was wondering whether this would turn out to be his 'birthday spanking'; he might not deserve any more tonight, although I had planned something similar to what I'd received during my birthday party.

Kathy won her first hand, and took the flogger to Sam. She was hesitant, and I got up and showed her the technique, letting it circle around, left-to-right, and then right-to-left. Sam flinched when he felt the hard strokes that I gave him, but Kathy was much easier on him; even so, she managed to redden Sam's hips, as well as his upper thighs, with her 30 strokes.

Then, Linda won another hand, and gave Sam 20 strokes of the hairbrush, alternating sides. Sam was groaning continuously, now, even through the hand spanking we gave him for our next ante.

I won the next hand, and gave Sam ten firm, but not very hard strokes of the tawse. That could be a very severe implement, but I went easy on him, and I'm sure he knew it. It didn't take much, now, to give Sam some pain, his bottom a deep red all over.

Julie won the last hand, and I showed her how to adjust her position so that the cane didn't whip around to Sam's hip. I decided to count down each stroke: 3, 2, 1, Now! Julie did a good job, giving Sam a definite sting, but not overdoing it. We were all impressed with what Sam took – although he had been strapped down, so had little choice in the matter.

And I was sure that we were all now feeling a bit sorry that we'd given Sam so much pain on his birthday. I took my friends into the kitchen, and proposed that the only 'birthday spanking' Sam would take later would be over my lap, using my hand. They readily agreed.

Sam was now beyond the worst of the physical pain he would receive today; but perhaps not beyond the worst of the psychological pain, as he had at least one more 'experience' coming – something that I was sure he didn't expect.

We went back into the pool room, and I took the blindfold off Sam's head, and decided to also take out the ball gag. Julie turned Sam to face her, and bent down to kiss him on the lips. "Did you like our 'spank poker' game, Sam? Now, you know what it feels like to be strapped down to this turntable thingy, and be spun around." Sam didn't say anything, just nodded his head.

I said, "OK, girls, do you think Sam has had enough on the Lazy Sam? Maybe we can give him some good prostate stimulation, and let him come again ... if he wants to?"

Everyone nodded, except Julie. "Don't you think he should be cleaned out, first?" Kathy was nodding, and Linda cracked a big smile, realizing that Julie was suggesting that Sam get an enema.

The ball gag out of his mouth now, Sam complained, "Please, Kelly ..."

I spoke to Sam quietly, and seriously, "Let me ask you, Sam: Don't you plan to give my friends an enema when they come over in a month?" I didn't know exactly what Sam had planned, but was sure he would 'clean them out' thoroughly at some point during the day.

Sam let his head drop, his forehead against the plywood of the turntable. "Well, uh ..."

I smiled, "Just as I suspected." I turned to Julie, and said, "I'll get it ready." I went down to the exam room, and prepared a bucket of lukewarm saltwater, and brought it, and one of the huge 200cc syringes, back up to the pool room. This would be similar to the enemas that Sam, Julie and I had experienced, in preparation for our ménage.

I placed the bucket on the turntable next to Sam, and drew about six ounces of water into the syringe. Placing it against Sam's butt, I quickly injected the warm liquid into him. Then, I handed the syringe to Julie, and turned Sam into position in front of her.

The process went quickly, as we each injected Sam and turned him to the person on our right. After a dozen syringes of water, Sam groaned, but we continued until he had taken 18 injections – about three quarts of liquid.

"Shall we let Sam expel it in the bathroom up here, while we visit?" Sam groaned again, and I offered, "OK, Sam. You can either do it while we all listen, or one of my friends can take you to the downstairs bathroom." Sam moaned, and said, weakly, "I'll use the bathroom downstairs."

I looked around the turntable at my friends, and Linda stood, "I'll take him." We unstrapped Sam, and he stood unsteadily; then, Linda took his hand, and led him downstairs.

I really hated getting enemas. But Kelly was right: Cleaning the girls out would be important to one of the main events that I had planned for their challenge. Good weather would also be important, as some of the events would need to take place in the backyard.

Linda held my hand firmly, as she led me down the stairs, and into the bathroom, and I realized that she was holding something in her other hand. She was nice enough to close the door behind us, but when I went to sit on the toilet, she said, softly, "Sam, you're going to have to wait; I need to use it, first."

I wasn't cramping anymore, and nodded, expecting Linda to pee quickly, and let me have my 'release'. She reached under her dress, and lowered her pantyhose, and panties. Then, she said, "Please turn around, Sam." When I cocked my head, she explained, "I don't mind peeing in front of you ... but I have to change my tampon. And, I'd appreciate it if you could give me a little privacy for that."

I nodded and turned around, facing the door, getting into the standing position. Linda did her thing, while I stood there, waiting. She flushed the toilet, and came around in front of me, her undergarments still around her thighs.

As she pulled up her underwear, and then her panty hose, she said "I'm sorry, Sam. Both Julie and I still have our periods. I had hoped I could give you a nice sex experience as a birthday present ... but maybe I can make it up to you when we come over in a few weeks?" She washed her hands and dried them, then leaned forward, giving me a light kiss on the lips.

Smiling at her, I replied, "That's a very nice thought, Linda. But you don't have to be sorry about anything. You guys are being great today, and I don't expect sex from anybody ... except Kelly. And, fortunately, she doesn't have *her* period today." I sat on the toilet, and let the water rush out of me.

A year ago, I would have been quite embarrassed doing this in front of anyone; but Kelly had increased my openness – probably as much as I'd increased hers.

I really liked Linda; perhaps she was a little overweight, but she had a great personality, and she was really a down-to-earth woman. She had been much more open – both in terms of her body, and in terms of doing sensual and sexual things – than I had expected when I'd first met her. And, I know that she had impressed Kelly, Julie and Kathy with her degree of openness, in her discussions and in her actions.

All of Kelly's friends had been great, each in her own way.

In between floods, Linda asked, "So does your bottom hurt, Sam?"

She knew it did. "Of course. But at least I set a good example for your challenge."

Linda laughed, "Not really; you were strapped down, blindfolded and gagged. So you didn't have much choice other than to take it. I know that you're turned on by us submitting voluntarily, holding ourselves in position, and not complaining."

She looked at me, "We've heard a lot of whining from you today." Then, she chuckled, "But I think it's great that you're willing to submit, also. I know that Kelly is turned on by having you submit to things that would embarrass you."

As I finished up, she said quietly, "And I think Kelly has a few more 'challenges' for you, today."

I could not imagine what they could be, and didn't really want to think about it. I was glad that my 'real' birthday had been yesterday, and that Kelly had treated me nicely. Today, I was willing to submit, at least in part because I had made Kelly and her friends submit on her birthday. Fair was fair.

Sam and Linda came into the pool room, Linda smiling, but Sam not so much. There was really only one more 'event' planned, and then we would pick up the dinner, and enjoy the evening together; perhaps with one last 'birthday spanking' for Sam.

"Are you ready for one more challenge, Sam?"

Sam shrugged, "Not really. But since I love you and your friends so much, I am willing to submit." Then Sam raised his eyebrows, "Just *one* more challenge?"

I nodded, wondering whether I had forgotten anything. "I think so. We'll see." Sam's shoulders sagged again.

Turning to my friends, ignoring Sam, I said, "So my Internet research on kinks and fetishes revealed one more thing that might be interesting for us. Kind of like having Samo, our little puppy." My friends did not yet know what I'd planned. I pulled a box out from under the desk and, as I opened the top, I looked up at Sam, "Are you familiar with 'ABDL'?"

Sam stared at me, and I could see the cogs turning in his brain, but he shrugged, and replied, "I think I've heard of it, but I can't recall what it means."

I smiled sweetly at him, and pulled the top item from the box, "It stands for 'Adult Baby Diaper Lover'; part of a fetish called 'age play'." I held up the adult-size diaper, and Sam gave me a withering look, then covered his eyes, as my friends laughed uproariously. "I think it'll be fun for my friends and I to take care of a baby for a few hours."

Now, Sam exploded, "A few *hours*? Kelly, don't you think I've taken enough today?" Sam looked at my friends, "I've been a good sport ..."

Julie smiled at Sam, and replied, "So have we."

I spread a towel over the desktop, and pointed to it, "Up here, young man." I chuckled, and rephrased my request, "I mean, little baby."

Sam shook his head, and hopped onto the edge of the desk. I pulled out the next item, which was a bonnet – meant for a child, and way too small for Sam, but I put it on his head, and tied it under his neck.

Then, I pulled out another package and opened it, holding the pacifier in front of Sam's mouth. "Open!" Sam opened his mouth, and I stuck the pacifier into it. Sam closed his eyes and shook his head. My friends were now gathered around the desk, and couldn't help but laugh. Sam was still nude, and really looked like a huge baby.

"Now, lie down, and we'll get you powdered and diapered."

Sam sputtered, the pacifier in his mouth, "Kelly ...", but when my friends gave him a dirty look, he laid back on the towel.

"Julie, can you please help me?" Julie and I lifted Sam's legs, and Julie held them up, while I took the bottle of powder from the box, and sprinkled it liberally on Sam's butt. "Kathy, can you hold his buttocks apart for me?" When Sam was well-separated, I sprinkled more powder on him, and rubbed it in.

Then, I had Linda come around to the opposite side from Julie, and they lifted Sam's legs until I could slide the diaper under him.

Sam had given up the fight, and was playing it up, sucking on the pacifier. As I tried to figure out how to work the diaper, Sam let the pacifier slip out of his mouth, and started crying like a baby.

"Wah, wah ..." Sam reached up and rolled his fists in his eyes. I finally got the diaper on him, making sure it was tight ... fluid-tight. Julie and Linda let go of Sam's legs, and he bent them, bringing his knees almost to his chest, as he cried. Kathy stuck the pacifier back into Sam's mouth, and he quieted, sucking on it, and looking around the desk at us with wide eyes.

I pulled out a baby bottle, and ran into the kitchen, where I filled it with one of Sam's beers. Not quite baby formula, but perfect for my 'big baby'. I laughed, thinking 'my little puppy' and 'my big baby', and realized that at some point Sam might be 'my li'l pony'. I took the pacifier out of Sam's mouth, and he held the bottle, trying to suck out the beer. Evidently only a tiny trickle was coming out.

I whispered to Sam, "We can't actually carry you, so please get off the desk, and down onto the floor." I had Julie and Kathy help me roll the turntable behind the file cabinets, while Linda disappeared upstairs. I gave Sam a baby rattle, which he shook, as he sat on the floor.

A few moments later, Linda reappeared, wearing a weird outfit: Black running shorts, and a white blouse, but still in her pantyhose. She smiled at us, and sat down next to Sam cross-legged.

"OK, little Sammy, let's get you into my lap." Sam sat in Linda's lap, and Linda surprised him by unbuttoning her blouse — no bra underneath, her large breasts now accessible to 'little Sammy'.

We all laughed; it was quite a sight. Little Sammy smiled, and immediately dropped the rattle, taking one of Linda's breasts into his mouth, and sucking. He closed his eyes, and Linda rocked — as much as she could with big Sam's weight in her lap.

I looked at my watch, and made an executive decision. I announced to everyone, "I had planned for Sam to finish a beer – or two – then lie on his stomach on a pillow, while we visited. Eventually, he would need his diaper changed." My friends were smiling, while Sam opened one eye, and shook his head, Linda's breast still in his mouth.

"Then, I thought we could bathe him, in the upstairs bath tub." I looked at Sam, and smiled, "And your reward, baby Sammy, was that the four of us would go topless, so we could bathe you without getting our dresses wet."

There was no reaction from Sam, so I continued. "But it's time for us to order dinner, and I'm not sure we want to wait until you pee in the diaper."

Then I gave Sam the evil smile, and added, "And, we all watched our little puppy, Samo, pee in the yard." Sam opened both eyes, surprised to hear this; he had thought that only Linda had seen him pee in the yard, his leg up like a dog.

Concluding, I said, "So, maybe we won't change your diaper." Sam smiled, and I added, "And, if it's OK with my friends, maybe we can all go in the sauna after dinner – and have a more 'normal' evening to finish your birthday party." Now, I gave Sam the evil eye, "Except for your birthday spanking."

Before I could ask my friends if they were OK with the revised plan, Linda said, alarmedly, "Baby Sammy is looking a little pale, and his forehead is hot; maybe he has a fever?" We all laughed, knowing what this meant.

Sam just stared up at Linda, who couldn't keep her laughter inside. As she broke into a belly laugh, Sam bounced around in her lap.

I said, "OK, baby Sammy, let's get you back up on the table. Then, we can take off your diaper, and take your temperature." This idea did not bother Sam in the least.

He crawled out of Linda's lap, and over to the desk, then stood, while we took off the diaper, and then he lay across the towel-covered desk on his stomach.

I ran down to the exam room and brought back the rectal thermometer and a tube of KY, handing them to Kathy. As Julie and Linda pulled Sam's buttocks apart from each side, Kathy smoothly inserted the thermometer.

I told her, "Sam thinks there should always be good contact inside, so we'll move the thermometer around a little." I proceeded to move the thermometer in and out, and around in circles, Kathy finally taking over the task.

When we were done, Sam looked over his shoulder at me, "May I dress for dinner, please?"

I laughed, and nodded, but Linda had other ideas. "Sam, don't you want to get washed up, before dinner? I know we're going in the sauna later, but why don't you let me bathe you. And, if you need it, perhaps I can release some of your tension?"

As Sam nodded, Julie and Kathy laughed, and I suggested they come with me to pick up our dinner from the Chinese restaurant.

As the others left for the restaurant, Linda led me downstairs again. We went into the shower room, and Linda took off her still-open blouse, her running shorts, and her pantyhose and panties. I turned on the shower, and adjusted the temperature of the rain shower and leg jets. Linda stepped in, and began bathing me, thoroughly and lovingly.

When she got down to my privates, she looked up, smiled at me, and said, "Kelly suggested that we 'reward' you, if you took your challenges well."

She took me in her hands, and stroked me – obviously intending to get me 'up'. I responded easily and, after washing me, she put me into her mouth. I rocked fore-and-aft, as Linda did a creditable job of giving me oral sex. She took me out of her mouth, and stroked me expertly, and my cum spurted across the shower. We hugged, and Linda continued bathing me, slowly and sensuously.

I offered to bathe her, but she declined, suggesting that I could do that after we all came out of the sauna, after dinner. I made sure that the sauna temperature was set properly, and we dried off, standing together next to the chaises in the shower room.

Before dressing, I took Linda in my arms, and hugged her. We held each other, cheek-to-cheek for a long while.

No words were necessary. Linda knew that I appreciated her attention, her openness, our intimate contact, and her sexually satisfying me.

Linda gathered her clothes, and we went upstairs together. I went up to the guest bedroom with Linda, and stood in the doorway, while she dressed, putting on plain white bikini underwear, a white bra, her white blouse, and a grey wrap-around skirt with a white palm leaf pattern.

Then, she came with me into the master bedroom, and into the closet, where I donned a pair of my European underwear, a comfortable Hawaiian shirt – also sporting a palm leaf pattern, and my usual black dress slacks.

We went downstairs into the playroom, and I opened a bottle of white wine. By the time I'd poured two glasses, we heard Kelly, Julie and Kathy coming through the front door.

We went upstairs, and helped arranged the dozen or so boxes of food on the kitchen table. Again, we had a magnificent buffet spread, but this time we used real china for our unreal Chinese dinner.

We ate in the dining room, taking up only half the table; the last time Kelly and I had eaten in here was the Christmas dinner with our families. I smiled, as I looked around the table at Kelly and her friends; this was another kind of family: Intimate, caring, and loving, although none of us were related, genetically.

I toasted everyone, and thanked them for coming to my birthday party. Kelly chuckled, and raised her glass, telling her friends something I'd said a few times – that it was nice to be thanked by someone, after she'd spanked and challenged him.

My bottom could still feel a dull pain from the spanking, and I was still a bit embarrassed that everyone had watched me pee like a dog, and wear a diaper. But I had also been rewarded by Kelly's friends. I'd had three orgasms in the past six hours, and was pretty certain that there would be more before the end of the evening.

After dinner, we went downstairs to the playroom, and sat around the coffee table, on the couch, loveseat, and chair. It looked more like a formal party, now that Sam was dressed.

In her usual direct way, Linda turned to Sam and asked, "So Kelly tells us that you want us to submit to another one of your 'challenges'. And she says that we'll probably be embarrassed. Haven't we already proven that we're willing to be 'open' with you?"

Sam thought for a moment, and replied, "Yes, Linda. You guys have been incredibly open, in playing with Kelly and I. There's really nothing that you have to 'prove'. But it still turns me on to see how people will react to unexpected challenges. And there are always more kinks and fetishes to explore ... although there are also some that I would never be interested in trying."

Linda looked dubious, so Sam explained, "For example, I don't like the idea of someone peeing on me – it's called 'golden showers' or 'watersports'; and certainly not anything to do with excrement; I would have rebelled, if Kelly had wanted me to poop in the diaper."

Linda wrinkled her nose in disgust, "Yuck!"

Sam nodded, "And I'm not into humiliating anyone – or being humiliated by them: Having to lick their shoe, or things like bukkake, or omorashi." Now, Kathy cocked her head, and looked at me to see if I knew what Sam was talking about; I didn't.

Sam smiled, "Doing things like several men ejaculating on a woman ... or forcing someone to hold their urine until they're really uncomfortable. And, I'm not into abuse or torture; or anything really dangerous, like asphyxiation or scarification.

"All of my fetishes ... well, at least most of them, are a turn on for me when done with dignity and respect. And consensually."

My friends were still dubious about these things. Sam continued, "I would never tie you up and *force* you to endure something that you hated." Sam chuckled, and looked at Kathy, "Although I might try to get you to accept things that you never liked – like taking a shot."

Now, Sam looked at me, "And Kelly is turned on by some of the same things. She has been on a mission – over the past year – to get me to open up to things I didn't like, or was embarrassed about. Like being on the toilet – for example expelling the enema in front of Linda.

"Or," Sam now smiled at me, "being intimate with another male."

Linda gasped. I wasn't sure that Sam was ready to share this, but I turned to my friends, and announced, "Yeah. Sam's really hung up about homosexuality, even though one of his sons is gay. But we recently got together with my friend, Fiona, and her fiancé, Justin, and had a pretty close 'couples' experience."

Now, Julie was staring at me, and smiling. I explained further, "Sam actually let Justin go down on him!" Sam winced, but my friends were grinning.

Sam coughed, "But there *are* a lot of different things that I *would* try with women – like tickling, or mud wrestling, wearing latex, or mummification." Sam glanced at me with a smile, "And Kelly and I haven't even tried shibari or kinbaku, yet."

Kathy's eyes went wide, and she stifled a giggle. Then, she chuckled, "Well, I wouldn't mind some tickling. And, I'd take you on in a mud-wrestling match, any day ... although you'd probably win."

Sam nodded, "OK, Kathy, you're on. Maybe not the next time we play, but I look forward to tickling you until you can't stand it any longer." Sam raised his eyebrows, "And, I'd *love* to mud-wrestle you! We'll have to plan on it, sometime."

Sam sipped the Diet Coke he'd brought down from the kitchen, and asked us if we wanted anything to drink. Everyone shook their head.

Linda blurted, "I'm holding out for the bubbly." Neither Sam nor I had mentioned Champagne, but it was a good idea. I was sure that Sam had some in the bar fridge. I looked at him, and he rose. saying, "I think that can be arranged."

As he went behind the bar to open a bottle of Schramsberg sparkling wine, Julie asked, "But what is 'kinbaku' and 'shibari'?" Kathy suddenly smiled again and, uncharacteristically, put her hands over her face.

Sam lined up glasses on the bar, and opened the bottle, as he answered Julie's question, "Shibari is tying people up. And, Kinbaku is the same, but usually meant to be artistic and intricate erotic bondage, sometimes with very fancy knots and rope work. And, sometimes, with the tied-up person being suspended in the air."

Linda put her hands over her face – the first we'd seen that gesture in a long time. Sam handed a glass of wine to each of us, and sat back down on the chair.

"Getting back to your upcoming challenge, most of it is catching you guys up to Kelly, in terms of learning my preferred formalism of spankings – the positions and implements ... although you guys tried most of them on me, today.

"And even though I spanked you lightly a few times during Kelly's birthday party, none of you has been punished to the point of getting turned on enough to come. Well, except Linda." We all smiled at her, and her cheeks flushed, as she looked down at her wine, and ran her finger around the rim of the fluted crystal glass.

We all toasted Sam, the pervert, and sipped the wine. Somehow, Sam never seemed to run out of ideas, or fantasies.

Then, I brought up another idea – something, now that I thought of it, I was surprised Sam hadn't asked for, already. Turning to my friends, I said, "Another thing Sam enjoys is hearing about women's fantasies. Maybe you guys can share some of yours?"

Linda looked up, and said, loudly, "Well, I've already shared mine. And, Sam made it real. It was hot!" We all laughed.

Julie said, "I'd like to be fucked by several men – at least three – all coming in me and on me. Forcing me into positions where I could satisfy three or four at a time." She sipped her wine, and appeared to be done, but then added, "But, I have to admit, the ménage with Kelly and Sam was hot – especially, when I pegged Sam, while he fucked Kelly in the ass."

None of us laughed at this – the image was just too powerful, and I knew that Sam, Julie and I were all visualizing the scene.

Kathy asked, "You 'pegged' him?"

Julie nodded, and explained, "I was wearing a strap-on, with a huge dildo." Linda had put down her glass, and had both hands over her face, again.

Julie continued, "While Sam was doing anal with Kelly, I stepped up behind him, and shoved the dildo into his ass." Julie smiled at us and sipped her wine, as if she were just talking about the weather, or a sale at the mall.

Continuing, Julie explained, "As Sam moved back and forth inside Kelly, he was moving 'forth and back' against me, with the dildo sliding inside him." Julie looked at Sam, and said, "That had to be a pretty stimulating experience for your prostate."

Sam swallowed some wine, and replied, "Yes. It was."

I turned to Kathy, and asked, "What about your fantasies, Kathy?"

She sneered, "My fantasy is to ride into the sunset with a macho guy who really cares for me, and takes care of me." She looked down, and back up at us, "And doesn't cheat on me." Again, we weren't laughing.

It was time. I asked Julie to help me upstairs, and we took out the birthday cake and stuck in 51 candles. Strangely, Sam had bought an ordinary supermarket white cake, decorated with pink roses and green leaves of icing.

We lit the candles and, with Julie carrying the plates and forks, and me carrying the cake, we walked down the stairs, and began singing 'Happy Birthday'. We put the cake in front of Sam on the coffee table.

When the singing was done, I announced, "I'll be giving Sam his birthday spanking in a minute. Just a nice, hard over-the-knee hand spanking." I smiled at Sam, and looked back at my friends, "And then, I'll take the hairbrush to his butt, giving him a stroke for every candle he doesn't blow out on the first try."

Sam groaned, but he was smiling. And, I was kidding him, although he didn't know it. He took in a deep breath, and blew, blowing out all but seven or eight candles. Then, he looked up at me guiltily, and blew again, this time extinguishing all the flames.

I went over to the small round table on the other side of the room, next to the spanking chair, and pulled a hairbrush from the drawer, then dragged the chair over to near the coffee table. Sitting down, I smiled sweetly at Sam, and patted my lap.

Sam stood, and stepped to my right side, unfastening his belt, unzipping his pants, and then pushing them down, along with his underwear. Then, he draped himself across my lap, his cock pressing onto my right thigh.

A moment later, he squeaked, "I'm ready for my birthday spanking, now, Miss." His bum was still a little red, but as this was only going to be a hand spanking, I intended to make it good. I smiled at my friends, and they smiled back at me, intently staring at Sam over my lap; Linda nodded.

With no further warning, I lifted my hand, and began Sam's spanking, raining spanks onto his butt as hard and as quickly as I could. The whole thing – 51 spanks – probably took about half a minute. Sam bounced around a little, surprised at the hard and fast spanking, but stayed in position, only breathing a bit heavily after the loud clap of the last spank had died out.

I put the hairbrush on his now-quivering bottom, and said, "You did very well, young – or, now, 'not so young' – man! I've decided not to punish you for your lack of wind power ... but I *am* going to give you the three last strokes with the hairbrush."

Turning to my friends, I said, "You guys can call them out." I lifted the hairbrush, awaiting the signal.

Together they yelled, "One for good health!" I brought the hairbrush down on Sam's bum, but not particularly hard. I was sure that he would be relieved. Then, "One for good wealth!" Another stroke of the back of the brush, on the opposite side. And, finally, "One for long life!" This time, I gave Sam a more serious swat with the hairbrush, and his bottom jiggled, but he still didn't make a sound.

I patted his bottom, "You may get up, now. Let's eat some cake!" Sam slipped off me, and stood, pulling up his underwear and slacks, tucking in his dress shirt, and re-fastening the belt. He had been slightly hard, and I'd half expected him to say, 'Take me to my boudoir ... and let *them* eat cake!'. But he just bent down, and kissed me sweetly.

Then, we cut and served the cake, and indulged. It may have been a commercial birthday cake, but it seemed to go very well with the sparkling wine. I was sure that we were all enjoying it.

Julie ran upstairs, and brought down the birthday presents my friends had selected for Sam. Julie gave him a dildo set, angled for optimal male stimulation. Linda presented him with a beautiful, modern-variety 'school paddle', made of clear plastic, holes drilled through it, with a rubberized grip. It was only ¼" thick, so would not be as severe as the traditional hickory ones.

And we learned why Kathy had smiled, when she handed Sam her present. Unwrapping it, Sam held up a large book, with an image of an intricately-tied and suspended woman on the cover. The title was 'The Art of Kinbaku'. We all laughed, and Sam nodded, "Thank you, everyone!"

Most of my presents to Sam were very minimal, compared to the ones he'd given me: Several pairs of sexy European underwear, and a very nice, velour robe that Sam could use instead of the generic ones stored down by the sauna. Over the left breast was monogramed, 'Sam', in gold, and on the back was a stylized 'Superman' logo, also in gold.

I had actually bought myself one, also, with my name embroidered on the front, and the same logo on the back. Sam hugged me, and my friends applauded.

As he was about to stand up, I said, "But, Sam, there's just one more thing ..." Sam looked at me curiously, and I handed him a small, wrapped box. I watched, with bated breath, as he opened it, and his eyes just about popped out of their sockets.

He held it up for everyone to see. "It's the new Apple Watch! That's incredible!" He leaned over and kissed me. "I thought these were in short supply, almost impossible to get?"

I smiled at him, and said, "I've been thinking about your birthday for a long time. I placed the order the first day they went on sale. And I *still* wasn't sure it would be delivered on time." Smiling at him, I added, unnecessarily, "I hope you like it."

It was the stainless steel version, with Milano band – very stylish, in addition to the techie kind of thing that Sam loved. Sam put it on, and showed everyone.

I was happy that I could make Sam happy. And I hoped that the birthday party had made Sam happy, despite the challenges we had thrown at him.

I wasn't sure that any of us were up for the sauna, and I thought about suggesting that we go in the jacuzzi, but when we brought the leftover cake and dirty plates back to the kitchen, I realized it was storming outside.

We went back downstairs, and I asked my friends whether they wanted to go in the sauna tonight. They all shrugged, and Julie offered, "We never got to bathe baby Sammy. Maybe we should just all get into the shower together, and give him a nice scrubbing?"

Linda and Kathy nodded, and Sam shrugged, smiling. I suggested that we all go upstairs to get undressed, and then meet back in the shower room.

Ten minutes later, the four women were bathing Sam, who stood, turning slowly, under the rain shower. We caressed his body, soap streaming down his masculine chest and firm abs, and through his ragged black triangle, then dripping from his enlarging manhood. Each of us took turns 'doing' Sam, and I wondered who would be getting him off, this time.

Kathy surprised us by asking, "Would it be OK if we didn't have Sam come in the shower ... and let me give him my *other* present?" We all stared at Kathy, and she shrugged, "Well, I'm the only guest that doesn't have her period ... and the only one of us who hasn't made-it with Sam."

Then, she laughed, and added, "And it doesn't look like I'm going to get any sex from a boyfriend, anytime soon!"

We dried off, and went into the playroom, and Sam helped me pull back and fold the spread of the king size bed, and put it on a long, low bench that was against the wall. I asked Kathy, "Do you want privacy? Or, maybe we can be a peripheral part of the action?"

Kathy smiled, "I'm open." We knew that she'd meant she was open to our being there, but that wasn't how it came out.

We all laughed, "Well, I'm glad of that!" Then, I said, more (or less) seriously, "Your 'openness' letting our puppy Samo lap you to orgasm was pretty impressive!" Maybe it was the wine, but we were all hysterical again.

Then, I remembered something ... "Hey, guys, Sam never got his big shots." Sam's head popped up; he was now sitting on the bed, and he glowered at me.

I smiled at my friends, "I think I'll give you guys the choice: We can give Sam the shots – I would suggest that Julie and Kathy do it, after Sam is inside Kathy. It's a turn-on for me to see him in simultaneous pleasure and pain.

"And, in that case, I think you should agree that he can give you one big shot," Now, I looked at Sam, "ONLY one shot – and no other needles – during your challenge in a few weeks."

Then I chuckled, "Or, we can let him off the hook – or the needle – and then insist that you guys don't get ANY shots or needles during your challenge." I didn't know which choice Sam would have made, but I would let my friends decide.

Julie said, "Sam's already gotten quite a few shots from us. But, we *are* trained, now." She chuckled, "And it *would* be interesting to give him two big shots at the same time. Kelly gave Sam shots, when he and I were having sex the first time."

She smiled at me, "I think it's something that is a real turn-on for Kelly ... or she wouldn't have suggested it."

Linda commented, "It would be fun for us ... and I don't really mind getting one more shot; I'm sure we're going to get a lot more than that when we're here next time. But it's Sam's birthday, so maybe we should delegate the choice to him?"

I looked at Sam, and he shrugged, "I don't know. My bottom already feels like a pin cushion ... but although I don't like the physical sensation, it might still be a turn-on for me; at least, when I think about it later."

Linda gave Julie and Kathy *her* evil smile, and added, "And you guys haven't experienced a really big shot: You got tiny ones at the clinic, and gave yourselves a small one today. So, it might be one last thing to experience as part of your 'training'."

Sam looked at Kathy, who sat on the bed next to him – both of them nude (as we all were), and looking ready to get it on. Then, Sam leaned over and kissed her. "If we do that, I would give you the big shot the night before your challenge."

Sam looked at me, and said, seriously, "And I promise to never ask you guys to take a shot again ..." He chuckled, "Unless you ask for it."

Then, Sam looked at Kathy, "But Kathy has been so open with us; she didn't complain about the shot training in the exam room earlier today, and now she wants to share her body with me, intimately, sexually. And, she's the one who hates getting shots; or even seeing them."

Sam breathed out heavily, "So, I will delegate the choice to *her*." That was a bit surprising, but Sam – *my* Sam – was a very considerate person, despite his perversions, and desire to see people submit. Once again, I was proud of him.

Kathy shook her head, "I don't know. I still don't like shots ... but I guess if I could give myself one, I must be getting used to it, and shouldn't make a big deal about them. I like seeing Sam get his comeuppance, but – as he said – he's already gotten a lot today, and it won't really be a big turn-on for me."

Kathy looked at each of us, "I guess, if Sam's willing to promise not to bother us with shots or needles again, it might be worth taking one more." She looked down, and shook her head, "So I guess I'll let you guys decide." The decision had now come full circle.

I offered my own perspective, "Maybe, Kathy is right: If Sam is willing to promise that one more shot for each of you will be the last of it ... then maybe it will be worth it for you." I chuckled, "And, of course, he has me to stick needles into, since he knows that I will always submit to him."

Now, Sam chuckled, "Always?" That was a good point; even I had my limits. But I trusted Sam not to go beyond them ... and, in the back of my mind, I still envisioned taking Mistress Elena's course, and challenging Sam many more times.

Julie and Linda looked at each other, shrugged, and nodded.

Then, Kathy asked, "Why don't you guys give us just a little time to ourselves, and I'll let you know when we're ready?" That sounded like a good idea. We left Sam and Kathy on the bed, and I closed the curtains; then, I went to the exam room to get the shots and other supplies, while Julie and Linda used the bathroom.

I looked at Kathy, and she smiled at me, "I hope I find a man someday, who will be as open as you ... but NOT as kinky!" She leaned toward me, and I kissed her lightly on the lips. She smiled at me, "You are an interesting man, Sam. And, you've had an interesting birthday party." Then, she inclined her head, and asked, "Has it been enjoyable, for you?"

Chuckling, I said, "I had a nice birthday, yesterday. Today was more of Kelly's idea. But it makes me happy to see her happy. And, I have to admit that I've been amazed at how much *she* could come up with ... to 'challenge' me. A year ago, this would have all been so unbelievable ..."

Kathy smiled, "For us, too, Sam. For us, too." She batted her eyes, and asked, "Shall we get started? You don't have to do this, if you don't want to."

"Kathy, you're a beautiful woman. And, since when wouldn't I want to make it with a beautiful woman?"

Unfortunately, Kathy answered me, "When you're afraid you'll get infected with an STD? When you don't want to share your body with someone other than Kelly? Or, maybe, if you think you can't get it up?"

I leaned into Kathy, and hugged her. "Maybe someday it will change, but Kelly and I have a very 'sharing' relationship. It wasn't something that I ever envisioned. In fact, a year ago I thought I would be happy just having a close, non-sexual relationship with one woman, who was willing to 'play' with me."

I had to shake my head, "And, now, I'm deeply in love with one woman, and have a sexual relationship with three others, with whom I feel very close. And I've 'played' much more than I could ever have dreamed."

I looked at Kathy and said, with mock indignation, "But I've *never* had a problem getting it up." Then, I had to slightly correct myself, "Unless, of course, I'd had way too much alcohol. And that's not a problem, tonight."

I pulled Kathy into my cross-legged lap, and hugged her, "But, it will be easier, if we don't talk, too much." Kathy nodded, and we kissed. I rocked with her, and then rocked forward, until she was laying on her back. Then, I rolled off her, and lay on my back next to her, closing my eyes. Kathy rolled against me, and stroked me with her hand.

I thought back to earlier today, when she had straddled the chair, and I had made her come using my tongue. Then, I saw the three girls bending over the exam table. And, I thought about their upcoming challenge – something that I'd vaguely envisioned, but not really planned.

Soon, I was hard, and Kathy took me into her mouth. Kelly's friends were all quite talented in using their hands and their mouths to turn on a man. I let myself relax, and enjoy the attention she was giving me.

A few minutes later, she straddled me, leaning forward, and we kissed, slowly. Then, she sat up, adjusted her position, and put me in her. Although she was well lubricated, she felt tight – in a good way. I thrusted upward, into her, as I took her B-cup breasts in my hands. Her wavy hair – light brown with blonde streaks, fell onto my chest.

Then, she lowered herself to me, and whispered, "Shall we turn over, now?" I continued thrusting, as I gave her an 'Ummm hmmm'. We rocked side-to-side, and finally all the way over, with me now on top. Closing my eyes, the feeling was glorious, Kathy's hands now holding my bottom, and pulling me to her; until she called out, somewhat loudly, "We're ready, now."

Was I ready? Actually, I *was* just about ready ... to come. I heard the curtains being drawn back, and opened my eyes to see Kelly and her friends climbing onto the bed.

Kelly said, "Please stop moving, now, Sam." It was almost too late to honor Kelly's request, but I forced myself to still, and felt Kelly's hands on my butt.

She whispered, "I'll start by inserting something that I bought for your birthday ... a 'crystal wand'. Then I'll let Julie and Linda do their thing."

I felt the angled, glass stimulator against me, and relaxed my anal muscles, letting the well-lubed device slip into me. Kelly twisted it until I moaned, the wand having 'hit the spot', and now doing it's magic. This felt really good, but I didn't want to think about the 'thing' that her friends were going to do, next.

I heard the ripping of the alcohol swab packages, and felt the cold, as the swabs contacted my bottom on each side. I closed my eyes, trying to stay still, deep inside Kathy; and, not think about what was going to happen next. I felt the minor sting of a needle on my right side and, almost immediately, another on my left side.

I decided to begin my motion again, pumping slowly into Kathy. She held my head, and smiled at me, and then we kissed ... as saline was injected, and I felt an uncomfortable pinching on both sides of my bottom.

My motion increased, as the pain increased, and then leveled. I put my cheek against Kathy's, as I felt Kelly moving the prostate stimulator around inside me.

My bottom hurt, the needles still in me, but now, all of the sensations melded, as I suddenly felt an impending orgasm approach.

I felt the needles sliding out of me, and Kelly pushing against the sensitive tissues deep inside me, as my thrusting accelerated, and Kathy put her arms around my back and pulled me even closer. My orgasm exploded, and I let out a long, involuntary, "Aaaahh" – just now realizing that there were five hands caressing my body. Kathy's PC muscles clenched me, and I continued pumping into her.

I let my entire weight relax onto Kathy, and she stroked my back. Kelly pulled out the crystal wand, and now I had eight hands moving over my body. My energy was spent, and I lay on Kathy like a rag-doll. We turned our heads to each other and kissed again, as the hands continued to caress me all over.

What an incredible experience it had been! A four-on-one group sex experience ... or maybe, it was a three-on-one-on-one experience? I now realized that I'd hardly felt the shots, my senses overloaded with everything else that had been happening. It was epic!

Too soon, I was shrinking, and slipping out of Kathy. Linda rolled me over onto my back, and Kelly cleaned me with a warm, damp washcloth. I closed my eyes. Kathy moved over, and Julie and Linda made a 'Sam sandwich', pressing their breasts against my arms, as Kelly straddled my legs, and lowered herself to me.

I was nicely 'smothered' by the women; it was a very warm experience, in every sense of the word. I opened my eyes, and Kelly smiled at me, then kissed me several times on my lips, my chin, and my cheeks. Julie's and Linda's hands were stroking my chest, my stomach, and my thighs. It was overwhelming.

"Wow!" It was all that I could say. I made an effort to express myself better, but what came out was, "Wowee!" I closed my eyes again, and felt the closeness with Kelly and her friends. Then, I opened them, and said, sincerely, "That has got to be the best climax to a birthday party I've ever experienced!" Kathy leaned over Julie and kissed me on the lips. Tears came to my eyes.

It was lame, but I said, "Thank you all, so much. It was incredible. I love you all." Kelly climbed off me, and the sheets were pulled up over all of us. The lights went off, and I was out.

At some point in the middle of the night, I woke and had to pee. The girls were still on the bed, one or two of them snoring lightly. I crawled down to the foot of the bed, and made my way to the bathroom.

When I came back, I crawled between them, and put my head on the pillow, spooning Kelly; at least I thought it was Kelly.

I woke in the morning to a still-dark room, and Kelly rolled toward me, her eyes opening, and a smile forming on her beautiful face. I raised my head, and realized the other girls must have gone up to their own beds during the night.

Kelly put her arm across my chest, and asked, "Was that a nice birthday celebration, Sam?" I smiled at her, no words being able to describe the experience I'd had. Kelly understood. She crawled on top of me, and treated me to 'wake-up' sex.

I chuckled as I'd had that thought, realizing that we'd never had to have 'make-up' sex. Despite the deepening relationship with her friends, Kelly and I had ever-increasing love for each other. And, openness, respect, and trust. No jealousies, and very few tensions.

It had turned into a unique relationship; one that we both hoped would continue forever.

CHAPTER 11: FIRST ANNIVERSARY

It had been less than two weeks since Sam's birthday party, and we were celebrating our first year of re-meeting; actually it had been a year since our first lunch at the bistro. My friends would return for their 'challenge' a week from next weekend – earlier than originally planned, with the hopes that none of them would have their period. But, I would; there were always compromises.

At least, I didn't have my period now. I was looking forward to showing Sam – again – how much I loved him, both mentally and physically. Actually, it seemed more 'spiritual', than anything else.

I'd spent a half day in the lab at school, and was now on my way back to the house. We planned to play around a little, and then go back to the bistro where we'd had our first lunch together, for dinner.

We'd agreed to not give each other presents on this occasion, except – of course – ourselves. Sam had given himself to me at his birthday party, and my friends and I had given him something back.

I realized that most women would never have shared their man, especially sexually, and especially with their friends. But Sam and I had a different relationship – one that seemed even more loving than that of most couples. A relationship of closeness, of openness, of respect, and deep love for each other.

I wasn't jealous of my friends; they were probably jealous of me. And, I was proud of Sam for opening himself to the possibility of having sex with multiple partners – something that he had been very much against a year ago, when I'd met him.

He had demonstrated that we could have a very intimate and sensual time together without having sex; which also demonstrated his control, and the level of respect he showed. But sex wasn't a big deal – as his vasectomy prevented his partner from getting pregnant, and he was obviously not infected with an STD.

I was also proud of his sexual creativity, as well as his stamina. I knew that my friends were impressed with Sam – in many ways, including his sexual prowess. And, I think they were especially impressed with Sam's considerateness, being willing and able to satisfy them, without putting pressure on them to return the favor.

When I walked in the door, Sam was waiting for me. He took me in his arms, lifting me from the floor, and spinning us around. When he put me back down, we kissed each other deeply.

"Happy anniversary, Kelly." We'd had to decide exactly which date we would celebrate: It could have been a year from my parents' party, when we re-met; a year from our first lunch at the bistro; or a year from our first lovemaking experience, when I'd come over for a long weekend with Sam.

It was hard to believe that it had already been a year since our first lunch together ... the purpose of which had been for Sam to help me with my career choices. I'd been intrigued, when Sam had suggested that we share our fantasies with each other, but put off when he'd treated me more like a child than an adult.

Sam asked, "So what would you like to do this afternoon, before we go to dinner? It's warm enough to go in the pool, if you like, and the jacuzzi is always fun." Sam looked up at the ceiling, and thought a moment, then said, "I don't think we've ever made love in the swirling water ... have we?"

I couldn't remember. "No, I don't think so. I wouldn't mind getting relaxed in the sauna, for a while, either." Sam nodded, accepting my suggestion immediately and, taking me by the hand, he led me downstairs. We undressed in the shower room, leaving our clothes on the chaises, and Sam adjusted the temperature control, before we stepped into the warm, cedar-scented chamber.

It had seemed very small, when several of us had been in here, compared to the huge saunas in Europe ... but it seemed cozy and perfectly sized for the two of us. We laid out our towels, and sat on the upper bench, as we listened to the flames of the heater starting up, and the rocks on the top of the heater crackling.

I leaned over and gave Sam a peck on the lips. "So, what do you remember about our first lunch, at the bistro?"

Sam scratched his head and smiled, "Well, the first thing, and probably my strongest vision, was of you crossing the street, as I looked out the window from the corner table. Your long hair was swinging back and forth, there was energy – vitality – in your steps, as you ran across the street.

"And then, as you approached the table, I saw your smile, your sparkling eyes, the smooth skin of your face. You were the most beautiful woman I had ever seen ... and you still are." Sam leaned over and kissed me, our mouths opening, and tongues doing a familiar dance.

Then Sam continued, "And, I remember you telling me things. Like how 'wild' you'd been as a teenager, and how your boyfriends never satisfied you, although one of them had spanked you." We were both chuckling. After all the spanking we'd done in the past year, I hardly remembered that I'd told Sam about that insignificant event.

Sam said, "And you said that you wanted adventure, experimentation, ... and 'rough' sex." Now, Sam frowned. "Actually, this is the first time in a year that I've remembered that part. We've had a little adventure," Sam smiled at me, "and quite a bit of 'experimentation' ... but I don't think I've ever given you what you asked for that day: 'rough' sex."

Sam was shaking his head, "Of course, I've spanked you and then helped you have an orgasm, or made love to you afterward, but I've always viewed sex as something caring and loving, not something that should be coarse or adversarial; although I'm aware that some women have rape fantasies.

"And *you* had your pirate fantasy – not exactly rape, but the way you described it, pretty rough before the pirate finally had his way with you."

I was nodding. And, Sam had done a good job of role-playing the pirate scene during my birthday party, even dragging me by my hair. But, as he'd said, he never really treated me rough *during* sex. Sam gave me the evil eye, and said, "Maybe, I should make it up to you ... and have some rough sex with you this afternoon?"

That sounded like it could be interesting; something different than we'd done. Which was amazing, as it seemed that we had 'done' almost everything, over the past year.

My mind filled with a blur of images of our 'playing' together – from hot wax and needle play, to electrical stimulation and sex toys. "That could be fun." I looked into Sam's eyes, "You know, Sam, I am willing to submit to you in any way you want, today. And always."

Sam shook his head, "Kelly, you might find this strange ... but I'm really not that interested in having you 'submit' to anything today. Let's just have a loving time together; maybe with a little rough sex, thrown in."

We laughed, and I maneuvered myself so that my legs were around Sam, one between him and the cedar paneling of the sauna, and the other across his lap. I lifted his dick vertically, and squeezed it against his stomach with my leg. Then, I put my arms around him, and we kissed; much more seriously this time.

When we came up for air, Sam chuckled, and asked, "So what do *you* remember, from our first lunch together?"

It was hard to believe, but thinking back, I actually remembered most of our time during the lunch being a discussion of biotech and genetic engineering, my school plans and career choices. But there *were* quite a few things I remembered about Sam, and our discussion after we'd finished eating.

"Well, I remember how handsome you were, although you seemed a little stiff." Sam cocked his head, and I added, "Until you told me how beautiful you thought I was, and that you wanted to make passionate love to me." I was laughing, now, remembering bits of our conversation.

Sam was indignant, "I never said anything like that!" He folded his arms across his chest, in a defensive posture, and his eyes told me that he was quickly getting upset.

As I laughed, I said, "Yes, you did, Sam. You told me you were heterosexual ... but then said we would probably never have sex." Sam squinted his eyes, and I could tell his brain was searching its databanks for memories of that discussion.

I continued, "You then told me there were a lot of things that two people could do that didn't involve sex, and you said that you were interested in 'fetishes'. You wanted to share fantasies, and said you would propose how we might play together."

Sam was shaking his head again. "That seems pretty 'forward' of me, for the first time we got together. I didn't *really* come on to you that aggressively, did I?"

I nodded, "Actually, Sam, you *did*. You were pushing pretty hard. At the time, I found it amusing, and just thought you were trying to demonstrate your openness. I didn't really think we would actually *do* anything together. But, I was intrigued to hear about your fantasies, especially after you said I might think you were 'psycho'.

"And I was also curious, after you told me that you defined 'sex' in a certain way, and that you wanted to sexually play, but without having sex. And, although you talked big, you seemed terrified to actually share your thoughts with me. It was confusing, but I considered you 'safe', so didn't mind having lunch with you again, to hear you out."

As the rocks on the sauna heater crackled, Sam wiped the sweat from his brow; it was getting hot in here. "It's amazing that I didn't scare you off, telling you all that."

I chuckled, "Well, you probably *would* have scared off most women. But, as you know by now, I have a lot of self-confidence; so I took it as a challenge." Now I laughed, and droplets of sweat flew from the tip of my nose, "I guess you've given me a lot of 'challenges', since then."

Sam laughed, too, and said, "And you've given me quite a few, also!" He shook his head, "Can you imagine if someone had told you a year ago about all the challenges you – and your friends – gave me on my birthday?" I shook my head.

No, I would never have believed it. In fact, I wouldn't have believed that I could be that close with my female friends; now, I'd had sex with one of them, and shared Sam with all of them. I was getting turned-on, just thinking about it. What a difference a year can make!

We exited the sauna, and took a lukewarm shower together, letting the water stream over our bodies. Wrapping towels around our waists, we went into the playroom, where Sam poured a can of low-cal lemonade into crystal glasses with tiny ice cubes from the freezer section of the bar fridge.

We sat down on the couch, and Sam asked, "So what are your most interesting memories from the past year of our being together?"

That was a good one! "Sam, there are so many memories, I can hardly organize them; and most of them are pretty 'interesting'!"

Before my brain could rewind, and pick out a few memories, Sam said, "Well, your 'first experience' here has to be one of them."

He chuckled, and offered, "I could fire up the computer and projector, and play back a few scenes from that day: How nervous you were, when I presented the 'contract'; your shock at the 'corrective' punishment you received, when you didn't follow my instructions at first; doing jumping jacks with the Ben Wa balls inside you; letting me bring you to some incredible orgasms ..."

I shook my head, "No, Sam. I really don't want to see those now." I smiled sweetly at him, "Maybe some other time." Then, I had to laugh, as I remembered, "How about when I punished *you* for bringing up the age issue, over lunch? That was pretty fun!"

Sam shook his own head, "I see what you mean. Maybe we can put off watching those videos." We were both laughing now, and remembering many other experiences we'd shared.

Sam suggested, "Let's go back for another course of the sauna, and we can share a few of our most vivid – or 'interesting' – memories?" I agreed, and we finished our lemonade, and walked back to the sauna.

It was really hot, now, and we both decided to sit on the lower bench, to enable a longer session. Sam turned over the wood-encased sand dial, the fine particles dropping in a narrow line through the waist of the glass tube.

I said, "Well, I'm sorry to say that this isn't really about you, or us ... but one of my most striking memories is watching Julie masturbate, lying over your lap after you gave her a sample spanking, the afternoon that Linda took her birthday spanking."

Sam nodded, "I agree. That was really hot. Actually, it was pretty hot having Linda volunteer for a birthday spanking, when I barely knew her. Of course, after her schoolgirl spanking experience last December, there's no doubt that she's turned on by it."

My mind whirled, "And, of course, I vividly remember our first lovemaking experience – you carrying me into the playroom, the soft lights, the Champagne, the path of rose petals (and the ones unnecessarily scattered on the bed), and that sensual music – Bolero. You had said that you wanted more than having sex with me ... you wanted to make *love* to me. That had to be the most romantic experience of my life."

Sam gave me a mock frown, "You mean, I haven't been romantic, since then?"

I slapped his thigh, playfully, "You know what I mean." Then, I thought about it, "Maybe you *haven't* been as romantic since then ..." Sam's frown returned, but I assuaged him, "But the first time is always supposed to be the most romantic."

I laughed, "Actually, I thought the pirate scene – with me in the Victorian dress, and you in the pirate outfit, pulling my hair, tying me to the mast to flog me, and then making love to me, as I bent over the boulder was pretty romantic ... even though it was in full view of my friends."

"You weren't in 'full view'! In fact, all they could see was your face." Then, Sam smiled, "But it seemed pretty romantic to me, too." He kissed me on the tip of my nose.

Then, Sam smiled, "And one of my most striking memories was you masturbating on top of me, while I was pinned to the bed, blindfolded, before we went to the French restaurant that first time. Now *that* was pretty hot!"

I smiled, and nodded. We'd had a lot of hot experiences together, over the past twelve months.

Then another thought popped into my head, "And something else that I remember vividly – again, not having to do with you – was my experience with Fiona, on the playroom bed. I guess you were there, taking pictures, but Fiona and I were totally into each other."

I couldn't help but let my hand drop, and finger myself, as these thoughts – and many others – flitted through my head.

Sam laughed, his own hand dropping to stroke himself, unabashedly, "And, although very little happened (and I couldn't actually *see* anything), another striking 'scene' was crawling to Linda and Kathy in the pitch black, and satisfying them, while you and Julie got it on, on the bed, the night of your birthday party."

Then, Sam laughed louder, and I saw that at least one part of him was serious, as his manhood expanded. He closed his eyes, obviously envisioning a scene, "And, one of the most incredible memories I have is of your friends going down on me the morning after your birthday. *That was amazing!*"

We smiled at each other, our own thoughts passing through our heads, and our own hands caressing ourselves. Then, suddenly, we simultaneously – in 'stereo' – blurted, "And the ménage with Julie ..." There had been so many experiences, but our minds were obviously on the same wavelength. It *had* been a long string of incredible experiences, for both of us.

"Sam, are we ready to get out of the sauna, and play around, a little? I'm almost ready."

Sam laughed, as we stood, and he held the smoked glass sauna door open for me. He said, "We should take a shower first. If you want, we can go down on each other." He gave me an evil smile, "But, I have a different idea, if you can hold out a little longer."

Kelly nodded, and I started the shower. We bathed each other under the warm rain shower, 'doing' each other enough to keep us both turned on, but not going too far. It occurred to me that this was almost like Tantric sex: Being brought to the edge, and then held there, not allowed to find our release, nor diminish our excitement. By the time our shower was over, we were both ready.

I whispered to Kelly, "We can take another quick shower later, and I'll brush out your hair." As she nodded, I said, in a loud, crude voice, "But now, wench, I'm taking you upstairs for some rough sex!" With that, I grabbed her hair, and pulled, hearing only a quick 'Ow!' before I made my way upstairs, Kelly in tow.

When we entered the bedroom, I pulled Kelly's hair harder, swinging her around, and then pushing her onto the bed. Before she could move, I jumped onto the bed, and pinned her down. She smiled, but then began wrestling with me, trying to free herself.

Kelly was really a strong woman, and our wrestling abilities were well-matched. She turned me over before I could flip her onto her back again, giving her a light slap on her cheek, and then letting my weight hold her down, as I forced myself on her, kissing her fiercely, biting her lip, and then moving down, and biting each of her nipples.

"No way you're going to rape me, you bastard!" She took a handful of my hair, and pulled; it really hurt! I loosened my grip on her, and she flipped us over again, her hair covering my face so that I couldn't see anything, and forcing me to close my eyes.

Kelly then kissed *me* roughly and, as I tried to kiss her back, she went down on me, putting my length into her mouth, and gently biting. "Maybe, I'll bite off this little wiener!"

"Little?!?!" Now, I was upset. Then, I had to laugh; I wasn't *really* upset. I reached up to grab Kelly's breasts, and she looked up briefly, giving me enough time to raise my knee, and flip us over again. I pinned Kelly down, her hands above her head, and my hands on them, as I again kissed her, then raised my head, and growled, a truly feral sound coming from my lips.

Kelly's eyes were wild, and then – in an instant – she was smiling, laughing. I slapped her again, a bit harder, this time, and reached for her hair, "Little!!?!?" I bellowed.

But slapping her meant I'd had to release one of her hands, and she again reached up and pulled *my* hair. I ran my nails across her chest, and down her breasts; although they were trimmed, they left long, white streaks. As I rubbed myself on her narrow 'landing strip', she scratched my back with her fingernails – which *weren't* short, and I growled again.

Kelly continued to laugh, and I pulled myself away, down her body, and lifted her legs in the air. I pushed my way into her depths. It was amazing that I was turned-on enough, but the sensual 'fighting' and my rubbing on her had been sufficient preparation.

Kelly put her legs around my back, squeezing hard. I crossed my legs, and reached down, my hands around her neck, and roughly pulled her into a sitting position, now in my cross-legged lap, as we rocked, my erection plunging deep into her warm wetness.

I held onto Kelly's hair, and growled in her face. Then, she took a handful of my hair, and growled at me. Suddenly, we were laughing, and then kissing, fervidly, savagely.

We continued to rock, our arms around each other's back, Kelly now thrusting into me. I looked into Kelly's hazel eyes, that now appeared black in the fading light of the bedroom: She was an animal, a wild, needy creature.

We both thrust toward each other, finally finding our joint release, and we alternately put our heads up and howled – like a wolf, or maybe a werewolf.

I kissed her on the ear and then, lowering my head, I bit her on the neck. Grabbing a handful of her thick, knotted hair, I pulled until she shrieked. We snarled at each other, and then laughed and kissed each other again, slowly, ardently, finally calming, and giving ourselves fully to each other.

As Sam slipped out of me, I kissed him on the nose. "Well, that was fun! Something different." Again, I had been amazed by Sam's creativity, his versatility. It had been an animalistic experience, like nothing we'd done together previously. We walked back downstairs, hand-in-hand, and took another shower.

When I turned Sam around, there were long streaks across his back, where my nails had made their mark. I washed my hair, and we sat on towels on the chaises, Sam combing the knots out of my hair, then brushing it, from roots to ends. Then, he fashioned a French braid, the best I'd ever worn.

We dressed casually, both of us in jeans, Sam wearing a Hawaiian shirt.

I put on a white blouse, leaving the top three buttons undone. It was strange to think that it would be 'sexy' for Sam, after all we'd done; he'd seen every square millimeter of my body. But the look he gave me proved that he was still excited by seeing me in a 'revealing' outfit. How funny!

Our dinner was nice, very casual. We each ordered what we'd eaten during our first lunch together – a hamburger for Sam, and a Salade Niçoise for me. Sam ordered a bottle of Merlot, probably not up to his standards, but still very pleasurable.

It would be fun to tour the French wine-growing regions together, as Sam had once suggested. In fact, he had suggested a lot of places that sounded nice – the Greek isles, Italy ...

It was a big world, and I still yearned for adventure. Maybe, someday, we could travel to India, China, Africa, South America. But, realistically, I had at least another year to complete my doctorate, and then get my first job in industry. It could be ten years or more, before I would have the freedom to travel. And, Sam would be ten years older then. I didn't want to think about it.

The best I could do was to keep a positive attitude, and work hard toward my goals. Realistically, that was *all* I could do.

As I'd told Sam when we'd had our first lunch together, I wasn't interested in having a family; but now, I realized that my body clock was ticking, and that having a family in ten years might mean *another* ten-to-twenty years being tied down.

I wondered whether I would ever be able to see the world, do the things that we were ready for, now.

I realized that I really didn't know what I wanted – except for my relationship with Sam to continue. My career was important to me, and I had no intention of giving that up to have a family.

Sam had plenty of money ... but if he had asked me to quit school and forget about my career, to travel with him, I really didn't know what I would do.

Fortunately, there was little chance that Sam would force that choice on me: He wanted to see me get my doctorate, and was as excited as I was about our business.

Hopefully, I could do it all, although it wasn't clear whether that was a reasonable goal. I was happy now, and – perhaps – that's all I could wish for; the future would have to take care of itself.

CHAPTER 12: PREPPIES

Sam and I discussed the plan for my friends' submission training experience. Sam had gotten a colonoscopy earlier this year, something that he did every five years. He wanted my friends to prepare, as if for a colonoscopy – clearing their bowels completely – but I'd objected. That was asking too much.

We'd compromised, and agreed to a 'mini-prep', where they would restrict their diet two days before the experience, then come over to the house, and take a laxative that would mostly clean them out – still very uncomfortable, but not as rigorous as actually preparing for a colonoscopy.

Sam told me that he wanted me to be prepped also, but he wouldn't require it; he said that I would be demonstrating some of the things that he would have my friends do, and that I should be prepared in the same way. I decided that if my friends were going to do it, then I would, also.

We instructed Julie, Linda and Kathy to eat lightly on Thursday, no fruits or vegetables, seeds or nuts, and they came over for dinner Thursday evening, prepared to spend a couple of nights at Sam's house. Sam made a spaghetti dinner – marinara sauce, but no salad, and popsicles for dessert. Then, my friends and I drank a cup of laxative tea, while we watched a movie on Sam's giant screen.

On Friday morning, we ate cereal, and for lunch, Sam made toast, and offered us a variety of jams and jellies. Then, we all drank a laxative solution, mixed with a sports drink for flavor. Sam gave us the rules for the spanking experience – similar to the 'contract' he'd given me before my first experience with him.

We all had iPads, and Sam sent an e-mail to us with links to videos that he suggested we watch while we were 'indisposed' the afternoon of our bowel cleansing. They were similar to the ones he'd shown me when I first came over, including spankings using various implements, and examples of some fetishes that were beyond even his limits.

We stocked the bathrooms with soft toilet paper and medicated pads. Our version of the prep wouldn't be as difficult as the one required for a colonoscopy, but it was still uncomfortable, each of us running to our respective bathrooms most of the afternoon. In the meantime, we played monopoly, only Sam being able to take all of his turns.

For dinner, Sam served a beef broth. Although he wasn't taking the laxative, he limited his diet to the same things we all had, mainly liquids, jello, and popsicles. My friends were good sports, but they were not happy, their butts sore, and their stomachs growling.

Sitting in the playroom after dinner, all of us wearing the pink tees that Sam had given us at my birthday party, we played charades, based on a list of words that Sam had devised. Then, Sam announced that it was time for the shots.

My friends nearly revolted at that point, but I reminded them that it would be the last time, and that there would be no needles during the experience tomorrow. Sam went into the exam room, and said he would call each patient in, when he was ready. We turned on the television, and watched a reality show on the big screen, as Sam made preparations in the exam room.

I walked out of the exam room wearing my white lab coat, with a small name tag that read, 'Dr. Johnson', just about the time the first commercial came on. I looked down at a clipboard, and called, "Julie!" Julie smiled at me, and stood up, then walked into the exam room. I smiled at the other 'patients', then followed her in, and closed the door.

Julie stood next to the exam table, still smiling. I explained, "I'm going to give you guys a medical check-up tomorrow morning, but you'll get your shots tonight. I'm also going to take your temperature ... rectally."

Julie shrugged, and I continued, "The shot will be a big one – like the ones Kelly and I took at the clinic before our trip; but I'll be using a thin needle, exactly the same as you guys used during my birthday party. So, the needle won't hurt much, but the injection will take a while." Julie nodded, blankly.

"Tomorrow morning, before you get out of bed, I'm going to come in and take your temperature again. Then, we'll have breakfast, and we'll finish your preparation and get started on the spanking training."

Grumbling, Julie said, "I just hope I don't have to go to the bathroom more than once tomorrow. It was a miserable experience, today."

I nodded, "I know, Julie. But I really wanted you guys cleaned out for one special 'event' that I have planned. And, you'll get to have a big lunch tomorrow – I know you'll be hungry."

Then, I instructed her, "Please lower your underwear, and lie down on the table, and we'll get started." Julie reached under her t-shirt, and lowered her white bikini underwear to mid-thigh, then climbed onto the table, and lay on her stomach.

I lifted the back of the shirt above her waist, and then lubed the rectal thermometer. "Just relax, now," I said, as I separated her buttocks, and slid the thermometer in, until only an inch was sticking out.

Then, I picked up the syringe, which was filled with 5cc of sterile saline. Pulling off the needle cap, I showed Julie the shot that she was about to get. "Are you ready for your shot, now, Julie?"

She said, unenthusiastically, "Sure, Sam."

I would be giving all the shots in the right hip. I swabbed the area, and let the alcohol dry. Then, I said, "Here it is," and inserted the needle. I checked for blood, then asked Julie, "How are you doing?"

Julie giggled, and said, "I'm fine, right now." She closed her eyes, and I began the injection.

As each cc was injected, I informed her. "That's one cc. Now, two cc." I continued, until the full 5cc was injected. "OK, Julie, you're fully injected, now. Please rate the pain."

Julie opened her eyes, "Like you said, it feels like you're pinching my butt. It's probably a 10 out of 100. It's not so bad." Then, she looked up at me, "But it's certainly not a turn-on. Are we done, yet?"

I chuckled, and pulled out the needle. "Yes, Julie. I'm just going to put a little bandaid on it, to keep it clean. I'll take it off in the morning, when I take your temperature." Julie closed her eyes again as I bandaged her, and then I moved the thermometer around, until the four minutes was up.

I pulled the thermometer out and read it, recording the temperature on her 'chart'. "You may get up, now. We're finished." Julie got off the table, and pulled her underwear up. Then, surprisingly, she put her arms over my shoulders, and kissed me on the lips. I opened the door, and Julie went back to the couch and sat down next to Kelly.

I looked at my clipboard, and called, "Linda!" Linda rose, walked over to me, and we went into the exam room, closing the door. I went through the same procedure with Linda, as I had with Julie. Linda took off her pink bikini panties, and lay down on the exam table. As I inserted the thermometer, Linda chuckled, "Well, I can't imagine that our experience tomorrow will be much worse than what you put us through today."

I moved the thermometer around, keeping Linda's large buttocks separated, and said, "I don't think you're going to have a problem with the spankings – you've already been through most of it during your schoolgirl experience. And, I fully expect you to get very turned-on by it."

Then, I explained, "The only other things will be getting an enema and your medical exam ... and there will be 'just one more thing' for you guys to do – sort of a competition, that will test your openness again. And, we'll have a nice lunch, and a special dinner."

Linda said, "Yeah. I'm already hungry." As I reached for her shot, and uncapped the needle, she added, "And I can't imagine how much more 'open' we can be; we've walked around nude in front of you, we've masturbated in front of you, you've stuck things up my butt, and you and I have even had sex."

She chuckled, and shook her head, "You know, Sam, you *really* are perverted. I've been telling Kelly that since I

317

came over that first time, when you gave me a so-called 'birthday spanking'. But, you continue to show us exactly how perverted you are. I don't know how Kelly puts up with you!"

I showed her the shot, and she just nodded. I swabbed her, and inserted the needle. Then, I let go of it, watching it wobble, as I told Linda, "Well, if *I'm* perverted, then Kelly's pretty perverted herself: She is actually turned on by many of the same things ... especially, when she's doing them to me. Like at my birthday party."

Linda nodded, and I began injecting the saline, calling out the number of cc, as I had with Julie.

When I asked Linda to rate the pain, she said, "I don't know, Sam. It's not that bad. We all get shots; it's not a big deal." I pulled out the needle, and Linda whined, "But this is the eighth shot I've taken in the past eight months ... for you."

I put a small round bandaid over the injection site, and then moved the thermometer around, watching the exam room clock.

I told her, "Well, six of them were really for you – they were a good idea medically; it was just that I was the one suggesting them. I'm surprised your doctor didn't give them to you. But doctors have to weigh the benefits for an individual patient against the cost to the healthcare system." I pulled out the thermometer, and read it.

Linda slid off the exam table, and put on her underwear. "Well, I'm going to hold you to your promise of not giving us any more shots!" With that, she walked out of the exam room, and back to the couch.

I prepared the last shot, and walked out of the exam room with my clipboard. "Kathy!" Kathy exhaled loudly, and walked reluctantly to me. We walked into the exam room, and I closed the door behind her. For the third time,

I explained what was going to happen – tonight, and tomorrow morning.

As Kathy pulled down her underwear, she looked at me, "I managed to give myself a shot, but I still think they're horrible." She lay on the exam table, and I inserted the thermometer.

I said, "You don't seem too disturbed by the needle stick. And the injection just feels like you're getting pinched." When Kathy looked at me doubtfully, I asked, "May I show you?" She shrugged. I reached over to her left hip, and took an inch of the flesh of her buttock between my fingers. "Like this ..."

I pinched harder and harder, Kathy eventually saying, "Yeah. I hate that feeling." Then, she surprised me by asking, "Sam, do we really have to do this?"

I put my hand on her shoulder, and said, "No, Kathy. You were great at my birthday party, and I won't force you to take the shot." I thought a moment, and suggested, "If you insist, you can watch me give the shot to myself."

Kathy's mouth opened, and her eyes showed her surprise. I continued, "But, if I do that, I'll ask that you watch. I won't tell your friends; I'll put a bandaid on your butt, so they won't know."

Then, I looked at her seriously, "But I *will* tell Kelly; I don't keep anything from her. I think she'll understand." I was reluctant to offer this to Kathy, both because I didn't want to be unfair to her friends, who had taken their shots, and because I wasn't looking forward to taking a big shot, myself.

Kathy closed her eyes, and shook her head. "I don't know, Sam. I guess I'll let you give me the shot." Then, her eyes opened, and she looked up at me, "But could you please do it quickly? And don't let me see it?"

I bent down and kissed Kathy on the cheek, "Are you sure, Kathy? It is not my intent to torture you guys ... just to challenge you a little."

Kathy squinted at me, "Well, the diarrhea we had today was torture. I've never sat on the toilet for so many hours in a single day."

Despite her whining, she was actually smiling at me. "OK, Sam. If we're going to do this, please do it now; and quickly." Kathy turned her head toward the wall, and put her arms around the pillow.

I swabbed her and, before the alcohol had dried, inserted the needle. I injected the saline as quickly as the small-diameter needle would allow; still, it probably took close to 30 seconds.

Kathy didn't make a sound. As I put the bandaid on her, she looked turned her head, lifting it off the pillow, and said, "Horrible."

A few moments later, I took out the thermometer and read it. Kathy got off the table and pulled up her underwear. I hugged her, and said, "I'm proud of you, Kathy. I won't make you take any more shots."

As we walked out of the exam room together, Kathy mumbled, "Thank you, Sam."

CHAPTER 13: TRYING TRAINING

Kelly and I were awakened by the alarm we had set for 6:30AM, and I tiptoed to the guest room where Linda and Julie were staying. With three thermometers, a small tube of KY, and tissues in my hand, I peeked in, and was surprised when Linda waved to me, and smiled. As I walked in, she flipped aside the sheet and blanket, turned over, lifted her nightgown, and pushed down her underwear.

I sat on the edge of her bed, lubed the thermometer, and separated her buttocks. I inserted the thermometer, and pressed the 'start' button of the 4-minute timer I had set on my new Apple Watch. I glanced over at Julie: She was still sleeping, breathing easily. When the alarm on my clock beeped, I pulled out the thermometer, and read it, then wrapped it in a tissue.

I looked over at Julie, and she opened her eyes and yawned. I held up the second thermometer, and Julie nodded; then, she turned over. I stepped over to her bed, and pulled down the covers. She was wearing nearly-transparent baby dolls, and no underwear. I lubed the thermometer, and pulled Julie's nightgown up a few inches.

I took Julie's temperature, as Linda lay on her side watching, the covers pulled up around her. Both girls were totally cooperative; but taking their temperature was not a big deal – I had done that at Kelly's birthday party, and even then they hadn't been particularly bothered by it.

We would see later in the morning how open they really were; but I doubted that they would be embarrassed by anything we would do ... at least until the 'event' I had planned for them in the afternoon. I pulled the bandaid off Julie's bottom, and said "Thank you, Julie."

I walked across the hall, and looked into the second guest bedroom. Kathy was just waking, and I waved to her. As I walked in, she sat up. She was wearing what looked like a men's dress shirt. As I began lubing the third thermometer, Kathy said, "I need to pee first, Sam."

I nodded, and she stepped out of the room, and walked down the hall to the guest bathroom. A couple of minutes later, she returned, and lay on the bed, on top of the covers. She hiked up the shirt and, like Julie, was wearing no underwear. I took her temperature, then took off her bandaid, and pulled the shirt down over her bottom.

Kelly and I took a quick shower together, and went downstairs to get the simple breakfast ready. By 7AM, we were all sitting around the kitchen table eating cereal with fresh fruit. Kelly's three friends wore the pink t-shirt they had been given at Kelly's birthday party, and white bikini underwear, as we had instructed.

As we finished breakfast, I took the opportunity to explain what we intended to accomplish today. "You may be wondering why we invited you here ..."

Linda slurped the remaining milk in her cereal bowl, and looked up, "To turn on a pervert?" Kelly and her friends laughed, but I didn't find it funny.

"No, Linda. There are several reasons. First, I think you guys are beyond being embarrassed by most things, since we've already done a lot together. If you hadn't been so open already, we probably wouldn't have been able to have this experience, today. But we're going to test your openness just a little bit more. I don't think any of you will have a problem with what we're going to do this morning."

I didn't mention what I'd planned for the afternoon. "Second, I want to 'train' you, as I trained Kelly, how I would like you to behave, when you're punished ... even if it's just for play." I looked at the blank faces around me.

"Finally, I'm hoping that, by the end of the day, you will understand how a spanking can sexually excite you. I realize that it will depend on your own views of what turns you on; for example, through our schoolgirl scene, we already know that spanking is a turn-on for Linda." She nodded.

"And, Julie has also shown us that she might get turned on by being spanked." None of us could forget Julie's masturbation performance after I'd given her a demonstration spanking ... except Kathy, who hadn't been here with us. Kelly and Linda were nodding.

"And, I'm hoping that we can turn this experience into something fun ... even if your bottoms hurt. We will start out with each of you getting the same spanking, but I'll also give you the chance to show us how much you can take. The day will turn into a competition – if you guys are 'game'."

Now, I looked at Kelly, as I told everyone something that I had not shared with her. "We'll have to see how it goes ... I'm not promising anything yet ... but I'm thinking of rewarding the winner of today's competition with a trip." Kelly's mouth dropped open.

Linda suddenly had a smile on her face, "Paris?" We all laughed.

"I wasn't thinking about Europe, Linda. Someplace a little closer ... but perhaps just as exotic, and erotic."

Everyone gave me a questioning look, and they turned to Kelly. She said, "Don't look at me. Sam hasn't discussed this with me, yet. I have no idea what he's talking about."

Kelly seemed a little perturbed, but I would certainly check with her, before I offered anything to one of her friends. "I should clarify something: I'm talking about taking one of you on a trip *with* Kelly and I. Your demonstration of openness, and training on how to submit to me ... to us ... will be important during the trip we might take." Now everyone was even more confused.

I finished my orange juice, and made one last point. "And none of this has to do with 'sex'." I glanced at Kelly, and laughed, "At least, sex as in intercourse. If you get turned on today, I hope you will let Kelly or I satisfy you ... or maybe you will masturbate for us."

Looking at each of Kelly's friends, I emphasized, "But nothing that I'm proposing – today's experience, or the trip – will be based on your willingness to have sex with me." I chuckled, "Even though I've already had sex with all of you. As far as I'm concerned, sex will always be voluntary – something that you do because you want to, not because of a competition, or a dare, or a condition." The girls nodded.

"So, shall we get started?" We got up from the table, and brought our dishes and silverware to the sink, and Kelly quickly rinsed everything and loaded the dishwasher.

Then, we walked into the pool room, which was mostly empty, but where I had set-up several special things for today's experience. Among them was the spanking chair in the center of the room, moved up from the playroom; and several sets of eyehooks mounted to the back wall, between the small bathroom and the sliding door.

Several pieces of equipment were in the corner, next to the massage table, and there were several boxes of 'accessories' under the massage table. Kelly and I had also carried the large armchair from the playroom, and the two from the living room, and they now sat next to the sliding glass door, on the other side of the massage table.

I asked the girls to line up an arm's length from each other, in front of the spanking chair. "This morning, we'll give you some 'basic training', some warm-up spankings, and a few medical 'procedures'." When Linda and Kathy groaned, I said, "Of course, not including needles or shots!"

I continued, "First, I want to confirm that you're all here voluntarily." The girls nodded, and their response was picked up by the video cameras I had mounted around the room.

"Second, I want you to each be aware that you can stop the action, if it gets too much for you, with a safeword. The safeword should be something you'll remember, and not a word that might come up in normal conversation. Kelly and I have been using 'horseradish'. You can use that, also, or pick one for yourself, if you prefer."

The girls nodded, looked at each other and shrugged. Julie said, "That sounds OK to me. I don't think I would use that word today, unless you're serving roast beef for lunch." Linda and Kathy nodded, and chuckled nervously.

"Third, I want you to know that my concept of a 'punishment' has three elements: The main punishment, any corrective punishment needed, and a corner time." Linda rolled her eyes. "The corrective punishment – if needed today – will be additional spanks with the same implement or a more severe implement."

I smiled fiendishly, "In the past, I've used needles or shots as a form of corrective punishment, but we won't be doing that today. Of course, 'corrective' means if you don't take the main punishment properly – for example, you get out of position, or don't follow my instructions precisely." The girls nodded, but appeared to be getting bored.

"Finally, the corner time is usually a rectal insertion – like a butt plug." Now Kathy looked at the ceiling. I continued, "You probably won't be having many 'corner times' today," I laughed, "But maybe a few ..."

Kelly was standing next to me, facing her friends. I smiled at her, and said, "Now, we'll show you a few of the 'positions' that you must learn. Kelly, please demonstrate the 'standing' position."

Kelly immediately put her feet a little more than shoulder width apart, stood up straight, faced forward, and put her hands on her head.

"Your hands may be on top of your head, or clasped behind your neck; or, if you get tired, you may put them on your hips. But your hands should never be in front or behind your body in this position." I looked at Kelly's friends, and said, "Please assume the standing position, now." They all complied.

"I will expect you to be in this position whenever we're doing spankings, if we haven't told you to get into a different position. Do you understand?" All three girls nodded.

"Now, Kelly and I will introduce you to some other positions, and implements. Then, we'll warm up your butts a little." I smiled at the three girls now lined up, awaiting their fate.

"You've already seen most of the implements, and felt them at a low intensity, so there shouldn't be anything surprising. I'll give your warm-ups on your underwear."

I laughed, "Of course, you guys are used to me seeing your bottoms by now ... but even a thin layer of material will give you some protection, and a little less sting."

I looked at Kelly, who was also in the standing position, and asked, "Shall we give them an OTK demonstration, now?"

Kelly smiled at me, "Yes, Sir."

She stepped to my right side, and I said, "We'll first show them the 'across the lap' position." Kelly bent down, and laid herself over me, her breasts just outside my left thigh, and her waist over my right thigh. "You can see that Kelly's head and legs are suspended in the air. I'll just give her a quick ten spanks, now."

I gave Kelly ten hard and quick spanks, and she held her position perfectly. "You can see that in this position, my hand is coming down on her bottom from above. That works OK, but if we add a "T" to the OK, we get 'OTK', the 'over-the-knee' position." Kelly groaned at my joke; nobody thought it was funny.

Kelly moved herself forward, so that her waist was over my left thigh; I straightened my right leg, letting Kelly's legs drop, her toes now touching the carpet. Kelly's head hung down, a curtain of hair surrounding it.

Looking up at her friends, I said, "In this position, I can spank her from right to left, giving more of a follow-through, the spanks coming up from under her.

"As you'll learn with the harder implements, spanks should never be given much above the middle of the butt – certainly not as high as the waist, and certainly not with solid implements, like the paddle or cane. That can cause damage, something we definitely DON'T want!"

I continued the lesson, "I will give Kelly a 'level 10' spanking, now – 200 spanks, but as it will be over her underwear, it will only count as a level 5. You guys may be surprised how much it hurts at first – except Linda; but as you start to relax and settle into it, you'll find it isn't really painful.

"We always warm the bottom with 'light' implements, like the hand, before moving on to anything more serious. Your bottom will get used to it, and even the heavier implements won't hurt that much, once you know what to expect."

I patted Kelly's butt, and looked down at the back of her head, "I'd like you each to let me know when you're in position and ready for your spanking, and to thank me afterwards."

Kelly shook her head to get hair out of her mouth, and said, "I'm ready for my spanking now, Sir."

I smiled at her friends, then focused on Kelly's bottom, as I began her OTK spanking – giving her one medium spank about every two seconds, and gradually building up to harder spanks about once per second.

After 100 spanks, I stopped and rubbed Kelly's bottom, then smoothed her underwear, as I told her friends, "You see that Kelly is remaining quiet, taking her spanking well, keeping her toes on the ground."

Kelly's hands were on the carpet, and she was being an excellent model, as I had expected. I re-started her spanking, now giving hard spanks, accelerating to about two per second by the end. The entire spanking had taken about three minutes.

Kelly tried to look back at me, but I could barely make out her face through the mass of hair, "Thank you for my spanking, Sir."

I smiled at her friends, and said, "That's how a spanking should be taken. Do you have any questions?" They shook their heads, none of them saying a word. I patted Kelly's bottom, and told her she could get up. She slid off my thigh, and stood, then bent down to kiss me, finally taking the standing position a few feet to my side.

Looking at her friends, I asked, "Who wants to go next?" I was not at all surprised, when Linda stepped forward, and immediately got herself into the OTK position, presenting her large butt to me. I folded her t-shirt back above her waist, and put a hand on her bottom.

She wiggled a little, adjusting her position, and then said, loudly, "I'm ready, Sir. You may begin." Smiling, I began her spanking, following the same routine as I had with Kelly.

After 100 spanks, I rubbed her bottom, and asked, "How are you doing, Linda?"

She chuckled, and said, "I'm doing fine, Sir. But I don't think my bottom is very warm, yet, Sir."

Now, I chuckled, and said, "Well, I'll just have to take care of that, won't I?" I re-started the spanking, giving her much harder spanks, alternating sides, and making sure that her bottom was covered, including some areas that weren't being protected by her panties.

Her butt cheeks bounced, and wobbled, but she held herself in position very well, as anticipated.

When she had received the full spanking, and I rubbed her bottom, she quickly said, "Thank you, Sir. My bottom is starting to warm up, now." We all laughed, as Linda clumsily got up, and stood before me, in the standing position. Then *she* bent over and kissed me.

When she stood back up, I said, "Thank you, Linda." Then I added, "I appreciate being kissed by a beautiful woman, but that isn't really required."

Linda looked down at me, and said, "I didn't mind it, Sir." Again, we all laughed, and Linda went back to her position, alongside her friends.

I think we were all surprised, when Kathy stepped forward, and said, "I'll go next, if you don't mind, Sir."

I looked at Julie, and she shrugged, smiling surprisedly. I replied, "That's fine, Kathy." Kathy stepped to my right side, and got into position. She made a few grunts, as I started spanking her, but she also did quite well. Of course, this was only the beginning of their warm-up, but it appeared that Kathy was going to show us all that she was enthusiastic about the experience.

Finally, it was Julie's turn. As anticipated, she also took her spanking perfectly, returning to the standing position afterward, then bending down, taking my head in her hands, and giving me an open-mouth kiss. She proudly pranced back into position, all three girls again lined up, their hands on their heads, awaiting the next warm-up.

Kelly and her friends moved the three armchairs into a line in front of the spanking chair, as I walked behind the desk and drew some columns on the blackboard – one for each of the girls. Then, I carefully drew horizontal lines, making at least a dozen rows. At the left of the top row, I wrote 'OTK', and filled in a '5' for each spankee.

When I returned, Kelly's friends were again lined up near the back wall of the pool room.

"OK. Now, Kelly will demonstrate the next two positions, and I'll give her a taste of the next two implements." Kelly got in the first position, and I told her friends, "This is the 'over-the-front-of-the chair' position."

Linda giggled, and I continued, "Kelly's feet are outside each of the chair's legs, and her forearms are down on the arms of the chair. That pushes her butt up and, because the arms are so low, forces her to bend her knees, which she has pushed against the front of the chair."

I looked at Julie, Linda and Kathy, and they nodded. "So, her bottom is now angled downward, perfect for getting swats with the Ping Pong paddle, which I will swing from low to high. I'll give her only 10 sample swats, but you're each going to get 20." I wasn't bothering with exact accounting, and would give them another 5 points, if they took the swats well.

I picked up the smooth-sided Ping Pong paddle, and placed it on Kelly's left buttock. Then, I swung it, coming up, and impacting her bottom with a 'SMACK!' I gave Kelly a couple of seconds to recover, then gave her a second swat on her right side. Looking back at her friends, I said, "I will mostly alternate sides, but every once-in-a-while I'll give two swats – one after the other – on the same side."

Kelly breathed in, and said, "I'm ready, Sir!" I paddled Kelly's bottom, over her white bikini panties, as she held her position perfectly. I gave her double swats on numbers 5,6 and 7,8, and finished with a hard last swat on each side. She quickly said, "Thank you, Sir!"

I told her she could get up, and relax, not having to get into the standing position. Kelly was being a good model, and the training wasn't for her benefit. But she would undoubtedly get turned-on, when she learned that *she* would be giving much of the punishment to her friends.

Kelly had said long ago that her friends deserved to be punished for getting her into so much trouble in high school; but our relationships were very different now, and I knew that her excitement would be in seeing her friends submit, and take part in our 'play' together.

I turned to Julie, Linda and Kathy, and said, "You may each get into position, now." The girls approached the chairs, and got into position, Kelly having to remind Kathy that her arms had to be flat on the arms of the chair. "Are you ready, ladies?" I heard a chorus of 'Yes, Sir'.

Julie was on the left, and I gave her a nice firm swat on each side of her butt. Then, I stepped to Kathy, in the center, and gave her the same. Finally, I stepped to Linda, and gave her slightly harder swats. Returning to Julie, I gave her four more swats, alternating sides; then repeated the process with Kathy and Linda. Next, I gave Julie eight swats, harder now, the two middle strokes doubles on each side. Again, I repeated this with the other two girls.

Stepping behind Julie again, I announced, "Here come the last six; I will alternate sides, and they will be much harder. But, remember, you're still wearing your underwear. The paddle will sting a lot more when given on the bare."

I quickly administered the last swats to each of the girls; although I heard a few quiet 'Ow!'s', they did very well. I glanced at Kelly, and she nodded and smiled.

I decided on one last warm-up, and told the girls, "You may stay in this position to watch Kelly demonstrate the 'over-the-desk' position, and take the tawse." As Kelly bent over the desk, pressing her chest down, and grabbing the far side, I showed her friends the leather implement, pointing out the three 'tails'.

"This can be a very severe implement, but I'll keep the strokes at a medium level, for now. Kelly will get six strokes, and then each of you will take twelve. We'll do it like we just did the paddle, starting with two strokes each, then four, and then the final six."

Walking behind Kelly, and placing the tawse across her white panties, I waited a moment, and she said, loudly, "I'm ready, Sir!" I swung the tawse, and it impacted her butt with a loud 'CRACK!'. Looking back at her friends, their heads raised just over the backs of the chairs, I saw three pairs of wide eyes. Linda was the only one smiling, Julie's face a blank, and Kathy looking concerned.

I continued Kelly's tawsing, giving her six rather hard strokes – certainly harder than I would give her friends. We were already building the tension, but I would give them a break after tawsing them – something different, while the pain in their butts subsided.

Kelly gave me a 'Thank you, Sir!", and rose to the standing position. I hugged her, and kissed her on the nose, saying that she'd done great, and could relax, now. At least, for the next few minutes.

"OK, ladies, you may take your positions over the desk, now." Kelly's three friends bent over the large wooden desk, and I pressed down lightly on each of their backs, to make sure that they were all the way down against the desk's surface.

Julie said, "Ready!", and this was followed quickly by 'Ready!'s' from Kathy and Linda. They were in the same order, but this time, I started on the right, standing behind Linda. I gave her two strokes of the tawse, and she exhaled loudly.

Then, it was Kathy's turn; when the first stroke landed, she emitted a squeal, and after the second stroke, she let out a not-so-quiet, 'Ow!' I moved to Julie, and she took both strokes well.

Julie was known for being the wildest of the bunch, but I had no doubt that I would be bringing her to her knees, very soon. I repeated the process, again starting with Linda and working my way left, giving them the next four strokes. They were now feeling it, and all of them had relaxed themselves onto the desk.

I lowered their underwear in back, and surveyed the damage: Surprisingly, their bottoms were just a nice shade of pink, not even red, yet. I rubbed each girl's bottom for a minute or so, then raised their panties and smoothed them. Finally, I said, "You're onto your last six strokes, now. Please focus on staying in position!"

Starting with Linda, I gave six firm strokes – not really that hard, but they certainly stung more than the hand spanks or swats with the paddle.

Again, the girls behaved very well, only Kathy raising her chest a couple of times, but then forcing herself down against the desk for the next stroke. I rubbed their bottoms again, this time through their underwear, and they all gave me a quiet 'Thank you, Sir'.

Walking around the desk, I filled in the chart on the blackboard, writing 'Paddle' and 'Tawse' in the next two rows, and filling-in another '5' for each of them. I then sat in the teacher's chair, and looked at the faces staring back at me. "You guys did great. Do you think your bottoms are warmed-up, now ... or should we try a few more implements?"

Kathy was shaking her head, as Julie shrugged, and Linda smiled. It seemed that Linda could obviously win the challenge today, but Julie was very competitive, and would undoubtedly rise to the challenge, if she wasn't still 'on her knees'. I chuckled.

Already by this point, I was reconsidering the reward; perhaps they *all* deserved to take a nice trip with Kelly and I?

I informed everyone that they could stand casually, and went to the massage table, grabbing a beach towel, then spreading it on top of the desk. "To prepare everyone for the afternoon's main event, I'm going to give you all a nice big enema." There were groans all around.

Even Kelly didn't know, yet, what I'd planned for the afternoon competition. I continued, "I will be using a 'Bardex' double balloon enema system."

I walked over to one of the boxes under the massage table, pulling one out, and showing it to Kelly's friends. Kelly had felt this device once, and she would now be demonstrating it, by taking an enema herself. But I would be giving her a break, as her enema would only be two quarts, while her friends would each get four quarts – a rather large amount of liquid.

Kelly got into a knee-chest position on the desk, her butt facing her friends, as I showed them how the bulbs could be squeezed to inflate each of the balloons – one inside them, and one outside, holding the device in place. Kathy again stared at the ceiling, shaking her head slowly, as Linda said, "Oh, my!"

I lubed Kelly's anus, and then squeezed the folds of the inner balloon together, spreading another dollop of KY on them, then pushing it against Kelly's ass.

It took a little maneuvering, but the balloon finally slipped into her rectum. I squeezed on one of the black bulbs a couple of times, until Kelly groaned. Then, I turned the screw to close the valve, keeping the balloon inflated inside her.

I slid the tubing a small distance forward and back, showing Kelly's friends how the balloon would retain the device inside her. Then, I squeezed the other bulb, inflating the smaller balloon against her anus.

I rolled an IV stand over to the desk, one of four I had prepared; this one had a red rubber bag containing two quarts of lukewarm saltwater, with a red rubber hose that I connected to the end of the clear tube from the Bardex.

Then, I opened the valve, and let the water flow into Kelly. Turning to her friends, I asked, "Do you have any questions? You guys will be getting yours, next." Once again, there were shaking heads, and nobody said anything; they just stared at the clear tube going into Kelly's rear, the slow flow of the solution clearly visible.

As Kelly's friends watched her take her enema, I pulled out three more beach towels, folding them into long strips, and laid them under the eyehooks I had mounted on the pool room wall. I then pulled a number of things out of one of the boxes under the massage table, and approached the girls.

"Please put these on your wrists and ankles." All three of them looked at me strangely, and I laughed, "They're just for the enemas. For everything else today, you'll have to hold yourselves in position. And, you may take off your underwear, now."

They looked at me suspiciously, but finally relented, and fastened the padded leather cuffs around their own ankles, and each other's wrists. The panties came off, each pair handed to me, and I placed them on the massage table.

Then, I brought Kelly's friends over to the beach towels, and had each of the girls lie down on their backs, their heads near the wall, and their feet pointing to the other end of the room, where Kelly was still in position on the desk.

I used a caribiner to fasten each of the rings in their wrist straps to corresponding eye hooks on the wall. Then, I brought over three leg 'spreaders', and fastened the rings on the ankle cuffs to each end of a spreader bar.

Finally, I hooked a pulley onto the top eye hook in the wall, about three feet over their heads, and ran a thin line from one side of the pulley to the ring in the center of the spreader bar, then had each of the girls lift their legs, as I pulled the other end of the line, and cleated it onto the wall.

Now, there were three females, lying on towels at the end of the room, their arms above their heads, fastened to the wall, their feet separated by the spreader bars, and their legs pulled back toward the wall, a little farther than vertical. "Are you all comfy?" I got a response of groans.

But I had made sure that I hadn't put them in an overly uncomfortable position, the most discomfort

probably being that they were now unable to move –
similar to when they were strapped down to the turntable,
during Kelly's birthday party.

One by one, I inserted the Bardex enema nozzles,
inflating the balloon until each girl groaned, then letting a
little air out, so that they would not be suffering too much.
I brought the IV stands over, the filled red bags hanging
from a lower level, so as not to make the flow too fast.

I connected the tubing, and opened the nozzles,
causing the girls to groan again. "You guys are going to be
really cleaned out!"

Linda harrumphed, and whined, "Sam, you cleaned us
out yesterday. There really can't be much left in us."

I nodded, 'Then the water should come out clear. This
shouldn't be too difficult for you."

Under her breath, Kathy mumbled, "That's easy for
you to say!" I chuckled, and went back to the desk,
squeezing the red back hanging above Kelly. It was now
empty, and I closed the valves and disconnected the
tubing. Then, I deflated the balloons, and carefully pulled
the device out of Kelly's rear.

I helped her off the desk, and she gave me a 'look', but
then whispered, "It doesn't feel too bad. Thank you for not
making me take a 'full load'."

Kelly smiled, as she turned and saw her friends lined
up near the wall, tubing running from red bags to their
rears, as they lay quietly, taking their enemas. She walked
over to them, and said, "I guess I shouldn't ask if
everything's OK."

Linda grumbled, "How perverted is *this*? And you
actually *live* with this man?" Even Julie and Kathy had
smiles on their faces, now.

Yes, there was no doubt – just looking at this set-up, and what my friends were going through – that Sam was perverted. Again, I thought 'But aren't we all?'.

Then, more sanely, I realized that he was way more 'out there' than most people could imagine. Of course, it was possible that many other men – and women – had perverted thoughts; but very few of them were able to act out their fantasies; especially, with several women simultaneously.

But my friends were special. They had endured a lot of nonsense from Sam ... and given him some back. Sam had been a good sport at his own birthday party, and my friends continued to be good sports, as they submitted to his kinks and fetishes.

Sam was now taking snapshots of my friends, in their unbecoming positions. But I had to admit that I was also turned-on as I looked at the scene before me.

Suddenly, I realized that my innards were aching, and not going to retain the enema any longer. I had planned to go to the master bathroom, but wasn't sure I would make it; so I went into the small bathroom, just a few feet from my friends, and left the door open a crack, so that they could hear what was to come, in a few minutes; come out of them.

Sam was right – the water coming out of me was clear; we had done a good job yesterday with the bowel prep. Now, we were all ready for colonoscopies.

If there had been a real medical reason for this, it wouldn't have been so bad; but it was a lot to put us through, just to play with us. Linda was unquestionably right: Sam was definitely a very perverted man. And, again, I thought: But he was *my* perverted man.

By the time I was finished, my friends were, as well. Sam removed the enema tubing, and unhooked them from the wall. Giving Sam and I both a dirty look, they marched off to the other bathrooms, one downstairs, and two upstairs.

I gave Sam another 'look', and shook my head. He raised his eyebrows, put his arms out sideways, palms up, and shrugged. I said, "Maybe you deserved to get even more challenges from us, at your birthday party?" Sam shrugged again, but this time he wasn't smiling.

Sam cleaned up everything, and washed up in the pool room bathroom. He brought chilled bottles of water from the fridge, and placed one next to each of the armchairs, which he pulled a little closer to the wall where my friends had received their enema.

He pulled the straight-backed chair into the middle of the room. Then, he went to the blackboard, filled-in the next row, 'Enema', and gave each of my friends another 5 points.

When my friends came back into the pool room, I showed them the 'chair' position – basically a knee-chest position, with my knees against the sides of the chair, and head resting on crossed arms on the low chair back.

They each got into position, and Sam asked that they all drink some water. "I don't want you guys to get dehydrated." Then Sam announced, "Now that you're cleaned out, I'm going to insert a small butt plug, to get you ready for the exam room."

Linda and Kathy groaned again, and Kathy said, "Haven't we done enough in the exam room, already?" Sam just laughed.

As my friends finished most of their bottles of water, Sam took his time lubing and inserting the butt plugs. When they were all in place, Sam pulled out the flogger – a spanking implement with a handle, and two dozen thin deer-leather 'tails'.

He said, "While you're getting dilated, I may as well demonstrate the flogger: You guys used it on me at my birthday party, and I used it on Kelly, when we did the pirate scene at her birthday party. I'll go easy on you guys."

Kathy harrumphed, and grumbled, "Nothing is easy with you, Sam."

Sam smiled, and said, "I'm not going to flog your back, or use it on your breasts – like I did with Kelly, or on your genitals. We're just going to keep your bottoms warmed-up for your next spanking challenge."

There was tittering all around, but Sam ignored it, and began swinging the flogger, lightly, back and forth across each of my friends' bottoms, moving from one to the next, in turn.

Initially, there were no complaints; in fact, Linda was giggling – something unexpected by us, and surprising Julie and Kathy. However, as Sam kept up the pace, swinging the flogger repeatedly across my friends' reddening backsides, there was some heavy breathing and, eventually, some groans.

After several minutes, Sam stopped the flogging, and sat in the spanking chair, in front of my friends, who were still in the 'chair position' in the armchairs, butt plugs in their rears.

"If you guys think you're warmed up enough, I'll stop the flogging." My friends were all nodding their heads, although Linda still had a smile on her face.

Sam continued, "So we'll need two volunteers: Who wants to come with me down to the exam room? And, who wants to get their first serious spanking – a 10-minute OTK over Kelly's lap?"

Kathy rolled her eyes, and looked up at the ceiling, but Julie offered, "I'll come with you, Sam."

And, Linda volunteered, "And I guess I'm ready to get over Kelly's lap." Then, she chortled, "My butt's plenty 'warmed up'."

I smiled at the three girls, "I think it's great for you guys to volunteer, and I'm going to give Julie and Linda one extra point. Please keep in mind that this is a competition."

Walking behind the girls, I pulled the butt plug out of Julie's ass, and then Linda's. Kelly sat on the spanking chair, and I instructed Linda to get over her lap, and Julie to come with me. I glanced at Kelly, and she smiled at me, and nodded.

As Julie and I walked toward the pool room door, I looked back at Kathy, and said, "I'll be back in ten minutes to take out your butt plug. Then, you can go over Kelly's lap, as I take Linda downstairs." Kathy closed her eyes, and shook her head.

I put an egg timer, and Linda's water bottle next to the chair in which Kelly sat, and started the timer for 10 minutes. I instructed Kelly to stop Linda's spanking when the timer went off, and massage her bottom until I returned. "Also, please make sure Linda and Kathy finish their bottles of water."

Once Linda was over Kelly's lap, she said, "I'm ready, Ma'am." Then, Kelly began spanking her, not very hard, and not very fast, at first; but I knew the intensity would increase, and a ten-minute spanking would be challenging – even for Linda. I started the timer on my Apple watch, and led Julie down to the exam room.

We entered, not bothering to close the door. As I washed my hands in the exam room sink, I said, "Julie, let me start by saying two things: First, you know that I'm not a medical doctor, and we're just playing here; I'm not trying to diagnose or treat you – it's just a game." Julie nodded, and smiled.

"Second, I could spend an hour 'examining' you, but we only have ten minutes. So, we'll dispense with the gown, your history, the blood test, and a few more details. Please take off your tee, now, and get up on the exam table." Julie complied immediately.

I took a cursory look at her breasts, and helped her lay back on the table; then, I did a quick breast exam, palpating both breasts, and asking her whether she knew how to examine herself, and how often she did it. As with most women, she knew what to do, but seldom actually took the time to examine herself.

Then, I pulled out the stirrups, and Julie scooted down the table, until her butt was nearly off the edge, and put her legs up, casually clasping her hands behind her head, and smiling at me. I conducted a quick pelvic exam, both external and internal, including a rectal, and then inserted and spread the speculum.

I had mounted a small LCD monitor on the wall, where we could both see it, and used my new USB microscope with a tiny LED light source to image her cervix. We could see the cervical OS, the entrance to her uterus. Julie seemed amused by the whole experience.

I had Julie turn over and get into a knee-chest position, and then inserted the 'proctoscope', a rigid, stainless steel tube, with a solid insert – called an 'obturator', which had a rounded tip that made insertion through her anus easy, once she was lubricated with plenty of KY.

The scope was only about an inch in diameter, about the same size as the butt plug that had been in Julie for the past ten minutes. While it was nearly 9 inches long, only about 6-7 inches was inserted into her rectum.

I pulled out the obturator, and fed my tiny microscope and light source down the scope, managing to get an image of her pink internal tissues. It wasn't much to look at.

Julie had taken everything in stride, and I pulled out the scope, and asked Julie to sit up again. "Can we do a urinalysis, now? If you're not ready, we can do it later."

Julie nodded, and said, "I think so ... as long as you don't need too much." I helped Julie off the table, and we went into the bathroom. She sat on the toilet, and I had her spread her legs widely. We dispensed with the alcohol swabbing, and I had her hold her labia apart, and told her what to do.

She peed a bit, and I told her to stop, and handed her a small plastic cup. Then, she peed into the cup, and I set it on the sink, and used a dipstick to check for any blood or protein in her urine.

I had her continue to hold her labia apart, as she finished peeing, and wiping herself. We both washed our hands, and I looked at my watch: The whole process had taken only 12 minutes. Julie put back on the pink t-shirt, and we went back upstairs.

When we entered the pool room, Kelly was rubbing Linda's bottom, and Linda and Kathy had both finished their water. Linda's bottom was now a medium shade of red all over, including her upper thighs. "It looks like Kelly did a fine job of spanking you!"

Linda harrumphed, and said, "That was a really long spanking. And, it hurt!" I let Linda get off Kelly's lap, had Julie get into the chair position, and then I took the butt plug out of Kathy's ass. Linda and I watched as Kathy got over Kelly's lap; when Kelly began Kathy's spanking, I re-started the egg timer.

Then, I brought Linda downstairs for her exam. We went through the same procedure, and Linda also seemed unembarrassed by the exam. As I inserted the speculum, Linda chuckled, "Are you having fun, Sam?"

I shrugged, "I guess you guys have been so open, and we've already done so much, that these things aren't much of a challenge for you, or a turn-on to me."

Linda smiled, and answered, "Well, Kelly's spanking was a challenge: I didn't think a hand spanking could hurt that much. It wasn't bad for the first five minutes, but it got harder, and it was difficult to stay in position by the end."

Then, she smiled at me, and said, "I wonder how Kathy is doing?"

When I inserted the USB microscope and light source through the speculum, Linda looked at the wall-mounted LCD, and exclaimed, "Well, *that's* pretty interesting. I've never seen my own cervix, before."

Linda did fine with the proctoscope, and we finished up with the urinalysis. As Linda put her tee back on, she smiled at me, "I hope we're proving our openness to you, Sam. I really don't think any of us has been so open with anybody, except perhaps our gynecologists." She chuckled, "*I* certainly haven't."

I hugged her, and agreed, "You guys have been fantastic." Looking at her sincerely, I admitted, "After today, I don't really think there will be any more ways I'll be able to challenge you."

That was true: I'd used-up most of my ideas, fulfilled more than everything in my fantasies. As we walked up the stairs, I added, "But I do feel very close to you guys; you're all good friends ... even more than that."

Linda chided, "Sam! We've all had sex with each other. And done everything in front of each other. There's not much 'closer' that we could be."

Again, Linda was right. The five of us had developed a very unique relationship, something I'd never experienced before. Even if we didn't call if 'love', it was definitely a deep friendship.

We walked into the pool room, and found Kathy sniffling, as Kelly massaged her butt. Linda got back into one of the armchairs, next to Julie, and I helped Kathy up, and hugged her. Kelly looked up, and said, "I stopped after eight minutes, Sam."

I held Kathy, and said, "That's OK. I'll give you a '4', instead of a '5', but you guys have taken a lot, already."

Of course, we hadn't yet started the 'real' challenge, with the school paddle, the switch, or the cane. Maybe it would be too much? I had to re-evaluate the situation; I had meant it to be a 'fun' experience, not something miserable for Kelly's friends.

Stepping back from Kathy, I announced, "OK. Here's what I propose. I will take Kathy downstairs for her 10-minute exam, while Kelly spanks Julie. As soon as Julie's spanking is done, you guys can go out to the pool, and Kathy and I will join you as soon as we're finished."

I looked at Kelly, and announced, "Kelly will put out a bowl of fruit we've prepared – cut-up melons, grapes, apples, orange slices, and mango.

"While you guys relax, I'll make lunch. We're going to have three fondues today: Cheese fondue and French bread for lunch, a fondue *bourguignonne* for dinner, and a dark chocolate fondue for dessert, with strawberries, and the fruit leftover from your snack this morning."

The girls were already salivating. Continuing, I said, "I think you'll all feel better when you've had something to eat. It's just after ten, now, and I can get the cheese fondue made by 11AM. Then, we can re-evaluate our plan for the afternoon." I looked around at everyone, "How does that sound?"

Linda blurted, "I'm starving; I'm sure I'll feel better after we eat."

Julie said, "The pool sounds good. It's a beautiful day outside, and we've been cooped up for the past 24 hours. And the fruit sounds pretty good."

I told Linda that she could get up and go outside, and asked Kelly to get towels for everyone before she spanked Julie. Both Linda and Julie came over and hugged me, "Thank you, Sam," Linda said quietly.

Then, Kathy said, sourly, "Ok, Sam. Let's get this over with." I brought Kathy downstairs, and did her exam. She didn't complain – she was resigned to it.

But I was determined to turn this experience around. I decided that there would only be the spanking competition, and one more 'wild' challenge; it was the reason I had wanted the girls cleaned out, in the first place.

Then, I would leave the rest of the experience to them.

CHAPTER 14: COMPETITIVE SPIRIT

I took a dip in the pool with the girls, everyone seemingly happy again – even Kathy. They had snacked on fresh fruit, relaxed in the jacuzzi, and were now playing around in the pool. We were all nude, and enjoying one of the first blue-sky days we could remember.

Kelly sat at the patio table, watching us frolic in the water. As I treaded water in the deep end, I waved to her, and she smiled and waved back.

We hadn't had a chance to talk, so I climbed up the ladder, dried off, put back on my running shorts and tank top, and invited her into the kitchen with me to fix lunch together.

Kelly cut the bread into one inch cubes, as I heated some white wine in the garlic-rubbed, heavy ceramic fondue pot, and began slowly adding the cornstarch-coated Emmental and Gruyère cheeses, stirring in a zig-zag pattern. Then, I poured in some Kirschwasser, German cherry brandy, along with a pinch of nutmeg and dry mustard.

I turned down the heat, and opened a bottle of chilled Gewürztraminer wine, as Kelly took out the plates and fondue forks, as well as the pink tablecloth and matching napkins. I also took four half-gallon containers of milk out of the fridge, leaving them on the counter.

When Kelly looked at me curiously, I filled her in on the last big challenge, which I hoped she would demonstrate, before asking her friends to submit, and compete. "Sam! That's terrible! I'm starting to think that Linda's right; I can't believe you can come up with these things!"

I shrugged, and replied, "It was something I saw on the Internet. And I thought it would be the most embarrassing thing – probably the *only* embarrassing thing – that I could ask your friends to submit to." Kelly shook her head.

Then, I said, quietly, "And, I will offer Linda and Julie the option to compete with an outdoor spanking challenge."

When Kelly gave me another dirty look, I said, "But I think we should take all of your friends on a trip, not just the winner of the challenge. Kelly stared at me, and I told her what I had in mind.

Suddenly, her eyes brightened, and she put her arms around me, "Now, *that* might make this whole day worthwhile for my friends! And, for me." I also told Kelly what I proposed for the rest of the afternoon, and she shrugged, "You'll just have to ask them. I'm OK with it, if they want to do it."

Kelly shook her head in dismay, as she brought everything out to the patio, and set the table. I brought out the base of the fondue set, and lit a can of Sterno, which would keep the fondue at the proper temperature.

Kelly's friends were lying on chaises, gathering some rays, and talking quietly. I ran into the pool room and grabbed my camera, and then asked them to lie on their stomachs for a couple of quick snapshots of their matching red bottoms.

Then, I announced that lunch was ready, and Kelly and I brought out the fondue and platter of bread cubes, along with a salad we had prepared earlier and quickly tossed with balsamic vinaigrette. I poured the wine, emptying the bottle – which amounted to only a small glass for each of us, split five-ways.

There were a lot of 'Mmms' around the table, as everyone dug into the cheese – literally. We chatted about a lot of things, but not the morning's activities ... until everyone was filled, and Kelly had cleared the table.

When Kelly returned to the table, she told her friends that I would explain my ideas for the rest of the day, and that what we did would be up to them.

Julie, Linda and Kathy stared at me, wondering what I would suggest, and I smiled at them, and sat back in the chair. "First, I would like to thank you for being so open this morning, and suffering through the punishment training, as well as letting me examine you. I don't think any of us has much to hide from each other, anymore."

Julie broke in, and said, "We never did, Sam. We've been open with you since Linda and I first came over." Linda was nodding vigorously.

I nodded, "Yes, I agree. You guys have been very open, and good sports with everything I've thrown at you." I glanced at Kelly, and she shrugged, knowing what I was about to say. "There's just 'one more thing' that I think would be interesting ... and about the only thing left that I can imagine might be embarrassing ... even for you, Julie."

The girls groaned, and Kathy looked up into the blue sky, and shook her head. But I continued, hoping that they would submit to the wildest thing I would probably ever propose. "I hope it will be a competition; I'll explain that in a moment."

Taking a deep breath, I continued, "I know that Kathy isn't interested in spanking; I had hoped we could get her to the point where it turned her on, but I admit defeat.

However, I know that Linda is turned on by it, and I think Julie might be interested in a little competition with her."

I looked at Linda, then Julie, "So, if you think your bottoms can take a little more, it would be fun to see you guys in a two-way spanking competition."

I explained, "You'll have to strategize it – how much you want to take with each implement, as each heavier implement will be worth more points." Julie and Linda looked at each other, and smiled, then shrugged.

"And, to cap off the day, if you do get turned on from the spanking, I would be happy – either alone with each of you, or all together – to make sure you're fully 'satisfied'. But, only if you want." The girls didn't say a word, but smiled at each other again.

"Then, I'll make dinner for you – a very different kind of fondue, that I think you'll enjoy."

Now, for the zinger, "And, Kelly and I have decided that the competition will be just for fun: We will take *all* of you on the trip, if you want to go with us." Now, there was tittering around the table, the girls' eyes wide, and grins on their faces.

Linda asked, "So will you tell us where you want to take us, Sam?"

I glanced at Kelly, and she nodded. I smiled at her friends, "Yes. We were thinking about a week in Hawaii, at the end of summer." Now, the table erupted in cheers and applause. There were even bigger grins, and nodding heads, all around.

I added, "Of course, we'll understand, if you have a boyfriend, or something comes up, and you can't make it. But it would be fun to all be together; mostly for a good time ... with maybe just a little 'perversion' thrown in." I had thought they might groan again, but the girls laughed, and continued nodding.

"I'm pretty familiar with the islands, and have a favorite that I'd like to share with you. I would really like to bring you to some special places, off the usual tourist route. I thought we could get a 2-bedroom condo, and maybe – if you're game – camp out one or two nights."

Kelly's friends jumped up, and surrounded me, each one hugging me, and then Kelly. Julie exclaimed, "That sounds fantastic, Sam. I've been to Hawaii once, with my family, but I was just a kid." She looked at her friends, and said, "But this should be a lot more exciting; if you know what I mean." We all laughed.

Kathy remarked, "I've been to Hawaii several times with my parents. But they always went to the same resort on Maui; it wasn't very exciting for me, either. And, I never got to see the other islands except, of course, Oahu."

Kathy finished the last of her wine, and added, "Hawaii is beautiful. But the places I've been were pretty touristy and crowded."

I wasn't going to go into the details of what I was envisioning, where I wanted to take them, and what we might do on the trip. But it would be the opposite of 'touristy and crowded'.

I suggested that we take another hour break – it wasn't even noon, yet – and then Julie and Linda could begin their competition, if they were interested in doing it. After that, we would have the last official 'event'.

The bevy of beauties lay in the sun, and swam in the pool, as I cleaned up the pool room, Kelly helping me to carry the chairs back into the living room and playroom. Then, Kelly and I went out to the pool, and lay in the sun with her friends.

It was now another skinny-dipping party, this one quite different from the one at Kelly's birthday party, and yet the same: One more unknown challenge awaited Kelly's friends.

Sam had managed to turn the atmosphere of the day around, my friends now excited to continue playing, and also to go on a trip with us. I was excited about visiting Hawaii ... but was nervous about how much time I would miss from school to do my research; especially, if I also took a month to study under Mistress Elena in London.

I would have to speak with Sam about that soon: It was almost June, and we would be traveling to Fiona and Justin's wedding in a month. I would need to schedule Elena's course for July, if she was available then.

And, I had to talk with Raj, my advisor, next week about my schedule; it seemed that I might be away most of the summer. I had only a couple of presentations to give in my seminar groups in the next couple of weeks, as the semester was nearly over.

I left Sam lying out in the sun with my friends, and went downstairs to his office, first e-mailing Raj to set-up a meeting for next week, and then e-mailing Elena to confirm that she still was willing to train me, and ask whether the month of July would be good timing for the course.

Elena really hadn't shared many details with me, and I didn't know whether I would be the sole student, or if she would be training several women – and perhaps men – together.

The idea of a benefactor funding my training, and my having to have a session or two with him was a non-issue: I had assumed that if I were trained as a Domme, then I would be dominating more than just Sam; although the idea of having Sam as my sometime slave still excited me.

Walking back upstairs, I went through the pool room to get out to the patio; we had left the sliding doors open, the first time we'd been able to do this in months. I was surprised to see Sam and Kathy standing by the desk, both nude, and apparently in a deep discussion.

Kathy was explaining, "I'm really OK, Sam. I'm not upset with you, at all. It just isn't my 'thing'. My upbringing was quite different than that of Julie and Linda – and probably most other people. The idea of hitting, or being hit, by someone just doesn't turn me on, even if it is done as a sensual experience."

Then, she laughed, "Although I wouldn't mind 'spanking' the guy I was supposed to be with in Mexico – and, I *do* mean 'spanking', as in tying him down and flogging him. Actually, I *might* get turned on, if he were here right now, and I could chain him to the wall and paddle or cane him until he cried."

Kathy shook her head, and said, "See: You guys are even starting to make *me* think in perverted ways!"

I walked into the room, and asked, "Am I missing anything?" Sam shrugged.

Kathy said, "Kelly, I like you guys – a lot. And it's been great that we could all be so open with each other – you, Julie, Linda and I; and Sam, as well. We've all gotten comfortable doing things together, from skinny-dipping to sex. And, I hope we keep our open relationship."

Kathy smiled demurely, and admitted, "I may be a little jealous that you're with such an open, considerate, and loving man."

Kathy glanced at Sam, who looked bewildered, and then smiled at me, "And it's neat that you can 'share' him with us. We've had some really fun times, although – as Linda keeps saying – they've included some pretty bizarro experiences." We all chuckled.

Kathy continued, "I haven't even minded Sam 'playing doctor' with me ... too much." Then, she frowned at Sam, "Probably the worst experience was getting our bowels cleaned out yesterday; that wasn't fun, at all."

I nodded, in complete understanding. I could see that Sam was still concerned about what Kathy would say next; whether she might leave the party, or not want to travel with us.

Then, Kathy explained, "But I just don't think spanking is much fun." She turned to Sam with a crooked grin, "Of course, if I really did something bad, and needed to be punished, I might choose to be spanked, rather than some other alternatives."

Then, looking back at me, she apologized, "I don't want to be a party pooper, but I just don't want to 'submit' to any more spankings today. My butt hurts enough ... and I could never compete with Julie and Linda, who are really into it."

Sam and I were both nodding, "We understand, Kathy," I said. Not everyone is into the same thing. And, you've been a really good sport about it." I looked at Sam, and said, "I wasn't going easy on my friends this morning, and gave them an OTK spanking like I gave you when we visited Elena."

Sam briefly scowled, and I realized that I should have said 'Mistress Elena', as he was jealous of my relationship with her, the fact that she had singled me out for additional attention. I continued, "So I might have overdone it, even though it was 'just' a hand spanking."

Now, Sam hugged Kathy, and said, "We apologize, Kathy. I think we both had hoped that you might find some sensuality in spanking," he chuckled, "and maybe even get turned on by it. I visualized 'satisfying' you, after your experience turned the corner from pain to pleasure."

Sam thought a moment and added, "The idea wasn't to force you to take a spanking, but to keep you involved long enough that it might have become pleasurable at some point." Sam shook his head, and shrugged, not being able to say anything more.

Kathy kissed Sam on the nose, and stepped back, "I don't think that's going to happen, Sam ... although I *might* try again, sometime; maybe without my competitive, spanking-loving friends around."

Sam smiled, although I really doubted that Kathy would give him another chance to explore the deeper feelings that spanking could cause.

Then, Kathy smiled brightly, and said, "But, if you really want to do something sensual with me, sometime, maybe you could give me a massage?" She pointed at the massage table, a few feet away, and Sam's mouth dropped open. Kathy laughed, "I might even let you give me a 'happy ending'." Kathy seemed serious; she was not joking.

Sam nodded, and offered, "I would be honored to massage you, Kathy."

He glanced at me and smiled, "In fact, if Kelly wants to visit with Julie and Linda for a while, I'd love to give you a massage this afternoon! Perhaps that would make up, a little, for the miserable time I've shown you in the past 24 hours."

Now, Kathy's mouth dropped open, and she turned her head to me; I smiled at her and shrugged. "I'm sure I could keep Linda and Julie busy for an hour or so." We wouldn't push Kathy, but if it was something she would enjoy, I knew it would be something that Sam would enjoy, also. And, he *was* very talented with his hands.

Sam said, "But I would suggest that we have Julie and Linda's spanking competition, before your massage." And then, after your massage, we can have the last 'official' event of the day."

When Kathy frowned, Sam quickly explained, "There's no spanking involved ... but it will require another 20-30 minutes of 'openness' from you." I shook my head slowly; Sam was really pushing it, now. He said, "And maybe just a little discomfort."

Kathy stared at him, and so did I; if he was going to ask Kathy to do this, he should at least explain what she was getting herself into.

Sam read my thoughts, and said, "Kathy, it's going to involve putting a little more liquid in your rear." Kathy's mouth opened and closed, and Sam explained, "But not a lot, and it will only be in you for a minute or two."

As I looked at Kathy, and slowly shook my head, she said, "Well, actually, I don't mind enemas that much. Occasionally, I even give myself one at home." Now *that* was surprising; after all this time, and as close as we'd been, here was something else that we didn't know about one of my friends.

Kathy looked at me, and said, "And, of course, there's no issue of embarrassment: Sam has seen me – inside and out," we chuckled, and Kathy went on, "and poked and prodded me, and gave me that huge enema this morning."

Then, she smiled at Sam, "I do want to 'play' with you." She quickly clarified, "As long as it doesn't involve spanking ... or shots."

Then, smiling again, and turning her head back and forth to Sam and I, she said, "And, if you give me a good massage first ... I guess I could do it. Whatever it is that you're planning."

Sam put his forefinger in the air, and said, "Just a minute." We watched, as he went out to the patio, and sat on a chaise, next to Linda and Julie and, standing in the doorway, we could hear him talking to them.

"It's not even one o'clock yet. But I'd like to propose that we do the first few rounds of your spanking competition now – outside. Then, I will give you guys another hour to lie in the sun and play in the pool ... and let your bottoms cool off ... while I give Kathy a massage."

Both Julie and Linda were sitting up now, and both of them raised their eyebrows at Sam. He explained, "That's my 'peace offering' to her; something that she said she would enjoy. If you guys don't mind me not being with you for an hour or so." Julie and Linda nodded.

Sam continued, "When we're done, Kathy can cheer you guys on, as you finish competing to see how much more your bottoms can take. And, THEN we'll move on to the last 'challenge' – something in which even Kathy has agreed to participate. It won't take more than 30 minutes. So, what do you think?"

Julie spoke up, "I think that's a good idea, Sam. It would be nice to give Kathy something *she* wants."

Linda piped up, "And, we can certainly take care of ourselves for a while. And visit with Kelly. And, play in the pool."

I smiled at these incredible women, and thanked them. Kelly and Kathy came out, and the four women put their towels on the chairs, and sat around the patio table, while I brought out some iced tea and cookies.

Kelly was the only one still dressed, wearing her birthday tee. She was near the end of her period, and I wondered whether she would agree to demonstrate what I had in mind for the final event.

I carried a couple of the large beach towels, the ones on which the girls had lain to get their enemas, and walked along the path around the pool; then I walked across the grass, to one of the large boulders that bordered the yard, next to the flowerbeds. I folded each of the towels, and laid them on top of the boulder, next to each other, half of them hanging down, almost to the grass.

Then, I went back into the pool room, and retrieved a few of the spanking implements, as well as the clipboard that I'd used in the exam room.

Sitting at the large desk, I clipped a ruled sheet of paper, and drew columns – one for Julie and one for Linda, then I numbered every third row, and wrote the name of an implement. I drew a vertical line, making a third, narrow column, and put '120' next to the top implement, then '110', '100', and so on, down to the last implement – the cane – where I wrote '10'. Then, I put everything into a small box, and put back on my running shorts and tank.

I walked out to the patio, carrying the box, and asked, "Shall we get started, then?" The girls looked at each other and shrugged.

I led them down the path around the pool, suggesting that Kelly and Kathy sit on the bench that was at the edge of the deck bordering the lawn. I gave the clipboard and a pencil to Kelly, and said, "You'll have to keep score." Kelly looked at the sheet, and shook her head.

As Linda and Julie stood next to the bench, I stepped onto the grass, and smiled at everyone. I was certainly smiling inside, anticipating that this competition could be very interesting.

I raised my hands, and said, loudly, in a circus barker's voice, "Welcome, ladies and ladies, to the First Annual KS Biotech spanking competition." Kelly frowned; as an afterthought I realized that I shouldn't have joked about the company, or associated it with our 'play'.

"Let me rephrase that: Welcome to the First Annual Kelly and Sam spanking competition." Now, Kelly smiled, and nodded. "The contestants will be Linda," I pointed to her and she bowed, "who has already demonstrated tremendous fortitude, as her beautiful bottom was tanned." Linda giggled and bowed.

"And Julie," I pointed, and she curtsied, "who is well known as the wildest among us, and a woman with a fierce competitive spirit. They are the finalists, by a margin of only two points over Kathy, in this morning's qualifying rounds." The girls were laughing, now.

I stifled my own laugh, and continued, "The final competition will be done in two sessions, one now, and one after an hour recess." Then, I whispered to everyone, "Or, maybe a little longer."

I led Julie and Linda to the towel-covered, flat-topped boulder, and said, "The competitors will now take their position." I whispered, "Please bend over the boulder, each one of you on a towel. Your feet should be apart, and your chest down on the towel, with your hands in front of you."

I helped get them into position, spreading their feet a little wider, and making sure that they were arching their back.

"As with all spankings, you will stay in position, keep your eyes forward, not move your feet, and *definitely* not put your hands behind you. You will also remain as quiet as possible; you may emit sounds, if you need to, but do not utter a word!" I whispered, "Except your safeword, if you need to use it." Julie and Linda nodded.

I turned to Kelly and Kathy, and said loudly, "I should have covered these rules this morning. Those will always be the 'rules of engagement' of a spanking … unless I ask you a question, or request that you count them out.

"Scorekeeper Kelly will count the strokes I give each of you, putting that number under your name, on the row corresponding to the implement I'm using. And Umpire Kathy will keep a count of each time you raise a foot, lift your body off the boulder, move your arms below your head, or say any word."

I looked at Kathy and Kelly, and suggested that the number of 'errors' be written below the number of strokes, for each contestant.

Then, I instructed Linda and Julie, "I'm going to give you a certain number of strokes with each implement. I'll start on one or the other of you, randomly. When I've finished a set, I'll call your name, and you can either say 'More!', or 'Stop!'.

"Each implement will be worth more points than the previous one – the first one will be worth one point per stroke, the next one two, et cetera. There will be twelve implements in all, the last one, worth twelve points per stroke."

I looked at Julie and Linda, now bent nicely over the boulder, next to each other, and then looked back at Kelly and Kathy, sitting on the bench. "Does everyone understand the rules?"

Everyone said, 'Yes', and then Kelly roared, "You always make everything so complicated! And so mathematical." She laughed, "Maybe my friends should refer to you as 'PS'?" When I looked at her enquiringly, she said, "Perverted Scientist."

Everyone was laughing again, especially Linda. But she would probably not be laughing in a few minutes, after we had begun the competition.

I called out, "Are the Scorekeeper and Umpire ready?" Kathy and Kelly yelled, 'Yes, Sir!'. "And are the contestants ready?" Julie and Linda yelled 'Yes, Sir!' together.

I scrounged in the box, and pulled out the first item, an ordinary, household flyswatter. Standing behind the girls, I announced, "Let the games begin!" With that, I gave Julie – who was on the left – 20 quick and hard swats with the flyswatter, followed up immediately by giving Linda 20 swats.

The implement was too light to have any effect on either of the girls. "Julie?" She yelled 'More!'. "Linda?" I heard another 'More!', then she was giggling. This time, I alternated between the girls, giving another 40 swats with the flyswatter. The impact barely made a sound.

I repeated the process another time, first giving Linda 40 swats, and then Julie 40 swats. Linda was still giggling. After another two 'More!s', I alternated between them, giving another 20 swats each.

Kelly yelled, "That's the limit for implement one, the flyswatter."

Linda bellowed, "Flyswatter? Is that the best you can do?" Julie was hysterical.

I heard Kathy mumble behind me, "If I'd known it was going to be that easy, even I might have done it!"

I pulled out the 18-inch wooden ruler, and asked, "Are the contestants ready for the second round?"

Julie and Linda yelled, "Yes, Sir!"

I gave Linda 20 hard strokes of the ruler, a tiny bit of pink now showing on her bottom. Then, I gave the same to Julie. Calling out their names, they both requested more, and I gave Linda another 40 strokes, and then Julie her 40. Once again, they requested more, and I alternated, giving one girl two strokes, then the other two strokes, until they'd each received a total of 110.

Now, their butts were definitely pink. I realized that whatever color they'd reached after the morning warm-up had completely faded.

Kelly yelled, "That's the limit for implement two, the ruler."

Next, I held up a wooden spoon, nearly as long as the ruler. A bath brush would have been a much harsher implement, but I was trying to instill a feeling of confidence in the contestants, before they graduated to more severe spanking tools.

I put the spoon against Julie's backside, and began her 'spooning', alternating sides, and including her upper thighs, until I had counted 50 strokes. Then, I moved over to Linda, and gave her 50 hard strokes of the spoon.

Once again, when I called out their names, they both requested more. I decided to give each of them another 50 strokes, alternating between the girls, and moving around each of their butts randomly. They were starting to breathe more heavily, and I could see that both their rears had a mottled appearance.

Kelly yelled, "That's it with the wooden spoon! The contestants are still neck-and-neck."

I looked back at her, and said, "From here, it looks like they're butt-and-butt. Or, maybe, ass-and-ass." Everyone was laughing again. Julie and Linda had to know that it would get harder, but they appeared to be enjoying the experience, so far.

Next, I found the 'loopy Johnny', a handle with several loops of thin black rubber, each a different length. "Are the contestants ready for round three?" Both girls affirmed that they were ready, and I started with Linda, giving her fast, hard strokes of the small device, moving around her bottom in a circular pattern.

Now, I heard a few quiet 'Owls', but Linda took 30 strokes with no problem. Julie got the same, not making a sound.

I called their names, and – again – both girls yelled 'More!'. This time, I started with Julie, giving her another 30 strokes, and then moved to Linda, giving her the same.

I called their names a third time, and there was some hesitancy in their responses. But they both finally yelled 'More!', and I gave them a final 30 strokes, starting with Linda, and moving to Julie.

Kelly called, "That's the limit." Then, she asked, "But what's that thingy called?"

I laughed, and replied, "This is called a 'loopy Johnny'. It's thin loops of rubber, but I'm not sure why the 'Johnny'."

Looking in the box, I found a slipper – in the U.K., it would be called a 'plimsol'. It was a rubber-soled, canvas-sided sports shoe. I bent it, and looked down at the two bottoms awaiting their slippering. I barked, "Are the contestants ready?" As I had expected, both girls yelled, 'Yes, Sir!'

This time, I began with Julie, giving her ten hard swats on her left side, then giving Linda the same ... and then repeating on their right sides.

There were quite a few grunts from both girls, and their bottoms were turning a nice rosy red, now – still light enough that I knew they were feeling it, but not really hurting, yet.

I called out their names, and both girls called out their 'Yes, Sir!'s. This time, I started with Julie, giving her another twenty swats, hard and fast, alternating sides. Julie was now panting, and emitted a few squeals by the end. Doing the same with Linda, I saw that she was not as bothered, perhaps breathing heavily, but keeping quiet, and in position.

Once more, I called their names, and they both agreed to take another 20 strokes of the slipper. Starting with Julie again, I kept up the pace and intensity; these girls were tough, and perhaps I had selected too light of implements?

But, before Julie's 60th stroke, Kathy called out, "Two fouls for Julie!" I finished the set, and looked back at Kathy. She said, "Julie lifted one foot, then the other." I nodded, and smiled at Kathy; she was really doing her job as umpire.

Then, I moved to Linda, giving her another 20 strokes, her large bottom now showing much larger and much redder blotches. However, once again, she remained in position, and I heard only some panting, and loud exhaled breaths.

When I was done, I called out Linda's name, and she immediately said, 'Yes, Sir!', and I noticed that Julie glanced over to her. Linda glanced back at Julie, smiling confidently. I gave Linda her last 20 strokes with the slipper, and this time, she let out a couple of howls at the end.

Moving over to Julie, I called her name, and she hesitated, "Um. I guess so, Sir." It wasn't exactly the proper response, but I put the slipper against her butt, and began her thrashing. Before she'd even received ten more strokes, she was emitting a string of sounds, 'Oooh!', 'Aaah!', 'Ow!'. Finally, the spanking was beginning to have an effect!

When I finished, Kelly announced, "Done with the slipper! Linda is two points ahead of Julie!" Julie shook her head, slightly, and I'm sure she was resolving to take the rest of her spanking without losing any more points.

But the next round would be challenging, and might finally show a difference in the two girls' capabilities to control themselves while accepting pain.

The handle of the crop was sticking out of the box, and I pulled it out, and slapped it once on my left palm; it really smarted! Since the first session was nearly over, I decided to use this implement as it had meant to be used; although, of course, it was *meant* to be used on horses!

"Are the contestants ready for round six?" Both Julie and Linda proudly called out 'Yes, Sir!' I nodded, and looked back at Kelly, who was smiling, and Kathy, who was shaking her head. She was probably glad, now, that she hadn't volunteered for this competition.

Even I was surprised that both Julie and Linda had taken their stroke limit, only Julie making a slight error in not holding her feet steady. I doubted that either girl would want to take the full 70 strokes of the crop.

I laid the end of the crop against the left side of Julie's bottom, and she flinched. Bringing it back, I swung hard, the strap whipping forward, with a loud 'CRACK!' against her flesh. She yelled 'Ow!', and I moved to Linda, and gave her an equally hard stroke. I only heard an 'Ugggh!', and Linda remained perfectly in position.

Then, I moved back to Julie, and gave her two strokes on her right side, one coming quickly after the other. She was quieter, but I was sure I heard a sniffle. Then, I gave Linda two quick strokes on her right side. There was a quiet 'Aaahh!', but again, Linda behaved very well.

Repeating the process, I gave three strokes on Julie's left side, then three on Linda's; then four strokes on each of their right sides. They had only taken ten strokes, and were both panting.

Moving to Julie again, I gave her another ten strokes, alternating sides, with each stroke coming about every two seconds. By the end, she was howling ... but still not saying a word. Then, I gave Linda ten strokes, the same way. She wiggled her bottom, but remained remarkably quiet.

I called out their names, and both girls again agreed to continue. I gave Julie another ten strokes, her bottom now splotched with bright red, against pink. She sniffled more, and near the end, lifted up her body, putting it down again, quickly.

But Kathy had spotted this, good umpire that she was, and called out, "One point foul against Julie!" Linda glanced at Julie and smiled, Julie just shaking her head.

Moving to Linda, I gave her another hard ten strokes and, on the seventh, she shrieked, "Ouch! That hurts!" Kathy called out, "Three point foul against Linda!" I gave her the final three, wondering whether 'ouch' should count as a word. But, I would trust my umpire; her decision was final.

"Another ten strokes, ladies?" They called out 'Yes, Sir!' in unison. I thought that Julie might have awaited Linda's answer before responding, herself, but she was an aggressive competitor, and probably was trying to intimidate her adversary. I *knew* they were both feeling some pain, now. But they were willing to continue on, resolutely.

I alternated between the girls, giving each a stroke on the left side, then repeating on the right side. Both girls were relatively quiet this time, indicating that they were beginning to feel the endorphin 'rush'.

"OK, you guys are impressing the crowd!" They had each now received thirty strokes of the crop. Perhaps I should have used the belt or switch, at this stage? "Now, I'll put some pressure on you: Who wants another *twenty* strokes of the crop?"

There was silence for a moment, before Linda volunteered, "Me, Sir!"

Another few moments of silence, and Julie mirrored, with "Me, too, Sir!" I was really surprised, now, and hoped that the competitive spirit wasn't driving both girls beyond their limits. But they both knew the safeword, and could call it quits, at any time.

I gave each girl ten strokes, and repeated the series again. Julie was sniffling throughout, and Linda was panting hard. On her second ten, Julie stamped her feet, and Kathy yelled, "Four point foul for Julie!" Then, on Linda's last stroke, she lifted her right hand, starting to bring it back, before pushing it down in front of her. Kathy hollered, "And, one point foul for Linda!"

This seemed too much: I didn't want to force either girl into a certain number of additional strokes. So, I offered, "The limit is twenty more, but I'm going to crop one of you, then the other, and you can call 'Stop!' when you've had enough. Please remember that there is one more implement in this session, and then the five hardest ones in the next session. Who wants to go first?"

There was silence, but finally, Linda volunteered, "I'll go first, Sir!" That was probably a tactical error, as Linda would have to take the full twenty strokes, or Julie could outgun her, knowing where Linda had stopped. I looked back at Kelly and Kathy. Kelly had a blank expression, and Kathy now had her hands on her cheeks.

Turning back to Linda, I applied one hard stroke every five seconds, alternating sides. Linda breathed harder, and was now letting out squeals after each stroke. After a dozen strokes, she called, "Stop!" I chuckled; there *had* to be a limit, and I guess Linda had reached hers.

Now, it was up to Julie. I positioned myself behind her, and began her cropping, again with one stroke about every five seconds. After eight strokes, Julie was whimpering, and at ten, she cried, 'No!'. But she had not used her safeword, so I continued. At twelve, she shrieked, 'Aiyeee!', and at fourteen, she hollered 'My God!'

Kathy called a two point penalty on Julie, but the cropping continued. At fifteen strokes, Julie screamed, "Stop! I can't take any more, Sir." She had beat Linda by one stroke, but there were still half the implements left. Julie did not get penalized for the additional words, as she'd already called 'Stop!'.

I rubbed the two bottoms, standing between them, Julie with my left hand, and Linda with my right. Then, standing behind each girl, in turn, I ran my hand underneath, stroking lightly, and feeling wetness on both of them.

I chuckled, and whispered, "We have one more implement to go in this session ... but if you guys want, when we're done, I'll 'do' both of you, together. Maybe you can have simultaneous orgasms?" I heard no response, but both women sniggered.

"OK, ladies, we're on to the last implement of the first session. The score is very close. Who wants to be in first place, going into the second session?"

Linda cackled, "Me, Sir!"

Julie was laughing again – a good sign, considering that her bottom must be smarting. She hooted, "No, *me*, Sir!!" Kathy and Kelly were laughing behind me.

I took the rubber paddle out of the box. It was a mean instrument, about four inches wide, and twelve inches long – not much different in size than the school paddle, but much more flexible. It might not bruise as much, but it would certainly sting.

I gave Julie and Linda one more chance to back out. "Are the contestants ready for round seven?" There were simultaneous, and apparently enthusiastic 'Yes, Sir!'s from both of them.

Stepping behind Linda, I proceeded to give her ten hard strokes, the rubber slapping against her bottom loudly. Now, *she* was sniffling, and Kathy called a one-point foul, when Linda lifted her middle off the boulder momentarily.

Then, I stepped to the left, positioning myself behind Julie, and administered her ten swats with the rubber paddle. Julie squealed and yelped after each stroke, but didn't get out of position. I was impressed; again.

"Linda?" She immediately responded with a 'Yes, Sir!', and I gave her another ten hard swats, moving the paddle around to even-out the redness of her bottom. She was howling, now after every couple of strokes, but stayed in position admirably.

"Julie?" Taking a bit more time, Julie finally answered, softly, "Yes, Sir!" Again, I applied ten hard swats to her quivering buttocks. Trying to avoid overlapping strokes, I gave her the last two on her upper thighs, one just below the other.

Julie couldn't help but begin reaching back with both hands, only remembering to put them back on the boulder after they were halfway to her butt.

Kathy screamed, "Two point foul for Julie!" Julie was shaking her head again, and sniffling. Maybe, I should bring some tissue out here?

Again, I stepped behind Linda, and called her name; and again, she gave me a 'Yes, Sir!', although much less enthusiastically, now. I gave her ten more swats, now waiting nearly ten seconds between each stroke. There was a lot of screeching, and finally some wailing, as she took the last few strokes. Linda had now received 30 strokes of the rubber paddle, halfway to the limit I had set for this implement.

I stepped over to Julie, and called her name. There was a lengthy delay, and I wondered whether she was going to give up, but she finally replied, "Uh, I guess so, Sir!" Again, I wasn't concerned about the correctness of her answer, as she showed her determination and willingness to continue.

I gave her the ten swats, waiting more than ten seconds between each stroke. She was whimpering and sniveling throughout, but took the spanking quite well, considering what she'd already taken.

Kathy called a two-point foul for stamping her feet, but it was truly impressive how much Kelly's friends could take ... and were *willing* to take, for a game.

I called, "Linda?" Another delay, but eventually she said, 'Yes, Sir!' hesitantly. I told her that she could call 'Stop!' whenever she'd had enough. I slowed down the paddling, taking 20-30 seconds between each stroke. Linda was howling by the second stroke, and on the third, she shrieked, "Oh God! Oh God!"

Kathy called a four-point foul. I gave her one more stroke, and Linda called a loud 'Stop!' I rubbed Linda's bottom, the entire surface now a dull, dark red.

Shaking my head, I called "Julie?" Again, there was a long delay. Finally, Julie looked back at me, and said, "I don't think so, Sir." I patted her bottom, and said, "You did a good job. I'm proud of you." Her bottom was a dark red, also.

I stepped back, and said, loudly, "I am really proud of both of our contestants. That was really a 'fight to the end' – the rear end!" Both girls were laughing, as were Kelly and Kathy, behind me. Then, I told Julie and Linda,

"Please stay in position, as we tally the score for the first session."

I walked to Kelly, and sat on the end of the bench next to her. It took some time, computing the score. They had received 120 points for the flyswatter, 220 for the ruler, 300 for the spoon, 360 for the loopy, and 400 for the slipper, less the fouls.

But Julie had taken 3 more strokes of the crop, and Linda had taken 4 more strokes of the rubber paddle. Altogether, Linda was only 10 points ahead of Julie in the raw score, but 17 points ahead, after taking the fouls into account.

Standing, I walked onto the grass, and announced the results: "Ladies, and ladies! Julie having taken 3 more strokes of the crop, and Linda having taken 4 more strokes of the rubber paddle, the score before fouls is Linda – 1950, and Julie – 1940. Linda had 9 fouls, and Julie had 16 fouls. So, the final scores are: Linda – 1941, and Julie – 1924. Linda is the winner of the first session!"

Kelly and Kathy applauded. Linda was nodding, and put her arms up in a victory gesture, as Julie shook her head.

Stepping next to the boulder, and leaning over, I said, "If you would allow me, I'd very much like to satisfy you, now ... with my fingers. If you prefer, I can take each one of you downstairs, separately, but it might be more fun staying here, and doing it together."

Then, I added, "And, we can either let Kelly and Kathy stay where they are, or ask them to go inside, or to the patio table, or into the jacuzzi." Perhaps I had given them too many choices?

Linda said, quietly, "I'm OK with us doing it together – this was quite a shared experience. But, I'd kind of prefer that Kelly and Kathy do something else."

Julie laughed, "I'm also OK getting fingered together. And, I don't care where Kathy and Kelly are – I'm not going to be thinking about them."

I walked to the bench, and suggested that Kelly and Kathy sit at the patio table for a few minutes. Kelly hadn't wanted to go into the jacuzzi, and this would give Julie and Linda a bit more privacy. They nodded, and retreated to the patio, while I stepped between Julie and Linda.

"I could blindfold you, if that would make it more private?" Both girls laughed, but neither commented. I put my hands under them, my left hand on Julie, and my right on Linda, as I began to stroke them together.

Both girls closed their eyes, as I slowly moved my hands, sliding my fingers alongside their labia, and up over their pubic hair, catching their hoods in the separation between two fingers, and then moving my palm in a circular motion. I pulled my hand back infinitesimally, squeezing their clits between my fingers slightly.

Pulling my hand back a bit more, I closed my fingers, and pressed gently, moving them around in small circles, then tapping lightly in the vicinity of their clits, then squeezing, and tapping some more. I was playing it by feel, my own eyes closed, and the feeling of their two sensitive areas a 'stereo' sensation.

I focused, and continued to stroke, now sliding my fingers between their folds, up and over their clits, pushing the hoods back, and then my fingers retreating, as they had advanced.

Julie and Linda were both very sensual creatures, the feeling of raw sex, now being exuded from their bodies into mine. I had been with Julie and Kelly during our ménage, but this was something new: Utilizing a miniscule portion of my appendages to stimulate, to sense, and to engage with the most private parts of Julie's body.

As I heard Julie breathing harder, I swirled my fingertips around the hard bump inside her, while I continued to make long strokes inside Linda.

Suddenly, Julie's breath caught, and I stilled my fingers, pressing down lightly. I continued to stroke Linda, my fingers now moving beyond her hood, until it caught between them, and I squeezed gently.

Then, I positioned my palms – according to my own proprioception – in the same place on both of their bodies, and very gently pressed upwards, rocking my fingers slightly, just barely, as Julie moaned. I gently slid my fingers back from her hardness, and slipped them into her, inverting my hand, and now putting pressure on her G-spot, pressing downward inside her.

My hands were now mirror-images of each other, pressing upward on   Linda's external tissues, and downward, inside Julie.

Julie came suddenly, creaming my fingers, which I held in place, applying gentle pressure, as she thrust slowly against them. As Linda heard Julie's response, she bucked against me, and I slipped my fingers into her, as well, again inverting my hand, and moving it along her, as I anticipated her response.

I slowly moved both of my hands within the two women, one having had her release, and stilling, while the other moved her lower body in a circular motion, positioning my fingers to her desire, as I held them still, only pressing gently downward, generating a small amount of friction between us.

It didn't take long for Linda to orgasm, bucking up and down, and thrusting forward and back, as I held my fingers within her. She was panting, and emitted a soft squeal, as I felt her pushing her secretions onto my fingers.

I inverted my hands again, while I was still inside both women, and then slowly pulled them back, out of them, and settling them between their folds.

I gently pressed upward, cradling them as if their entire bodily support depended on my holding them from underneath. Linda's eyes opened, and she chuckled, causing Julie to glance at her, smiling a satisfied smile.

Both women were satiated, and I was glad that I was successful in bringing them to the peak of sensation, and then the release of all the tensions in their bodies.

They both glanced back at me, and I brought my hands out from under them and smiled – satisfied, myself. They backed off the rock and stood, and I hugged Linda, and then Julie; then Linda again. We all held each other in a sensual embrace, and they leaned their heads on my shoulders.

Julie ran her hand through my hair, and said, "Thank you, Sam. That was wonderful. Kelly was right, when she told us how talented you are." Then, putting her hand behind my head, and pulling, I turned to her, and we kissed. It wasn't a long kiss, but both of us were very sincere.

Linda smiled, and then pulled me to her, kissing me on the cheek. "Thank you from me, too. I am glad that Kelly is willing to share you, at least for a short time."

She shook her head, and looked at Julie, "I still don't understand *why* Kelly is willing to share her man with us." She turned to me, "I know it turns you on, and maybe she's just willing to satisfy your desires ... or maybe she's also turned on by seeing you satisfying another women. I don't know."

Then, she ran her hand lightly down the back of my tank, "But I'm not complaining." I kissed both women on the cheek, and took them by the hand, leading them back to the patio.

Sam walked back to the patio table, Julie and Linda in tow, all three of them smiling a secret smile; but not that secret. I could not remember how many times Sam had satisfied my friends, taken care of their needs without worrying about his own; but I knew that he could narrow his focus, putting all of his energy and determination into the task.

And, I could not remember a time when Sam had failed to arouse, and then satisfy me, or my friends, when he had put his mind – and body – to it.

Sam poured some iced tea, the ice now mostly melted, and drank it in one long swallow. I guess it had been hard work ... although, looking at his running shorts, I knew that he wasn't – and probably hadn't been – hard, himself.

Sam got the massage table ready, and brought Kathy into the pool room. I remembered that Kathy got professional massages in Mexico. But Sam had proven his abilities with the few massages he'd given me, and also with Alex, who was a massage connoisseur.

Kathy had joked with him about giving her a 'happy ending', but I had no doubt that Sam would make that a reality. By dinnertime, he would have satisfied all three of my friends.

Linda and Julie sat down at the patio table with me, and we chatted – about spanking experiences (including Linda's schoolgirl role-play), some of our experiences together (including Julie's ménage with Sam and I), and eventually turning to the domme experience that Sam and I had had with Mistress Elena in London.

They'd heard a little about it during our Europe show, but I shared a few more details – especially some of the things to which Elena had subjected Sam. But I also told them how Sam had offered to take part of the caning that Mistress Elena was going to give me.

Sam was a baby, but he was strong; he was considerate, but he pushed people to their limits; and he loved sex, but was willing – and capable – of enjoying very intimate non-sexual relationships.

It was a beautiful afternoon, warm and clear. After a while, Julie and Linda decided to go into the jacuzzi, and I sat on the edge, dangling my feet in the warm water, continuing to chat with them.

We shared our summer plans, both of my friends planning to stay in town – at least, until we left for Hawaii. We speculated on what Sam had in mind, but I couldn't add any information to what Sam had already told us.

I mentioned our upcoming trip to Fiona's wedding, and how Sam had suggested that we see Niagra Falls, then drive up to Quebec, before driving down to Boston through the White Mountains of New Hampshire. None of us had been to any of these places.

I told my friends how I was concerned about traveling almost the entire summer – Eastern Canada at the end of June, London – I hoped – all July, and Hawaii in August; it would be virtually impossible to make any progress on my research project.

Linda couldn't understand; she told me there was no rush, as Sam was supporting me, and I would finish my dissertation and graduate with my doctorate eventually.

But I explained the competitiveness of the field, the data needed to file more patents, and the urgency in developing a product that our company, KS Biotech, could commercialize.

I felt compelled to move as quickly as possible, and had guilt feelings that I would be 'enjoying' the summer, without accomplishing much.

It seemed that we had been out here a long time, and I glanced back to the pool room, through the open sliding glass door, to the massage table; the patio table and chairs were blocking most of my view, but Sam was still working on Kathy.

I hoped she was enjoying her massage, a small compensation for what Sam had put her through in the past day, from spending hours in the bathroom yesterday, to giving her a big shot last night, to spanking her this morning, to giving her a pelvic exam.

I shook my head, at how ridiculous those series of events sounded. Then I realized that it had been the long, and hard OTK spanking I'd given her that made her finally rebel.

But Sam had turned the situation around, cutting short Kathy's spanking experience, proposing the trip to Hawaii, and offering her a massage. I could tell that she actually had enjoyed watching Linda and Julie compete, bent over the boulder, to see how much their bottoms could take.

And, I hoped that Kathy was enjoying the massage that Sam had been giving her for nearly an hour.

I was nearly finished massaging Kathy, and I could see that she was relaxing and enjoying it. In fact, I don't think I'd ever seen Kathy as contented as she looked now. I had offered to drape her, but she'd just looked at me, and asked, "Are you kidding?"

I had only wanted to be professional, but Kathy was right: I'd seen her walking around nude for two full days, and – of course – had seen every part of her body intimately. And, I was trying to give her a relaxing experience without any pressure or anxiety about it turning sexual; but she had already told me that she would enjoy a 'happy ending', which I would be delighted to give her.

Working my way up her left leg, I made long strokes, the coconut oil allowing my hands to glide over her tanned skin and work her well-toned muscles. The aroma was tropical, making me think about Hawaii, and some interesting experiences I could share with Kelly and her friends. I let my hands circle her thighs, moving up to her crotch, but just grazing her womanly parts.

Then, I leaned over her, bringing my hands around her hips, and up her sides, pulling them down, my hands diving under her, and finally pulling up her bottom, as they exited at her thighs. I repeated this stroke several times, my eyes closed, as they had been for much of the massage.

When I opened my eyes, I realized that I was staring at Kathy's sparse, blonde pubic hair which, from a distance made her appear to have bare pubes. I slid my hands over the top of her hips, and up her middle – over her stomach and, putting one hand over the other, between her relatively small breasts, around them, and down her sides again.

After a few more strokes, I moved to the end of the massage table, and massaged her forehead, ears and neck again; I had already covered this area, but wanted to give her just a little more, as she looked so relaxed.

Finally, as I held her shoulders, I leaned over and kissed her very lightly on the lips. I whispered, "How are you doing, Kathy?"

She opened her eyes, and smiled at me, "It was really nice, Sam. My whole body is tingling." I nodded, and smiled at her, then bent down, and whispered in her ear,

"Would you still like a happy ending? I would be delighted to get you off, but it's entirely up to you." Kathy smiled, and gave me a single almost imperceptible nod.

Stepping to the other end of the table, I leaned over, and reached to her hips, putting my hands around them and slightly under her, and pulled her down the table, Kathy raising her middle to lessen the friction. Her legs were now hanging down from the end of the table, with me standing between them.

I used the thumbs of both my hands, sliding over her oiled skin, outside of her labia, then coming together around her clit. Using my best technique, I got her going. Then, my hands around her hips, I went down on her, licking, lapping, swirling my tongue. Kathy's eyes were closed again, and she began moving her body, slowly, in an undulating, wave-like motion.

I put my mouth against her clit, and blew out, letting my lips vibrate against her. Kathy giggled a little, her motions increasing, as I began flicking my tongue under her hood, and then swirling it around her clit again.

It didn't take long; I focused on my task, and Kathy focused on hers, finally bringing her own hands down next to mine, and taking over, coming violently, as her middle thrust up toward the ceiling.

Leaning against the end of the table, I let my hands slide up her middle, cupping her breasts. I could barely reach her face, as I lowered myself, rubbing my nose on her chin.

Kathy lifted her head, and kissed me, and then I pulled her into a sitting position. I put my arms around her back, and she put hers around my head, pulling me to her. We kissed each other, and I helped Kathy down from the table.

She laughed, and asked, "Are you going to bathe me, now?" That was a great idea ... but we had one more event, so I promised to bathe Kathy after she and her friends had completed the final 'challenge'. Kathy laughed again, and said, "Well, Sam, at least you've gotten me in a good mood for it. Whatever 'it' is."

I led Kathy outside, and Julie and Linda climbed out of the jacuzzi. I told Kelly to take them to the bench, while I got a few supplies. First, I placed a yardstick on the grass next to the boulder, and began putting small stakes in the ground every foot for three yards.

Kelly and I went back inside, and I put the rest of the supplies in a pail, and then Kelly and I carried out the four half-gallons of milk that were now at room temperature, having sat on the kitchen counter since lunch.

I stopped in the pool room to put on some flip flops, then went out to the boulder, and spread the towels across the top, completing the preparations.

I stood in front of the bench where Kelly's three friends sat. Before I could say anything, Julie looked at me, and said, "Sam, I am willing to concede the spanking championship to Linda." Linda looked at her sharply, but Julie kept her eyes on me, and added, "Do you think we could skip the second spanking session?" I looked at Kelly, and she gave me a nod and a smile.

Replying in a mock whine, I said, "But, Julie, you haven't felt the belt, the hairbrush, the switch, the school paddle, or the cane!"

Julie chortled, "I *have* felt the school paddle, as I'm sure you remember." Of course, I remembered; I'd had to give Julie a real punishment at Kelly's birthday, when she had revealed that Kelly was an adopted child.

I nodded, and looked at Linda. She stood, raised her hands, and said loudly and proudly, "I accept the victory, as 'spanking queen' of the Johnson estate." Then, she turned, looking over her shoulder, showing us her still-red bottom. She said sincerely, "I'm OK with that, Sam. I think Julie and I have taken enough spankings for one day."

"OK. The majority rules. Let's complete a last non-spanking challenge, then we can all go down and take a shower together, and you guys can dress for dinner, while I get the next fondue ready."

Linda said brightly, "You mean we can actually get dressed? Wow! *That* will be different!"

Everyone was laughing, now in a good mood, so I decided it was time to explain the last planned event of the day. "The last event is something I saw on the Internet, done by young girls in Japan. And I thought you guys should try it. In fact, it's the main reason I wanted you cleaned out. You've all been prepped, so now let's have some fun!"

Kelly's friends didn't know yet what I was proposing, and were dubious about whatever it was being fun. I looked at Kelly: She gave me a dirty look, then shrugged, and nodded.

"Kelly, please get in a knee-chest position on top of the boulder." Kelly was shaking her head, as she walked across the grass, and took her position on the towel, her ankles at the edge of the huge rock, and her butt high in the air.

I took the supplies out of the bucket, and poured a half-gallon of milk into it. Then, I lubed one of the huge 200cc plastic syringes, which had a conical tip. I drew in a full syringe of milk – about six ounces – and walked over to Kelly, carrying the pail.

Looking back at Kelly's friends, I smiled, then turned and stuck the tip of the syringe through Kelly's anus. I pushed the plunger, and injected the milk into her. Whispering my intentions to her, I filled the syringe again, and injected another load of milk into Kelly's rear. Then, I took the syringe and pail, and returned to the bench.

Julie looked up at me, "You're kidding!" Linda now had her hands over her face, and Kathy's mouth hung open, as she slowly shook her head.

Making sure the challenge was clear, I said, "No, I'm not kidding. In a minute, you three are going to get into position next to each other on the boulder, and I'm going to shoot some milk into you. Then, Kelly will do a countdown, and you'll squirt it out your rears. We'll see who can squirt the furthest." There were groans all around.

Linda squawked, "That's sick!" Then, she clarified, "And I don't mean in a good way! Bizarro!" Julie cackled, and Kathy was still speechless.

I had to admit that it *was* really bizarre; but we'd done so many things together it was starting to get difficult to come up with something new, something that might be embarrassing, challenging. I turned to the boulder and said, "OK, Kelly, are you ready?"

Kelly replied with a negative-sounding, "Yes, Sir."

Julie, Linda, Kathy and I were all staring at Kelly's butt. "Then let 'er rip!" I commanded. A moment later, a stream of milk shot out of Kelly's rear. I estimated that it had reached nearly six feet from the boulder.

Kelly's friends were beside themselves – literally, and figuratively. Linda cried, "Oh, my God. That's really perverted!" Julie was now laughing hysterically, and Kathy was shaking her head ... but I detected the hint of a smile. I clapped, and the three girls joined me.

I shouted, "Do you want to try again, Kelly?"

Kelly responded by shaking her head, "Not especially." Now, all her friends were laughing, despite knowing that they were next.

Kelly stood, walked to the side of the boulder, and jumped down, avoiding the trail of milk that she had left on the grass. I turned to her friends, and said, "OK, you guys are up next!"

Then, I offered, "If you insist, I can let each of you try it separately, first ..." They didn't answer, just rose, and marched down the side of the grass, climbing up onto the boulder, and getting into position.

There was a little jostling, but now there were three asses high in the air. As they adjusted their positions, I ran back to the pool room, opening the desk drawer, bringing out my phone.

I took a few snapshots, and was a little sorry I hadn't set my DSLR on a tripod to catch the action. But I realized that I could take a few short videos with my phone; that would have to do.

I walked over to the boulder, behind the girls, and injected two syringes of milk into each of them. They were surprisingly accepting of the challenge, not even groaning. I hurried back to the bench, and held my camera up, ready to take a snapshot, as the milk was released.

Kelly counted down: 3, 2, 1 ... and a moment later, there were three streams of milk.

I was pretty sure I got the picture. Nobody else would be seeing it, but I knew it would produce a few laughs from Kelly's friends at some later date. Kelly and I clapped, and I shouted, "It looks like Julie might have won this round, with a distance of seven feet!"

Then, we repeated the process. This time, I injected two syringes of milk into each girl, then went to each one again, injecting a full syringe of air, and a third syringe of milk. I ran back to the bench, and set the phone for video.

Kelly counted down, and three jets of milk shot across the yard, at slightly different times, and in several spurts from each girl. "I think, this time, Kathy was the winner." It wasn't easy to see how far the milk had gone, but I estimated, "She shot her milk at least eight feet!" Kelly and I clapped, and I whistled.

"One more time!" Now, there were groans. I was pushing the women, but they had done so well, so far ...

This time, I had them lay on their backs, with their feet pulled up to their chests, their butts at the edge of the boulder. I injected four syringes of milk into each of them, about 24 ounces, with no air.

Then, I went back to the bench and aimed the phone again, as Kelly counted down. Julie and Linda shot out their milk in a spray and, about ten seconds later, Kathy shot hers in an amazing stream.

Again, I wasn't sure of the exact distance, and perhaps exaggerated a little, but I hooted, and yelled, "Kathy's the winner again, with a distance of *nine* feet!" Kelly and I clapped, hooted, and whistled. I hollered, "Outstanding!"

The event was over, and I allowed the girls to climb down from the boulder. I hugged each of them, and they were actually smiling; except for Linda, who scowled at me ... and *then* smiled.

We all went downstairs, and I started the rain shower and all the leg jets. Kelly and I took off our clothes, and joined Julie, Linda and Kathy in the shower – which wasn't really big enough for the five of us; but we jostled around, and bathed each other.

I rinsed off, then stepped out from under the shower, drying off, as I placed four fresh towels on one of the chaises, and said, "I'm going to get dinner started. You guys can take your time, wash your hair, or whatever, and get dressed. When you come back downstairs, I'll open some wine, or make drinks – whatever you want."

I smiled to myself as I climbed the stairs to the master bedroom, went into the closet, and put on a pair of dress shorts and a Hawaiian shirt. I considered the day to be successful, even though Kathy had not gone through with the spanking challenge, and we'd cut it short for Julie and Linda.

But, once again, they had been great: They were more open, enthusiastic and fun than Kelly or I would ever have believed.

Just a year ago, I had hoped to meet one woman who would 'play' with me. Since then, my life had undergone an amazing transformation. I still missed Sarah, but now I was embarking on a new life with Kelly. And her friends.

CHAPTER 15: DREAMS OF PARADISE

My friends and I took our time in the shower, as Sam had suggested. Then, we walked upstairs, and they went into the guest rooms to dress, while I continued into the master bedroom. It had been a day of crazy, ridiculous experiences ... but in a way, it had also been amazing.

Sam had agreed that there would be no more shots for my friends and, I hoped, no more needles. I would now propose that he promise that there would be no more enemas.

Sam had challenged my friends enough, and they had taken almost everything with good humor. The trip to Hawaii sounded nice, but I was a little suspicious of what Sam had in mind for my friends. Maybe, we could just have a nice, friendly, *normal* trip?

We all assembled down in the kitchen, as Sam cut a tenderloin into small cubes, putting them in a bowl. Then, he made several different sauces – there were at least half a dozen of them.

Sam told us that we would be dipping the beef into oil, cooking each piece ourselves, then dipping it into our own glass bowls of sauces, that would form a semicircle around our small plates. It was a fondue *bourguignon*, like we'd had in Interlaken, Switzerland, during our amazing European tour.

When Kathy asked about the sauces, Sam reeled them off: "I'm making a Remoulade sauce, a spicy red sauce, an oriental sauce, a Spanish sauce with saffron, a tartar sauce, a sour cream and mustard sauce, and a garlicky aioli." Kathy's eyes went wide, and her mouth fell open – not for the first time, today.

Linda seemed unusually animated, "Sam, can you make margaritas? We could still have wine with dinner if you want."

Sam laughed, "Sure, Linda." He looked around, "Does anybody want anything else, while I'm making drinks?" Everybody shook their heads, but Sam said, "Kathy, if you'd like something a bit more healthy, I could make a tequila sunrise for you? We have fresh orange juice."

Kathy chuckled, "Thanks Sam. That's very thoughtful of you. But I think I'll have margaritas with everyone else."

Sam whipped up – literally – a pitcher of margaritas, and poured them into wide mouth glasses; he had wiped the rims with Cointreau liqueur, and then rolled them in a pile of large-grained salt that he'd spread on wax paper.

Handing them to us, we all toasted to a very 'interesting' day. The pitcher was empty after the five glasses were filled, and Sam made another pitcher.

Linda exclaimed, "This is the best margarita I've ever had!" Sam explained that he'd used both tequila and a little brandy, the 'sweet and sour' and margarita mix he'd pulled from the fridge in the garage, and he had added plenty of Triple Sec, and also some Grand Marnier.

There was barely room for the ice in the blender, but the consistency had come out sensually smooth. I had to agree that these put the margaritas at the Mexican restaurant to shame. Sam always strived for the best, regardless of the effort that it took. But he also made everything look so easy!

I suggested that we eat outside, the weather being so good, but Sam was concerned that the table would be too crowded, with all the sauce bowls. Then, I suggested a creative solution: We could put Sam's turntable on the glass table, making a huge table, plenty big enough for all of us.

Sam thought that was a great idea for the future, but said that we should all be able to dip our meat in the hot oil, without having to rotate the table.

Not ready to give up, Julie and I decided to see if everything would fit. We put the pink tablecloth over the glass patio table, set out salad-size plates, and seven small Pyrex glass bowls around each of the plates.

I was amazed that Sam had so many of the small bowls, but he explained that Sarah had used them to make large batches of individual desserts, when their kids had been in school, and they'd hosted some big parties.

Julie and I were successful in fitting everything onto the table, leaving the pink cloth napkins on each seat, and putting a fondue fork across each plate. We were able to fit wine glasses, and put the fondue set – the grate and Sterno can – in the center of the table. Now, it was completely filled; not even a wine bottle would fit.

Sam put oil into a metal fondue pot, and heated it on the stove, adding a few cloves of garlic, and some sprigs of thyme. Then, he opened a nice bottle of a red wine, letting it breathe.

My friends had originally planned to go home after dinner, but I was pretty sure, as Linda poured the second pitcher of margaritas, that they would be spending a second night here. It was Saturday night, and I didn't know of any reason why they had to rush home.

I went downstairs, and turned up the sauna temperature. Then, I went out to the backyard, and flipped on the pool light and tree lights ... although the days were getting longer, and we were having an early dinner.

We all chatted, and enjoyed Sam's margaritas. It was amazing how simple Sam made the dinner preparation look. He said he normally would have made a salad, but we'd already had one with lunch.

Julie said, "Relax, Sam. We'll have plenty to eat. It looks fantastic."

Linda added, predictably, "And we have to save room for the dessert fondue you told us about."

We were all laughing, and relaxing even more due to the margaritas we were drinking; Sam didn't skimp on the alcohol and, as I yawned, I hoped that we wouldn't fall asleep before dessert.

Kathy was effusive about the massage Sam had given her, saying it was better than most of the professional massages that she'd had. She said that she and her mother always got one or two massages when they went to Mexico on their Christmas vacations, noting that they'd had both masseuses, and masseurs.

She didn't tell us whether Sam had given her a 'happy ending', but I was fairly certain that Sam would not have passed up the opportunity to satisfy Kathy.

Sam adjusted the heat of the oil, and took all the sauces out of the fridge. He put a spoon in each of the large bowls, and we all took one, and went out to the patio. Sam insisted that we arrange them in a specific order, and we walked around the table, each filling one of the small glass bowls around the plates.

Sam brought the oil and some matches out to the table, and lit the Sterno, as I filled the last bowl of sauce for each of us. Then, Sam brought out another five small bowls, putting one in the middle of each plate, and filling them to overflowing with the raw filet.

With one more trip to the kitchen, Sam brought out the wine, and filled each of our glasses, emptying the bottle. When I gave him a 'look', he shrugged, and said, "We don't have room on the table for it, and this way, we won't have to get up and down." It was a lame excuse, as he could have put it on the deck next to his chair.

Sam announced that dinner was ready, and we sat down at the table. He fiddled with the flame under the pot of oil, adjusting it so the oil would maintain the right temperature to cook the meat.

Finally, he raised his wine glass, and we all followed suit. "I want to thank you all for being such good sports – again. I know that you didn't like everything we did ... and you *still* haven't experienced everything that Kelly did, the first time she came over. But I hope you found it interesting."

We sipped the wine, and Linda said, "You could say that." She picked up the long, wooden-handled, double-tined fondue fork, as we all chuckled. Then, she skewered a piece of meat, and dipped it in the oil, causing it to bubble and sizzle. Julie and Kathy began cooking a piece of their own meat.

Sam had whispered to me when we came out together the last time that the oil would maintain its temperature better, if there were only three or four pieces of meat cooking at one time; so we sipped our wine, and watched my friends twirl their skewers, putting our own meat in the oil only after they had pulled theirs out.

The meat was very hot, but cooled rapidly, when dipped into one of the cool sauces. It was delicious, and special: Sam and I had eaten a fondue like this in Switzerland, but Sam's sauces seemed even better than the ones we'd had there. For the second time today, there were 'Mmms' around the table.

Linda asked, "Sam, where did you learn to cook like this?"

Sam shrugged, and explained, "Well, Sarah was a good chef, and we often cooked together. And, we've traveled many places in the world, and collected recipes. I also have a pretty good library of cookbooks." He smiled, and I could see he was figuring out what he would say. He concluded, "I guess I've had a lot of practice."

I instantly decoded that as 'I'm pretty old'. But that might not have been his train of thought; perhaps it was mine?

I suddenly saw Sam in a different light, a fifty-year-old man playing with a bunch of mid-twenties girls. I shook my head. That wasn't how I usually saw Sam: He was fit, and active, and very sexual. I saw him as more of an equal, and I realized that, in many ways, I was his superior.

Julie dipped her meat in one of the sauces, and commented, "Sam is a man of many talents."

Kathy looked down, and agreed, "Yes, he is." At that moment, I knew that Sam had satisfied Kathy, undoubtedly bringing her to an explosive orgasm – on the massage table, right behind us.

Linda now looked at Julie, and nodded, "I'll drink to that." She sipped her wine, and my friends all smiled; but they didn't laugh. Sam had challenged my friends, but he'd also rewarded them.

The dinner was long, with surprisingly little conversation. Of course, we all had to cook our own meat, but the sauces were delicious, and I was sure that my friends enjoyed the fondue *bourguignonne* that Sam had prepared.

As we had eaten early, it was still light outside when we finished. We cleared the table, and washed the dishes, the job taking only minutes with all of us working together.

We went downstairs to the playroom, and sat around the coffee table. Linda asked, "Sam, are you now convinced that we're open? And, maybe you can just have fun with us, without feeling the need to 'challenge' us?" Kathy was nodding.

"Yes, all of you have been extremely open with Kelly and I." He glanced at me, "And, I don't think we'll need to have any more 'challenges'," he said, as my friends clapped and cheered. "But we still could do some kinky things, as long as you are interested in playing with us.

"For example, Linda's schoolgirl spanking experience was pretty interesting – and exciting for her, as well as Kelly and I. And, the ménage with Julie was an incredible experience – the first time Kelly and I made it with someone else, and the first time we'd ever been part of a ménage."

Then, Sam turned to Linda, "And it might still be fun to have some 'special' birthday parties ... and, of course, give each other birthday spankings." Sam raised his eyebrows and, looking into Linda's eyes, added, "And, you have a birthday coming up soon, Linda; in a couple of weeks, if my memory serves me ..."

Linda snorted, "Well, that might be OK." She looked around at her friends, and smiled demurely.

Kathy laughed, "You already missed mine, Sam, while you and Kelly were in Europe." She stuck out her tongue at Sam. Then, she glanced at Julie, and said, "But Julie's is coming up ... in August. Maybe we can have a birthday celebration for her in Hawaii?"

Sam nodded, "That sounds like a great idea!" Julie just smiled.

Now, Linda asked, "So what are your ideas for the trip to Hawaii, Sam?" We all looked at Sam expectantly; even I had no idea what he had in mind.

Sam smiled, and stood, then walked to his desk, fiddled with his computer, lowered the giant screen, and turned on the projector. As he walked back with a Bluetooth keyboard, and sat in the chair, he said, "Sarah and I went to Hawaii quite a few times ... and had some real adventures."

He tapped the keyboard, and began a travelogue of one of their trips, an aerial view now on the screen, showing a lot of tall buildings along the beach, and some very blue water off the coast.

"I want to tell you about my favorite island, but maybe I can build up to it by showing you the other islands, and giving you a little background?" Linda nodded, and the rest of us stared at the screen.

"This is Waikiki, of course, taken from the plane, as we were landing, with the Diamond Head crater on the right. Oahu is the most populated island, with nearly a million people, and freeways with diamond lanes. There are some good restaurants, and great shopping, but a crowded beach like this is not *my* idea of Hawaii.

"Of course, there are nice beaches on Oahu ... but the island is so populated, and has so many tourists, that some iconic places, like Hanauma Bay – which used to have spectacular snorkeling – have nearly been ruined. There's Sea Life park, on the east end of the island, which is similar to Sea World." Sam advanced to the next picture.

"And, on the north-east shore, Kailua Bay is beautiful; I have a friend who has a multi-million dollar home in Lanikai, and they have great paddle boarding and kayaking. And, as you drive to the north end of that shore, you have the Polynesian Cultural Center." Sam was now flipping through the images quickly.

"Here, on the north shore, are the beaches famous for the huge winter surf – like Sunset Beach, the Banzai Pipeline and, to the west, Waimea Bay. It *is* beautiful, and I always recommend that people going for the first time to

Hawaii stay on Oahu at least a day or two, to drive around, and see Pearl Harbor and the USS Arizona memorial."

Sam flipped through more pictures, and suddenly the images changed completely, a desolate, lava-covered expanse before us. "I think the best island for someone new to Hawaii is the 'Big Island', the Island of 'Hawaii'. It's the biggest island, and has an incredible variety of things to see and do, including snorkeling or diving on the Kona coast, which you see here."

Then, Sam laughed, "I have a riddle for you: What states are the farthest north, the farthest south, the farthest east, and the farthest west, in the United States?" We guessed, Julie naming Maine as farthest north, and Kathy telling her it had to be Alaska; Julie then said, "But Maine has to be the farthest East!"

Linda guessed Florida as the farthest south, and then dithered ... saying it might be Texas. And we all guessed that Hawaii had to be the farthest west.

Laughing again, Sam said, "No! Hawaii is the farthest south." The next picture came on the screen, "This is the South Point lighthouse on the Big Island – it's the most southerly point in the U.S."

Now, in a belly laugh, Sam answered the riddle, "And, like Kathy said, Alaska is the farthest north." Kathy sat back, looking self-satisfied, and Sam continued, "But Alaska is *also* the farthest east and the farthest west!"

When we all stared strangely at him, he explained, "Alaska crosses the International Date Line, at least the Aleutian Islands do. So it is both the farthest east, and farthest west of any state!"

Linda chided, "That was a trick question! No fair!"

Sam chuckled, and then asked us another question, "And, what do you think is the tallest mountain on the earth?"

Linda quickly answered, "Mount Everest, of course! Everybody knows that!"

Sam was belly laughing again, now starting to choke, "Wrong again! Now, *this* would be a good game, if you guys were rewarded for your correct answers ... and had to pay a penalty for the wrong ones!" We all groaned, knowing what 'penalty' Sam was talking about.

Sam tried to stop laughing long enough to give us the answer, "The peak of Mount Everest is the highest point on the earth above sea level ... but the tallest mountain – from base to peak – is Mauna Loa, on the Big Island!"

Linda fell back on the couch, and was now laughing almost as hard as Sam. "That's *another* trick question! And we're not paying 'penalties' for not being able to answer your trick questions!" We were all laughing; again.

Sam continued, "Along this southern coast is Hawaii Volcanoes National Park, where the Kilauea volcano is still erupting. You can take a helicopter ride over it to see the lava flowing, if you're lucky; or, you can hike out into areas of steaming lava, and maybe even see it flowing into the ocean.

"It's a great place to hike – down into the Kilauea Crater, through huge lava tubes, and across desolation wilderness, which is covered in volcanic ash. There are strange formations, called 'lava trees', and in some places the lava flow is still threatening homes."

Again, more flipping through the pictures, and there were images of beautiful and lush rainforests on the screen. "On the east side of the Big Island is Hilo, where you can visit orchid gardens, and macadamia plantations."

Linda blurted, "I *love* macadamia nuts!"

Sam nodded, "They're my favorite, also. But, did you know that they can't be eaten raw from the tree? They have to be processed and roasted."

Linda smiled, "And the chocolate-covered ones are great, too." Linda twisted her nose, and asked, "Isn't it almost time for the chocolate fondue?" Now, we were all hysterical again.

Sam replied, "Let's just finish this tour of Hawaii, first. Then, I'll make the fondue." Linda nodded, reluctantly, and Sam continued. "Another question: Where is the largest ranch in the U.S.? Actually, I'm talking about the largest private cattle ranch."

Julie guessed, "It has to be in Texas."

Sam laughed again, and said, "You guys are so easy! The largest private cattle ranch is in the north of the Big Island, the Parker Ranch. It's below the third major volcano of the Big Island, Mauna Kea."

More images flipped by on the screen, and Sam said, "And, on the northeast shore of the Big Island is Kohala, where some of the most elegant hotels in Hawaii are located."

There was another aerial view, "As I'm sure you know, the Big Island is the most easterly of the Hawaiian Islands. The next island to the west is Maui. The Big Island and Maui both have a population of around 150,000. This aerial view is of Kahului, where the airport is, and on that coast are some of the best windsurfing spots in the world – for experts."

Sam flipped through a bunch of images, "On the west end of Maui is the town of Lahaina, and the long stretch of hotels on the Kaanapali coast. Farther north are more condos and hotels in Kapalua."

There were more images, and Sam said, "On the south shore are some nice hotels in Wailea and, farther to the east is my favorite Maui beach, Makena." He chuckled, and said, "It's not very crowded, and most people stay on 'big Makena' ... but just to the west, over some rocks, is 'little Makena', which is a famous nude beach on Maui."

Sam now showed another rainforest, with a huge rocky spire, "You may know that Maui looks like two islands joined, with a waist, or 'isthmus'. Just to the west of this is a place that not many people visit, called Iao Valley."

There was a close-up of the spire, and Sam explained, "What you're seeing here is called the 'Iao Needle'. Sarah and I actually stayed in a tiny motel here on our first trip to Hawaii, a couple of decades ago; there was a stream flowing right under our room!

"And, the huge volcano on the east side of the island is Haleakala, where there is an incredible national park — that can take many days to hike through. At the top of Haleakala are some famous astronomical observatories."

More images, this time of waterfalls and beaches, "Finally, you can drive the Hana Highway, along the northern shore to the eastern tip of Maui, where you can stay in the village of Hana. And, just a little farther are the 'seven sacred pools'."

Sam looked at us, "So Maui is also a very diverse place, and a nice place to tour — as long as you get out of your resort hotel, and drive around." Of course, it's also one of the great golf meccas.

Now we saw some different pictures, including one of Sarah on a mule, going down a steep trail. "The next main island to the west is Molokai. I don't have many pictures, but this one is Sarah and I riding the mules down to the Kalaupapa peninsula, where there used to be a leper colony."

More images flitted by, "And this is when we got lost on the east side of Molokai, in Halawa valley. We had hiked to a waterfall, and misjudged the time; the sun set behind the mountain, and we couldn't make it back before it was pitch black under the canopy of trees in the rainforest. I'll tell you about that another time."

Sam hadn't told me about any of his experiences in Hawaii. I guess there were a lot more things we could share with each other; at least, things that he could share with me.

Now, a beautiful image appeared on the screen: A deep bay, with jagged mountains in the background, and incredible pastel-colored clouds – most likely near sunset. Palms and ferns were in the foreground, and a sailboat heeled as it made its way out of the bay, and into open ocean. It was magnificent!

Sam breathed in deeply, and said, "And this is my favorite island: Kauai, which is to the west of Oahu." As he flipped through a few more images on the giant screen, my friends' mouths dropped open: It was literally drop-dead beautiful!

Sam didn't narrate – he just flipped through a couple dozen images – of white sand beaches, vines hanging from a sheer cliff over a cave, a winding trail hundreds of feet over the ocean, and jagged peaks in the distance, with the sunset beyond.

Just as we were getting absorbed into the images, Sam turned off the projector, the screen suddenly black. He closed his eyes, and breathed deeply.

"I'm not going to give you a tour of Kauai, the 'Garden Isle' ... you're just going to have to experience it for yourselves. It's the most remote, tropical island of the main (accessible) Hawaiian islands. The central peak – a now-extinct volcano, named Mount Waialeale, is known as the wettest spot on Earth: It gets somewhere between 450 and 600 inches of rain per year."

He looked at each of us, "That's about 50 *feet* of rain – about a foot per week. The water accumulates on the top of the island, in a place called the Alakai Swamp, and flows over the mountains on the north side, creating dozens of waterfalls, which flow into streams, then rivers, emptying into the ocean.

"The island of Kauai has about 60,000 people, but on the north shore – about 20 miles of coastline – the population is only about 6,000." Sam chuckled, "Plus tourists, of course."

He breathed deeply again, and I could tell that talking about Kauai was an emotional experience for him. "But I know quite a few spots where we will be alone, with nature, in an incredibly remote-feeling place."

Sam's eyes appeared damp, and he wiped them with the back of his hand. He said, in an emotional tone, "And, I'd like to share it with you."

I leaned over and hugged him.

He pulled back, "Sorry. I'm just remembering times with Sarah, on the 'garden isle'. Sam covered his face with his hands, all of us silent. Obviously, a lot of feelings were being released, and there was nothing we could say. I held Sam, as he sniffled, then pulled back.

"I'm sorry. But it has a lot of meaning to me. I had intended to share it with Kelly, alone ... but you guys have become special to me ... and I wanted to invite you to get a taste of Kauai, if only for a week ... or two."

My friends were awestruck: They had never seen Sam so emotional. And, I'd only seen him like this a couple of times in the past year.

Julie rose, and stepped between the couch and coffee table, bending down, and hugging Sam. "We would love you to show us your favorite island, Sam." She kissed him on the cheek, and returned to her place on the couch.

Linda – who usually was very direct, and somewhat abrasive, said softly, "Sam ... we would be honored, if you would let us come with you; if Kelly doesn't mind."

I didn't know what to say. Sharing Sam with my friends was not an issue, but I wondered whether this was something too intimate, too close to him, too emotional to be shared.

Sam wiped his eyes again, and looked at us. "My concept for the trip is to give you a tour of *my* Kauai ... not sexual, but intimate. We would share a condo, and perhaps Kelly would let each one of you spend a night with me; just being close. And, as I mentioned, perhaps we could have a couple of days of hiking, and exploring one of the remote valleys, together."

Sam continued, "It's not about challenges ... but I would count on your openness, the closeness between us all, a level of intimacy that will give you a feeling for why I'm so emotional about this magical place."

Sam straightened, and said, less emotionally, "I'm sure there are many other 'magical' places in the world – perhaps Tahiti, Bali ... probably dozens, or even hundreds of places. But this one is very special to me. And, it would be a demonstration of *my* openness to share it with all of you." Sam looked at me, "As Linda said, if Kelly will share it with you."

I didn't know how to react; this was unexpected. I'd already shared Sam with my friends, and they had achieved a level of openness and intimacy rarely seen, even with couples who had been together for many years.

Of course, I would share Sam ... but I wondered about the deeper significance of this place, the island of Kauai; why he had been so emotional. I moved next to Sam, and hugged him, as he composed himself.

He said, sheepishly, "I'm sorry you guys. I guess it's been an emotional day for me, too." Then, he brightened, "Would anybody like some chocolate fondue?"

We all smiled, and Linda said, "I've been waiting patiently for you to offer that!" Linda was really something; but so were all of my friends. I guess we all had our own identities, very special, and very unique.

We rose, and went upstairs into the kitchen, where Sam began the preparation, again being very efficient, and having the fondue ready in just a few minutes.

I wasn't sure what had come over me, although I always became a bit emotional, thinking of some of the times that Sarah and I had shared. And I also got emotional about Kauai – not just what Sarah and I had done there, but the sheer beauty, the 'feel', of the island.

Pulling out a small cast-iron pot, I poured in the heavy cream, and dropped in a dollop of butter, a dash of cocoa powder, and a pinch of cayenne, and turned the burner on the stove to medium. I quickly chopped two 70% chocolate bars into small bits, and dumped them into the heated cream mixture.

Closing my eyes, and thinking of Kauai – and Sarah – I stirred the chocolate, until it had melted. Then, I turned the heat as low as it would go, and poured in a small shot of Frangelico, and another of Kahlua. I continued stirring, finally turning off the burner, and grabbing matches from a kitchen drawer.

Kelly took out the fruit leftover from lunch, along with a bowl of beautiful strawberries, and carried them out to the patio table, as I lit the Sterno, adjusted the flame, and set the chocolate mixture on top.

Everyone sat down at the table, and I ran back inside for a surprise ingredient, marshmallows, which I poured from the bag into another bowl. Then, I carried them outside, with the fondue forks, and a stack of small glass plates. Kelly passed the plates and forks around, and everyone began skewering pieces of fruit, and dipping them into the dark, rich chocolate.

No instructions were necessary and, once again, there were a lot of 'Mmmm's, and very little discussion, as everyone enjoyed the dessert. I offered coffee, or espresso, but got no takers.

Kelly said, "I know you guys were going to go back home tonight, but you might consider staying over, and leaving in the morning."

Kathy put her hand to her stomach, and said, "That sounds like a good idea." Julie and Linda nodded, without halting their preparation of more chocolate-covered fruit.

I noticed that Kelly had already turned on the outdoor lights and pool lights, and I got up, and turned off the patio lights. Then, I walked along the path bordering the pool, and lit the Tiki torches.

It was now getting dark, a half-moon low in the sky, the temperature perfect, and the air still. It was an 'enchanted' evening ... but not as enchanting as the thick, sensual atmosphere on Kauai. I closed my eyes, seeing the full moon setting over the Bali Hai ridge, the dark waters of Hanalei Bay in the foreground.

Once again, I became emotional; I couldn't explain it. But I looked forward to sharing these experiences with Kelly and her friends. Perhaps they would understand?

We never went into the sauna, nor the jacuzzi or pool. Maybe the coffee would have allowed us to stay up longer.

But it had been an emotional day of ridiculous, incredible experiences, and Sam's emotions created a melancholy feeling that slowed the pace of the evening.

After cleaning up the dessert, we hugged each other, and climbed the stairs, my friends going into the guest bedrooms, and Sam and I into the master bedroom. We undressed silently, and got into bed. Sam spooned me, and we fell asleep without making love.

My last thoughts were of the images that Sam had shown us of Kauai, the sunsets and water, the rich foliage and atmospheric color. I looked forward to the trip with Sam, and my open and adventurous friends.

Thank you for reading Book 6 of the Experiences series. If you enjoyed it, please take a moment to leave a review at your favorite retailer. And, if you liked this story, you'll LOVE the continuation in Book 7: Island Experience!

- Simone Freier

Discover other titles by Simone Freier

Experiences Series Book 1: Origins of a Fetish

Experiences Series Book 2: First Experience

Experiences Series Book 3: Weekend Experience

Experiences Series Book 4: Birthday Experience

Experiences Series Book 5: European Experience

Experiences Series Book 6: Friends' Experience

Experiences Series Book 7: Island Experience

Experiences Series Book 8: Domme Experience

Connect with the Author

Follow me on Twitter: http://twitter.com/SimoneFreier

Friend me on Facebook: http://facebook.com/SimoneFreierAuthor

Subscribe to my blog: http://SimoneFreier.com

Favorite me at Smashwords: http://smashwords.com/SimoneFreier